FLIGHT of
the SIREN

by
Brendan Myers

NORTHWEST
PASSAGE
Books

Gatineau, Quebec, Canada

Flight of the Siren

ISBN: 978-1-9991146-2-6

Published by
Northwest Passage Books
Gatineau, Quebec, Canada

Publication history:
First published 6th November 2020
Revised 17th December 2020

For all enquiries, please visit:
brendanmyers.net

Acknowledgements

My sincere thanks go to Meg Elison, Nicole Luiken, Shirley Meier, and Carla Sulzbach, for their comments on various drafts of the text, and their confidence in me as a writer. Special thanks to Nathaniel Hebert, designer extraordinaire, and to Jordan Stratford, editor, proofreader, writing mentor, and most enthusiastic cheerleader for my work.

I owe the most special thanks to my partner Andrea Lobel, whose comments on the first draft, whose encouragement, and whose love, empowered the Siren to fly.

I am also deeply grateful to the 126 people who provided financial support for professional editing and design services through Kickstarter.com, the internet-based crowd-funding service. Among them I owe special thanks to Robert Hart, Robert Meeks, Alfred, Kimberly Hawkland, Sara Korn, Levar Jones, Cory Hutcheson, Albion Gould, Rosmairta Kilara, Yewtree, Joe Roy, Gillian Shields, Jennifer Gibson, Turlough Myers, Ivo Dominguez Jr., Eric Hortop, Stan Yamane, Pat Bellavance, John Bookwalter Jr., Sionain E McCann, Frank L Jenkins, Todd McGrattan, Tara Egan, Paul Elliot-Magwood, Lars Nohrstedt, Tony Schlisser, Barbara Pott, John Hoke, Joel Belland, Brian K., Thomas Schwartz, Zara, Todd Pote, Elaine Stutt, Mark-Anthony Page, Sian Reid, Lindsay Harris, Bridget Gole, Chris McLaren, Gwendolyn Guth, Lisa Bland, Catherine Haynes, Iona Reid, Scott Tizzard, William Apple, Jonathan Colvin, JD Ferries-Rowe, Ezekiel Zong-Han Azib, and two supporters who remained anonymous. I remain forever grateful to everyone for their kindness and support.

After things reach their prime, they begin to grow old,

Which means being contrary to Tao.

Whatever is contrary to Tao will soon perish.

—Lao Tzu, *The Tao Te Ching*.

First Transmission: Pluto.

A dwarf planet in the Kuiper belt. Discovered in the year 1930; the first and the largest object of its kind ever found.

Perihelion / Aphelion distance: 30 / 49 astronomical units.

Orbital Period: 248 years. Eccentricity: 0.2488. Inclination: 17.16 degrees.

Population: Uninhabited.

§ 1.

"Aren't we supposed to be alone out here?"

She turned off the cabin lights, so that the glare would no longer wash out her view of the stars. Indicators on control panels became new stars: some flashing and bright, some glowing dim yet steady. She leaned over the flight deck dashboard, careful to avoid tripping any switches or keys, and pressed her face to the cupola window. The stars ahead seemed to turn around an orange and beige dwarf planet, as though it was the timeless and eternal centre of the universe. But the low hum of the ventilators, and the quiet but persistent electronic bells from the control panels, rooted the moment in the present.

"There's no one out here but us," said the captain.

"Look at the tactical," Lorelei replied.

The captain looked. The tactical display showed two, possibly three more ships orbiting the small world ahead. Lorelei folded her arms and imagined that the force of her silent disapproval would be enough to chase the trespasser away.

The captain pressed a button that silenced the tactical display's alarm chime.

"It's probably nothing. These old systems glitch all the time," he said.

"It's not a glitch. Someone's out there." Lorelei said.

"Nobody's there, Lorelei," Captain Xiao insisted. "No one has ever come this far from the sun before. There are very few ships that *can* come this far. No one's going to take this moment from us."

A new alert from the ship's system interrupted the captain's thought.

The comms officer frowned at it. She put on her headset: one earcomm, and an augmented reality glass over one eye.

"Someone's hailing us. On the *short* range frequency," she said.

"All right, someone *is* there," the captain admitted.

Lorelei smiled.

"Handshake protocol says Republic of Arethusa," said Sitara, the comms officer, reading the report at her terminal. "Typical. Our flag isn't planted yet and they've already built a mall."

Lorelei's smile disappeared.

"*Kai'tzeen!*" the captain swore. He touched a button on the comms screen and opened a channel. "This is the CNH Expeditions Ship NavCom Seven, Captain Jiandong Xiao commanding. Who am I speaking to?"

The voice that replied was deep, harsh, and quick. "NavCom Seven: this is the ASDF *Scavenger*. Report your status."

Jiandong saw the puzzled and judgmental looks of his companions. He shrugged his shoulders in reply. "Our status? We were supposed to be the first ones out here. Is there a problem?"

"No problem." replied the *Scavenger*. "We are here to observe your mission, and we're not going to get in your way. But we're sending a team to secure your LZ for you."

"Secure our landing zone? What the hell for?"

As the captain argued with the Scavenger, Sitara floated to a seat beside Lorelei.

"Fuck those flyboys," she muttered. "We trained for this mission for years. We were supposed to be here first!"

"But it's strange," said Lorelei. "If they made the first footprints here, then why didn't they tell the world? Where's the big announcement? Where's the video? They didn't even log a public flight plan."

"That *is* strange," Sitara agreed.

"And why is a warship defending an ice rock with no resources, this far out in space? Maybe there's something down there that they don't want us to see," Lorelei said.

Sitara examined the tactical display, and cast a wider search area to look for other ships. "I doubt it," she said. "If there was, we would know about— what are these?"

The tactical display showed new contacts: three large metallic objects in high elliptical orbits. It also showed a scattering of smaller objects, like a halo around the planet.

"I'm going downstairs to take a closer look," said Lorelei, and she left the flight deck. She floated through the hexagonal corridor, politely greeting colleagues on the way, but slowing to chat with none of them. Only nine people, most of them technicians, called the ship home: but the many storage bins hanging from nets on the walls made the spaces feel cramped and crowded. In some spaces, burned-out lights had not been replaced, allowing the hanging containers to cast long shadows. The flight deck and other spaces of the central fuselage were always weightless, but the ship rotated to provide the illusion of gravity to a ring of labs and crew quarters in the midsection. Lorelei felt her body weight returning as she slid down the ladder to the ring. Arriving in the ship's main science lab, she ordered the computer to show her the radar contacts orbiting Pluto. One was a military corvette, carrying light weapons for short-range targets. The other three were labelled 'undocumented objects': telescope pictures showed them tumbling along their orbits, as if rolling down a steep hill. Wreckage.

Lorelei examined the planetoid. She created a holographic map of its surface above the work table. Its ancient yellow-white flatlands, and dark orange-black mountains, were hers to explore. Having had months to study this map, she knew it well, and had given her favourite features private names. A neon-green square indicated the landing zone; Lorelei zoomed the image into it, and studied the surrounding landscape.

Not far from the site, and by the edge of a range of charcoal and orange foothills, Lorelei saw a large circular feature, and a row of perfectly aligned rectangles beside it.

"Abacus: Give me RADAR and LiDAR scans of this area," she said.

Digital grid lines passed over the holographic image, sharpening and clarifying the landscape. The rectangles turned into blocks resembling the kind of prefabricated housing units common to off-world colonies. The circular feature became a large geodesic dome with hexagonal frames.

"Abacus: overlay infrared. Give me the interior temperature of these structures."

The hologram faded into shades of red. The dome and row of blocks remained sharp, and glowed much brighter than the surrounding landscape. A block of text appeared in the hologram next to the buildings: *Infrared Spectroscopy. Temperature of*

3

structures: minus-5 degrees Centigrade.

"How many people are down there?" she asked.

Body-heat signatures = zero.

"Well, if they're in space suits, their heat wouldn't show, anyway," Lorelei reminded herself. She moved closer, and magnified the image. A vague heat-shadow of something inside the dome resolved into view. The shape was long and curved, like a crescent, with a jagged round shape near the middle that reminded Lorelei of the sail of an ancient wooden sailing ship. She worked the magnification controls some more, but could not resolve the image any clearer.

Jiandong stepped into the lab. He was one of the few on the ship who always kept his belt buckle shined and his shirt buttoned up to the top of his neck: a formality that he felt his position required of him. But a touch of rebellion showed in the way he let his hair grow slightly longer than regulations allowed. "Lorelei, I need you to— what are you doing?"

Lorelei showed him the image of the structures she found. "Where there appears to be nothing, there's always something," she said.

He nodded. "I spoke with the captain of that warship. He told me we might notice those buildings. And that they're a Class Two radiation hazard. It's not safe to go near them."

"Abacus: overlay a radiation hazard map," Lorelei said. Observing the results, she turned back to her captain. "Radiation normal," she told him. "Did they really believe we wouldn't notice that? We're a science ship."

Jiandong grinned, but sighed. "It doesn't matter. We're going to land, plant the flag, and build the relay, like it's an ordinary day."

"Those buildings shouldn't be there. We were supposed to be there first! The International Treaty on the Exploration of Space says that no one is allowed to land on any celestial body until—"

"—until after the Conference claims it for all humanity," Jiandong finished for her, as his patience thinned. "I know the law."

"We have a duty to report this," she concluded. "Think of what will happen to us if we don't."

Jiandong sighed and shook his head. "We've been touring the Kuiper belt for almost two years. If we report this, we'll have to stay here six more months, to investigate. I want to go home. So does everyone else. Let it go."

The captain moved to the door, but Lorelei followed him. "In my last job, my supervisor put his name on my research and left my name out. Before that, I taught a master class in early modern philosophy, and they paid me with a gift card for a hairdresser. Now we've got the Arethusans openly breaking international law— they're not even trying to hide it. I signed on for this mission to leave that kind of nonsense behind."

Jiandong gripped the door frame. "I don't like this any better than you, but I don't want anyone on my crew getting shot because they were curious about some empty boxes. Do your job, nothing else. For at least one more day. Then we can all go home. Please?"

Lorelei glared at him, and gritted her teeth.

Jiandong took a memory card and downloaded Lorelei's discovery on to it. "Here. In case they EMP us and wipe our data," he explained, as he handed her the card. "Later we can talk about it. Today, we do what the men with the guns tell us to do."

He swept out of the lab. Lorelei folded her arms, shook her head, and turned her attention back to Pluto.

§ 2.

NavCom Seven's landing shuttle detached from its moorings and drifted away. Its thrusters fired, taking it down to the surface of Pluto. A moment later, a heavier and bulkier shuttle detached from the Arethusan corvette and followed them. The Scavenger ordered the shuttle to orbit Pluto one more time, so that the Arethusans could land first.

The region around the landing zone was a field of yellow-white rock, covered with a thin regolith of pebbles, and nitrogen snow. The pinpoint-sized sun made the landscape as bright as a dawn or a twilight back home. But the atmosphere was no more than a haze, leaving most of the sky above as black and star-scattered as interplanetary space.

Sitara Kula had been chosen to make the official first footprint on the farthest world from the sun visited by humanity. She stepped off the platform, making a slight bounce as she landed in its tiny gravity.

"With these small steps on this new world, the human adventure continues," she said. For weeks she had worked on what she would say, and had made her final decision only moments before saying it. She paused to take in the view, and to feel the billions of eyes watching her through the landing shuttle's exterior cameras. She planted a flagpole on the frozen ground and raised the banner of the Conference of the Nations of Humanity: a sky-blue field with an icon of a person holding up one arm in greetings, drawn with only three curved white lines, like an ancient rune.

"Well done," said the Arethusan lieutenant, who had been standing behind the camera with his soldiers. "Your name will be on the history books of the world forever."

Sitara only glared at him, and kept walking.

The bright crescent of the nearest moon filled a quarter of the sky. But the soldiers did not give anyone much time to admire the view. The technical team rolled their equipment out of a shuttle. Lorelei unpacked her sampling kit and wheeled it out beyond the blast radius of the shuttle's landing rockets, to find an uncontaminated sample. One of the soldiers, however, followed her.

"No samples," he said.

"This is my job," Lorelei stated.

"No samples. Radiation," the soldier repeated, and he raised his rifle, not high enough to shoot, but enough to make his point.

"It's also my job to report to the Council when people break the treaty laws," she said, as she put the sample kit away. She went to help the technicians attach the relay unit to its various cables and peripherals, and lay out the scaffolding for the dish antenna field. A short distance away, Sitara dug a trench where the relay station's nuclear battery would be buried. Several soldiers patrolled the perimeter of the work site. Whenever Lorelei looked over her shoulder, she always found one of them watching her. When she thought there was a free moment to do so, she waved to Sitara to come closer. She touched their helmet visors together, so they could speak without using their suit radios.

"My radmeter still shows no unexpected radiation," Lorelei said. She showed Sitara the readings on her radmeter.

Sitara sighed. "I was checking the OS on the main router, when one of them pulled me off. He said he wanted to look for spyware devices."

"They're laughing at us. They know there's nothing we can do," said Lorelei. "But I want to take some photos, anyway. Quietly, secretly."

"These soldiers will probably arrest you. Might even shoot you, if you get caught," Sitara warned.

Lorelei disagreed. "They're not watching the starboard airlock on our shuttle. I can slip out, and be back before we finish our work. If the admiral finds out we knew about those buildings, and didn't report them—"

Sitara turned to see what the soldiers were doing, and whether any of them were near. Lorelei gently guided their helmets back together.

"Here, take my transponder, so they don't track me," said Lorelei, as she handed Sitara an attachment from her suit, "and distract them while I break out the rover."

Sitara hesitated, but Lorelei pressed the transponder into her hands.

"Quickly. I don't want to give a speech at your funeral."

A crackling in their suit radios caught their attention. "You two, by the shuttle! What are you doing?" the lieutenant in charge barked at them.

The scientists looked up and saw that one of the soldiers was recording a video of their meeting with his suit camera. Another marched over and snatched Lorelei's radmeter from her hands. Aghast, she marched over to the lieutenant, who was supervising the placement of the nuclear battery in its trench. "One of your men took my radmeter."

"Are we interfering with you?" The lieutenant's cold tone implied the answer he was expecting was *no*.

"Obviously. You shouldn't be here at all," Lorelei answered.

"You have your mission, we have ours."

"And what is your mission, lieutenant? The way your people wave their guns in our faces like fresh new recruits— no discipline, no professionalism— you're going to hurt someone, whether that's your mission or not. So get your people in line, and let us do our job."

Having said what she hoped would be enough, Lorelei returned to her colleagues. The work was nearly finished now, and it appeared that the technicians didn't need her help anymore. She looked at the lieutenant, then to the nearest of the soldiers, and then to the horizon. The moon's crescent had grown slightly, as the sun crawled along its slow course in the sky. On a distant hilltop, she saw the glitter of fresh snow.

"NavCom Seven, this is Lorelei. There's something on the horizon that I would like to sample," she said, and she walked toward it.

A nearby soldier took a step toward her. "No samples. Radiation," he reminded her.

Jiandong, listening from orbit, radioed back to her: "Lorelei: NavCom Seven. Reading you five-by-five. What is it?"

"Captain, I—" Lorelei took another look behind her. Some of her colleagues, and all of the soldiers, were watching her now.

"Doctor Verlassen, whatever you're about to do, don't do it!" the lieutenant ordered, holding his hands open to her. "If you stay here too long the radiation will kill you." Through his helmet visor she could see his face: round and dark and bright-eyed, with a bushy brown goatee and a sincere expression. But she could not ignore the heavy rifles carried by the men under his command. She looked back to the horizon again for a wistful moment, then turned back to the building site.

The lieutenant sighed. "NavCom Seven: Lieutenant Glaive. Situation under control," he told Jiandong.

"Roger that," Jiandong replied.

As the NavCom crew continued their work, Sitara persuaded one of the soldiers to help her lift some awkward equipment. The move left part of the NavCom shuttle unobserved. Lorelei reasoned that it would take only half a minute to unfold the shuttle's ground rover. And the sound, she reasoned, would not carry in the sparse atmosphere.

Moments later, she was in the driver's seat and speeding away.

The rover was only a metal frame with two seats and an electric motor, but it was swift enough to carry her over a low hill and out of sight before anyone at the work site noticed she was gone. Following a navigation pin that she programmed into her suit's display, she sped alongside the yellow-white snowbanks, sometimes bouncing in her seat as she struck a hidden shelf of stone.

She found the forbidden base camp after ten minutes of driving. She bit her bottom lip as she stared at it, as if that would help her see through its walls.

"If they didn't want us to see this," Lorelei wondered, "why let us come down here and plant the flag so close to it? Why the lie about the radiation? Why didn't they just kill us while we were still in orbit?"

She parked the rover near the large circular building: a geodesic dome the size of an aircraft hangar. Its lattice of metal beams held a stiff inflatable material in place, which vibrated slightly with the work of the air pumps inside it. Lorelei activated her spacesuit's body camera, and looked around. The snow around the base had been freshly cleared and swept. It sparkled yellow in the feeble sunlight, and blue-white with the moon. The rectangular buildings, she now saw, were the beginnings of a small permanent base: housing, labs, equipment maintenance, a power plant. Radiation hazard signs written in Hindi, and the badges of military agencies from Gayatri Pradesh, decorated the doors. But the flagpole flew the banner of Arethusa.

Looking around some more, she noticed several people in space suits lying in the snow, a short distance away. She stepped closer, and found Gayatrian Space Force patches on their shoulder, and burn marks on their chests. She drew the clear conclusion.

She touched the dome's airlock, giving herself a moment to decide not to turn back. She turned the heavy lock wheel on the door, and stepped inside. The airlock whirred into action, and Lorelei's heart quickened when she felt air pressure embracing her suit again. She took off her helmet when the pressure equalized, inhaled, and opened the inner door.

The air was cold here, and smelled vaguely of matchsticks, hot metals, and rum— the smell of space. The floor was a lattice of steel laid on top of a layer of insulating materials, to prevent the ground from sucking away all the heat in the air. The only light came from the red glow of several space heaters, arranged around the edge of the dome, revealing only silhouetted shapes of machinery, and the bars holding up the geodesic dome. As with the doors, all the equipment in the space had Hindi labels, and Gayatrian military symbols.

In the centre of the space, standing twice as high as herself, was the monumental object that she was not supposed to see. The largest part of it was a dish antennae, wider than Lorelei's outspread arms. This was attached to a spherical box with triangular faces, half-hidden in a lattice of support beams and attachments. Cameras and other sensors bristled from its arms. But she saw nothing that resembled fuel cells or reaction thrusters. The longest of its broken arms extended out in opposite directions, and at their ends they each held a sphere, about the size of her helmet, made of a smooth black material that was somehow glass but also somehow ceramic: not quite one or the other. The whole object gave Lorelei the impression of an ancient cairn: a witness to the endless and terrifying depths of cosmic time and space, bearing a sacredness that its new surroundings could not diminish.

Looking around the wall near the airlock, Lorelei found a light switch, and turned it on. Powerful spotlights on the dome's ceiling glowed to life, picking the crates of equipment out of the darkness, and casting the grounded space probe into clarity. She walked closer, and saw that the dish was dented and holed from thousands of tiny asteroid impacts, and that the core was similarly battered. Many of the lattice beams were bent into sharp angles, probably from the crash.

Then she saw the oval-shaped plaque on the bottom of the probe's core. It appeared to be made of a reddish-golden metal, though it too had been damaged from long exposure to space. Several lines of symbols and characters were inscribed on one side, and on the other side the lines of characters formed three concentric circles, and several radiating lines of different lengths. At the top of the plaque there were two small circles, with lines inside them resembling the continents of a planet. At the bottom, there were three humanoid figures outlined: two adults and a child.

Lorelei turned on her suit's lamp to get a better look. The letters on the plaque belonged to no language she recognized, and the planet in the portrait was not her home world. Looking at the three humanoid figures at the bottom, she noticed they had three digits on their hands instead of five, and three toes on each foot.

Lorelei looked at her own hand, then back to the plaque. Her eyes widened, her mouth hung open, and her shoulders sagged. Her breathing, she noticed, had become fast and shallow, and she willed herself to slow down and breathe more deeply. She removed her gloves and touched the upraised hand on one of the humanoid figures. She smiled, and let a tear flow.

"We found you," she whispered. "We found you! Oh my stars, we found you!"

Changing indicator lights on a panel near the airlock caught her attention. Someone was entering the dome.

"*Scheisse*!"

She dashed around the probe, putting it between her and the door, and crouched low to the ground. Fear widened her eyes and accelerated her heartbeat.

Lieutenant Glaive entered the dome, removed his helmet, and immediately powered on his rifle. He raised it to his eyes, and scanned the room, looking for Lorelei.

"Doctor Verlassen!" he called. "If you had stayed here less than a minute, took a few photos and then left, then you might have got away with it."

Lorelei grimaced; she knew the soldier was right. She touched the probe, and looked up at its dish antennae. Had the dome contained anything else, she would not have lingered so long.

The lieutenant moved about the perimeter, searching for her. "You better let me arrest you and take you back to my ship before the radiation kills you," he said.

"There's no radiation," Lorelei told him. "It's a cover story. And a stupid one!"

The lieutenant checked a readout on his suit panel on his left arm, and saw that she was correct. "I have to arrest you anyway," he told her.

Lorelei stepped out of her hiding place, her hands in the air, and said, "Can I show you something first?"

"No," he growled.

"Then I want to say thank you."

"For what."

Lorelei lowered her hands. "The three minutes I had in here. They have been the most important three minutes of my life."

"Why? What's so important about— whatever this thing is? A dead space probe?"

"They didn't let you in here, did they?" Lorelei realized. "They didn't tell you what this is. Look at that plaque there, on the bottom," she told him, and she pointed to it.

The hardened and loyal Arethusan soldier glared at her for a moment. Then he moved to examine the plaque. He turned on the spotlight on his rifle and leaned in for a closer look.

"Look at the planet pictured on the top," she showed him. "Then, look at the people. Count the fingers on their hands."

Glaive looked. He lowered his rifle. His legs lost the strength to hold him, and he fell on his seat. He scrambled away on hands and knees for a moment, then pulled himself to his feet with help from the latticework of the dome.

"*Kai'tzeen*!" he swore. "Jesus Christ! What the hell is that thing?"

"It's the answer to the most metaphysical of all questions,"

Lorelei said. "Why the great silence? Is anybody out there? This probe is the answer. The answer is yes. It's yes! Isn't it wonderful? Centuries of searching, and now we know. It's yes!"

The lieutenant collected himself, but stayed near the edge of the dome. "How are you staying so cool about this?" he asked.

"Because I've always known a discovery like this is possible," Lorelei explained. "Basic mathematics tells us the galaxy should be swarming with life. It was never really a question of *whether* we would find it. Only a question of *when,* and *how.*"

"So who built this?" the soldier asked, his attention absorbed by the probe. "How did it get here? Why did they send it? Does any of it still work?"

Lorelei crouched near the probe's dedication plaque. "The fact that it's *here*, at all, is what interests me. The universe is larger now, because of it. And we ourselves are smaller."

"I don't get you."

Lorelei collected her thoughts. "Through most of history, we thought our planet was the centre of the universe, and that it was created especially for us. Then we discovered the centre of everything was the sun. Then a hundred years after that, we found out the cosmos has no centre. It goes on forever. And all the stars have planets. Yet we still thought we were special, because of our intelligence, our ability to reason. But now, we have proof that there's at least one other world out there with intelligent beings like ourselves, and there could be millions more worlds like it. Which means there's nothing left to make us feel special. But it also means we are not alone."

Glaive walked around the probe, as though in a daze. "I have orders to arrest anyone who sets foot even *close* to this place, never mind who gets inside. And to kill them if they resist."

"They'll kill you too, if they know you were in here with me," Lorelei supposed.

"Give me your suit camera," he ordered.

Lorelei had forgotten her camera was still recording. A trill of dread passed through her. She switched the camera off, unclipped it from its attachment just under her neck, and hoped that the lieutenant did not notice that she palmed the memory card and dropped it into her suit.

The soldier tossed the camera to the ground and crushed it under the butt of his rifle.

"You were never here, and neither was I," he said, as his

discipline returned.

"Thank you," she said, and she reached out to touch his arm. "Go."

Lorelei put her helmet and gloves back on, and returned to the airlock.

When she was gone, the lieutenant found a chair and sat down. He gave himself a moment to reclaim his professionalism, then tapped his communicator. "Glaive to Scavenger. FOB is secure."

§ 3.

In the NavCom Seven's lab, Lorelei showed Jiandong and Sitara the footage from her spacesuit's body camera.

"There's nothing obviously alien about this, Lorelei," said Sitara.

"The big dish antennae looks like the one on the Traveller probes. The third? Or maybe the fourth?" said Jiandong.

"It's none of them," said Lorelei. "Look at the core. And the spheres at the two ends. They're different. We didn't make this." When the video came to the plaque, Lorelei froze the picture and said, "This is the reason the lieutenant made me swear on my life not to tell anyone. But I'm telling you anyway. It's too important to keep secret. And when we get back home, we have to tell the world."

The crew examined the image. Lorelei zoomed into the three humanoid shapes at the bottom of the plaque, and then scrolled up to the diagram at the top.

When Sitara realized what she was looking at, she spilled her coffee on the floor.

"It's a fake," said Jiandong. "No other explanation."

"If it's a fake, why try to scare us away from seeing it?" asked Lorelei.

"Maybe it's a distraction," said Jiandong. "It's there to let the Arethusans test their secret new technology, and blame any sightings on aliens."

"It's not a fake," Lorelei insisted, her anger mounting. "Look at the density of the micro-meteor damage. It must be hundreds of years old. I'm telling you what I saw!"

Jiandong shook his head. "I cannot understand why you find this paper tiger so convincing. We found more than ten thousand planets orbiting other stars, all within a hundred light-years.

None of them show evidence of civilization. You know this."

"Ten thousand planets within a hundred light years," said Lorelei. "That's— how many planets in the galaxy as a whole? And you say none of them with intelligent life? As an ecologist, I can tell you that's impossible. Life always appears when the conditions are right for it."

"I'm not saying no other planets have intelligent life," Jiandong defended himself. "I'm saying we've never found any."

"We've found microbes and bacteria on three other bodies in our own solar system."

"But nothing that can build a rocket. Nothing with a brain!"

Lorelei pursed her lips. Then she looked at Sitara. "You're the card-player. What are the odds?"

Sitara rubbed her forehead for a moment, to think. "I'm with the captain, on this one," she said. "If there are any aliens out there, it's mathematically very likely that some disaster collapses their society before they can launch anything that we will ever find. Their resources run out, or they pollute their climate, or they blow themselves up in a nuclear war. So, I'm sorry. You're right when you say that life is probably common, throughout the galaxy. But Jiandong is also right when he says that probably none of it has come to the same level as us. If I had to bet on one of you, I'd bet on him."

"But what about this," said Lorelei, as she pulled her own hair and searched for the words. "The limits of one planet don't have to be the limits of all civilization. What if that limit is the whole galaxy?"

"If that were true," said Jiandong, "then we would see signs of intelligent life everywhere. But we don't."

"And where there *appears* to be nothing, there's always something," said Lorelei, smiling as though she had won a small victory. "We could be looking at a galactic civilization that has only now begun. And our world, and the world that created this machine, are only the first two of billions of planets, each of them with billions of people."

"I want you to be right, Lorelei," said Sitara. "But wanting something to be true doesn't make it so."

Lorelei pursed her lips. Then she said, "The Arethusans are sure the probe is alien."

"If that's true, then we should expect to hear from them, any moment now." said Jiandong. "They're going to want some assurance that you kept their secret."

A polite chime sounded in the lab: the ASDF Scavenger wanted to talk. Jiandong moved to a comms panel, but looked at Lorelei before he took the call. "It feels good when I'm right about these things," he said, though his frustrated tone revealed his true meaning.

Lorelei made an exasperated face, but Jiandong opened the comm channel before she could reply to him. "NavCom Seven, receiving your signal," he said into the radio.

"NavCom Seven: Lieutenant Glaive. I need to board you."

"Negative, Lieutenant," said Jiandong. "We are burning for home. I'd rather not have to do our orbital calculations all over again."

A heartbeat after Jiandong spoke, red alarm lights lit up on every panel and monitor in the lab, and an alarm rang. Jiandong checked the panel nearest him and said, "They've put a weapons lock on us!"

"It won't kill you to do those calculations twice," said the lieutenant.

§ 4.

"The air from their ship smells like a gym locker," said Sitara, as the airlock doors opened.

It was Glaive, the lieutenant who confronted Lorelei in the dome on Pluto. Lorelei caught her breath, and willed herself to avoid eye contact with him. He marched on board with the precise steps of a professional soldier.

"Welcome aboard the NavCom Seven. I'm Captain Xiao," said Jiandong. "And you are?" asked Jiandong, as he extended his hand.

The soldier's hands stayed behind his back. "Glaive, Lieutenant, Arethusan Space Defense Force," he introduced himself. "And this must be the rest of your command staff. Doctor Lorelei Verlassen, Ph.D in philosophy, post-doctoral degree in ecology. Strange combination."

Lorelei moved a stray lock of hair out of her face and said, "Not really. If you take a close look at the logic of complex systems, you'll find—"

"Our file on you says that you were orphaned at three years old, and that your legal guardian was a boarding school."

"You seem to know a lot about me," Lorelei said.

"Standing orders," the soldier explained. "To know the weaknesses of both our enemies and our allies. For example—" he turned next to the short-haired, brown woman standing next to Lorelei, "—Sitara Kula, operations specialist, comms officer. Master's degree in mathematics. Previously employed as a dealer in a well-respected casino. A position you resigned to join the NavCom fleet. Our file on you would be of great interest to a forensic accountant."

"I'm sure I don't know what you mean," said Sitara.

"And you, Captain, are a mechanical engineer with some interesting family connections, and a citizen journalist," the lieutenant said next. "Award-winning, I'm told."

"And now, perhaps you could say something about why you need to come on board?" Jiandong inquired.

"I have been ordered to accompany you on your return flight home," the lieutenant explained. His voice was clipped and clear, as if he was reporting to a superior. But he spoke quickly, as if trying to get every word out at the same time.

"I know you have extra hibernation pods, for emergencies," Glaive continued. "I'm bringing my own food and water, and an extra oxygen recycler."

"I'll have to clear it with Fleet Operations," Jiandong replied.

"And what will you do if they say no?" said the lieutenant, as he widened his stance, daring the captain to move him.

"Depends on what mood they're in." Jiandong studied the lieutenant. "I might lock you in your pod so that you can't wave your guns in the faces of my crew—"

"I am unarmed," the lieutenant interrupted, and he showed his hands. "I won't interfere with your work."

Lorelei stepped forward. "And why have you been ordered to fly with us?"

"My government wants to know the state of CNH space operations. I am here to observe and report."

"We post everything we do on the grid," Lorelei said.

"Everything?" asked Glaive.

Lorelei didn't answer.

Glaive straightened his spine. "That's what I thought."

"You can bunk in the cargo bay; there's room in there now," Jiandong said, and he pointed the lieutenant to a corridor. "I'll let you know if the admiral tells me to space you."

"Thank you, Captain."

As the lieutenant and the captain left the main deck, Lorelei left for the flight deck. Sensing something was wrong, Sitara followed her. When they were alone, Lorelei released a long-held breath.

"This makes no sense," said Sitara. "We're only going home, and we'll spend most of the time in hibernation. There's nothing for him to observe and report about."

"He's lying," Lorelei said. "He's here to make sure we don't say anything about the probe. And to kill us if we do."

"No, that's not it, or not all of it," said Sitara. "In the years I worked at the casino, I learned to read people. Did you see his hands? Did you hear his tone of voice? He's afraid of something."

§ 5.

That night, Jiandong couldn't sleep. He opened Lorelei's video on his private terminal and examined the image of the plaque on the probe. But he scrolled away from the humanoid figures; their eyes made him shudder. He moved the video to a frame which gave the clearest view of the probe's dish antennae. He zoomed the image closer, then leaned forward in his chair.

Signs of radiation exposure, micro-meteor damage, metal fatigue. Were those lines metal whiskers? He could fix this thing's age, if he could measure them.

He went to the lab, and found Sitara already there.

"Can't sleep," Sitara told him.

"Neither can I," said Jiandong. He poured coffee for them both, and opened a new task on a terminal. "Abacus: access virtual engineering lab. Estimate the surface appearance of a sheet of spacecraft-grade aluminium after one hundred years exposure to interstellar space."

An image of a sheet of metal appeared on the monitor. It slowly filled with impact dots and corrosion.

"Two hundred years."

The impact dots on the image of the metal grew more numerous, and larger ones appeared among them.

"Five hundred years. One thousand years."

The metal tarnished further from the simulated space-borne gas and dust. Jiandong compared the image to the picture of the probe on Lorelei's video. He played with the brightness and contrast controls for a moment. Then he saw the level of damage on the probe was almost exactly the same as his thousand-year simulation.

"Still think it's a hoax?" Sitara asked.

"Balance of probabilities still says yes," Jiandong answered.

"My turn," said Sitara. On another terminal, she searched Lorelei's video of the probe to find the best image of the plaque on its side. Taking a look at the inscribed lines on its left side, she zoomed in and examined the symbols there. The top line consisted in a series of short marks: some vertical lines, some horizontal, some diagonal; and as they progressed from right to left, the symbols appeared in pairs, threes, and fours, and then crosses and circles and triangles appeared.

"See that? It's a number sequence," Sitara realized. "They're teaching us their math."

"As hoaxes go, this one's really professional," Jiandong said, impressed.

Sitara reached for a pencil and notepad and wrote down as much of the sequence as she could read from the corroded surface of the plaque.

"Base Twelve," she wrote her notes. "Makes sense. More factorals than Base Ten. Easier to do simple divisions. So they count on their fingers, and then what? Their knuckles?"

She began copying the lines on the plaque using the familiar number symbols, and entered them into a database.

"Abacus: translate these numbers from Base Twelve to Base Ten."

The numbers on her display changed in a cascade.

"What are you looking for?" Jiandong asked.

"There must be some universal constants in here somewhere," she muttered. She leaned closer to her monitor, and found a number that looked familiar. "Abacus: this looks like it might be the ratio of a circle's diameter to its circumference. Translate into our units, and translate everything else the same way."

The numbers on her database changed, and then more familiar figures appeared. The atomic weight of hydrogen. The charge of an electron. The speed of light.

"There! That's the key to decoding the rest of it," said Sitara.

"Doesn't make it alien," Jiandong reminded her.

"But who would make a code like this and hide it on the most distant body in the system? What would be the point? And why are the Arethusans defending it with a gunship?"

"Those are good question," Jiandong admitted.

Sitara's mind ran through possible answers. She idly scrolled the image on the plaque over to its right side, with the diagram of concentric circles and radiating lines. Zooming in closer, she saw that the lines were made of the same number symbols, and that the lines terminated at different lengths, each with a hexagon containing the same number. She wrote these new numbers into her spreadsheet, and contemplated the translation. Then she pushed her chair away from her desk, as if she had been jolted with electricity.

"Interstellar distances," she said. "This is a star map!"

§ 6.

Lorelei lay awake in her cabin, not wanting to sleep. Her mind was full of the alien probe she had found. Whenever she opened her eyes, she found her quarters empty; but whenever she closed them, the three humanoid figures from the plaque seemed to be standing around her. Their eyes were large and dark; their fingers long and spindly.

She sat up in her bed, took the memory card from its hiding place inside her pillowcase, and turned it over in her hands. The soft light from a control panel near the door, alternating in green and cyan, made the card look alien in her hands. She held her hands before her eyes and examined them. She wondered how they could have evolved into a tech-intensive civilization with one less finger. How did they make stone tools? How did they become apex predators? Did their brains evolve differently? All the evolutionary advantages of having four fingers culminated in her being there, at that moment, with all of her knowledge, in a bunk on an interplanetary space ship orbiting an ice rock in the ass-end of the solar system— somehow they made the leap from interplanetary to interstellar without those advantages. How did they do it? Her mind was a maelstrom of questions. She looked out her small cabin window, and wondered how many of the stars she could see had planets like Earth, and how many of those planets had someone like her, looking out her window at the same stars.

A knocking on her door broke her solitude. She twitched involuntarily with the sound. Her colleagues would have called her using the ship's intercom; a knock on the door could only mean someone she didn't want to see. She sat very still and silent: perhaps the visitor would think she was asleep and would go away. But the knocking persisted.

"Lorelei! It's Glaive."

Lorelei quickly hid the memory card in her pillow case and opened the door.

"Can I come in?" said the lieutenant. He was still dressed in his duty uniform as an Arethusan military officer, but it was disheveled and partially unbuttoned, and his feet were bare. "I want to discuss the Conference's first contact policy," he stammered. He could force his way into her cabin if he wanted. But he was pacing up and down the narrow hallway, wringing his hands and massaging his face, clearly agitated. Conflicted.

"It's 'Doctor Verlassen,'" she told him. "And whatever you need will have to wait until morning." She edged her door closed.

Glaive pushed her door open again. "You're a scientist, you must know what's supposed to happen. Who gets notified first. How the evidence is checked and confirmed. How the news goes out to the media. What happens when their ships appear in the skies of our planet!"

"Please, Lieutenant, do you want to wake up the whole ship?" Lorelei implored him.

"Right, sorry." Glaive turned around in a circle and breathed deeply. "Can we talk in your cabin?"

Lorelei stepped into the corridor and closed the door behind her. Her blonde curls, normally tied in a tail to control them in the ship's low gravity, now fell gently on her shoulders. Dim green and blue light from nearby monitors contrasted on the sharp features of her face, and in her steel-blue eyes. Standing nearly as tall as the soldier, she told him with her posture that he was in her world now. She would decide what happens.

"The policy must include a threat assessment," the soldier continued. "Because, it's obvious that whoever built that thing is more advanced than we are. Who knows what kind of weapons they—"

"It's only a space probe," said Lorelei. "We sent out lots of our own, for the same reason. To explore space. To say 'hello'. To just get out there."

"But what if it's not just a probe? What if they deliberately put it here on Pluto, so that it would signal its people when we found it? So that they know when we've developed space travel. And then they can come here and put the boots on us before we get advanced enough to challenge them."

"There's no evidence for that."

"No evidence against it either!"

"An absence of evidence does not logically prove the existence of anything," Lorelei taught him. "It's a common fallacy called—"

"My orders were to keep you and your crew away from that base camp, until the Arethusan Science Foundation arrived," the lieutenant interrupted. "But now I think we should keep *everyone* away. I need to tell my commander to blow it up."

"This is the most important scientific discovery of all time. You know it is!"

"It's also the most important security threat of all time."

"The probe is in no condition to signal anything," Lorelei argued, as she chased after him. "It can't use its antennae."

"How do you know?"

"It's got thousands of holes in it. You saw that yourself. If it was signalling anything, we'd have picked it up. Centuries ago, if it's been sitting there that long. We would have pinged radio from it before we got to the Moon. If it ever had a transmitter, it's dead now."

"So it's damaged," the lieutenant conceded. "That doesn't mean it's completely nonfunctional. There's only one way to be sure it never signals anyone."

Lorelei stood still and watched the lieutenant march away from her. "How can you be so—"

"Paranoid?" he sharply interjected.

"I was going to say: how can you be *sure*?"

Glaive stopped and turned to face her again. "It is a fundamental principle of military intelligence," he explained, "that you have to assume your enemy is smarter than you are, and that he is deceiving you. So who is to say the probe wasn't deliberately placed there for us to find, and it only looks like it crashed?"

"*We* are to say. Science, and scientists," Lorelei chastised him.

"You understand nothing," he told her, marching away. Lorelei watched him for a moment, her voice sputtering, torn between indignation at his last comment and the search for something to say that might reach him. Before he was out of sight, the latter effort won. She ran to catch up with him.

"Wait. Destroying it might be exactly the signal its creators are looking for," she told him.

"I don't follow," he replied.

Lorelei stepped in front of him, to block his path. "A Deadman Switch. Think about it. Let's assume for the moment that the probe *is* a trap, like you say. And right now, it's emitting no signals we can detect. But that's because it might be more advanced than it appears to be. Maybe it uses some kind of quantum effect, or subspace, or something else we can only theorize, to stay in constant contact with its creators. If you destroy it, you will interrupt that signal, trip the alarm, and the creators will know we're here. Even in your scenario, the safest thing to do is to not touch it at all."

Glaive looked up to the ceiling, lost in thought. "It didn't look all that futuristic to me," he said.

"*Ja*, well, if you were designing a trap for a primitive civilization, what would you want it to look like?" Lorelei reminded him.

He thought about this for a few breaths. "I need to talk to my commander," he concluded. He marched away, in search of a comms terminal.

"I'll take you to the lab," said Lorelei.

§ 7.

The hologram table and other nearby work stations in the lab were now nearly covered in hand drawn sketches, and piles of notes which guessed what numbers might lay beneath the centuries of corrosion.

"This line, the longest one, pointing to the spiral symbol, could mean the origin planet's distance to the centre of the galaxy," said Sitara. "So these other lines lead to other objects. The nearest bright stars, perhaps?"

"Can't be that," said Jiandong. "A pattern of stars like this could appear a hundred times across the galaxy."

"Black holes, then?"

"Doubtful. Most of our galaxy's black holes are clustered in the core. And look at the last number at the end of each line. It's expressed as a fraction of the speed of light. Now why would the probe's creators want us to know how fast these objects are moving, instead of what they are?"

"Don't know," said Jiandong.

Sitara touched a few controls, and displayed on the hologram table a record of an object approaching Pluto, and getting caught in a long elliptical orbit. "And here's another question," she said. "I've been looking through the public records for any sighting of something crashing on Pluto. I found a thirty-day gap in the record." She displayed a row of deep-space photographs, and moved it back and forth between the two records on either side of the gap.

"There could be hundreds of reasons for that," said Jiandong. "Equipment failure. Orbital maneuvers taking the cameras out of range."

"For thirty whole days, exactly?" Sitara objected. "No. Someone messed with the records. And they did a sloppy job of it, too. Look here: in the days before the gap in the record, you can see a Gayatrian prospector ship arriving in orbit, deploying surveyor drones. After the gap, the prospector is gone, there's a halo of metal debris orbiting in its place, including these three big pieces. And there's the Arethusan corvette."

"They covered up a battle," Jiandong concluded with a gasp.

"A battle for possession of the probe, I would bet," Sitara said.

After a moment of reflection, Jiandong closed the tactical display. "That changes nothing. The probe has to be a fake," he said.

Sitara looked him in the eye and whispered, "But what if it's *not*?"

At that moment Lorelei and Glaive arrived at the lab. The lieutenant saw the handwritten copies of the probe's plaque, as well as the holographic images captured from Lorelei's suit camera. He rounded on Lorelei and said, "You swore you would tell no one. You gave me your word."

"I have a moral obligation as a scientist to be truthful to and about the evidence," Lorelei stated. "And you were pointing a gun at me. So I was under duress."

Glaive pushed Lorelei out of his way and quick-stepped down the corridor. Lorelei picked herself up and chased him. The corridor was narrow, and the variety of bins and packages hanging from the walls and ceiling narrowed it further. The lieutenant pulled several storage nets down, to throw more obstacles in Lorelei's path. If another crewmember got in his way, he pushed them to the wall, though it often forced him to bounce off the opposite wall.

"Where are you going?" Lorelei shouted at him.

Glaive didn't answer. The chase continued to the ladder that led up to the ship's central core, where there was no gravity. The soldier kicked off from a handrail and sliced ahead toward the bow, appearing to corkscrew through the air as the ship rotated around him. Lorelei did the same, but she was thrown off by a storage bin that the soldier dropped in front of her. When she regained her momentum, the lieutenant had shut himself behind a sturdy bulkhead door.

Lorelei reached for the nearest internal comms panel. "Captain: he's locked himself in the flight deck!" she warned.

Back in the lab, Jiandong heard the message. He rushed to a terminal. "Abacus: transfer all command and control functions from the flight deck to this lab. Authorization: Captain Jiandong Xiao. Passcode: Oscar Whiskey Tango One One Six."

A readout on his terminal said, *Command and control functions transferred.*

"Freeze all outgoing communications."

The intercom bell sounded, and then Glaive voice spoke through it. "Too late, Captain."

Jiandong entered another command. The video feed from the flight deck's security camera appeared on the monitor, showing that the lieutenant was seated at the comms station, sending a text message to someone.

"He's signalling his ship," Jiandong surmised. "Sitara: can you stop him?"

"I'll try," she said, and she sat down at the lab's main terminal and got to work.

Noticing that two of the technicians gathered by the door, listening and concerned, Jiandong picked one of them. "Lance: suit up for EVA. I might need you to sabotage our antennas."

Lance nodded, and left for the airlock.

Jiandong turned back to the comms. "Listen to me, Lieutenant. If you try to take over my ship, I will cut off your air supply," he threatened. His companions glowered at him, surprised by the threat. "I have a duty to protect the ship," he explained.

Glaive howled back at Jiandong, "Try it, and my commander will launch an EMP on your systems and cripple you adrift." He typed a text-message to his commander on board the Scavenger: *FOB Sentinel compromised. Have seized flight deck but locked out of helm control. Awaiting orders.*

"Fry us with an EMP and I'll still leave you locked in the flight deck," the captain told Glaive. "With no gravity. Your bones and muscles will waste away to nearly nothing. When you get back home you won't be able to walk for a year. Your soldiering days will be done."

"Imprisoning someone in zero-G is a war crime, Captain."

"It's *you* who are threatening *us*, Lieutenant!"

Then the lieutenant received a text-message reply from his commander. *Lt Glaive: Scavenger Actual. Message received and understood. Summoner be kind.*

Glaive leaned back away from the monitor, folded his arms. He typed a reply to his commander, but deleted it before sending it. Then he knocked on the bulkhead door, and spoke through an intercom: "Doctor Verlassen, are you still on the other side of this door?"

Lorelei was floating away toward the ladder, but she paused when she heard him.

"If you can hear me," he continued, "I just want to say, for what it's worth, you're welcome."

Lorelei moved to the intercom panel to talk to him. "For what?" she said.

"For those three minutes. I'm sorry that I couldn't give you more."

Lorelei acknowledged this with a moment of silence, then said, "So what happens now, lieutenant? Is your ship going to open fire on us? Even with you on board?"

"It's not how I would have wanted to go," said Glaive. "But when the Summoner calls, well, you have to answer. Glaive out."

"Lieutenant Glaive!" she pleaded. "Answer me! You want your people to fire on a Conference ship? An unarmed scientific ship? Do you have *any* idea the size of the shit-storm you're about to start? Arethusa at war again, only this time against the entire Council?"

She waited for him to answer, but none came. Thumping on the bulkhead didn't help.

"Of course you won't answer, because you think you're going to die," she said to the bulkhead door, as if he might hear her anyway. She floated back to the ladder, and returned to the lab to rejoin Sitara and Jiandong.

When she got there, the hologram table was showing a tactical display of the ship's position. Some of the crew crowded around it, grim-faced and worried, counting down the seconds until the warship came within weapons range.

"Twenty-three minutes," said the captain, gesturing toward the rangefinder's estimate.

"We can escape in a shuttlecraft," Lorelei suggested.

"Our shuttles don't have enough air to get us to the nearest station," Jiandong reminded her.

"Escape pods," Sitara reminded him.

"The only ship in range that could pick us up— is the Scavenger," Jiandong said. He stood still for a moment, and looked out a window. "Summoner be kind," he whispered.

"Hmm. Never knew you were religious," Sitara remarked.

"Something like that, but it's complicated," he said. "You?"

"No," she replied. "I always thought it was enough to live a good life. To have as much fun as you can without hurting anyone. Can't ask for more than that, I suppose, except— it's just not fair that it's ending like this. What about you, Lorelei?"

Lorelei said, "Am I religious? That depends on what you mean by religion."

"How can you talk like that?" Sitara said, her voice raised louder than needed to make the point. "We might all be dead in twenty minutes."

Lorelei bowed her head. "I— I don't always feel things the same way other people seem to do. I've always been like this. But it doesn't mean I feel nothing—"

Sitara said, "In twenty minutes, everyone on this ship is going to feel nothing, and it's your fault—"

Jiandong rapped his knuckles on a counter to get their attention. "Let's not spend the last minutes of our lives arguing," he said. "I'm going to record a message for my family. Both of you should do the same." Then he left the lab.

Sitara calmed herself. "I should record something for— someone," she said. And as she floated out of the lab, she paused by Lorelei's side. "Sorry."

Lorelei acknowledged it with a nod.

"You have anyone at home? You want to record something for them?" Sitara asked.

"No, there's no one," Lorelei said. It was a plain fact about her life that she had accepted since her teenage years, but rarely mentioned to others because of the stir that the statement often created.

Sitara hugged her friend, and left the lab.

Lorelei stepped into the corridor, to watch her go. In one direction she saw Lance arguing with Jiandong about whether the situation was hopeless. In the other direction, two technicians were kissing each other and pulling off each other's clothes. They didn't seem to hear Lorelei apologize for interrupting them.

She returned to the lab, and replayed the video of her encounter with the alien probe. She smiled, pleased to have been given the three minutes in the dome to study the discovery, but shook her head when she remembered she might have no chance to tell anyone else about it. She paused the video when the plaque came into view, then closed and rubbed her eyes.

After a breath, she snapped her eyes open and looked at the image again, analyzing. All the numbers at the ends of those lines were expressed as fractions of the speed of light. But why use a speed measurement, instead of coordinates? They can't be moving through the galaxy very fast. What if it's not speed?

What if it's *frequency*?

Lorelei moved back to the hologram table. "Abacus: show me a map of the galaxy." The holographic map appeared above the table.

"Now show me the positions of all known neutron stars within—" she checked one of Sitara's notes, "—within five percent of twenty-five thousand light years from the centre of the galaxy." On the hologram, boxes singled out hundreds of neutron stars along a ring half-way between the centre and the edge of the galaxy.

"Exclude all stars whose rotational period is not within five percent of one of the following," Then she read the numbers from the diagram. The majority of the boxes in the hologram disappeared; those that remained gave the impression of a necklace around the middle of the galaxy. Looking closer, Lorelei found a part of the necklace where fourteen pulsars clustered close together. She zoomed into that area: sensors in the hologram emitter detected the movements of her fingers to guide the image where she wanted it. The map from the plaque joined the hologram. Playing with its size and camera angle, she found that the position of the pulsars matched the angles of the radiating lines on the map. At the place where the radiating lines converged, there was a star.

"There you are," she whispered. "Abacus: Display in this map the position of Sol."

A different coloured box picked out another star in the hologram. Lorelei saw it, let out a reflexive yelp of surprise, and started to laugh.

"That's Rhinemaiden 74-B. Only nine light years away! Only nine— that's so close!" She ran to the comms panel. "Jiandong, Sitara, come back to the lab! I found something— and it's wonderful!"

Moments later, Sitara and Jiandong gazed in awe upon the image of the galaxy with the position of Lorelei's discovery.

Jiandong said, "Abacus, is this star registered on the exoplanet catalogue?"

A text box appeared saying that the star hosted two gas giants and an as-yet undetermined number of terrestrial planets, but had not yet been studied for signs of life.

Jiandong was still skeptical. "Then why are there no radio signals, no signs of civilization?"

"Maybe they're too weak for us to detect," Sitara suggested.

"I'll tell you what it is. It's a *testable hypothesis*, that's what it is," said Lorelei.

Jiandong said, "We don't have the equipment for the kind of test we'd have to do."

Lorelei stepped up and said, "But other people do. So let's broadcast the evidence. Let everyone can see it for themselves, and decide. It might not save our lives. But at least our lives would be *remembered*. That would be something, wouldn't it? We send out the whole package. Raw data, our analysis, the location, the logs, everything."

Sitara looked to Jiandong and said, "Can we do that much, at least?"

Jiandong meditated for a moment. "Yes."

§ 8.

The first to see the transmission from the NavCom Seven was Glaive, who sat in the captain's seat on the flight deck and wondered grimly when the end would come.

Next, the transmission reached the crew of the Scavenger, surging ahead on the constant push of its nuclear fusion thrusters, its gun ports open and ready to fire. Its commander watched the first ten seconds of the video, then turned his monitor off. "Well played," he said.

Like stepping-stones across space, the transmission touched the receivers at NavCom stations across the solar system. Within an hour it reached the relay orbiting Saturn, and the mining stations collecting ice from its moons. Next it reached the mineral-mines on Ganymede, and the research station studying the micro-biome in Europa's ocean. Around the same moment, the transmission reached the comms arrays orbiting Mars, and the thousands of people living in the pressure-domes of Troth Base and other stations on its surface. Finally, the signal reached the third planet, orbiting opposite the sun from Pluto: the blue and gold and green world of Earth. Within hours, ten billion people in every city, town, colony, station, and starship saw the faces of the NavCom crew, fronted by two women and one man, each from a different nation, standing together in the lab of a ship that flew the flag of all humanity. They introduced themselves and their ship, each in their own language.

"My name is Doctor Lorelei Verlassen; I'm from Éostray," said the last to make an introduction. "We would like the world to know: on the surface of Pluto, there is a crashed exploration probe from an alien starfaring civilization. It had this diagram attached to it—" she held up one of the sketches of the plaque "—and we think it's a map showing us how to find where it came from. We have evidence to believe the probe is proof that humanity is not alone in the universe."

"Here on our ship," said Sitara, "we don't have the equipment to search for life around that star of origin. But some of you out there do. So take a look, and tell us what you find. Attached to this message is a data stream with everything we know about it. Photographs of the probe, its map, and copies of the notes we made while we studied it. Think of this as a science project the whole world can do together."

Finally Jiandong spoke. "We would like to thank the crew of the ASDF Scavenger, who met us in orbit around Pluto. They made us understand the necessity of sharing this discovery with the world. They are now flying in formation with us, as our honour guard. We're coming home now; we will be happy to see you."

§ 9.

On the flight deck, Glaive received a message from his commander: *Scavenger to Glaive. Cease hostilities and stand by. Keep the watch.*

The lieutenant closed his eyes and breathed deeply. He pressed the intercom.

"Captain Xiao?"

In the lab, Jiandong answered: "Xiao here."

"My commander has just informed me that we are not going to die today."

At almost the same moment, an indicator on a lab computer went dark. The Scavenger had disengaged its weapons lock.

Jiandong closed his eyes and grinned. "All right. We're going to live," he said.

Sitara laughed, and pulled her companions into a group hug. Then Lorelei slipped away from them, to find a nearby window.

"Everything is going to change," she whispered.

"So, Captain," Glaive asked over comms, "I wonder if you might let me out of here?"

Moments later, the bulkhead doors of the flight deck opened. Lorelei stepped in. "Would you like a more comfortable cabin for the flight home?" she said.

Glaive smiled as he floated himself out of the flight deck and followed Lorelei down the passage. "That message of yours was was quite the gamble," he said. "I don't mind admitting I'm glad it worked."

Lorelei chuckled softly. "So am I."

Glaive sighed. "But now I have another problem. You broke your word to me. I can't just let that go."

Lorelei gripped a nearby zero-G handrail and turned to face him. "You saw what's down there. You know what it means. I had to tell someone."

"Perhaps you did," the lieutenant said. "But a broken promise is a broken promise. So now you owe me."

"I owe you? But I did the right thing. So did you."

"You owe me," the lieutenant repeated. "So I'm going to call in a favour from you some day. And you will not refuse it."

"I promise," she said after a pause.

"I'll take it, for now." He pushed past her. "Cheer up, Lorelei. That home movie of yours is going to make you famous!"

Second Transmission: The CNHS NavCom Seven.

Length: 35 meters.

Propulsion: Fusion-reaction engine.

Max Operational Range: 128 astronomical units.

Crew Complement: 9 (technicians and scientists).

Max Time Between Resupply: 28 Months.

Primary Mission: Chart all astronomical bodies in the solar system, install communication relays and navigation beacons, and conduct deep space search and rescue, as per CNH Expeditions Council mandate.

§ 10.

The sun steadily brightened as the NavCom Seven spiralled through space, ever closer to the inner worlds of the solar system. The ASDF Scavenger hung by its side, to all appearances an escort, though it held the NavCom ship in an invisible electronic leash. The crew of both ships spent most of the seven-month homeward journey in their quarters. A mild narcoleptic gas delivered through a breath mask kept them in a dreamless sleep for a month at a time, and a nutrient solution from a drip-feed in their arms kept them alive. Abacus awoke them in rotating watches for food and exercise. Most crew members returned to their bunks after a day, as there was no one to talk to, and nothing much to do. Jiandong wrote for his news column during his turn on night watch. Sitara recorded video-letters to her friends. Lorelei, however, wandered the ship alone for several days at a time. She read books and research papers downloaded from online libraries, and she filled the lab with her handwritten notes, sketches, and calculations. She searched the news networks for any report about the probe, or about the star that it came from. She found only the usual flood of sitcoms, sports replays, and shouting politicians.

A few hours before they were due to arrive in orbit around Earth, Abacus awakened everyone from hibernation. They stretched their arms and legs, visited the latrines, and gathered in the galley to drink their post-hibernation glucose solutions and to socialize. Sitara searched the cupboards for something more interesting to eat than dry-biscuit rations.

"Okay, everyone: orbital insertion maneuvers in one hour," Jiandong told the crew through the intercom, when everyone was awake and settled. "But I'm stopping the gravity rotation now."

When they were weightless, Jiandong and Sitara gathered on the flight deck to look ahead. Earth and the Moon were crescent from their point of view, since the ship approached them from outside the Earth's orbit. The crew easily picked out Earth's continents by the lights of all the cities, as well as some of the industrial bases on the moon. Round the Earth, a thin ring of dust and broken satellite parts glittered in the blackness between stars, flecked with highlights when some larger object reflected the sunlight at just the right angle.

Sitara pointed to a cluster of lights that were moving nearby, against the backdrop of stars. "What's that?"

She brought up an image of the moving lights on the ship's monitors, and zoomed in. They saw a large cylindrical cage, open at both ends, containing tanks and pods and various machines. Several drones and worker pods swarmed around it, moving parts into position and securing them in place. Around the middle of the cage they saw a gigantic half-finished sphere.

"It's an orbital construction platform," said Jiandong. "Big. Looks like they're building the largest fusion reactor core ever."

"It's a starship. Someone's building a *starship*!" said Sitara.

"With five or six engines like that, you could fly all the way to Lorelei's star."

"Yeah— in ten thousand years."

"Speaking of Lorelei's star," said Jiandong, "Where's Lorelei?"

They found her in the lab, making pencil sketches of the probe, from a model projected over the hologram table.

"I couldn't sleep," she explained.

"You couldn't sleep?" said Jiandong. "Was something wrong with your hibernation pod?"

"No. I lay down, and then the dreams came, and they were too full of shadows. I couldn't sleep."

"Nobody dreams while in hibernation," Jiandong said.

"I do."

Jiandong rolled his eyes, but decided better than to pursue it.

"How long have you been awake?" Sitara asked her.

"I'm not sure. Maybe— maybe twenty days?"

"Twenty days!" Jiandong blurted. "So that's where all the food went."

Sitara said, "You weren't lonely all that time?"

"Not really," Lorelei admitted. "I know how to live with it. I need it, sometimes. I had things to think about."

Jiandong still couldn't understand her. "You just sat and thought about things for twenty days?"

"I took breaks to watch movies," Lorelei shrugged. "I've been trying to understand something. Sitara said it was mathematically likely that an alien civilization would destroy itself before it sends out any signals that we could detect. So I had to know: exactly how close are *we,* to the same end? I made a list of the big global problems that can face a global civilization. Climate crisis, resource depletion, pandemic, nuclear war—"

"It can't be healthy, to look into the darkness like that," Jiandong remarked.

Sitara agreed. "Especially when you're alone. You should have waited until everyone was awake," she said.

"I needed the time, the quiet," Lorelei said. "I can't be myself when there's too many people around. Can't do my own thinking."

"I don't know how you do it, Lorelei," said Sitara. "If I'm by myself for too long, I get crazy. Can't even sleep."

Jiandong sighed. "What was so important that you needed the whole ship to yourself for twenty days?"

"I think I discovered something. Something important," Lorelei replied. She sorted through her paperwork, intent on sharing her discovery. "I looked up the numbers for a dozen of the world's social and economic indicators— global trade volumes, political stability, wealth and poverty ratios. And I analyzed them using ecological models: eco-footprint size, carrying capacity, trophic pathways. I created an equation that measures the fragility of complex systems. I call it the Threshold of Cultural Entropy. Here I can show you—"

Sitara said, "We can look at the numbers later. Tell us your results."

Lorelei held her breath for a moment, and then said, "I predict a ninety-nine percent chance of *Kulturdammerung* in sixteen years."

"Sixteen years!" Sitara blurted.

"No one can predict a thing like that," Jiandong said.

"I just did," Lorelei corrected him.

Sitara's voice quivered as she asked, "You're really sure of this?"

"There's a small margin of error," Lorelei conceded. "But I'm about as sure as any good scientist can be sure of anything. To explore outer space you need global supply chains, global political cooperation. But global civilizations face global problems. Strategic resources start running out. Transport systems break down. *Food* and *water* starts running out. People get desperate, and frightened. They lose trust in each other. They start to care about their own survival above all other things, and then, so do their leaders. They look for scapegoats to blame, and they spend more time attacking imagined enemies than solving real problems. And as things get worse, we grow more vulnerable to catastrophes—"

As Lorelei spoke, Jiandong examined some of her notes. "Sixteen years? That must be wrong. It's too *soon*—"

"But there is a way to survive," Lorelei explained. "Not only to survive: to flourish and prosper. To do *better* than only surviving. Like *they* did."

"Like who?"

"The aliens who built the probe," Lorelei said. "They're a proof of concept. They must have had all the same problems that we have. But somehow they *solved* them. Or, at least, held them back long enough to send one sign of their existence into the universe, where we could find it. And that means there's a chance that we could make it through *our* problems, at least long enough to send out a sign of our own. So I made another calculation—"

As she searched through her papers again, Jiandong said, "This is all too much. Waiting for aliens to save us is almost as bad as waiting for God."

Lorelei dropped her papers. "This is not prophesy or magic," she insisted. "This is *science*."

Realizing his annoyance was unhelpful, Jiandong paused, and breathed. He said, "The reason I'm being so hard on you right now, is because I will have to explain to the admiral why you took twenty days of ship resources for this. You know what kind of man he is."

"*Ja*, I know," Lorelei said.

"So what do you want me to tell him?"

Lorelei pointed to another paper and said, "That although threshold of *Kulturdammerung* can cannot be voided, still it is not inevitable: it can be changed. Pushed further into the future, or pulled closer to the present. If there was another force at work in our culture— a force of *reason,* and *moral aspiration*, strong enough to counter the forces of survivalism and complex system breakdown— then we could push the threshold farther into the future. And because of the probe, I know what that force is."

"So what is it?" asked Jiandong.

Lorelei said, "Star travel."

"*Kai'zeen's beard!*" Jiandong swore.

Sitara laughed and shook her head. "That's too much for me, too," she said.

"I'm serious, and I'll show you," Lorelei retorted. She opened a photo of the probe on the hologram table and showed it to her companions. "Do you see?" she asked.

"It's the probe," said Jiandong.

"*Ja.* Look at it. Do you see?"

"See what?"

Lorelei made an exasperated sigh. "Our NavCom ship can cross one AU in about seven days. So to cross nine light years, we would need— what? Ten thousand years?"

Sitara did the math in her head. "Ten thousand, nine hundred and fifteen."

"Great. Okay. But according to Jiandong's analysis of micrometeor damage," said Lorelei, "the probe is only around a thousand years old. That means it can fly around eleven times faster than we can. Sitara, is that right?"

"Close enough," Sitara confirmed.

"So! When it crashed on Pluto, why didn't it smash into millions of tiny pieces?"

Everyone turned to face the hologram of the probe, surprised by it a second time.

"Strange, it's the same but it looks different now," said Sitara.

Lorelei smiled. "I think there's something on that probe which allows it to break the laws of physics as we know them," she concluded. "Something which allows it to travel faster than light. And to slow down enough to soft-land on a dwarf body like Pluto."

"Crash land, you mean," said Sitara, with a smirk.

"Soft land— badly," Lorelei amended herself, with a touch of embarrassment. Returning to her calculations, Lorelei said, "But this is another proof of concept. If the people who built this found a way to get around the speed of light, then so can we. And our search for it could be a force of optimism and cooperation. My calculations show that if we can pull ourselves together and build a starship, then a lot of good things will happen for us. New ideas and new confidence will enter our culture. New resources for the economy. New communities on new planets— the greatest land-rush in all of human history. And the year when the threshold of entropy reaches ninety-nine percent will be pushed more than five hundred years farther ahead into the future. Long enough for us to solve our biggest problems. Stabilize the climate crisis. Dismantle the nuclear weapons. Lift everyone out of poverty—"

"Bring the dead back to life," Sitara continued for her.

"I know what it sounds like," Lorelei said, with a grin. "But I am not saying star travel will save us. I'm saying, we are walking on the edge of a knife. The smallest touch, the tiniest quiver to one side or the other, and we rise up to join the gods, or else we fall into oblivion."

A spiritual silence held them, as they contemplated the implications.

"All right, I'm convinced," Jiandong declared, when the silence grew too loud for him. "Maybe this thing *did* travel faster than light. But as for your confidence in *people*— I don't know. What if this probe is all that's left of them? What if sending it was the last thing they did before they destroyed themselves?"

Lorelei thought about that for a moment, and said, "What if it's not?"

Third Transmission: Arethusa

Government type: Military-Industrial Complex

Military: 32,000 active duty personnel, in four branches: army, navy, space defense force, and cyber defense force.

Mercenaries on contract: 2.7 million ground force and space force personnel.

Deployed nuclear weapons: 1,300 land based, 200 space-based (estimate).

Largest City: Newgarten.

§ 11.

When their orbital insertion maneuvers were complete, a planetfall shuttle docked with the ship, and took the crew to the planet below. Designed to take off and land on aircraft runways, the shuttles that served in Earth's orbit took more time to reach the ground than rockets, but provided a more pleasant experience for passengers. Twilight was falling over the city of Newgarten as the shuttle descended. The crew, and the unwelcome lieutenant, got a long look at the forest of skyscrapers and towers poking their pinnacles above a thin blanket of smog. They turned golden-red and purple in the sunset, and hundreds of other colours in smaller patches as the towers turned on their animated billboards and nightly hologram shows. No green earth appeared anywhere in the urban sprawl: where a space in the smog allowed a view of the ground, asphalt and concrete and steel possessed it, from the edge of the ocean to the far horizon.

Two colossal statues, one clad in armour and holding a shield and spear, the other wearing a crown and holding a sceptre, stood like sentries on opposite banks of a brown river, near where it emptied into the sea. They gave a sense of dignity to the dazzling urban spectacle behind them, though their forms were half shrouded in the smog. A long retaining wall of black metal enclosed the coast and the riverbanks, and portals along its length spat a stream of floodwater back into the sea.

Lieutenant Glaive accompanied the crew on their flight down

to the city. "Anyone ever been here before?" he asked, hopeful for conversation.

No one answered for a moment. He looked to his soldiers; they only shrugged.

"I came here on a school trip, once," said Lorelei. "I was twelve, I think."

"I was born here," said Glaive, pleased that someone accepted his bid. "See the statues of The Prince and The Soldier? We used to call them The Boss and The Blockhead."

"You never called them that when there was a priest nearby," said Jiandong.

"Oh, *Kai'tzeen*, no," Glaive laughed. "When I was a kid my friends and I used to go to the foot of the Boss, and dress up like animals and give offerings to The Wild, just to watch the priests lose their shit. So much fun. I wonder if local kids still do stuff like that."

"My parents were priests," said Jiandong.

"I bet that was fun" said Glaive, with a smirk.

"My childhood was quite pleasant, in fact. Until the war."

Glaive understood, and said nothing more.

The planetfall shuttle landed on a pad upriver from the city's main downtown core. A gangway rolled out, and the passengers could see Admiral Din Mbemba waiting for them at its foot, as well as a few armed guards stationed around the edge of the pad.

"Welcome home!" said the admiral, as the NavCom Seven crew disembarked from the shuttle.

Two men dressed in the severe black uniforms and helmets of Arethusan border officers approached the crew. One carried a footstool, the other a metallic briefcase. The man with the footstool put it down in front of Captain Jiandong. "Place your right foot here," he said.

Jiandong folded his arms. "What's this for?" he said.

"Arethusan law requires that foreign nationals be fitted with transponders," said the officer. The second officer opened the briefcase, showing that it carried the transponders: round metallic clamps designed to fit around the ankle, which twinkled with operating lights as the officer switched them on.

Jiandong noticed Mbembe wasn't wearing one. "Why don't you get one?" he asked.

"CNH senior officer; diplomatic immunity," he explained.

"What if I refuse to wear it?" Sitara said.

"They'll throw you in jail. Until you stop refusing."

As Lorelei stepped up for her transponder, she asked Mbembe: "Did anyone look at the star we told you about? Did anyone find anything?"

Din gave her a patronizing smile as he guided everyone to a nearby limo, which was arriving at the hangar doors. "Please follow me."

The limousine was flanked by armoured vehicles in front and behind. They drove through the city, past the late night bars and gun shops with their flashing holographic billboards, the pawn shops, self storage centres, and payday loan lenders. Every sidewalk and square had its party-goers and hawkers and drunks, no matter the wealth of the buildings behind them. The guards on the motorcade ensured that the pedestrians and slower traffic got out of the way. It drove a few more blocks, passed through a guarded checkpoint, and entered a neighbourhood of marble porticoes and glass towers, where no one was out and about at all. It stopped in front of a small hotel, half-hidden in a nest of soaring office towers.

"Here we are," said the admiral.

The crew followed him into the building. The admiral led them up a flight of stairs, to a hallway outside of a meeting room. Porters scanned their fingerprints and eyes, took breath samples to capture their DNA, and assigned everyone a visitor's badge.

"Why here? Why not Expeditions Council headquarters?" Lorelei asked.

"The Council often uses this hotel for VIP business in Arethusa," explained the admiral.

Sitara eyed the armed security guard at the stairwell, and said, "What kind of VIPs?"

The porters opened the meeting room doors. Inside, Sitara saw a long table, with four well-dressed people, three men and a woman, seated behind it. On the table in front of each of them was a small flag for the countries they represented. Behind them, the flag of the Conference hung from a floor pole.

"The Council!" Lorelei exclaimed.

"Just the four permanent members, and myself," said the admiral.

"What is this?" Jiandong demanded.

"Your disciplinary hearing."

§ 12.

Lorelei saw the members of the council in the meeting room, and marched over to their table before the porter had finished taking her biometrics. "Did you look at the star?" she demanded of them. "Did you find anything?"

"Doctor Verlassen," said one of the councillors, a dark man with short white hair that was so precisely styled it might have been cut with a laser. "My boy told me all about you."

"Your son?"

The man gestured to Glaive.

"Doctor Verlassen, this is my father," said the lieutenant.

"Sturgeon Bediako Glaive," the father introduced himself. "Perhaps you've heard of me?"

"No, sorry, I don't follow politics much," Lorelei disappointed him.

"I wasn't always a Senator. Back in the day, I was a rallyfoot player. Made MVP ten years in a row."

"I don't follow sports much, either," Lorelei said.

Sturgeon was genuinely puzzled. "No sports or politics? What else is there?"

"Philosophy, science, literature, art—"

The Senator, instantly bored, glanced at his gold wristwatch, and then turned to a nearby personal assistant android. "You there! How long do I have to wait until someone brings me a drink?"

The android left the room. The other councillors moved around the table to their seats. One sat down and began grooming his thin hair with an oil-slicked comb, to paste it over the balding top of his head. Another, a woman with big brown curls and a face of such sharp features and pale complexion that it might have been moulded from plastic, was talking to someone on her comms. "It's two degrees too cold in this room. I measured it myself. Did they not read the official policy for optimal negotiating conditions?"

A third panelist, a man with a heavy beard, dark complexion, and and a velvet sash over his shoulder, leaned toward the admiral. "How long do you think this will take? I've an appointment with some high-value clients in an hour."

Lorelei addressed the entire panel. "What did you find out about the probe? And the star it came from? Did you look at the star?"

The woman on the call looked at Admiral Mbembe. "You didn't tell them?"

Escorted, Sitara and Jiandong entered the room.

"I have questions too" Jiandong said.

Sitara said, "And why can't we go home?"

"Let's get this hearing officially underway," Admiral Mbembe began. He switched on a recording device. "As Admiral of the CNH Expeditions Council fleet, I call to order this ad-hoc disciplinary committee, on this fifteenth day of October, the year 2120. For the record: will the members of the committee state their names and representations."

"Sturgeon Glaive of Arethusa," said the white-haired man, as he accepted a drink from an android butler.

"Gretel Von Richter of Éostray," said the doll-faced woman without looking up from a radmeter. "And it's still too cold in here."

A man with the heavy beard was typing something into his pane, and had to be nudged by Gretel to give his name: "Alankar Sen of Gayatri Pradesh."

Finally, the man with the oil-slicked hair introduced himself: "Hanfei Gao'Fu, representing the People's Republic of Chang'ren," he said.

"Would everyone please be seated," said Mbembe. "Captain Xiao, if you would speak on behalf of your crew."

Jiandong stayed on his feet. "I don't know what we're accused of," he said.

Sturgeon Glaive waved to the wall display. "Breach of the International Treaty on the Exploration of Space," he said. "Specifically, the articles about trespassing on extra-terrestrial property."

"And it seems there's a clause in the treaty which makes this meeting mandatory, at the earliest convenience of all parties." the admiral added.

"This is not convenient for us," said Jiandong. "We've been given no time to prepare. We haven't seen a lawyer. We landed here less than an hour ago."

"You had the last seven months, while flying home," said Sturgeon.

"We were in hibernation."

The admiral cleared his throat to interrupt them. "You three, the officers of the Expeditions Council Navigation-Communications Ship Number Seven, trespassed or authorized the trespass upon an extra-territorial property. During which, you also broadcast images of the interior of the same property, also in contravention of the same treaty."

"So you admit you landed on the planet first," said Lorelei.

Jiandong pressed her point. "It's against the same treaty to land on a planetary body before the Conference does. We have an admission of treaty violation by Arethusa here, on the record."

"Now, gentlemen," said the admiral, "this meeting is not a place to trade irrelevant accusations. We must keep our eyes on the facts."

"It's a fact that they broke the law and we exposed them," said Jiandong, pointing at Sturgeon Glaive.

"But they are not the ones on trial here," the admiral countered.

"So this *is* a trial," said Jiandong.

"No, it's a hearing."

The NavCom crew exchanged worried looks. "I think it's a circus act," said Sitara, giving voice to her friends' growing frustrations.

"Now, if you want this to be over quickly, don't be difficult," said Sturgeon.

"And since we have officially begun," said Gretel Von Richter, "and in accord with CNH policy for hearings like this one, I should like to request an adjustment of this room's temperature." Some of her colleagues groaned, but she continued. "Policy requires that it should be fixed at the scientifically-determined optimal temperature for negotiations. We simply can't work in a room as cold as this. It's impossible." Gretel's pronounced vocal fry gritted against Lorelei's ears.

Some of the councillors chuckled quietly. Din Mbembe said, "Do we actually have a policy for that?"

"We do, and it's your job to know it," said Gretel, still smiling.

Din turned to a nearby android and said, "Bring me the policy manual." The android handed him a Q-link.

Lorelei looked at her companions and said, "What's happening here?"

Alankar Sen shook his head, then said "While we wait for that very important clarification—" he smirked at Gretel— "let me say that my government thinks it is *very* relevant that Arethusa had a presence on Pluto, in breach of international law."

Jiandong smiled to hear him say it.

"There is no proof of an ASDF base on Pluto, at the time in question," Sturgeon said, "but for the disinformation spread by these troublemakers."

"Disinformation?" Jiandong blurted. He pointed to Lieutenant Glaive and said, "We have the whole mission logged, with ship ID, vectors, and video. He was there too!"

"That's right," said Lorelei. "He was in the dome with me. He saw the probe, just as I did. You can see him in my body-cam footage."

"Paladin!" Sturgeon grunted at his son.

The lieutenant stepped forward. "My ship, the ASDF Scavenger, was in orbit around Pluto at the time the NavCom Seven arrived."

"There, you see!" said Lorelei.

"However," the lieutenant continued, slowly and carefully, "at that time, there was no physical installation belonging to the ASDF on the surface."

The crew of the NavCom Seven jumped to their feet, already arguing with him.

"You want us to believe that a building with the flag of Arethusa beside it somehow does not belong to Arethusa?" Lorelei stated.

"Your video feed also shows the door covered in Gayatrian symbols," said Sturgeon. He grinned, and glared at Alankar Sen.

"I'm telling you, it's all fake news. Manufactured in a simulation," Alankar said. "From the mutinous crew of a pathetic technical ship, desperate for attention."

"Then who did build it?" Lorelei asked.

No one answered.

Seeing Lorelei's aghast face, Admiral Mbembe said, "I think we have strayed off the agenda for long enough. Shall we move on?"

Gretel, without hesitation, said, "Admiral, we have not yet had a decision on the temperature of the room."

Alankar said, "I'm comfortable. Everyone else looks comfortable. Stop wasting our time."

Gretel rose to her feet and said, "I invoked a point of order, to see that CNH policy is followed correctly. I have the right to do that," she seethed.

Alankar coughed to get attention. "I want the record to show that this committee recommends to the council that there ought to be a policy regarding how many times someone can interrupt a hearing on a point of order."

"I'll second that," said Sturgeon. "And I would like to chair the sub-committee to draft the language of the policy."

"*This* is the sub-committee," Admiral Mbembe reminded them. "And I am its chair."

Hanfei Gao'Fu, the representative for Chang'Ren, put down his oil-comb. "Then let us return to this committee's proper business. We are here to discuss—"

"—The trespassing charges," said Sturgeon Glaive.

"No, we're here to discuss the illegal structures on Pluto," said Gretel, at almost the same moment.

"The signal from Rhinemaiden 74-B, colloquially known as Lorelei's Star," said Hanfei.

And over Hanfei's voice, Alankar said, "On a point of order, Admiral, but is this the policy committee or the disciplinary committee?"

As the committee debated whether or not Alankar was speaking rhetorically, Lorelei turned to her friends and spoke quietly. "Who are these ridiculous people?"

Gretel overheard Lorelei's question. "We are the authorities."

The implications of this statement struck Lorelei in the stomach. "But— since the moment this meeting began, you've been talking about nothing!"

"I quite agree," said Sturgeon Glaive, seizing what he saw as an opportunity. "And while I find all of this digression endlessly entertaining, shall we get back to work?"

"Thank you, Senator," said Din Mbembe. "Now, this committee was convened to discuss—"

"—what we found when we looked at Lorelei's Star," Hanfei Gao'fu finished for him.

"No we weren't," said Din Mbembe.

Lorelei pulled her chair closer. "What did you see? Why won't anyone tell us? What did you see?"

Sturgeon's voice grew strained. "Absolutely nothing of relevance to what you did on Pluto!"

"But you did see something—!" Lorelei guessed.

"We did," Gretel confirmed. "Something of the very highest relevance to all the world."

"We can have that meeting some other time," Sturgeon shot back.

"Éostray has demanded that meeting for seven months," said Gretel, "And so has Chang'ren. So, when, exactly? When? I'll schedule it right now."

"Not today," Sturgeon grinned.

"Yes today!" said Gretel, as she thumped her hand on the table. "Why are we sitting here trying to decide how to punish these good people for making the scientific discovery all humanity has been waiting for? I'll tell you why. Because Arethusa doesn't want to admit it broke the law!"

Then Gretel noticed her thumping of the table created a small dent. She covered it with her Q-link.

"Gentlemen, gentlemen, and ladies," Admiral Mbembe said, with his hands in the air to call for peace. "This hearing has only one item on the agenda. What should we do about the crew of the NavCom Seven and their violation of the treaty?"

"I say we give them a parade, in every major city in the world," said Gretel. "That's what we give to heroes, in Éostray."

Hanfei said, "I think it's about time we told the crew here what we found." Seeing Sturgeon about to object again, he added: "It *is* relevant, no matter what you say. It's the *reason* the defendants broke the treaty."

Sturgeon pursed his lips and glowered at Hanfei. "Some people think they can do what they want at meetings like this."

"As you know," said Hanfei, addressing the NavCom crew, "the technology to detect exoplanets is much better now than it was when we first looked at your star fifty years ago. So when we looked at it again, we found that there is at least one terrestrial rocky planet, just on the inner edge of the habitable zone. We estimate it's about ten percent larger than Earth, and its orbital period is about twenty days shorter than ours. Relative time dilation is negligible."

"You found the planet." Lorelei whispered, grateful for the news.

Hanfei continued. "Our spectrograph analysis showed us an elevated infrared signal coming from it, as well as the chemical signatures of oxygen, carbon, nitrogen, phosphorus. And liquid water."

"The compounds of organic life!" Lorelei grinned with genuine excitement.

"And the Expeditions Council named it after you. Lorelei's Planet."

Lorelei's crewmates patted her shoulder and congratulated

her. Lorelei struggled for a moment with the irregularity of the naming convention, as irritated as she was flattered. Sturgeon scoffed quietly.

Lorelei sat down in her chair. "Any signs of communications? Technology?"

Hanfei shook his head. "I'm sorry to tell you that we are not detecting any organized information signals. No evidence of microwaves or laser transmission. Not even radio."

Lorelei looked down to the floor. Then she looked to the nearest window and said, "But you found a planet."

Jiandong said, "So why is there nothing about this in the news nets?"

"The Council decided not to tell the world everything all at once, but instead to release a little bit at a time," said the admiral. "To give everyone time to think; to let things settle in. But between us—" he looked at Alankar, "—I think certain councillors would rather we told the world nothing at all."

Lorelei shook her head. "Do they not understand how important this is?"

"And is that why we were brought here under guard?" Jiandong asked. "To make sure we don't talk to the press?"

"The security is for your protection," said the admiral. "There's a lot of people out there who want a piece of you, for all kinds of reasons. We received over twenty million hate messages and death threats— they overwhelmed our traffic. But on the bright side: if there's a celebrity anywhere on Earth you'd like to meet, chances are they want to meet you too."

"I don't want a photo-op. I want answers," said Lorelei.

"We *are* answering your questions as best we can," Admiral Mbembe defended himself.

Lorelei looked out the nearest window, and said, "Actually, I want to *go* there."

"It's nine light years away," Hanfei Gao'fu reminded her.

"But the council is already building a starship, *ja*?" said Lorelei.

The admiral paused. "No, we're not."

Lorelei's brow furrowed. She looked back and forth between the admiral and her colleagues. "We saw one under construction, in orbit," she said.

Before anyone else could speak, Alankar Sen intervened. "Ah, that. I get a lot of questions about that. My government is building a new orbital arcology, nothing more."

"An orbital arcology?" said Jiandong. "With the biggest nuclear fusion engine ever built?"

"It provides electricity, not thrust," Alankar replied.

"But—"

"It's an arcology," Alankar insisted.

Lorelei looked to the admiral and said, "Then our starship is in the planning stage?"

"I'm sorry, no," said Din Mbembe. With a sidelong glance to Alankar, he said "The proposal to build a starship and visit your planet has not made it out of the agenda-setting committee."

"But that's not right," said Lorelei. "Don't you want to know what's out there?"

The rest of her crew agreed. "Doesn't the Council have a *mission* to explore space?" said Sitara.

"And doesn't the same law apply— that the first landing on the planet would have to be a Conference ship?" said Jiandong.

"We seem to have strayed off topic," said Admiral Mbembe. "Again."

"Far off, indeed," Sturgeon announced with pleasure. "There's no reason to discuss Lorelei's Planet any further. Lorelei–"

"Doctor Verlassen," Lorelei interrupted.

"—couldn't have known about the probe before she entered the base—"

Gretel saw an opportunity. "Do you want to admit something about that base, Senator Glaive?"

Sturgeon held up an angry finger to stop her from saying anything more. "My government," he said, "has been completely open about everything we're doing out there. That base on Pluto was not built by us. We've been telling you that for months."

Almost everyone reacted to this at the same moment. Gretel thumped the table again and accused Sturgeon of lying. Alankar pushed in front of everyone some photos of what he insisted was an arcology. Hanfei sat back, observing from over the top of his glasses. And Sturgeon, at the centre of it, folded his arms, gazed on the ceiling, and waved people away when they came too close to him. In the midst of the ruckus, Lorelei felt her arms and legs trembling, her belly twisting with disgust at what the councillors were doing. Her friends Sitara and Jiandong wore similar feelings on their faces, but seemed powerless to move.

She rose to her feet to face the councillors. "What's *wrong* with you!"

The chaos stopped. Several of the councillors made a slight recoiling motion. Gretel touched the small gold flower that hung from her necklace. Lorelei had posed The Madman's Question: an intimate, spiritual affirmation to more than half the room.

Sturgeon rose to stand taller than her. "You have no right to raise that poisonous question to me, or to any of your betters," he growled low. To his colleagues he added, "Madness, indeed!"

Alankar clenched his fists and glared at Lorelei. Gretel, however, was watching Alankar and Sturgeon. A small smile grew on her face. But as she was about to speak, Hanfei stood up. "Councillors, please! Perhaps now would be a good time to take a recess," he said.

"It's been less than ten minutes!" Admiral Mbemba objected.

"And in that time we have said and done nothing," Hanfei insisted. "Perhaps we may attempt to begin again after a few moments of restful reflection."

Those who had glared angrily at each other moments earlier now focused on the Chang'ren ambassador with suspicion. Admiral Mbembe turned off the recording device. They all moved to leave the room.

Lorelei got up to follow them out. Before she could step into the hall, one of the armed guards moved into her path. The guard's hand was on the holster of his sidearm.

Seeing the guard's hand on the holster of his sidearm, Sitara moved to Lorelei's side. "Easy there, cowboy. You wanna shoot an unarmed scientist in the Council chambers?" she asked him, disgusted. "Do you Arethusans get any training at all, or do they give you picture-books?"

"Let's just sit down, Sitara. It's not worth it," Lorelei advised her friend. Sitara made a defiant face at the guard, and sat down.

Gretel put a gentle hand on Lorelei's shoulder and led her back into the room. "A word between us, Doctor? May I say, I'm proud of you. Pressing The Madman's Question on him like that. It was perfectly timed, perfectly said."

"I suppose it *is* one of the Twelve Noble Questions. Is he religious? Did I offend him?"

"He's religious enough during elections," Gretel grinned. "And don't worry about offending him. It's fun to see him get angry." Then she gestured toward Hanfei. "Now may I introduce my colleague Hanfei Gao'Fu, from Chang'ren," she said.

Hanfei greeted them with open hands. "I called for a recess because I have seen enough of what your character is like. I am satisfied that you are all civilized people, and I wanted a chance to speak with you privately."

"So what is going on here?" Lorelei demanded.

"My dear Doctor Verlassen," said Gretel, "You may be the smartest person in this room, but you have no idea how to run with the big dogs. Do you honestly think I care about the temperature in the room?"

"But this *isn't* a race," Lorelei said.

"It is to *them*," Hanfei explained. "It is, in fact, the only race that matters. And for you, it's a chance to force the representative from Arethusa to admit on record that his government has known about the probe for months."

"During your hibernation," Gretel explained, "they've said the base was built by us, by Chang'ren, by various corporations. Even the Communion. But they still threaten to shoot down anyone who lands near it."

"There's wreckage, in Pluto's orbit. A Gayatrian ship. They're not kidding."

Hanfei said, "If you can help madam Von Richter and I to force a confession from him, then we will ensure that none of you will be punished for anything."

Jiandong was pleased to hear it. "I think we can do that. Sitara?"

Sitara gave a tired smile in reply. "This whole thing is unbearable anyway."

Lorelei, however, was cautious. "I don't know how I feel about being used like that," she said.

"We're not asking you to lie or to withhold anything," said Gretel, as she put her child-like smile back on her face. "But to continue pressing the questions on him. You could ask him to state exactly which sections of the treaty you are accused of breaking. Hanfei and I can finish the case from there."

"Sounds straight-forward enough," said Jiandong. "We have the right to know exactly what we are accusing of, down to the sub-section."

"And now, we had best step outside," said Gretel. "Can't let the others get too suspicious. In the meanwhile, I imagine you three probably haven't eaten since you landed? I'm sure that was Sturgeon's intention. To keep you uncomfortable, and on the defensive."

Hanfei said, "After this unpleasant business is over, you are all welcome to join me for dinner at the embassy. It must have been a a few weeks since you had a proper meal—"

Hanfei was interrupted by the sound of shouting coming from the hallway. The door burst open and Lieutenant Glaive marched in. Behind him came his father, his hands on his son's shoulders, apparently to ensure the lieutenant did not turn around and leave.

"—all be over in less than two minutes if we stick to the agenda. I can't stand these meetings where all we do is take breaks. Nothing gets done. It's all talking and more talking, and nothing gets done!"

As the councillors sat behind their table again, the admiral re-activated the recording device. "Meeting resumed after a short recess," he said.

Lorelei nodded toward the representative of Chang'ren, and then addressed Sturgeon. "Sir, may I ask you to read the exact sections of the treaty that we are alleged to have broken?"

Sturgeon did not expect the question. His momentary look of surprise made several people in the room smile. "You really want me to sit here and look it up?" he asked.

Din Mbembe said, "They have the right."

Sturgeon looked at Admiral Mbembe for help. The admiral pointed to the Q-link on the desk, which displayed the contract on its screen. Sturgeon grimaced, and flipped through the pages. When he found the clause he wanted, he read it aloud: "Section three, subsection nine, paragraph four. Signatories on this treaty agree that while the land-surface of any celestial body cannot be owned by anyone or any corporate or state body, structures placed on the land-surface can be owned by that agent who places them there. Further, that no person may enter said structures without the permission of the owners."

"Sounds quite comprehensive," said Lorelei. "Yet you claim you had no presence on Pluto."

"Well then, sir," said Gretel, smiling, "If that building isn't yours, then our Doctor Verlassen didn't need your permission to enter it."

Sturgeon's face turned slightly red. "You're splitting hairs."

Gretel grinned. "You gave us a deliciously big hair to split."

Sturgeon glared at his colleagues for a few heartbeats, and then pointed at Gretel. "Your people must have done it. You must have made the video in advance and ordered your agent—" he pointed at Lorelei, "— to transmit once they got there."

Gretel grinned and shook her head. "You know what I love

about you Arethusans? Your audacity. You don't care whether you're right or wrong. You just love to make things happen. It makes you feel like you're in control."

"We *are* in control," Sturgeon growled back. "We have the largest military, and more off-world colonies than any other nation." He sat back, and smiled with pride.

"The biggest mouths, too," Sitara whispered to her friends.

Hanfei said to Sturgeon, "You may sit on top of the world now, but you will not sit there forever."

"Is that a threat?" Sturgeon hissed.

"It's a prediction," Hanfei said. "Some day very soon, the largest military and the largest colony network will belong to whoever conquers Lorelei's Planet. That nation will also enjoy all the minerals, all the energy, all the farms and manufacturing: everything they need to dominate the human race for a thousand years. But that nation will not be Arethusa. And it won't be Éostray, or Gayatri," he continued, eyeing Alankar Sen as he spoke, "or any of those disorganized, disunited, and primitive nations cobbled together less than a century ago from—"

"It *will* be Gayatri," said Alankar, slapping his hand on the table. "We are tired of being treated like we can never be more than second-best! We are just as much a player in the race as any of you. And I promise you, when our starship reaches that planet, the first words spoken by the first human to walk on it will be in our language—"

"So your government *is* building a starship, after all," Hanfei interrupted cooly.

"It's an arco—!" Alankar insisted. But he saw the way his colleagues looked at him, and he knew the mistake he had made. "Strike that from the record," he ordered.

"We can't do that, and you know it," said Hanfei.

Sturgeon grinned happily.

Gretel looked at Hanfei and said, "You might have warned me you were going to do that," she said.

Hanfei smiled, and shrugged.

Admiral Mbembe tapped the table to get everyone's attention. "I think a great many issues have arisen here tonight, which ought to be discussed by the council as a whole, and not by a sub-committee like this one. We still have the outstanding matter of the actual business this hearing was supposed to be about. Now, since it seems there is no plaintiff in this case— unless, of course, Mr. Glaive has anything more to say?"

"Arethusa withdraws its complaint against the crew of the NavCom Seven," said Sturgeon.

Din Mbembe was glad to hear it. "Captain Xiao, you and your crew may resume your duties as usual. This meeting is concluded."

The crew rose to their feet and loudly congratulated each other. They reached out to the council members to thank them. Sturgeon also applauded the conclusion, but grew impatient as no one of the NavCom Seven crew came to shake his hands. He folded his arms, then gathered his devices and marched out of the room, pushing one of the guards out of his way as he left.

Lorelei moved to face the admiral. "So when do we fly to the new planet?"

"My android will bring you your hotel room keys and your dinner tickets," the admiral said, ignoring her question. "Feel free to enjoy the attractions of the city. But don't stay out too late. Press conference in the morning. Goodnight, and welcome home!" He shook everyone's hands again, and followed the other councillors out of the room. The NavCom crew found themselves alone.

"Do you still believe a starship can save them?" Sitara asked Lorelei. "Because I think they don't want to be saved."

§ 13.

In her hotel room that night, Lorelei enjoyed stretching her arms to their full extent and spinning in a wide circle. Full, normal gravity, for the first time in two years! Food which was not freeze-dried! A shower without a shut-off timer! But a concierge told her she had to keep the ankle monitor on. Even when she went to sleep.

The next morning, a car took her to the press conference. She arrived in the media theatre to find Sturgeon Glaive and Din Mbembe arguing over the fact that Sturgeon was wearing an Expeditions Council flight jacket.

"You're not a member of any NavCom Crew," said the admiral.

"I'm showing solidarity and respect to the brave men and women of the Expeditions fleet," Sturgeon grinned.

"You're making it look like you're one of them— which you are not!"

As Lorelei approached, Sturgeon took her elbow in his arm

and said, "What's the big deal? Lorelei is a member of the fleet, and she doesn't mind."

Lorelei let her mind be known by jerking her elbow out of Sturgeon's hands, and glaring at him. "In fact I *do* mind," she told him. "I had to earn that uniform."

Sturgeon smiled at her. "Now Lorelei, don't be such a stickler for the petty things. Come sit next to me for the press conference. Show the world that we are all friends here."

As Sturgeon, Admiral Mbembe, and the NavCom crew took their seats behind the press conference front table, Lorelei chose to sit with an empty chair between her and Sturgeon. The senator noticed, but turned to the cameras and put his smile on. An android combed his grey hair into a side-part with a fringe in front, and sprayed it with a chemical whose smell made him wince.

Lorelei opened a Q-link that had been placed on the table in front of her, and found that it contained several pages of text, photographs of the probe, and various charts and graphs. "Why didn't we get a copy of the press kit until now? There's no time for us to study it," she asked Admiral Mbembe.

"You don't need to study it," he answered, as an android brushed the lint from his uniform jacket. "You're here to help us set the image straight. That's all."

"What does that mean?"

"It means you let the ambassador and I do the talking. If anyone asks you a question, you keep your answer brief, and you let one of us finish it."

Lorelei wanted to argue the point, but an android stepped behind her and began brushing her hair. In only two strokes it caught a knot in her curls. Lorelei pushed it away; Sturgeon laughed quietly at her for it.

The admiral introduced everyone at the table to the press gallery, and he reviewed the information about Lorelei's planet that was already in the public domain. Then Sturgeon took the podium, and talked the journalists through an animated slide show about the planet's size and atmospheric composition. Lorelei began to daydream. She took a pencil and drew on the tablecloth a sketch of a starship.

When Sturgeon's main presentation was done, Mbembe opened the floor to questions.

"Claire Bennett, Times of Newgarten— How did you discover all this?" asked one of the journalists.

"Arethusan scientists at the National Observatory made the precise quantum-level spectroscope analyses of the light from the star filtered through the planet's atmosphere," said Sturgeon.

"As if he knows what that means," Sitara whispered to Lorelei.

"As if that means anything at all," Lorelei whispered back. "Quantum spectroscopy— did he just make it up?"

"He did. On the shitter this morning," said Sitara.

Sturgeon spared half a second to give the two women a patronizing smile and a wag of his finger.

"Any signs of civilization?" Claire asked again.

"None so far," said Sturgeon. "We continue to monitor the planet using the orbital telescopes at the Lagrange points around Mars, so as to detect the longest wavelengths. As you know, our National Computing Lab has the world's biggest quantum-logic mainframe, and we've got it searching for patterns in the data. But so far, nothing meaningful has emerged."

"What about the infrared signal, that you mentioned? The organic compounds in the atmosphere?"

"Our scientists have already determined that it doesn't mean anything."

Lorelei looked up and said, "It could be the heat dissipation from the industrial base of an advanced society. Or it could be hydrocarbons in the upper atmosphere. The chemical signature of industrial pollution. Fossil fuels. Global warming," Lorelei explained. "Any *one* of those is a sign of civilization."

The journalists mumbled among themselves, and whispered into their recording devices.

Din Mbembe leaned in front of Sitara to hiss at Lorelei, "What are you doing?"

"I'm answering the reporter's questions," she said.

"That's Senator Glaive's job."

"But he's not a scientist."

Claire Bennett asked her next question. "Senator, why didn't you mention this before?"

Sturgeon said, "Because this is still speculation," he chuckled. Then he glowered at Lorelei.

Lorelei didn't notice; she was quivering from the glare of every journalist in the room, and all their cameras and lamps.

"I only thought of it now," Lorelei admitted.

"There, you see?" Sturgeon smiled. "Only a theory. Nothing real. Next question."

"That's not what the word 'theory' means," Lorelei said. But Sturgeon only smirked at her.

Another journalist had the next question. "Grant Molloy, Eagle Eye News. Would you tell us, Doctor Verlassen, how did it feel to be the first to touch an alien artifact?"

"Well, it's probable that I was *not* the first; after all, someone built the dome where I found it."

"So you admit you were trespassing on someone's base."

"Someone's *illegal* base," Lorelei reminded everyone.

Grant Molloy addressed Jiandong next. "Captain Xiao: do you think what Doctor Verlassen did— trespassing on that base — was right?"

Jiandong paused, pursed his lips, and drew a breath. The clicking of camera shutters grew louder. "What Lorelei discovered there," he said, "was of such universal importance— it legally overwhelms—"

The journalist interrupted to say, "But she can't have known about the discovery before she broke into the base. Unless someone told her what she would find?"

"No one told me anything," Lorelei said.

The reporter addressed Sitara next. "Miss Kula," he asked, "isn't it true that you signed on to the NavCom fleet to avoid compulsory treatment for gambling addiction?"

"What? No!" Sitara seethed.

Jiandong spotted Sturgeon and Grant Molloy exchange knowing looks. He turned to his admiral, gesturing for help.

Din Mbembe said, "Next question, please."

Another journalist took a turn. "Mary Drake, The Contact. Doctor Verlassen. Tell us about your outfit today. Is that a Kaspar Chase designer dress?"

"I don't know," said Lorelei, as she fingered the neckline of her dress. "I had it printed here in the hotel this morning."

"Royal blue dress, high heel knee boots, and your Expeditions Council jacket. Very adventure-chic. Our subscribers love it. They want to know why you chose it."

"I didn't have clothes like this when I was a girl, so I like having them now," Lorelei explained. "Why does it matter?"

"Could you stand up and let us take a full head-to-toe picture?"

Lorelei glared at the reporter, and stayed in her seat. Her undisguised annoyance caused the room to quiet down. "We discovered physical proof that there's another intelligence in the galaxy besides our own. Don't your viewers care about that?"

"Let me remind you," Sturgeon interrupted, "that to the best of our knowledge, there is *no* life on Lorelei's planet. No *intelligent* life, that we know of."

"That doesn't mean there's nobody out there," Lorelei said.

Sitara chose that moment to distinguish herself as a scientist. "Look at it like this. A thousand years ago here on Earth, we were still using sailing ships, horse carts, and water clocks. We couldn't have detected the laser-nets and microwaves that we use now— we couldn't have imagined them. In the same way, we today might not be able to imagine the technology that we ourselves will use, a thousand years from now. And that might be where the aliens are *today*. If they're out there at all, then it's likely their technology has advanced so far that we don't even know what to look for. Who knows— maybe they are already watching us, with technology so advanced we cannot know that we're being watched."

Sturgeon's way of looking at her changed from annoyance to calculated interest.

"And if they're out there, "Lorelei finished, "we have only sixteen years to find them."

"What happens in sixteen years?" asked Grant Molloy.

"The threshold of cultural entropy reaches—" Then Lorelei's voice drifted, as a new thought appeared in her mind. She held her breath for a heartbeat, to give it time to take shape. The press gallery waited for her to speak. Sturgeon glared at her. Then she said, "But this calculation will change, very soon. Because the Conference of Nations is going to build a starship."

The press gallery filled with gasps and frantic voices speaking quickly into transcribers. Camera flashes filled the room with stars; Lorelei involuntarily shielded her eyes for a moment. Mbembe and Sturgeon gaped at Lorelei. Her crewmates shifted uncomfortably in their chairs.

Din Mbembe stood up and walked to Lorelei's side, to speak into her microphone. "What Doctor Verlassen means, of course, is—"

"—exactly what I said," Lorelei finished for him.

Lorelei saw how everyone in the room was looking at her. One of her legs began to vibrate nervously.

"Excuse me," said Claire Bennett. "This announcement isn't in the press kit you gave us."

"But it *is* what's going to happen," said Lorelei. "It's what *has* to happen."

Din Mbembe took the main podium and said, "Ladies and gentlemen, that's all the time we have today. Please direct your remaining questions to the press office. Thank you."

Then to Lorelei, he said, "Follow me."

§ 14.

Din Mbembe led Lorelei to a stairwell. Once they were both inside and the door was closed, he rounded on her with an accusing snarl: "Explain yourself!" When Lorelei took a step back from him and didn't answer, he said "Do you think the Council will do what you want, just because you told them to?"

Lorelei found her voice again. "I was only describing what's going to happen."

"And how do you know what's going to happen."

"Isn't it obvious? Because, now that everybody knows about the planet, they're going to want to go there. Because it has to be a global effort— something all humanity can call their own. Because it's the right thing to do. Because if we don't do it now, we never will."

"You don't make policy. The council does," Din reminded her with finality. "After your stunt on Pluto, some of the councillors wanted to stick you with a desk job. But today, the entire general assembly will want to space you out an airlock. I want your letter of resignation in one hour."

"But, sir!"

"Either you resign, or I fire you. Now which of those do you want on your record?"

§ 15.

Sturgeon left the press conference without speaking. He marched to his limousine, waiting for him in front of the hotel. He slammed the door shut more forcefully than was necessary, and activated the auto-tint on the windows to make it impossible for the reporters to photograph him. His smile fell off his face like an old coat dropped on the floor.

"Take me home," he ordered the car.

At the Glaive family penthouse, on top of one of Newgarten's tallest condominium towers, Glaive was lifting weights in the gym. Sturgeon announced his arrival by turning off his son's music.

"Were you watching?" Sturgeon asked.

"The presser? Yes, sir," said Glaive, sitting up from the bench and reaching for a towel. "I think it went very well for us."

"No, it did not," Sturgeon grumbled.

"We didn't have to say anything on record that we didn't want to."

"What you need to understand," Sturgeon said, "is that people only ever hear what you *don't* say. Because they can fill that empty space with the very worst possible interpretation of what you *did* say. So, no, it did not go well; it went intolerably badly!"

Glaive looked to the cityscape, to give himself time to think of what to say next. The building which housed the family penthouse gave an excellent view of the city's skyscrapers and super-towers, stretching on to the horizon. The lone brown river that sludged between them was the only space on the ground not covered by asphalt and concrete and steel.

"Are we going to build a starship now, too?" he asked.

"Let's say, whoever has the probe, has a head start," said Sturgeon.

Glaive's mood perked up. "So we *are* building a starship!"

"I didn't say that."

"But I heard what you didn't say."

Sturgeon chuckled. "Catching on! I am at this moment drafting a letter to our Minister of Science and Weapons Development, asking him to put you in charge of building it."

Glaive let out a small gasp. "Sir? In charge of— I don't know anything about engineering. Or project management. I thought you wanted me in the army, so that I'd be eligible to run for Senate."

"You don't have the boots to be a soldier," Sturgeon snapped back. "I read your report— the classified one— I know what *really* happened. Your duty was clear, boy! And you let that Éostray girl's pretty face talk you out of it. Why didn't you shoot her?"

"Because— the probe was—"

"Yes, of course, the probe," said Sturgeon. "That's the excuse for everything these days. Now give me a real answer, to a question that matters. Did you notice anything on the probe that looked like it was still active?"

"It's all in the report, Sir."

"Answer my question, son."

Glaive sighed before answering. "No. Nothing obvious, anyway."

"Nothing? Did it have any lights on? Was any part of it warm to the touch? Anything?"

"I was too busy thinking about what Verlassen was doing."

"Not good. When you take over as director of the Space Research Agency, you'll have to notice everything. But listen— this is important— tell me again how long was that woman in the FOB before you got there."

"About three minutes— why do you ask?"

"Three minutes," Sturgeon cussed. "Long enough to hide things from us."

"What's this about, Sir?"

"Something that their comms officer said to the press a moment ago. It's obvious Lorelei and her crew know things that they're not telling us. Listen— it's been seven months since news of the probe went public. It's about damn time we stopped assuming that just because we can't find the aliens that they're not out there."

"We don't know anything about the people who built the probe—"

"The *aliens*, son. Not people— aliens. But you're right that we don't know what their real intentions are. And as a soldier it is your responsibility to keep our nation safe. Now put those two thoughts together and tell me what you get."

"You get the seventh standing order, sir," said Glaive. "In the absence of good intel, always assume your enemy is smarter than you and that he is deceiving you."

"Very good. Now, when you take over the starship project, you'll find that we have been working on it for almost a year. Right now it is designed only for science and colonization. I want you to ensure that it will *also* be designed for war."

Glaive paused before replying. "Why do you want me to do it, Sir? I thought, after what happened on the Seven—"

"You are still on probation for that one," Sturgeon growled. "But a new space race has begun. I need someone in charge of our mission who reports directly to me."

§ 16.

Lorelei returned to her hotel room, wrote the resignation

letter, emailed it to the admiral, and packed her few possessions into a suitcase. When she opened the door to leave, she saw Gretel Von Richter standing there, smiling and greeting her with open hands.

"He sacked you, didn't he?" said Gretel.

Lorelei nodded. "I suppose he was right to sack me," she sighed.

"I'm sorry to hear that," said Gretel. "Do you have any plans?"

"Right now I want to go home," Lorelei said.

"I understand completely," said Gretel, as she took Lorelei's hands. "But what you did in the press conference— well, let's say, some influential people took notice."

"I'll never go into space again," Lorelei predicted unhappily.

Gretel led Lorelei back into the room, so they could speak more privately. "Ever since the discovery, I've been trying to get the Council to do exactly what you told the world it must do. Maybe the council will listen to *your* voice, more than mine. I'm putting a new proposal on the agenda for the next meeting, and if it passes— well, would you like to stay in the race?"

Lorelei perked her eyes for a moment, then her gaze returned to the floor. "But who would hire me?"

Gretel took Lorelei's hands and said, "I would."

Lorelei looked up.

"I have a job for you," said Gretel. "I want you to lobby the other members of council to agree to my proposal. Most are already on our side; they just need a little extra persuasion."

"How many do I have to talk to?" Lorelei asked.

"Half the council, but that is not the problem. The problem is that the Gayatris can't hide their starship anymore, so they are likely to exercise their veto. It will be your job to make sure they don't. Here, take this—" Gretel handed Lorelei a Q-link— "and study it tonight."

"What is it?"

"An intelligence report on every member of the council."

Lorelei flipped through the documents on the screen. "Here's a profile Sturgeon Glaive," she observed. "I met his son. He was the lieutenant guarding the base on Pluto."

Gretel said, "You'll find a dossier on him in there, too."

Lorelei closed the folder and asked, "Why are you doing this for me?"

Gretel smiled. "Because you're perfect for this job. Smart,

experienced, pretty, more than a little bold. And now, you're world-famous, too. Éostray needs leaders like you. But we also need to clean you up. Change your image a little bit. You look good— don't get me wrong— but we need you to look *right*."

Lorelei looked at Gretel's hands and said, "Clean me up— do you mean— cybernetic skin, like yours?"

Gretel smiled. "You noticed? Perceptive, too. I also had my arms and legs replaced with biotechnics." She rolled up her sleeve, revealing that her arm was made of flesh-coloured carbon-fibre plates attached to thousands of long and thin servomotors.

Lorelei's hands slightly recoiled. "You're not going to—"

"No, no," Gretel grinned, as she closed the panel and put away her pen. "We'll just get you some better clothes. Hand-sewn, and designer made. Nothing home-printed like this—" Gretel gently tugged the shoulder of Lorelei's flight jacket.

Lorelei made an annoyed face. "What does that have to do with my job?"

"In the world of diplomacy, your looks can show how serious you are," Gretel explained. "That you respect yourself and whoever you're talking to. And dressing up can be fun! Oh, and you really should consider upgrading yourself. You want to win the honours race, you need every advantage you can get."

Lorelei shook her head, then turned her attention back to the documents Gretel gave her. "When is the next meeting of the council?"

"Tomorrow. There's an informal dinner first, and I'll make sure you are there."

"That's not much time to prepare."

"I have faith in you," the representative encouraged her. "Just tell them why you think a starship for all humanity is important. Maybe say something more about your Doomsday Argument—"

"It's called the threshold of cultural—"

"And try The Madman's Question on them again. It was so beautiful when you did that at the hearing yesterday. They won't be able to squirm out of answering. And there will be quite a few important people taking account of who gives you a straight answer, and who does not."

Lorelei nodded. Then she looked around the room and sighed. "I have nowhere to stay tonight."

"It's already taken care of," Gretel said. "The embassy is paying for your hotel room now. Just charge everything you need. We've added you to the diplomatic account with the concierge. I'll meet you here tomorrow. Get some rest. You're going to be fine."

§ 17.

"You fired her?" Sitara exclaimed.

"Of course I fired her," said Mbembe. "After what she did today, what would you have done!"

Mbembe stood behind the desk of the now-empty press room. He leaned forward, his hands on the tablecloth, as if his effort held the desk back from flying up and crushing the two officers before him.

"When were you going to inform me about that? I'm her captain!" said Jiandong.

"I'm informing you now," Mbembe told him. "And you, Captain, are walking a razor's edge too. You will have your chance to tell your story, soon enough. We have a packed schedule of public appearances for you, starting later this week. Science conferences, presidential galas, prayer breakfasts. Every university in the world wants to give you an honorary doctorate. Hell, the king of Éostray offered you a knighthood. Everybody has their own ideas of what the discovery means, and they all want you to validate them. We have to be very careful, so that you don't say the wrong thing."

"And what is the wrong thing?" said Jiandong.

"I shouldn't have to tell you," Mbembe said. "Now, tomorrow you'll be given a package of briefing notes and talking points. Whatever you say, you stick to them. Whatever questions anybody asks, whatever your opinions— hell, whatever your feelings— you stay on message."

"What about Lorelei?" asked Sitara.

"What about her?"

"You can't stop *her* from talking to the press. You fired her."

"She is about to be buried neck-deep in lawsuits," Mbembe retorted. "She won't be saying much of anything very soon."

"Will that be all," said Jiandong.

Din said, "Tomorrow morning, you'll be invited to an informal breakfast meeting with the whole council," he told them. "Until then, don't leave the hotel, and don't talk to anybody."

§ 18.

Lorelei's new job held no interest for her at all. She sat in a chair near the window of her hotel room, with her feet up on another chair. Her boots lay on the floor beside her, underneath a small scattering of papers torn from her sketch pad. In her hands she held the Q-link Gretel gave her, and as she read from it she underlined any noteworthy passages with a light pen.

"So that's when he fired you?" said Sitara, who sat on a nearby desk.

"I probably deserved it," Lorelei replied.

"What will you do now?" said Jiandong, who was leaning on a wall near the door.

"I got a new job already. With the embassy of Éostray."

"Well, that was fast," said Sitara. "I guess you're a national hero now."

"The ambassador seemed very keen to hire me," Lorelei explained, as she stood and dropped the Q-link on the desk beside Sitara. "And my first responsibility is to read these papers. Technical reports. Financial planning reports. Personnel briefings. All written in corporate baffle-talk. Hardly one sentence out of every ten actually *means* something."

Sitara picked up the dossier. "This is high-level classified intel. And the ambassador just handed it to you. Like it was nothing."

Lorelei paused for a moment, then said, "I suppose that was a little unusual."

"Can I see them?" Jiandong asked.

Lorelei gestured to the Q-link, to show she didn't care if he read them. Jiandong took it and scrolled at random. Finding a document that interested him, he said "This one is a material stress-test report. Someone put a lot of work into it."

Sitara said, "And I saw some write-ups about every member of the Expeditions Council. Their whole lives are in here— their friends, their vacations, their food allergies."

"She wants me to find some dirt in here on the representative of Gayatri Pradesh," said Lorelei, "so that I can stop him from using his veto. The vote tomorrow evening," said Lorelei. Then she dropped herself back into the chair by the window, and looked outside.

"This is what you want, Lorelei," Sitara observed. "A chance to go back to space again. To go to the planet you discovered. I'd have thought you would be more excited."

"It's the politics," Lorelei complained. "There's this phrase I've been hearing rather often, these last few days. 'The honours race'. You've heard it too? Whatever it is, Gretel wants me to be part of it. But all I want right now is to go home."

"If joining the race gets you what you want," Sitara shrugged.

"It just seems so pointless," Lorelei said. "They're racing to see who can stand on top of the world longer than anyone else. But the stakes of their race are actually very small. Above us, there's an ocean of stars that goes on forever, with planets everywhere— *life* probably everywhere too. We could be going out to explore it."

Sitara moved to Lorelei's side and said, "If you want to explore the galaxy, then *that's* what you have to tell the ambassador. You have to help him see the world the way you do."

"I've never been very good with people," Lorelei lamented. "In fact I don't really *like* people. When I was a teenager and the other girls had boyfriends and went to dance clubs, I went to the forest, and sat in the hunter's platforms half way up the trees, and made drawings of the valley, until the sun went down."

"Did any of those girls get to discover an alien probe on Pluto?"

"No," Lorelei admitted.

"There, you see? If you can do that, you can do anything."

Lorelei's eyes remained downcast, but she smiled.

Jiandong, who had been listening from a respectful distance, said, "Tomorrow evening, Sitara and I are meeting most of the council for a formal dinner. You should come."

"Mbembe will kick me out," Lorelei predicted.

"I won't let him," he promised. "I'm the captain, and you are still part of my crew until I say otherwise."

Lorelei smiled. She offered her hands for her two friends to clasp. "Still a team," she said.

"Still a team," Sitara agreed.

At that moment, a news camera drone buzzed outside the window, invading the room with its lamp and its camera. Lorelei waved at the glass, turning it to a mirror, and the lights in the suite grew brighter in compensation. "I should get back to studying. I should work on what I'm going to say."

"You don't want us to help?" said Jiandong.

"Thanks. But if you don't mind, we were squeezed together in that spaceship for over two years. I'm glad to have some space to myself. Even if only a hotel room."

The three friends said their goodbyes for the day, and then Jiandong and Sitara left Lorelei to her thoughts.

§ 19.

When the door closed, Jiandong turned to Sitara. "Do you think she can do it?"

"Maybe. Yes."

"You don't sound certain."

"If she goes to a council meeting, she's likely to say or do something absolutely mad. Again."

Jiandong agreed. "Maybe we should have our own plan."

"I think I may have one," Sitara suggested. "I got a look at the dossier for Alankar Sen. He's bleeding cash, heavily in debt. He's paying support for three ex-wives. We used to eyeball players like him back in my five-card days. He needs money. And there's a really good casino not far from here."

Jiandong stopped walking and turned to face her. "I know what you're thinking. Don't do it."

"But I'm good at it!" Sitara retorted. "I paid for university and everything, by sharking people in casinos all over Gayatri. On the grid, too."

"This time, you're talking about bribing a diplomat!"

"It's not the main plan anyway. It's the backup plan. The *main* plan is whatever Lorelei's going to do. Unless you can think of something better?"

Jiandong thought about it for a moment, then said, "Yes, I think I can. Meet me in the lobby in half an hour."

"Why— what are we doing?"

"We are going to meet the Godspeaker of Newgarten."

§ 20.

The autotaxi carrying Jiandong and Sitara stopped in front to the city's largest cathedral: an imposing fortress-like structure of heavy black and yellow bricks, sitting in a garden enclosed by a wall of watchtowers and battlements. The front portal was surrounded by statues of various saints and religious heroes, and above it there glowed a large stained-glass window featuring

The Soldier.

"Jiandong, didn't you tell us you were not religious anymore?" asked Sitara.

"I said it was complicated," Jiandong replied, and he ascended the steps to the cathedral. "But at the moment I'm a citizen journalist, and I want to ask the Godspeaker some questions."

"You won't get to see him so easily," Sitara doubted aloud.

"Not all complications are bad."

An acolyte met them at the portal, and saluted them by touching his heart, his lips, and his forehead. Jiandong returned the salute, and recited a ritual greeting: "Hail, gatekeeper— we are two pilgrims seeking shelter from the storm."

"Welcome home, wayward children," the acolyte replied. Then the acolyte caught his breath, as he suddenly realized who he was talking to. "Aren't you—"

"I am," Jiandong confirmed. "But my associate here doesn't know the rest of the ritual, so do you mind if we just step inside?"

"Of course, sir," said the acolyte. "We have heard of your discovery. All of humanity rejoices in the news."

Jiandong winked at Sitara and said, "Told you they'd let us in."

They entered the cathedral. The main space was laid out like a parade ground for a company of soldiers, with regimental banners hanging from the rafters, and shrines to various militant saints filling niches along the walls. Candle light and incense wafted through the air. At the far end another large stained-glass window let in the last of the day's sunshine. It depicted a trinolay: a yellow flower with three petals, and a long stem and stamen.

"Why is the trinolay the symbol of the Communion?" asked Sitara.

"One petal for the Celestials, one for the ancestors, and one for Kai'tzeen, the first Godspeaker. The circle in the centre is for the One-And-All," the acolyte explained.

Below this window was a stage featuring statues of the seven Celestials, with offering bowls and candles at their feet. A short line of people waited for a turn to place coins, flowers, short handwritten notes, and other offerings at the feet of their gods. Nearby, another acolyte stood at a lectern and read aloud from a book with a gentle and melodious voice: *Every day we live, we give thanks to the seven Celestials, first-born from the One-And-All, who gave us the virtues of true civilization: The Midwife who gave us generosity, The Merchant who gave us fairness, The Soldier who gave us courage—*

The acolyte who led them in said, "Now, what brings you to our sanctuary?"

"We would like an audience with the Godspeaker," said Jiandong.

The acolyte smiled. "Of course! Please wait here. And may I say again, it's an honour to meet you!"

Jiandong and Sitara took a seat on a bench near one of the side shrines. They listened to the acolyte on the altar recite from his book.

"I haven't heard that prayer since I was a little girl," Sitara said.

"It's a tradition from the years after Kai'tzeen met the Summoner, that someone would read from the Chronicle of his life, every day at high noon," Jiandong explained. "In the old tradition people would gather for the reading and talk about it afterwards. Argue about it, sometimes. But in Communion churches like this, you listen, and think about it. That's all."

Before Jiandong could continue, the Godspeaker arrived. At first all they saw of him was his legs, bare but for his socks, since the rest of him was caught in the ritual cloak that he was desperately trying to pull on correctly. The acolyte who they already met was at his side, trying to help. "Please let go, I can do this—"

When the Godspeaker got his head through the top of the robe, he saw that Jiandong and Sitara were right in front of him. Sitara suppressed an urge to laugh.

"Welcome. I'm Jerome Rafferty, the new Godspeaker of Newgarten. You must be Captain Xiao, and officer Kula. What an extraordinary privilege to meet you!"

"Your cloak of office is inside-out," offered Jiandong

The Godspeaker looked at himself, laughing. "Oh dear, so it is. You don't mind if I—?"

"Not at all," said Jiandong.

Rafferty twisted his outfit around. "You may have guessed that I'm new at this job. Three weeks ago I was a spot-welder. Now, I'm told you wanted to see me?"

Sitara said, "I'm sorry, did you just say you were a spot welder?"

"That's right," he said. "His Holiness the High Godspeaker usually appoints people who spent half their lives in a monastery. But since your discovery, the Communion wants people who understand life outside the cloister."

"Oh, okay," said Sitara. "I thought it might be that nobody studies theology anymore—"

Jiandong winced, and nudged her.

The Godspeaker only made a soft chuckle. "It's fine. Now that we're settled, allow me to put to you The Teacher's Question," he said. "What are your questions?"

Jiandong activated recording on his Q-link, placed it on the shrine beside him. "For my column," he explained, and the Godspeaker nodded. "First, does the Communion have a position on whether there is intelligent life elsewhere in the galaxy?"

"Good question," said the Godspeaker, as he fumbled in his robe to retrieve something from his pocket. "It's a scientific question, of course, not a religious one. But if it turns out that there *are* aliens, the teachings of the Communion remain the same. The One-And-All creates the universe by shining it out from his spirit in every moment. And so he must surely sustain whatever aliens might be out there, same as he does for us." Finding his ceremonial chain handed to him by his acolyte, he draped it over his neck.

"If the One-And-All spoke to one of them, like he spoke to Kai'tzeen—" Jiandong gestured to the Godspeaker's medallion, "—then it will be interesting to read their Chronicle, wouldn't you agree?" Jiandong mused.

"There is only one Chronicle," the Godspeaker said. The smile disappeared from his face for the first time. "In all of history, only one man has heard the voice of the One-And-All."

Sitara said, "You seem very sure of yourself on that point."

"I said I was a spot welder, not an atheist," the Godspeaker replied, his grin returning.

"Of course," said Jiandong. "It's just that— when the Conference starship reaches Lorelei's Planet, we will likely find they have their own religion. What might that say about ours?"

Rafferty looked up to the ceiling for a moment. "Well! There's a plan for a starship already in the works? I didn't realize things were moving ahead so fast."

"The decision is coming up in the next meeting," said Jiandong.

"Interesting," said the Godspeaker, still looking to the ceiling and thinking. Then he looked to Jiandong and said, "Have you spoken to your parents yet?"

"My parents?" said Jiandong, startled by the question. "You know them?"

"I met them at a gathering in Trinothal. Lovely people. They told me you left the Communion and joined the Cosán Eolais."

Jiandong paused to think of how best to answer. "We were all young once, Godspeaker," he said.

The Godspeaker grinned. "Well. You are always welcome to return home, to us."

"Thank you. But for now, I think we must go."

The Godspeaker stood and held out his hand in a gesture of blessing. "May the Celestials guide you, and the Nocturnals spare you, now and forever." Then he turned to his acolyte, who nodded in confirmation.

Jiandong saluted the Godspeaker with a hand gesture to his heart, lips, and forehead. Then he turned to leave.

"By the way— when did you say the vote on the starship will happen?" the Godspeaker asked.

"Tomorrow," Jiandong said. "Evening session, after a formal dinner."

When they had left the cathedral and the door was closed, Sitara turned to Jiandong. "Okay, what just happened in there?"

He smiled. "The Communion is not only a religious group. It's also a multi-national corporation. It has lobbyists and campaigners in more than a hundred countries. And we just leaked to it some inside information."

"You could be fired for that. We *both* could be fired."

"But we won't be," he assured her. "The Communion protects its assets."

"You're a dog in the honours race, aren't you?"

Jiandong shrugged. "Not by choice. I'm leveraging what I have for my crew, and that includes you. The discovery promoted us to the big league. Right now you can bet that man is on comms to his superiors, telling them everything we told him. By tonight, every lobbyist on their payroll will pressure every member of the council to vote in favour of our starship."

"How do you know they'll want the vote to go our way?"

"If there are aliens out there, the Communion will want to preach to them. The Godspeaker said as much."

Sitara sighed. "Will it be enough?"

"Maybe. The rest is up to Lorelei."

Pressing a few icons on his Q-link, Jiandong summoned an autotaxi, which pulled up almost instantaneously.

"Do you mind if I don't go back to the hotel with you?" Sitara asked. "We've been in space for so long, I want to walk around for a while, maybe go to the sea wall."

"As you wish. See you at dinner tonight," Jiandong agreed.

When his autotaxi was out of sight, Sitara summoned another for herself.

"Newgarten City-View Casino," she told the car.

§ 21.

The autotaxi carried Sitara through a neighbourhood of pawn shops, payday loan lenders, and temp agency offices. A narrow road ended at the gate to the City-View Casino and its parking lot, where the holograms of playing cards, roulette wheels, and rolling dice outshone the streetlights. A large stained-glass window set above the front doors depicted a woman with a top hat, welcoming visitors with an open hand. Above the building, holographic fireworks exploded with gold coins and colourful paper banknotes. Statues of two Nocturnals flanked the door: The Gambler and The Magician.

A concierge met Sitara at the door. "Welcome to— Oh! you're Sitara Kula!" He waved at another nearby staff member. "Look who it is! From the NavCom Seven! Get the manager!"

By the time Sitara was less than ten steps inside the casino, she was surrounded by a crowd of admirers, all taking her picture.

The manager parted the crowd, flanked by security guards. "Ms. Kula. Welcome to the City View! Can I get you a drink?"

"I was cooped up in a spaceship for two years. I thought I'd sneak out of my hotel and have some fun."

"We are honoured to have you. Where would you like to begin tonight?"

Sitara looked around the gaming floor and spotted a cards table where one of the players sat hunched over the table, as if he did not want to be seen. But Sitara knew her target: Alankar Sen.

"I'll start with a few rounds of five-card finangle," she said, pointing to Sen's table.

"Right this way."

Along the way, she passed the counter where the casino sold its gambling chips, and she noticed that more than half the people waiting in line were not paying in cash. Instead they carried Q-links, laptops, and game consoles. An in-house pawn shop traded them for chips, and bottles of clean water. The few patrons buying their chips with cash were mostly soldiers.

"That's new," Sitara observed quietly.

The manager heard her. "We make a small profit selling the metals and plastics to recyclers," he informed her. "Of course, you're a VIP, so the dealer will trade your money for chips at the table. And your first drink is on the house. So: A shot of westiller? A cocktail? What's your pleasure?"

Sitara smiled and ordered a cocktail.

The small crowd which met Sitara at the casino door had grown around the cards table, and their whispering was growing louder.

"She's the one who cracked the code on the alien probe, right?"

"Or is she the one who found the probe?"

"No, that was the other one, the blonde one."

"Quiet, I wanna watch."

Sen turned away from Sitara when she sat next to him.

Sitara addressed him in Gayatrian. "Interesting to see you here, Ambassador Sen."

Alankar Sen, replied quietly in the same tongue. "Ms. Kula — what are you doing here?"

"I got two years of back pay today," she said. "I want to spend it on something fun. What about you?"

He tensed to rise from his seat. "Until a moment ago, I was enjoying some private time away from it all. Now, if you will excuse me—"

Sitara put a hand on his arm before he could get up. "Please stay. I've been on that ship for so long, I need to talk to people who aren't my crewmates."

He acquiesced. "Do *not* tell anyone you saw me here."

"I swear to the Prince, I won't," she promised.

By now, the small crowd which met Sitara at the casino door had grown around the cards table, and their buzz was growing louder.

Alankar lowered his head against the unwanted attention.

"Don't worry," she said. "They can't record anything in here. Their comms won't work and any images will be wiped once they walk out that door."

"You know a lot about casino security."

"I wasn't always an officer," she said, settling in and tapping the table twice.

The dealer welcomed the players to her table, brushed her hands to show she was not hiding anything, then passed out five cards to Sitara, the other players, and herself. She placed four of her own cards on the table face-down, and one of them face-up. "Leading with crowns," she announced, in accord with the suit of the face-up card.

Four players took their turns at the game. Sitara continued in Gaitreyan. "You've chosen a very noisy place to escape the noise of work."

"You can't escape the noise anywhere," Alankar explained. "But I like it. In places like this, you never know what's going to happen."

"Do you mind if I ask you: at that hearing yesterday—"

"Yes, yes, we're not building an arcology, we're building a starship," Alankar admitted. "It was never much of a secret anyway."

"Why lie about it? Why not admit it was a starship?"

"If people knew we were working on FTL technology before the world knew about the probe— well, it doesn't matter now."

"Who *really* discovered the probe?" she asked. "Who found it *first?*"

Alankar studied her face for a moment, as he considered how much to tell her. "Not the Arethusans," he revealed.

"You know, don't you?"

"But I can't tell you."

They played a round of the card game, which Sitara won. "Sixteen in swords," she announced as she laid her hand on the table.

"The sixteen in swords wins," the dealer confirmed, and the onlookers applauded.

Sitara gathered the chips she won. Alankar nodded in approval. "You're good at this."

"Oh, this is all for you," she grinned. "What would it take for you to vote for the Conference to take over the starship?"

Alankar tensed once more. "You're very smart, confronting me here like this, where I can't get away. So let me ask you, since you can't get away either: do you love our country?"

"That's not the point—"

"We have been the kicking-dog of the world ever since the end of the war. And we were not even involved."

"Didn't our national bank finance both sides—?"

"—But no one will laugh at us when we reach Lorelei's Planet first," Alankar concluded.

Sitara grasped his point. She pressed the Ambassador. "If you veto the Conference mission, other nations will build their own starships, and they can build them faster. Unlike us, they are not recovering from a banking crash."

"I'm not hearing this," Alankar said, and he studied his cards, pretending to ignore her.

"It takes money to build a starship, doesn't it?" Sitara reminded him. "Money we don't really have. You, yourself, are more than six million rupees in debt—"

"Your intelligence is thorough," he growled. "Too thorough for mere fleet officer."

"Never mind. Listen. I can win some of that right here, at this table, tonight. And if I do, can I count on your vote?"

Alankar paused. He studied Sitara's face, to see any sign she might be bluffing. "Let's just see how well you do before midnight. Then we'll talk."

Sitara smiled.

An hour later, Sitara's winnings formed a small hill of chips and counters, and she had more than doubled the crowd of spectators surrounding the table. The dealer could no longer contain her excitement at Sitara's presence. "I know we're not supposed to make small-talk with the guests," she said, "but can I just say it's lovely to meet you? Can I call you Sitara?"

"Sure. Nice to meet you," Sitara replied, shaking hands.

"So, we're all going to die, right?"

Sitara stopped arranging her cards. "What?"

"You said on TV today that the aliens might be watching us," said the dealer. "Actually, you know what I'm really wondering? Lorelei found the planet after looking at the probe for only one day. Maybe that's because she already knew where it was."

"What do you mean?" Sitara asked.

The dealer leaned forward and asked, very seriously, "Is Lorelei an alien?"

Sitara laughed. But then they saw that everyone surrounding the table was completely serious, and expecting an answer. They whispered their own opinions.

"Maybe Lorelei was sent here as a baby."

"Or, maybe she was visited by aliens and they told her where to look."

"That's ridiculous!"

"What if the all Celestials were actually aliens?"

"The Nocturnals, too?"

Sitara pulled her shoulders and elbows closer to her body.

§ 22.

Lorelei put down Gretel's notes and looked out the window, over the skyline of Newgarten. Her second sunset back home after two years, and she'd lost her commission and gained embassy status. The setting sun gave an orange-golden glamour to the brutal surfaces and rectangles of the skyscrapers. Some were starting up their nightly holographic displays: surfaces of smog-blackened concrete and steel turned into flowerpots or trees or waterfalls. She took up her sketch book and made a quick drawing of the city skyline, and the rising of one of Eostray's moons behind it. As nighttime fell, some of the skyscraper hologram shows became military recruitment videos, advertisements for beer and liquor and firearms, and short videos of criminals confessing their crimes and accepting their jail terms. Sounds from outside reached her only dimly, through the double-paned, bullet-resistant glass: the laughter of party-goers, the buzz of camera drones, tires of speeding cars, anti-theft alarms, sirens, gunfire, wind.

A drone buzzed up to her window. It was marked with the logo of Eagle Eye News. The flash of its camera shot a dozen bursts of invasive light into her face. She gestured the window glass black, then rubbed her eyes. She took up Gretel's Q-link again, and stared at its blank screen for a while. A mirror in the dim room.

Then she opened the dossier on Sturgeon Glaive, and found an unlisted comms ID for the Glaive family penthouse in Newgarten. She called it on the hotel room comms. An automated voice asked her whom she would like to speak to.

"Paladin Glaive," she replied.

The system connected her to his comms.

"Glaive?"

"Who is this?"

"It's Lorelei."

"How did you find this ID?"

"It was— lying around. I— um— have a question for you"

Glaive paused, then said, "Are you calling from a secure line?"

"Also, I need to know which way your father will vote at the council meeting tomorrow."

"This isn't a secure line, is it?"

"Lieutenant, I need to know."

"Why do you ask?"

She paused. "I have to give a presentation at that meeting, and— I don't understand those people."

"Fair. What *do* you understand?"

"That none of them can win the starshot race. Not when they're competing against the whole world. No one can win like that. But there's another race they *can* win."

"What race is that?"

"The one we *all* win. The one with everyone on board the same ship. Everyone, together. Coordinated effort."

Glaive considered this for a moment, in silence. He cleared his throat. "Lorelei, this is the honest truth: I have *no idea* how my father will vote."

Lorelei put the comms down for a moment, and looked at the window, still gleaming black. She brought it back to her ear.

"You still there?" Glaive asked.

"Yes, I'm here," she said. "Thanks for telling me."

"Please keep this comm ID secret," Glaive asked her.

"I will."

"Thank you. But— call me if you need me. Now— um— good night, Doctor."

"Good night, lieutenant."

The line disconnected. Lorelei flipped through the dossier on Sturgeon Glaive again, and then tossed the device away and moved to the window, waving it clear once more to reveal the endless urban skyline. She looked up to the sky. There were no stars: only the mottled prismatic stew of city lights reflecting off the clouds of grey-brown smog.

In the study of the Glaive penthouse, the lieutenant put down the Q-link and dropped himself into a nearby chair.

Across the room, Sturgeon smiled. He put down the Q-link he'd used to eavesdrop on his son's conversation, then opened a liquor cabinet and poured two glasses of westiller. He handed one to the younger Glaive. "I'm proud of you. You've remembered how to lie for your country. Some day you might actually live up to the name I gave you."

Glaive accepted the glass. He swirled it in his hands, contemplating the shapes the amber liquid made.

§ 23.

The fifteen members of the Expeditions Council, along with their assistants and advisors, gathered in the hotel's ballroom to receive the NavCom crew for dinner. A long table had been laid for them, with a white cloth and fine silverware. The crew of the Seven, as well as their admiral, Din Mbembe, wore their formal dress uniforms: a white jacket with gold buttons, a white beret, a gold sash and belt around the waist, navy trousers for the men and skirts for the women, and black knee boots. Rank insignias were clipped to the shoulders and lapels, and fleet badges were sewn on the arms and the berets. Although every councillor was dressed smartly too, the hotel staff stood up straighter when a NavCom officer passed by.

"Good morning everyone," Mbembe welcomed the council. "Don't wait to take a seat, there is no agenda right now, no special need for any formalities."

"No formalities— but we all thought to wear formal dress," Sitara said, leaning into Jiandong's ear.

Admiral Din Mbembe introduced Jiandong and Sitara to the group of dignitaries, and they applauded as they heard each name. But as Mbembe moved to introduce lower-ranking crew members, Hanfei Gao'Fu stepped forward. "Excuse me, where is Doctor Verlassen?" he asked.

"Unfortunately, she is no longer associated with the NavCom Fleet," Mbembe said.

A noise of disappointment rose from the group. Some asked questions among themselves about whether Lorelei quit the organization, or was fired, or where she might have gone.

Gretel Von Richter said, "But she'll be here soon." When she saw Mbembe's annoyed look, she added, "I invited her."

Mbembe saw how Gretel's gaze dared him to challenge her. So he turned back to the whole table and smiled. "But please, ladies and gentlemen, take a seat, wherever you like. There's no official place setting here today, and no reason to wait."

The councillors, dignitaries, and NavCom crew members wandered to their seats. Gretel complained to a neighbour that the water glasses were made of glass and not crystal. Hanfei poured the water from the decanter and into his glass through a filter he took from his own pocket, then examined the filter with a magnifying eyepiece.

Sitara swiftly moved beside Alankar Sen, the ambassador from Gayatri Pradesh, just before he could sit down.

Alankar grinned brightly to see her, and took her elbows in his hands to show his respect. "Miss Kula! Our nation stands a little taller today, knowing that the code on the alien probe was cracked by one of our own." Then he leaned closer to whisper, "We did *not* meet at the casino last night. Agreed?"

Sitara showed her agreement by nodding. Then she placed a small cloth pouch in his hands and said, "Consider this a contribution to the cause."

Alankar heard the gambling chips in the pouch make a muffled clank. He looked inside. "These chips are worth a hundred credits each," he observed, impressed.

"There's a lot more in my locker at the casino. And here's the key. Yours to cash out, or play with, as you choose. If you are willing to do the right thing."

Alankar played with the chips in his fingers. "How many more?" he asked.

"Twenty thousand credits."

Alankar considered this. He fidgeted with the key in his fingers. Then he asked, "Are you married?" he asked.

"I'm divorced," Sitara replied, puzzled by the question.

"I'm sorry to hear that."

"I'm not. I'm the one who did the divorcing."

"I have two wives," Alankar smiled. "One works with me at the embassy. The other's back home. A man of my rank is allowed to have as many as he wants."

Sitara guessed what he was implying. "I won't be your third," she told him.

"You are the smartest and most beautiful woman I have ever met," Alankar crooned. "And by my side you would have anything you may want. New clothes every day. Diamond and pearl jewelry. A private car with your own driver. Anything a girl of your class can imagine."

He reached for her hand, but Sitara folded her arms before he could touch her.

"And how will you pay for those things?" she taunted him. "With my winnings at the casino?"

Alankar's face twitched for a moment. But he recovered his

control quickly.

"You're good," he muttered. He pocketed the pouch of casino chips and walked over to another chair, to talk to someone else.

Sitara decided to interpret that as a win for her. She looked for an exit, and saw that a commotion had grown by the main ballroom doors: Lorelei had arrived. Within a moment, nearly everyone in the room gathered around.

Admiral Mbembe pushed his way to the front of the crowd and confronted her. "This reception is for Council members and the crew of the Seven. You can't be here," he hissed in her ear.

Gretel stepped in front of him and said, "She's here at my invitation."

Lorelei smiled awkwardly and said, "Hi, Admiral. Sorry for surprising you like this."

Mbembe shook his head and walked away.

The growing crowd of Lorelei's admirers had questions. Lorelei looked to Gretel for some guidance. Gretel said, "You're not on trial here today, and the media's not watching. Come, enjoy yourself."

Lorelei cautiously stepped to the breakfast table and took a seat. Gretel sat by her right side, and waved at Alankar Sen.

"You really must get to know Ambassador Sen, from Gayatri," said Gretel. "Before he entered politics he was a businessman, and very successful. He could tell you some stories!"

Lorelei remembered the job Gretel wanted her to do, so she smiled to Alankar and motioned for him to sit beside her.

"I hear you're a philosopher, as well as a scientist," said Alankar.

"I am," Lorelei confirmed.

"But isn't everyone a philosopher?"

Lorelei inhaled sharply, and considered how to answer without causing offense. "Well—"

Alankar offered Lorelei his business card and spoke again. "I'm a banker, myself. Lalkeela Pathfinders Bank. My great grandfather started it with five million rupees and a talent for bluffing. Now we are the third-largest bank in Gayatri Pradesh."

"Hence, his appointment to the Expeditions Council," Gretel explained.

Lorelei smiled. "I read Gayatrian economic theory when I was an undergrad," she said. "Is it true that the most important government jobs are sold at auction?"

Gretel made an awkward smile.

Alankar chuckled and said, "The Raj can bar you from entering the auction, if he wants. But yes. It's how we get financially responsible people in those positions."

Sturgeon Glaive, seeing his competitors monopolize Lorelei's attention, took a champaign glass from a waiter and moved to offer it to Lorelei. "Doctor Verlassen, the world's most celebrated scientist— I am so glad that we could meet under friendlier circumstances."

"Thank you, Senator."

"Oh, please feel free to call me Sturgeon. And I believe you already know my boy—" Sturgeon waved for his son to take a seat beside him "—who tells me he is a great admirer of yours."

Lorelei looked to Glaive. "You are?"

"Everyone admires you," Glaive said, carefully.

"It's true," said Sturgeon. "My office received over three hundred comms calls, and a hundred times as many emails last night, all from people who somehow seemed to know about the vote we're to take later today."

Alankar Sen said, "So did I, now that you mention it."

Gretel said, "And my office, too."

Lorelei opened her hands to protest her innocence. "They didn't find out from me, I promise you."

"Oh no, not to worry, I don't think it was you at all," said Sturgeon. "In fact I think it has something to do with your former captain. All those calls started coming just after the news nets reported that he visited the Godspeaker of Newgarten. I just found it curious that they all seemed to agree with you, that the Conference should build a starship."

"We *should* build a starship," Lorelei affirmed.

Gretel smiled and said, "And I agree. Doctor Verlassen, why don't you explain?"

As Lorelei began to speak, Alankar interrupted. "So, you hired her as a lobbyist?"

"A consultant," said Gretel.

Alankar folded his arms, but he listened.

"Well I think the most important reason—" Lorelei had to catch herself from stuttering, as she felt the gaze of a dozen globally-influential dignitaries in the room, "—is that we'll find answers to some questions about ourselves. Where we came from, where we might be going."

"Ha! We already know who we are," Sturgeon said. "We're

the winners in the struggle for survival. And we're going wherever the hell we want."

"But now we're not the only ones," Lorelei reminded him. "There's at least one more intelligence in the cosmos besides our own. If we can find them, imagine what we could learn from them!"

"True," Sturgeon acknowledged. "They might have advanced technology. But they might also have more powerful weapons than we do. Have you thought of that?"

Alankar was ready with the answer. "If they wanted to conquer us, they'd have done it by now. And I'll tell you why they haven't: they're gone. They don't exist anymore. As we already told you, we looked at your new planet and found nothing. Sending out that probe was probably the last thing they did before they destroyed themselves."

"Then why are you building your starship?" Sturgeon asked him. "You can't trade with people who don't exist."

"Mineral prospecting," Alankar replied. "Scouting colony sites. Winning the race!"

Sturgeon expressed his opinion of that with an inarticulate noise through half-smiling lips.

"There's a deeper matter that you're both missing," said Lorelei. "If we build a starship, we will be able to compare ourselves to any other civilization we find out there. And that will tell so much! What problems might be ahead of us? How to be ready for them? Are we near the end of our history, or the beginning?"

"The end of history?" Sturgeon scoffed. "I read that paper of yours, the one about the doomsday argument. You're obsessed, aren't you?"

Gretel came to Lorelei's rescue. "I read it, and I thought it was brilliant. Lorelei, why don't you explain it to us?"

As Lorelei prepared her thoughts, Sturgeon jumped in again. "I read it too. And let me tell you, it was wrong about everything. The world is not going to end in sixteen years. The economy is growing, not shrinking. And the planet is doing fine. Just smell the air in here. Full of oxygen, delicious."

"The air in this building is filtered and oxygen-enriched," Lorelei reminded him. "Every door in this building is an airlock, to keep out the smog. And the only reason the economy is growing is because we are cleaning up after the war. That's not real growth. That's just replacing what was destroyed."

"She got you there," Gretel said, and waved a finger in Sturgeon's face.

Sturgeon made a loud laughter, more for the benefit of his fellow Arethusans. "Do you hear that? She wants to leave the world broken. I've heard smart people say stupid things before, but this one wins the race!"

"You still have it wrong, Sturgeon," Gretel said. "There's a way to avoid a collapse in sixteen years. And Lorelei has the answer for that, too."

Lorelei straightened her spine, and laid out what she believed was the cornerstone of her argument. "If we build a starship, we will create something fundamentally new. And we will come together as a unified world to do it. But if we don't do it now, we have almost no chance of avoiding collapse."

Gretel added, "In sixteen years." She nodded to Lorelei and smiled.

Sturgeon looked at his colleagues. Lorelei thought that since his brow was furrowed with thought, that she had persuaded him. She smiled.

"Building a scientific starship is a good idea, no one denies that," Sturgeon announced. "But a *better* idea would be— a *military* starship."

Lorelei perked an eyebrow. "Why military?"

"Isn't it obvious? Because we don't know what's out there."

"That's why we should send scientists."

"Scientists? Lorelei, you're an intelligent woman. You must realise the aliens might be hostile."

"We have no reason to believe that," Lorelei told him. "The probe has no weapons. It has cameras and sensors. They sent it only to explore—"

"The probe has no weapons; I'll give you that. But now that we found it, we have to assume the aliens who built it also found us. And who is to say your probe wasn't an advance scout for a larger force?"

"*We* are to say, that's who," said Lorelei, with growing exasperation in her voice. "We can infer a lot about the society that built it just from the fact that it exists."

"Like what?"

"That they are advanced enough to build it," said Lorelei. "They gave us a map to their home world; that tells us they they want us to find them. The probe is like a message, and it says: 'We are here; is anyone else out there?' And it doesn't have to say anything more. A message like that is beautiful enough."

"But they're *not* there anymore," Alankar insisted. He turned to Sturgeon and said, "So we don't need a military ship. We need prospectors. Surveyors. Developers. Colonists."

Sturgeon said, "You want to send prospectors out there—that's fine, send them. But like I told her: send them after our fighters clear the path."

Lorelei said, "And what would sending fighters tell the people on that planet about who we are?"

"They're *aliens*!" Sturgeon insisted. "Stop calling them people. They're not human. They're aliens." Then he noticed that his near-loss of his temper startled some of those able to hear him. He sat back in his chair, and smiled, as if it was all a joke.

Lorelei looked to Gretel for some support. In her kindest voice, Gretel said "They *are* aliens, Lorelei. Whatever else they may be, they're not us."

Lorelei gave her a puzzled look.

"But whatever we choose to call them," Gretel continued, "we really should try to *find* them." She turned to Alankar and said, "Ambassador Sen, think of the business opportunities. Imagine the technology they might have. Imagine the resources waiting to be developed!"

Alankar grinned. "I admit it's an appealing thought," he said. "But there's at least one major obstacle in the way."

"What's that?" asked Lorelei.

"The Expeditions Council," said Alankar.

"Aren't you *on* the Council?" Lorelei asked.

"Yes, I am," he confirmed. "So I know better than most how useless it is. You know that law that says the Conference must be the first to land on every new planet? It was fine back when the only new planets were pathetic airless icebergs that no one cared about. But a *real* planet should be explored by anyone with the will and the means to explore it. Free, open, and fair competition — that's what brings out the best in people. And in whole nations, too."

"We already have that," Lorelei countered. "As soon as the Conference claims a new planet for all humanity, anyone can go there."

"Space doesn't belong to all humanity," said Alankar. "It belongs to those who get there first."

"Isn't that how the war started?" Lorelei said. Her words

caused a small stirring of ire among her listeners, not at the implications of her question, but at her audacity for saying it. Sturgeon spoke up to contradict her, but his words were lost in Hanfei Gao'fu's interruption.

"Space belongs to no one," he said, his voice not raised but nonetheless silencing all others. "But only because, outside our own solar system, no one can get there. The best engines ever built would need more than ten thousand years to reach your star. So the whole question of who owns it is quite empty, whatever the laws might say."

"Then we build something that can go faster," said Lorelei.

Alankar grinned. "And we have people working on that very problem, right now. Our engineers think they can bring the travel time to Lorelei's Planet down to fifty years."

"Fifty years still won't be enough," Hanfei reminded everyone. "Because the round-trip would be one hundred years. Even with the best hibernation technology, the crew will die of old age. What we need is an engine that can break the speed of light. But there is no such engine. And there never will be."

"The probe builders had one," Lorelei said, confidence and smiling.

"They cannot have had one— it is a scientific impossibility," Hanfei contradicted her. "The speed of light is the speed you'd reach if you had all the energy in the universe for your acceleration. Even if you were moving only one proton, you'd need infinite energy to make it go that fast. That's energy no one can produce in an engine."

"That's physics as we know it *now*," Lorelei agreed. "But what else is out there? Wormholes? Tesseracts? Time travel? We've already discovered gravity waves coming from colliding black holes. What if they found a way to bend the speed of light?"

"Who?"

Gretel gently swatted his shoulder. "Who do you think!"

Hanfei grinned, but said nothing more.

"Friends, we are distracting ourselves," Gretel declared. "We've been asking about how to fight an enemy that might not exist. Asking about who owns the resources on planets nobody can visit. We should be asking a simpler, yet deeper question. A more *noble* question." She nodded towards the reluctant celebrity scientist.

Lorelei understood the hint that Gretel was dropping for her, but also felt the press of expectation. Sturgeon, more than the rest, drilled his gaze into her; he also made a subtle shake of his head: *don't do it.* Lorelei glanced around the room, searching for her friends. Her eyes happened to spot the ornamental icons of the seven Celestials that decked the window frames. One of them, she realized, had a much better question than the one Gretel wanted her to ask. So she said: "What inspires you?"

Gretel reached for her trinolay necklace: Lorelei had posed a Noble Question, as she asked, but not the one she expected. She took stock of who appeared to find the question important, and who tried to laugh it away. Sturgeon made a quiet dismissive roll of his eyes. Hanfei and Alankar looked to each other, to see if one of them understood what Lorelei was asking. They both made annoyed smirks.

"What inspires you?" Lorelei repeated. "What do you dream about? Winning wars? Making money? Something else that isn't really that important, under the aspect of eternity? We now have proof that we are not alone in the universe. Proof that faster-than-light travel is possible. So, where is your imagination? Where is your sense of wonder? The great immensity of the cosmos is only an arm's length above our heads. If we can climb to it then think of what else we could do on the way. Build whole new societies. Make new art and new music. Learn from whoever else might be out there. Find new perspective on the meaning of life. We could be *better* than who we are now. We could be more *human*."

As Lorelei finished her outpouring of frustration, she found that the entire room was now silent. She said, "I suppose that's not what you wanted to hear me say. But think about it. If we can—"

As she finished, someone made a dismissive snicker. A second voice made a whispered comment to a neighbour, causing them both to laugh. With the precedent set, more muffled laughter spread across the room. Hanfei and Gretel looked at each other, as if asking for permission to join in. Lorelei looked to her friends for help, but they only shrugged their shoulders and made sympathetic faces.

Lorelei collected her handbag and jacket, and fled the room.

The guests returned to their champaign and empty pleasantries. Gretel studied her colleagues. When she thought the time was right, she tapped a spoon on a glass.

"Lorelei is right," she said. When her words and her glass-tapping got everyone's attention, she continued: "You can laugh at her as much as you want. I was laughing, too. But her discovery *will* change us, one way or another. I was prepared to veto anything that any of you put on the table, without considering it— without even looking at it. Just to give my country a few extra days. But why does it matter who gets to Lorelei's Planet first, when there are surely plenty of planets out there for everyone? So let's vote for a starship for all humanity. Let's vote for it *right now.*"

While most of the councillors muttered about the impropriety of Gretel's suggestion, Alankar toyed with a casino chip in his fingers. He sighed, and then stood up to speak next. "I agree with the member for Éostray. We have a full quorum in this room, and no need to wait until after we finish eating."

Admiral Mbembe scanned the room, and found what appeared to be a growing consensus among the councillors. He turned to his android assistant and said, "Bring in the official transcribers. Let's get started."

Sturgeon set his champagne glass on the table with an impolite thump. "Let the record show that Arethusa refused to be part of this insanity," he announced to the room. He grasped the younger Glaive by the shoulder and pulled him up from his chair. "Come along now, boy. We're leaving."

The councillors who remained gathered in a circle around Gretel, who smiled.

§ 24.

Jiandong and Sitara caught up with Lorelei in her hotel room. Lorelei packed her modest belongings into her worn CNH mission bag.

"Come on, Lorelei! The council wants to see you," said Sitara.

"No they don't," Lorelei insisted.

"Yes, they do! Please, come back down to the dining hall."

Lorelei followed her friends back to the dining hall. As soon as the councillors and dignitaries saw her, they rose to their feet, and applauded.

Gretel strode forward and said, "The vote was nearly unanimous. Only Hanfei voted against us."

Lorelei needed a breath to digest this news. Her gaze swept the room: it was now full of smiles for her.

"We're going to take over the ship the Gayatrians are already building. And—" Gretel rubbed her arm affectionately, "—we want *you* to be in charge of it."

Lorelei dropped her suitcase. Gretel hugged her; Lorelei kept her arms at her side, unsure whether she had been given good news. Then the other councillors stepped forward, to shake her hand and thank her.

As the applause settled down, Jiandong approached Admiral Mbembe. "Sir? I want to be transferred to the design team. I've wanted to go to the stars ever since I was a boy—"

"If Verlassen wants you, she can have you," Mbembe grumbled. He looked to Sitara. "You want to transfer out, too?"

"If you'll let me go," Sitara said. She noticed Mbembe was not smiling. "Why aren't you happy for her?"

"I wanted that job for myself, honestly," Mbembe replied.

"You're the admiral of the fleet," Jiandong said, confused.

"Yes, but no one will care about that anymore," Mbembe lamented. "So go enjoy yourselves. I've got paperwork to do." He marched out of the dining room.

Alankar approached Sitara. "You still have those winnings?"

Sitara glanced quickly at Lorelei to be sure she wasn't looking, and handed Alankar the key to the locker at the casino. "But I will not marry you," she reminded him.

"Another wife would be too expensive anyway."

Sitara felt her skin hairs rise.

"But here's something else you can do for me, and for your country," he said. "You make sure that my bank is named the exclusive provider of financial services to the starship project."

Sitara decided it was better than his alternative demand. "I'll try to arrange it," she said.

"You *will* arrange it. Unless you want the Raj to find out about *this*," said Alankar, and he held up the locker key in front of her. Sitara grimaced, but said nothing.

"As it is, he won't like the way the vote went," he said, making conversation. "But an exclusive contact with one of our banks will help soften the blow."

"The Raj doesn't have to like it. It's still the right thing to do," Sitara told him.

A short while later, Lorelei and Sitara and Jiandong enjoyed a celebratory drink with Gretel and some of the other councillors. Glaive returned, and cleared his throat to let them know he had something to say.

"My father would like to know how the vote went," he said.

"We won," said Gretel, grinning.

"And I would like to know—" he said, hesitating for a moment, unsure of the right words, "if I could join you? I won't be offended if you say no— I mean, just a few months ago, some of you here were nearly killed because of me—"

"Of course you can join us!" Gretel said, and rose to pull out a chair for him.

Glaive glanced at Lorelei, silently asking her permission.

Lorelei nodded, and gestured to the chair.

Sitara and Jiandong eyed Lorelei with mixed curiosity and discomfort, wondering what she was doing by inviting him.

Glaive noted their reaction. "Want to know who *really* discovered the probe?" he asked.

That got everyone's attention. "Yes! Please tell us!" said Lorelei.

Glaive looked left and right, as if checking for eavesdroppers. He said, "I have absolutely no idea."

This produced the laughter that he was hoping for. He relaxed, and accepted a drink.

Lorelei captured the moment in her sketchbook. She included the three aliens from the probe's dedication plaque in the scene.

Fourth Transmission: Gayatri Pradesh

Government type: Constitutional Oligarchy.

GDP: 7.234 trillion rupees. Growth: -4.1%. Inflation: 23.9%.

Largest industry: Financial services (82.0% of GDP).

Largest City: Lalkeela, population: 10.25 million.

§ 25.

A parade carried the alien probe from Newgarten spaceport to a downtown armoury hall, along a route that thronged with the celebrating people of the city and of the world. Amid the flying streamers, trumpet blasts, and media drones, the flag of Arethusa flew from the top of the float that carried the probe, much to Sturgeon Glaive's delight. The flag was navy blue, and featured Arethusa's national crest in the centre: white, with a black minotaur holding a battle axe. This crest was flanked by the figures of The Solder and The Prince, and topped by a white star.

In the hab module of the starship's orbital construction platform, a pair of engineers finished their last work shift of the day, and gathered to watch the parade on the vid screen in the rec room. One hit the exercise machines as they watched: a necessary daily routine for maintaining muscle mass in zero-G.

"All humanity will see pictures of this parade for centuries to come," said the engineer on the weight machine. "And they'll see our flag planted on the probe."

A second engineer said, "But whose flag will be the first planted on an exoplanet? *That* flag will be seen for centuries, too, Rob."

"You can bet it won't be *your* flag, Phil," said Rob.

"It could be," Phil protested.

"Nope. Won't be. Because—" He stopped as most of the lights in the rec room went out. "What the hell?"

"Probably tripped a breaker. Third time this week. My turn to check it out," said Phil. He floated down the corridor toward a service module, carrying his sandwich wrap in his mouth so he could use both hands to push off the walls.

Lights throughout the hab were flickering, or dark. A few monitors cast a multi-coloured aura about the walls. Phil touched off from a panel that made him stop: it was vibrating, and making a quiet knocking noise. He opened it, and found a hose coming loose from its attachment to a pump.

"What flathead put that thing in there?" he muttered. As he leaned in for a closer look, the hose broke free. High-pressure gas caused it to flail about, knocking Phil's tools out of his hand, then striking a cluster of cables and wires. One of the cables came loose from its junction, and snapped with electric sparks.

Phil pushed himself away and hit the nearest alarm button. Red emergency lights flooded the corridor.

"O2 line leak and exposed sparks in Module 9," he shouted down the corridor. He grabbed the hose by its root and reached hand-over-hand to its end, to plug the spray with his thumb.

As Rob arrived with a repair kit and two oxygen masks, another loose hose broke free from its valve. It hissed with high-pressure gas, which ignited when it touched the sparking wires.

The hose became a flame thrower. Its burning jet engulfed a cluster of tanks.

The tanks exploded, rupturing the module walls and exposing the hab to space.

§ 26.

"Sorry to disturb you, Lorelei," said Gretel, as she rushed into the office, "but you need to see this."

Lorelei's office was on the top floor of an early modern castle near the centre of Vogelsberg, in Éostray, which now served as the headquarters of the starship construction program. Hardwood panelled walls, antique lighting fixtures, a circle of chairs by a fireplace, and a retractable wall leading to an open-air terrace, made the space seem less like an administrator's office and more like a nobleman's salon. Gretel pressed a button on a control panel, and one of the wall panels rolled away to reveal a large monitor. She tuned it to a newscast, showing a live video feed of the CNH orbital construction platform. Several streams of burning gases jetted out from one side, along with bits of debris.

Lorelei dropped her notebook.

"This will set us back a few months, at least," said Gretel.

"How many people were hurt?" asked Lorelei.

"Don't know yet. Comms are down."

"There might be a hundred people up there! How soon until the rescue ships arrive?"

"Rescue ships? By the One! We don't have a budget item for a rescue."

Lorelei held her breath, deciding whether to answer Gretel's cold question. On the monitor, Lorelei saw some astronauts in space suits emerge from an airlock on the starship, and walk on magnetic boots toward the accident site. They carried toolkits for patching the leaks.

"The reason we *have* rescue ships," Lorelei reminded Gretel, "and the reason the NavCom fleet's mission includes space search and rescue, is in case of accidents like this. We're supposed to be there when no one else can be."

Gretel inhaled sharply. "Lorelei, the Security Council is saying it might not be an accident."

§ 27.

In an armoury hall in Newgarten, Sturgeon Glaive watched the probe being lifted from the parade float and onto a display platform. An aide approached him and whispered in his ear. His breath shortened, and his eyes darted around the room. Then he smiled.

His son stood beside him. "What's the matter?"

"I just got some unexpected good news," his father answered. "What news?"

Glaive noticed the other dignitaries and observers in the crowded hall were checking their comms and reacting with shock and surprise. He checked his own, and saw the news report about the accident.

Mary Drake, the nearest journalist, moved to his side. "I assume you just heard? Any first thoughts?"

Sturgeon's face instantly snapped into the shape of deep sympathy. "It's a terrible tragedy," he said. "Our thoughts and prayers go out to the families of everyone who died up there."

Glaive showed his ire with a hard glare. Sturgeon resumed. "Schedule another press conference. Tell them I know who caused this."

§ 28.

Lorelei and Gretel ran to the fleet operations control room, in what once had been the ballroom of the castle. Three massive displays were mounted on the walls, along with other monitors and readouts for technical information. One of the monitors displayed an image of a large hole in the side of the platform, and the glow of burning gases from exposed pipes and hoses, dispersing into space.

"Two explosions so far," Jiandong told Lorelei. "Comms are still down. But the workshops and habs on the construction platform are now exposed to space. It's likely everyone who wasn't on the starship or wearing a space suit is now dead."

"How many?" said Lorelei.

"Twenty or thirty, maybe more."

"And the rescue ships?"

"Still at least ten minutes away."

Lorelei pulled her own hair in frustration. "Can't we do *anything?*"

"Not until they lock down that fire."

She gripped a nearby hand rail, and watched the scene in space unfold on the control room's wall-sized screens. "Launch one of our planetfall shuttles, to pick up survivors," she ordered.

"It takes an hour to prep one for launch, another three hours to get there," Gretel reminded her.

"There may still be people needing rescue by then," Lorelei countered. She turned to Jiandong. "Captain? I'd like your technical team to be on that shuttle."

"I'll lead the team myself," Jiandong volunteered.

As he turned to leave, the monitors showed another part of the orbital platform exploding away, carrying two astronauts with it. Several more astronauts were saved by their tethers, but one of them swung into the fire jet from the first explosion. It ruptured his suit and silently engulfed him in flames, as his suit atmosphere burned away. Another astronaut's face visor was struck by fast-flying debris, turning his visor into a jet that spun him head-over-heels, and suffocating him in the vacuum of space. Everyone watching the monitor recoiled in horror; Sitara covered her mouth; Lorelei turned away.

Gretel declared, "This has to be the Arethusans. Where's the rest of the NavCom fleet?"

Sitara could not move her hands to enter the commands into

her terminal. Her attention was fixed on the images from the orbital platform. "All those people," she stammered.

Gretel shouldered Sitara out of her station and entered the commands herself.

"Hey!" Sitara objected, snapping out of her trance.

Gretel said, "Stay awake, Officer Kula."

Knowing they could do nothing about it, Lorelei and Sitara exchanged sympathetic glances.

A tactical display of the solar system appeared on the big screen. "Two of our ships are in orbit around Jupiter, one around Mars, one on its way to Neptune, the rest are in parking orbits," Gretel reported.

"None of them are under attack," Lorelei observed.

Gretel said, "That changes nothing. The Arethusans have never cared about your vision for a unified humanity. They think they're in a race. And they want to win. The attack on the station has to be them."

§ 29.

A light cloud of debris surrounded the orbital construction platform: coffee cups, power tools, and other scraps which floated out of the holes after the explosions had done their damage. They clattered on the windows and walls of the rescue ships. Survivors in space suits clung to the superstructure, some locking their legs around support trusses as their tethers were broken. Single-seat pods flew from the rescue ships to collect the astronauts: those still tethered to the platform and those floating free, those still alive, and those now beyond help. Other pods attended to the platform, to apply a gel-cement on the remaining gas leaks. The gels quickly froze solid and stopped the bleeding. When the cleanup was done, the pods checked the rest of the platform for any other signs of damage, while tugboat pods grappled the platform on long cables and pulled it into a higher orbit.

Jiandong piloted his shuttle into the platform's docks manually, as the platform's guidance system was still down. He and his team climbed into their space suits and prepared to enter the platform's hab deck, still open to the vacuum of space. The shuttle latched on to the platform's airlock with a quiet thud. Lance set the docking clamps with the hand crank, and opened the platform's inner door. The corridor greeted the team with a collection of weightless debris: Q-links and other devices, socks and T-shirts, ice crystals from flash-frozen water. Red alarm lamps rotated like beacons on a path through a foggy night.

"Comms open. Pick a partner to stay in a line of sight," Jiandong instructed his team. "I don't know what else has been damaged in there, and I don't want anyone getting hurt or lost."

At the first branching of the path, Jiandong chose the left corridor and sent two of his teammates to the right.

"*Kai'tzeen!*" yelped one of the technicians.

"What is it?" Jiandong called back.

"Somebody's hand," the technician called back. "Severed from his arm."

Jiandong swallowed, and pursed his lips. His suit readout told him that his heartbeat rose.

"Is that Lance?" said Jiandong, recognizing the voice of one of his NavCom Seven crewmembers.

"Yeah, Captain, it's me," said Lance Crassus. "Don't know if I can take another shock like that."

Jiandong understood. "Now listen. It's okay to be afraid. I'm afraid, too. But we are going to do this anyway. You flew in the Seven with me for two years, so I know you can do this. Besides, you do *not* want to vomit in your space suit."

"No, sir, I do not," Lance agreed.

The team could be heard through the comms, chuckling. When Jiandong heard Crassus chuckling with them, he smiled. "If you can laugh, you can feel less afraid, and so get the job done."

The team explored deeper into the hab. Jiandong found the galley, and in it he found more floating debris, including several frozen human bodies.

"I need someone to take these people back to the shuttle," he said. No one volunteered. "Very well then. *I* will take these people to the shuttle. The rest of you, find the site of the first explosion and then call me."

He had moved all the bodies from the galley to the shuttle's airlock when Crassus found the first blast site. "Captain? Zone six, at the end of the corridor," he reported.

"Coming, thank you," said Jiandong. When he arrived, he found a hallway blackened with flame damage. Its wall panels were twisted. All the lights were out; Jiandong took out a lamp to examine the area. Wires, conduits, and torn sheets of metal stuck out like teeth. Behind and between them, Jiandong could see the gel-cement which stopped the leaking gases. With help from his team, he pushed as much of the floating debris out of the way. Then from his tool kit he produced a fist-sized multifaceted ball, and gently released it into the middle of the weightless hallway.

"I'm taking a holographic scan of the area," he told his team. "Everyone stand back and close your eyes."

The team retreated a few steps. Jiandong pressed a button on his spacesuit control panel. Strobe-lasers shot out from some of the facets on the ball, while cameras on the other facets recorded the laser's reflections on every surface. Small micro-jets propelled the ball down the corridor.

"Okay, you can open your eyes again," he said, when it was gone.

"So, we're done here now?" said Lance.

"Check out the other blast site," said Jiandong. "I want to examine this one a little closer for a while."

"Sir," Lance agreed, and left.

Jiandong gave himself a moment to breathe and manage his stress. When his suit readout told him that his heart rate was back to normal, he turned on a lamp and inspected the damaged wall. He took samples of the metal and other materials, packaging them carefully in evidence bags.

"All the blast radius lines here make it seem as if we were struck by something from outside," he said, recording. "A small asteroid, or maybe a satellite collision? But on the outside, everything is twisted the other way. As if the blast came from the inside."

Jiandong stepped back, and held himself still for a moment, as the implications of those two facts came together in his mind. Then he packed up his gear and pushed himself back down the corridor and toward the nearest airlock.

"Everybody, stay right where you are," he ordered. "Nobody move! Don't even wave your arms!"

"Sir, what's going on?" A voice Jiandong couldn't place.

"The explosion came from inside the walls. The platform is rigged with explosives."

§ 30.

"Evacuate the campus," Lorelei ordered from the CNH control room. A bomb on the starship platform could mean a bomb in the project itself. "Security: search for suspicious packages. Full sweep for explosives."

"Yes, ma'am," said a security officer, heading for the door.

Lorelei continued: "Everyone in the command centre will have to stay here. We still have to co-ordinate things."

"What if there's a bomb right here in this room?" asked Sitara. Most everyone else showed in their faces that they had the same question.

"Then we have to find it," Lorelei said.

Gretel leaned close to Lorelei and said, "Can I have a private word?"

Lorelei nodded. "In my office," she agreed.

They strode through the castle's long corridors, still exhibiting the original wallpaper and mahogany furniture, though the ceiling hung with data cables and LED track lights. Lorelei and Gretel wove around the stream of designers, engineers, and scientists rushing to evacuate. When they reached Lorelei's top-floor office, Gretel closed the door. "We have a saboteur working for us."

Lorelei sighed. "That's one possible explanation."

"But I think you agree now, that it's not an accident?"

Lorelei hesitated, then nodded. "On balance of probability, that seems likely. But how did you know?"

"I've been expecting something like this," said Gretel, as she sat in a chair near Lorelei's desk. "The Security Council briefings have been a little dark, lately."

"Why aren't I getting those briefings?" Lorelei asked.

"You don't need the distraction."

"Has anyone on the security council read my paper on the Threshold of Cultural Entropy?"

"I read the executive summary," Gretel answered.

"If people understood it properly, they would see why our starship is important, and the bombing will stop."

Gretel tried to suppress a wave of patronizing laughter. "My dear girl, the world does not work like that," she said. "Now, what are you going to do about our saboteur?"

"We'll need to set up security checkpoints at all the campus entrances," she said. "Deploy drones at altitude, protect the airspace. A security dome."

"That's better," Gretel agreed. "And we should have a few checkpoints inside the campus as well. Certainly at the door of the command centre. Also at the main lab, and the—"

"No," said Lorelei. "Checkpoints at the entrances, but not inside the campus."

"Lorelei, we are under attack."

"We have gathered over a hundred and fifty of the smartest people on the planet. They won't do their best work if there's an armed guard looking over their shoulders. I want the campus to be comfortable and welcoming for them. A good place for thinking, and for listening."

"Listening to what?"

"To your own mind."

Gretel shook her head with a smile. "They told me you were a strange one." She looked around Lorelei's office, then said, "We should do something about the decor in here. Take out the plants, the old furniture. Bring in a scale model of the starship. And a portrait of the King. And some potted trinolay flowers. Right now your office looks like a college seminar room."

"What does that have to do with security?" Lorelei asked.

"Appearances," Gretel said. "Your office is where you represent this organization to society. You're not a grad student anymore, darling. You're the head of an important international agency, with a multi-billion mark budget, and the eyes of the entire human race watching you."

Lorelei looked at Gretel for a moment, as if Gretel had suddenly become a stranger. "You appointed me to this job, but you don't seem to think I can do it."

Gretel adopted a friendlier tone. "Oh, Lorelei, I think you're perfect for this job. Motivated, smart, outspoken. You believe in this project more than anyone else. You're not very good with people—" Lorelei smiled at that, "—but for that part of the job, I am here to guide you."

"Fine, get some newer furniture in here."

"Good girl," said Gretel. "And no more staff meetings in the pub."

Lorelei's head snapped up. "We should call the police—" She reached for her comms, but Gretel held up a hand to stop her.

"Not yet. Keep the investigation in-house," Gretel recommended.

"That's ridiculous— there might be a bomb right here in this room—"

"If we have to ask for help," Gretel said, interrupting her, "it will look like we can't solve our own problems."

"It's not irrational to ask for help in an emergency."

"It's not just what's rational that matters. It's also what *plays*."

Lorelei gave her a furrowed look. "What *plays*? People are dying. Nothing else is relevant."

"More important than the appearance of your clothes or your office, is the appearance of the organization. We have to show the world we are professional, capable, and absolutely in charge of our own affairs."

Lorelei grimaced, but did not verbally disagree.

"Here's what I recommend," said Gretel. "You ask the police to sweep the campus for bombs. The same for all our subcontractors and suppliers. But after that, you appoint one of our own to investigate who *planted* the bombs. And once we've caught the creature, the world will see that we really *do* know what we're doing."

Lorelei pursed her lips, and looked at Gretel for a few heartbeats. Then she said, "Do your security council briefings suggest any suspects?"

Gretel smiled. "The usual bag of charming young idiots. Colony rights activists, Cosán Eolais groups, Will-Of-The-One groups—"

"Who are they?"

"Will-Of-The-One? They think that upgraders like me—" she stretched out her artificial arms, "—shouldn't exist."

Lorelei perked an eyebrow.

"But let's keep our eyes on the finish line," said Gretel. "You want to know my favourite suspect for our saboteur? There's another starship being built somewhere, in secret. We don't know by whom. But whoever they are, it seems they want to get ahead in the race by pushing us behind."

§ 31.

Weightless, Jiandong's team stood still and waited for their captain to give them their next order.

"Nobody move," Jiandong repeated. "We don't know how many more bombs there might be, and we don't know what triggers them. So, nobody move."

"Captain, what should we do?" asked Crassus.

"We're going to take thirty seconds to breathe— get your heart rate down to normal— give me a chance to think."

"Okay. Breathe. I can do that. I can breathe."

"Good man, Lance, you're doing fine."

Jiandong closed his eyes and thought about what to do next. "Ground control, do you read?" he said.

In the CNH Expeditions control room, Sitara put on a headset and pressed a button to answer. "We read you, Captain. Be advised CNH Security Council is sending a bomb disposal squad."

"Got an ETA?"

"Two hours."

"Copy that," he replied. "Two hours, two hours," Jiandong whispered to himself.

"Do we have to stand here for that long?" Crassus again, panic returning to his voice.

Jiandong gave himself a few more breaths of time in which to think. "We have some choices. We can stand here and wait for the rescue. We can carefully crawl back to the shuttle— no magnetic boots, floating zero-G, very slowly, lest we trigger something. Or, we can suck up the risk and do our jobs: find the rest of the bombs as quickly as we can."

"I don't know how to defuse a bomb," Crassus said.

Jiandong pressed a button on his suit controller. The magnets on his boots disengaged, allowing him to float free of the deck. Carefully, he pushed himself down the corridor towards the technician.

"We're only going to mark them for the disposal team," he said. "You know what the machinery behind these wall panels should look like. So we search behind these panels for anything that doesn't belong. If there's anything that looks strange to you — anything at all, no matter how small— draw an X. And take your time."

"We could be here for hours, sir."

"We've got at least two, so we should start."

Crassus took up the tools he needed from his tool belt, and faced the nearest wall panel. After a moment, it was apparent he was frozen with fear. "Captain, I— I can't do it."

Jiandong turned a corner and found Lance. He touched their helmet visors together, so they could speak without using the radio. "Yes, you can. You have already done at least three brave things today that more than half of humanity will never do. You put on the Expeditions uniform this morning. You flew into space, with almost no time to prepare. And you stepped on to this platform, knowing it was dangerous. You were brave enough to do those things, you are brave enough to do *this* thing. Okay? Lance— okay?"

After a ragged breath, Crassus replied. "Okay."

"All right," Jiandong said. He pushed slightly away from Crassus to address his team. "Now, everyone, we will start at the far ends of every corridor, and work our way toward the airlock with the shuttle. Mag boots offline. Move slow. Deliberately, carefully. Let's get to work."

Jiandong picked a corridor and gently pushed himself along its length, to the end, scanning every wall panel with his radmeter. There he found air supply hoses, power conduits, and data cables. Nothing he saw there was unexpected. He picked one panel at random and removed it, and shined his lamp into the wall cavity for a closer look. He still found nothing that shouldn't be there.

"That's one," he said, and he put the panel back in place, and marked it safe.

"Captain?" called a crewmember. "Notice that each corridor section has only two air hoses each. One for new air in, the other for old air out."

"Why is that strange?" asked another.

"Because there should be six of them." Jiandong answered. "The main system, and two emergency backups. Good find, people. Keep looking for things like that. Record everything. This is a crime scene. Take your time."

The team got back to work. They scanned every panel, and the floor and ceiling panels, with increasing courage as time went on.

Half an hour later, the team had finished searching most of the platform, and they found nothing else unusual. The last area to survey was the platform's nuclear power plant.

"I got this last room," Jiandong told his crew. "The rest of you, start a second scan of the whole platform. Just to be sure."

"I'll do the power plant room," volunteered Crassus.

"Glad to hear it," said Jiandong, and he stepped aside to let the crewmember through. Jiandong moved to another corridor and began to scan the walls.

"Sir? There's something wrong here," said Crassus. "A power plant of this size should have three independent cutoff systems, ready to shut the core down in case of emergency."

"And?" Jiandong asked.

"There's only one. And it's in the box."

Jiandong paused in his work. "No one installed it?" he asked. "No one *unpacked* it."

"Well that's unprofessional," Jiandong mused.

"I'm going to hook it up," said Lance.

"Negative. We'll leave that to the repair crew."

"It won't take a moment."

"I said *negative*. The power core is still active. You could accidentally trigger a surge—"

"I'm not seeing any explosives in this room. It will be fine. It needs to be done, in case the core overloads while there's no one here to prevent it."

"Lance, don't do it. I'm on my way."

Jiandong put his radmeter away and flew toward the nuclear power core. He arrived in time to see Lance turn around and smile, after having installed the cutoff device.

"Done. I just had to—" Crassus said. But before he finished his last syllable, the cutoff device suddenly shook with electric arcs, bouncing between it and the power core. One of the arcs struck his backpack. He screamed just as his suit mic cut out; his body convulsed as all the oxygen in his suit caught fire. The face plate shattered, and as the burning oxygen escaped the suit he was sent spinning in the zero gravity.

Jiandong gasped, and choked with shock. Bile rose from his stomach to his throat. The other team members arrived behind him, but only in time to see Lance's floating body, and his burned face inside his helmet. Some of them shrieked and jerked their faces away; others froze in place, paralyzed by the grisly sight.

"Is— is that Lance?" asked one of them.

"Give me a moment, will you?" Jiandong asked them. The other engineers floated back to the shuttle.

Jiandong stayed for a moment. He closed the sun shield on Lance's helmet, covering his face.

"Summoner be kind," he said.

§ 32.

Lorelei finished her call to the police and returned to the control room. Sitara was waiting for her at the door. "You have to see this," she said, and she pointed to one of the large monitors on the wall. It displayed coverage of Sturgeon Glaive's press conference.

"Ladies and gentlemen, thank you for coming," Sturgeon told the journalists, who had assembled for him in his office. "I know this meeting was called with very short notice, but I suppose by now you have all heard of what happened on the Expeditions platform."

The journalists nodded and voiced their acknowledgement.

"And you all know that my government, and especially I myself, have been against the construction of a Conference ship, right from the beginning. Now I can tell you the real reason why."

At a wave of his hand, several aids entered the room, and handed out press kits. As the journalists opened them and read the executive summary, murmurs of worry and incredulity spread across the room.

Sturgeon puffed his chest with pride. "Ever since the discovery of the probe, our planet has been under attack by aliens."

The word rippled in soft whispers across the press conference. The sprinkling of camera flashes became a deluge.

Glaive, sitting at the table just behind his father's podium, studied his Q-link and hoped that none of the cameras were pointed his way.

"You might remember," Sturgeon continued, as his audience of stunned journalists recorded his confidence voice, "that the aliens who built the probe are a thousand years more advanced than we are. It stands to reason that they could be watching us, even walking among us, without our knowledge. Gentlemen, and ladies, today's incident is clear proof that they're here. And that they want to *prevent* us from reaching the stars. Now, we can speculate all day about exactly *why* they want to hold us down—"

"Senator Glaive," said a journalist, interrupting, "Do you have any *evidence* for what you're saying here?"

"Evidence?" Sturgeon blinked. "The evidence is currently on fire in orbit."

"Sir, if there's no evidence of alien involvement—"

Sturgeon cut the journalist off. "The aliens of Lorelei's planet are *dangerous*. An advanced civilization, with unimaginable technology— how could they *not* be the most serious threat to human life in the history of the world? They're more advanced than us, they're smarter than us, they're probably more numerous, and now they're attacking us. Why aren't you reporting *that*?"

"Mr. Glaive— excuse me, Mr. Glaive!" said Claire Bennett, another journalist. "If what you say is true, then is the government going to— I mean, do you have any—"

"I will meet with the President tomorrow morning, along with other members of the military advisory committee," Sturgeon explained. "We will present him with a policy that we've been working on during these past few months. We hope the President will sign it."

"Can you tell us what's in it? And who else is involved?"

"You'll find out, soon enough," Sturgeon grinned. "And until then, I invite everyone to call the President's office tonight, to urge him to support it."

Grant Molloy said, "What will you do if it turns out the attack on the platform was *not* aliens?"

Sturgeon glared at him, controlled his anger with a deep breath, and said, "I know that many of you will not want to believe what I'm telling you is true. But you need to set aside your doubts and questions. You know, today's attack may even turn out to initiate a great new age for a united humanity. For if you look at history, you'll see that nothing unites a divided people quite like a common danger. Diplomacy, trade, and religion: they all help, of course. But this is a common *existential threat* to all humanity, a challenge to which we must rise. You may not see it clearly right now. But in a hundred years people will look back on this day— the day we brought the alien probe home, the day they attacked us, the day we got organized to defend ourselves— and they'll say it was the day all humanity became one people, one nation, with one clear purpose and one strong will."

In the back of the room, a dozen people began clapping; some of them cheered out loud.

The journalists looked at each other in puzzlement.

"Who are those guys? Ever seen them in the pool before?" Claire asked her colleagues.

"No, never," Grant replied.

§ 33.

"I think we've seen enough, don't you?" Gretel said, switching off the press conference.

Lorelei nodded. "So. Aliens," She shook her head.

"I lay the odds of that, at a million to one," said Sitara.

"That ridiculous man thinks that a million to one odds are pretty good," said Gretel.

"Aliens," Lorelei repeated. "I don't understand how he can *say* that. It's— it's just— just the most—"

"I don't often see you at a loss for words," Sitara told Lorelei.

"Do we still have a channel open to Jiandong and his team?"

"We do," said Sitara, and she pressed a button on her console to bring Jiandong's suit camera footage back up on the control room's main screen.

The image which appeared there was Crassus' burned face. Everyone gasped; Lorelei yelped out loud.

"Jiandong, was there another explosion?" asked Sitara.

"No," said Jiandong's voice, crackling over the intercom. "This man died while attempting to repair the power core."

"What was his name?" said Lorelei.

"Lance Crassus," said Jiandong. "The same, who was with us on the Seven. I told him not to do it—" his voice faltered.

"Bring your team home, Captain," said Lorelei. "Chang'ren is sending a warship; we'll let them finish the job."

"Thank you," Jiandong agreed. He addressed his team. "NavCom technical team: did you hear that? Return to the shuttle."

Sitara turned off the video feed from his suit camera.

Gretel turned to Lorelei. "We can't allow the world to know about this."

"We *have* to tell the world," said Lorelei. "We're an international public service organization; we are not allowed to keep secrets."

"You saw Sturgeon Glaive's press conference, didn't you? When he finds out about that boy's death, he'll turn it into propaganda."

"Then in response, we tell the truth."

"No one cares about the truth, Lorelei!" said Gretel. She turned to Sitara. "Can you explain it to her?"

Sitara grimaced. "When Jiandong comes back planetside, the press will want to know if his team found any evidence of aliens up there. But we all know there will be no such evidence. And then the biggest army in the world will make it their official policy to call us liars."

"Then we will have to find the truth; and find it quickly,"

said Lorelei. "And then, we'll have to stand by it."

Gretel made a patronizing smile. "I used to think that way, once. I'd explain it to you, but I have to go. A family just lost their son, and they need me to comfort them."

When Gretel had left the room, Lorelei gripped the railing around her station, and pursed her lips.

§ 34.

The gym in the Glaive penthouse was part martial-arts dojo, and part spa: hardwood floors, potted plants, lavender oil in the air, antique melee weapons on the walls. Wide windows with softwood frames opened to holographic images of verdant farms along a riverside, though one of the windows flickered with an error message: *File not found.* Glaive worked the bench-press machine, keeping his body fighting shape as the standing orders required, and keeping his mind occupied.

Sturgeon marched in and dropped an envelope on his son's chest.

"What's this?" Glaive asked, putting down the weights and grabbing a towel.

"It's your chance to earn my respect again."

Glaive opened the envelope. It contained a printed itinerary: airline ticket, hotel reservations, a car rental contract.

"You're going to Lalkeela, in Gayatri Pradesh," Sturgeon explained. "You're to look for any industrial sites, with potential for investment."

"And what will I *really* be doing."

"Since you will already be there, you might find out whether any of your targets are— let's say— working on anything that is not part of their usual business model."

"Do you think that's actually happening?"

"I have my suspicions," Sturgeon said. "But I need eyes in the field."

"That's all? Reconnaissance?"

"For now. I'm giving you a simple task. We'll see how you do from there."

Sturgeon turned to walk out the door. Glaive interrupted him. "Sir, about today's press conference— I have to ask—"

"Second standing order!" Sturgeon muttered. He turned to Glaive. "Earth is under attack. That means Arethusa is under attack. And *that* means you, and I, are under attack."

"Do you honestly believe the alien story you told the press?"

"I know what we're going to do about them."

"Have you— have you actually *seen* any evidence of aliens?"

"Just focus on your recon mission," Sturgeon reminded him. "It might have a part to play, in coming days. So trust in that, pick your targets, and then we'll see if you're ready to sit at the grown-ups table again."

§ 35.

"I've got the report here from the police forensics lab," said Lorelei. "They studied the samples that Jiandong took from the bomb sites. And they say— I don't know how— that they found *no* trace residues of explosive material."

"Could that have been a mistake?" asked Sitara.

"Not likely," Lorelei answered. She opened a different document on her Q-link and sent it to Sitara. "Because I've also got the report from the bomb squad on the platform. They didn't find anything either."

Sitara skimmed the report. "It's as if there was no bomb at all," she said.

"There was *something*," said Jiandong. "And it killed a lot of people. Including a member of my crew."

Lorelei and Sitara moved to stand by Jiandong's side. "It's not your fault," said Sitara.

"Yes it is," Jiandong countered. "I was in command. I was the one who—" he stopped himself, as his sense of shame pulled on his voice. He took a breath before continuing. "I wasn't on the front line, during the war. But I saw a lot of people coming back from the line, burned and broken, just like him. So when they made the service compulsory, I joined logistics, so that I would never do that to anyone. But now I've done it anyway."

Lorelei reached out to him, but retracted her hand before touching him. "Do you want to take a few days off?"

"No," Jiandong answered. "I need to go back up there. Find out what happened. Bring some peace to the people who died, and to their families."

"CNH Security is on it now," Lorelei told him. "And if I saw a man burn to death in his space suit, you'd tell me to take a few days, wouldn't you?"

"I suppose I would," Jiandong reluctantly admitted. "Have you made a statement to the public yet?"

"My statement is prepared; it will be released this afternoon."

"Good; before you release it, I'd like to—"

A knock sounded from the office door; before anyone answered it, Din Mbembe entered. "Doctor Verlassen," he said. "Hiding in your new office, while some terrorist punches holes in our platform."

"We're investigating," Lorelei told him, and she handed him her Q-link, to show him the forensics reports.

"Oh. No bomb," said Din. He returned the pane and said, "You know what the Arethusans are saying?"

"We heard. We have no evidence of *that*, either."

"I know it's absurd," said Mbembe, "but the Arethusans are permanent members of the Council. People will believe whatever they say. I want your investigation to emphasize the aliens angle. Prove them wrong."

"Wouldn't that be a waste of time? We already know that they're wrong."

"We can't let them control the message," Mbembe said.

"We can interview everyone who had been to the platform in the last month, and ask them whether they saw anything unusual. Nobody's going to report aliens, so we can run with that."

"Thank you, Lorelei." He walked to the edge of the terrace, and breathed deeply. "I really like it here. Such a clean country, your Éostray." He smiled again, and left the office.

Sitara and Jiandong leaned closer to Lorelei. "There's something he's not telling you," said Sitara. Lorelei nodded, agreeing with her.

"He's the fleet admiral. If we can't trust him, who can we trust?" said Lorelei.

"If you're looking for people who have been to the platform in the last thirty days—" Sitara showed her friends a Q-link displaying a list of names to her, "—that list includes *him*."

§ 36.

Most of the city of Lalkeela was built on platforms the size of city blocks, standing a few meters above the ocean, connected to each other with long bridges for cars and trains. The tallest of its skyscrapers rose from what had once been the old port neighbourhood, but now lay under two meters of ocean. The spaceport was the largest of the city's platforms: its runways and launch pads roared with the engines of dozens of rockets, jets, choppers, and drones. Glaive's sub-orbital shuttle took him to the largest and busiest terminal, where he was photographed, scanned for biometrics, quizzed on his business and final destination, and at last charged fifteen different landing fees, before being released into the arrivals concourse. Breathing normally again, he tried to order an autotaxi online. Instead his screen filled with ads for male virility products, appearing faster than he could close them. Then he noticed no one else in the spaceport was using a Q-link: people merely walked out to the road and waved their hands at passing cars that had the word "Taxi" on a sign on the roof.

He waved down a taxi for himself the same way, climbed inside, and found a man already sitting in it. "Sorry, didn't realise this one was taken," Glaive said.

"I'm the driver," said the man, equally puzzled.

Glaive got in. "People still *drive* in this country?" he said.

"You can get an autocar if you want," said the driver. "but some of them are programmed to lock you inside, and make you pay a king's ransom to get out."

Glaive thought it possible the driver was bluffing, but he stayed in his seat. "The Crown Summit Hotel, please."

"Yes, boss. Here we go." The driver placed his hands on the control surfaces built into the arms of his seat. The touch-screen dashboard, spanning the width of the cab, lit up with maps, various readouts, and music options. The car took to the road: Glaive's mission was underway.

The roads from the spaceport to the city were built on raised bridges and carriageways two or three stories above the original roads, now drowned under several meters of ocean. They snaked between the sleek office blocks and condo towers of the old downtown core, some connected to each other by walkways for pedestrians, giving Glaive the impression he was driving through a forest full of spiderwebs. A new downtown emerged from a century-old suburb on higher ground: semi-detached houses with shops in their ground floors stood between new office blocks, some of them topped with wind turbines made from scrap metal. Local people crammed the streets with their market carts, selling used tech, fruits and vegetables which, the sellers promised, were grown in hydroponic ranges and not printed by synthesizers. After a few blocks and roundabout turns, Glaive and his driver found themselves in a dead-stopped traffic jam. Several car-lengths ahead of them there was an ambulance, with its lights and sirens blaring, yet it was stuck like everyone else.

"Why isn't anyone getting out of the way of the ambulance?" Glaive asked the driver.

"Because it might not be going to the hospital," the driver explained. "Somebody might have paid the driver to take him to the spaceport."

"Does that happen often?"

The driver shrugged. "These things are just understood."

Glaive noticed the street hawkers and pan-handlers who had surrounded him since they stopped. They called out sales pitches for trinkets, wooden animals, jewelry with colourful stones, handmade clothes. Most were speaking a language Glaive didn't understand. He rolled up the window to escape them.

"See the ones with the long brooms?" said the cab driver, pointing at some of the street people. "If you're going to give money to anyone, give it to them."

"Why, what are they selling?"

"Not selling. Serving. They're the ones who clean up the garbage on this street every day. You need to tip them."

Glaive tapped his Q-link. "Do they take Arethusan credits?"

"That's all you have? Arethusan credits? Get out of my car!" The driver powered down the vehicle.

"No wait, wait!" Glaive tried. "I can get you rupees at the hotel. Maybe I have something else you could take as collateral. What about my watch? Limited edition, hand made—"

The driver looked at Glaive. "Your coat."

"My coat?"

"Arethusan army, isn't it? Radar absorbing, plasma burn resistant— You don't see a coat like that here very often."

"It's yours. When we get to my hotel."

"And your watch. Right now."

Seeing little choice, Glaive handed over his watch. The driver smiled, and started the car again.

The Crown Summit Hotel was a repurposed low-rise apartment building. There were a few well-tended flowerbeds in front, but a number of bricks were missing from the outer wall, and several spent syringes lay on the sidewalk. A window near the front door had a long crack in it, held down with a length of tape.

"Your destination, boss," said the driver.

Glaive transferred a few items out of his coat and into his

trouser pockets, then gave the coat. "Thank you," he said.

The driver gave him a printed business card in return. "Call me if you need anything. Another tour of the city, a new coat, some greenrock, anything. My number is right there."

Glaive thanked the man again, pocketed the card, and stepped inside.

The concierge was ready for him. "Lieutenant Glaive?" he said. "Welcome to the Crown Summit Hotel. Our best room is ready for you."

The concierge held out a Q-link; Glaive touched the back of his left hand to it. An embedded chip lit up beneath his skin.

"You are now checked in. Your chip will serve as they key to your room," said the concierge.

The room was decorated with cracked plaster mouldings, and wallpaper patterned with garishly coloured lines and polka-dots. Glaive sat on the bed. The springs creaked under him. He opened the curtains and found a sliding glass door leading to a balcony, but a line of yellow 'Caution' tape advised against stepping outside. Clearly, his father was still punishing him.

He unpacked his army-issue dufflebag, and found an ordnance survey map of the city, which he spread out on the desk. Points of interest had been marked there for him by his father's assistant: Police stations, army reserve halls, comms towers, bridges— all infrastructure and security targets. He picked the location nearest the hotel and noted its coordinates on to his Q-link. Then he packed the map away again, organized a simple recon bag, and returned to the lobby.

"Is my rental car here?" he asked the concierge.

"It's waiting outside," came the reply. "What kind of driver you want? Male, female, android, human—"

"I'll drive myself, thanks."

When he stepped to the door, the concierge stepped with him, with his Q-link held out.

"Right," he said. He touched the back of his hand to the device, to tip the man. It registered the transaction; Glaive didn't bother to check the amount.

"Have a lovely day, sir," said the concierge. "Don't forget to tip the bot."

The android that delivered the car opened the door only after receiving another tip. It also handed Glaive a business card.

"*Kai'tzeen!* Even the robots!"

"It's for his owner," the concierge explained.

Glaive got into the car and drove away from the hotel, heading to the area of the city that lay on solid ground. His first target was a police station. He parked his car in the far corner of its parking lot. Then he set up his camera on a tripod in the passenger's seat, with the video output displaying on his Q-link. He pressed a button on it, and opened an audio recording app.

"Day One of mission. Surveillance of target number one, starting at thirteen-hundred-and-fifty-two hours, local time," he dictated to his Q-link, as he drank a coffee from a thermos. "Nothing to report at this time. Except that I already hate this job."

§ 37.

The terrace beside Lorelei's office offered an excellent view of the campus green, the main entrance, and the cobblestone streets beyond that led to Vogelsberg's downtown. Lorelei watched scientists and researchers at the gate, waiting in line to have their bags searched, their ID cards checked, and their bodies scanned by radmeters: procedures Gretel implemented through the Council, so that Lorelei could not prevent them. Technicians installed new security cameras on every lamp post. Police drones buzzed overhead. Lorelei shook her head at one that came too close to the terrace, so that her disapproval of their presence would thus be on record somewhere.

"We've interviewed everyone who works on campus now," said Gretel. "Scientists, office staff, janitors. Even the truck drivers who work for our subcontractors. And at our other sites, everyone who has been to the platform in the last sixty days. And they all have alibis. However—" she pressed a few buttons on her own tablet, and sent a document to Lorelei, "—there's something about these six people. I think we should investigate more closely."

"Why them?" said Lorelei.

"Because of their previous jobs," Gretel explained.

Lorelei looked. "Aerospace engineering, nuclear physics, AI programmers; the perfect people for starship design," said Lorelei.

"The perfect people for your *competitors*," Gretel said.

"They have the talent, the experience," said Lorelei. "That's why we hired them."

"They might not have the *loyalty*."

"Well," Lorelei sighed, "let's interview them again."

"And this time," Gretel recommended, "we use a neurographic feedback scanner."

Lorelei raised an eyebrow. "That's a little too much, don't you think?" she said.

Gretel said, "It's only a lie detector. It measures the synaptic energy in the cerebral cortex of the brain."

Lorelei said, "It also leaves people with lasting migraines."

"The newer models are much safer. They don't *cause* any pain. They create a low-level biofeedback loop, reflecting to the subject the state of their own thoughts. So if people tell any lies —"

Lorelei held up a hand to stop her. "I still don't like it," she said.

Gretel said, "You can't have another bombing on our platform. Can't risk one here on campus, either."

Lorelei sighed. "Agreed."

Gretel smiled. "I'll make the arrangements for the Communion to send us one of their scanners. We'll have it set up and ready to work in less than an hour."

"I want one of my people to supervise," Lorelei said.

"Naturally," Gretel agreed.

True to her word, in less than an hour Gretel had the neurographic feedback scanner assembled in a seminar room. Its four long legs, arranged in a half-circle, raised the machine high enough for someone to sit beneath it. The machine itself was a large orb made of black glass, inside of which several small foggy lights blinked on and off. When Sitara entered the room, the sight of it caused her to stop and stare.

"Lorelei asked me— to, uh—"

"Supervise me?" Gretel finished for her.

Sitara nodded, her eyes fixed on the machine.

"Ever seen one before?" Gretel asked her.

"Only in photographs," she admitted. She approached it cautiously, and examined a status readout panel on one of its legs. "Why does it look like— some kind of *creature*?"

"Psychology," said Gretel. "Some people secretly *want* to tell the truth. And when they sit under it, they admit all their lies before we turn it on."

Sitara turned from the machine to Gretel and said, "If the person sitting in it doesn't like it— if *I* don't like it— then it stops."

"Of course," said Gretel. Then she took one of the antique chairs from the side of the room and set it underneath the scanner's central orb. "We're ready for our first interview."

Gretel opened the door for the first suspect: a middle aged man whose work shirt bore the logo of a software company. He approached the neurographic feedback scanner and examined it. "Never seen one of these before. Heard about them, though. Fascinating technology. One day we'll use kit like this to read people's minds in real time."

"Mr. Crane? Please have a seat," directed Gretel.

Crane sat down. Gretel pressed a few buttons on her Q-link. Various panels flipped open on the machine's legs. From behind them emerged an array of lamps, sensors, and sharply pointed probes, all on delicate robotic arms. He made a startled jump in his seat. The probes and sensors followed his movements precisely. Above him, another hatch opened on the bottom of the orb. A crescent-shaped device lowered down, carried by cables and robotic arms from all of the machine's legs. It clamped itself across the man's head like a band, and then released several probes and sensors of its own.

The man in the chair was startled at first, but quickly became curious. He touched the head clamp and said, "What does this part do? I'm curious as to—"

"Hold still and try to relax," Gretel instructed him.

Crane resettled himself in the chair and folded his hands politely on his lap. "Okay."

"Now, the first questions will be easy," Gretel said. "Tell us your name, and where you're from, and what you do here."

"Eddy Crane, I'm from Arethusa. I'm a software architect, working here in health and safety compliance. Actually, it's Edison Crane The Ninth, because there's a slight chance I'm descended from old Éostray nobility—"

"The simplest answer is all we need."

He nodded politely.

"Now, just so you know what will happen, tell me what year you were born, and lie to me."

Crane looked up to the orb above him first. The lights flickering inside it were brighter and more numerous now, and their arrangement resembled a brain.

Gretel said, "Don't worry about it. When it's over, you'll be no worse than when it began."

"I'm— I was born in the year 2072," he tried. Then he

squeezed his eyes shut and let out a surprised yelp. His hands reflexively covered his temples.

"That was not so bad," Gretel said. She moved her chair closer to him, and petted his knee.

"It felt like someone poked the inside of my head with a needle," he said.

"Just try to remember: it's not the machine hurting you— it's your own thoughts, hurting yourself. Remain calm, tell the truth, and this will all be entirely painless."

Sitara signalled her opinion by clearing her throat and glaring.

Gretel ignored her. "Now, Mr. Crane, please tell me about your last visit to our starship."

"It must have been two weeks ago. Yes, that's right. Well, it must be right, since this headband didn't shock me—"

"And what were you doing?"

"Writing code for the life support computers. Working on the new escape pods, too. They have a built-in next-generation hibernation system, that could keep you alive and asleep for almost an entire year."

"How long have you worked for us?"

"About a year, I think. More or less."

"How long were you up there?"

"Ten days," he said. "The platform is zero-G, so we aren't supposed to be there for more than two weeks at a time. Your muscles start to waste away. You know what it's like." He looked up to the orb again, and made a sigh of relief that the machine didn't respond to his words.

"You're doing fine," Gretel encouraged him. "Now, tell me, what did you do before you were hired to work on our starship?"

"I worked at Legacy Aeternim corporation, R-and-D section."

"What did you do for them?"

Edison paused and said, "Whatever they asked me to do. Ow!" He winced again as a needle of pain pricked his temples.

"I'm sorry, Mr. Crane, but that's what happens when you don't tell the *whole* truth."

Gretel paused, and gazed on her captive for a moment. Sitara, watching nearby, began to wonder how far Gretel would push him.

"Have you ever been a soldier?" Gretel asked.

"No, never," Eddy answered. Then he howled out loud, as the

machine delivered a shock to his temples again. "That was painful."

"I know, I know," Gretel soothed him. "Don't do this to yourself. Just talk to me. Just tell me the truth. That's all you have to do."

Edison looked to Sitara and said, "Does the director know about this?"

Sitara said, "She told me to stop this if I thought it went too far."

"But we're almost finished," Gretel said to him. She put her hand on her captive's thigh. "You can do this. Be brave, tell me the truth, everything will be fine."

Edison closed his eyes and said, "I was never a soldier. But I worked for the army, once. Everyone in Arethusa works for the army for a while, that's just how it is."

"What did you do for them?"

"I wrote code. Mostly for logistics. Nothing special."

"Anything to do with starship design?"

"No. Mostly I was moving around cargo containers full of supplies. Helicopter blades, power cells, toilet paper. You know."

Gretel tried a different approach. "What did you do for Legacy Aeternim?"

"Supply chain management. More of the same, really. Nothing to do with starships— ow!"

Gretel smiled. "Interesting," she said.

"Okay, I was working on starship stuff," Eddy admitted. "But I'm still not allowed to talk about it."

"We're almost finished," Gretel promised him, with a wide and beautiful smile. "Just a few more questions. Are you still working for them?"

"No," Eddy answered, after a few breaths of hesitation. "But they can call me up again if they need me. It's part of the contract."

"Did you mention that when you applied to work here?"

"No."

"No? Why not?"

He winced. "Black ops project."

"You were working on a starship, weren't you?"

Edison did not speak.

"It's all right, you can tell me, you can trust me," Gretel said. "How long were you working for them?"

"Since maybe a week or two after they found Lorelei's

planet."

"Why did you transfer here?"

"The Conference pays better. And there's a ship. It's a dream project."

Gretel grinned. She touched Edison's hand. "I have to ask— did you plant the explosives on the platform?"

He laughed. "No, obviously. My job is about keeping people *alive*, not— oh, there's that needle in my eye again. This thing is not working properly."

"It's not the machine. It's your own thoughts. That little sting means there's something relevant that you're not telling me."

"I don't know what else I *can* tell you— oh, there it is again, and a little sharper. That one was kind of uncomfortable."

"You *know* something," Gretel concluded. She shifted her chair closer to him and placed her hand on his face. "It's safe to tell me. This room is a sacred place; there is no judgment here. Only truth. What do you know about the explosives on the platform?"

"About the explosion— nothing. But— aaoww! This thing— it's still hurting me. I'm telling the truth, I don't know anything about the bombs."

"The machine is only reflecting your own false thoughts back to you. You're doing this to yourself— and it will stop as soon as you tell me what you know."

"I don't know anything," he repeated, and then he shrieked with pain again. His eyes squeezed shut. He reached for the band on his head and tried to pull it off, but it would not move.

"Oh, Mr. Crane, you can be a better man than this; don't do this to yourself," said Gretel, as she caressed cheek.

Sitara shifted in her chair, and looked around the room, as if there were others who could share her discomfort. "I don't like this," she said.

"He's fine, it looks worse than it feels," Gretel reassured her.

"I don't know anything about the bombs," said Edison. The pain subsided a little, and he opened his eyes again. "At least, it wasn't me who blew up the platform. And I don't know nothing about anyone else. It's something different. Look, I'm a health and safety programmer. Do you understand what that means? Do you understand what I have to *do,* sometimes, to— Aaaa!" His face squeezed into a tight grimace, and his voice strained as he cried.

"Oh Mr. Crane," said Gretel, as she placed both her hands on his face. "I can't bear to see you hurt yourself like this."

"Get this thing off of me," he demanded, and he pulled the metal band on his head again. But as before, its grip on his skull was unshakeable.

Gretel gently grasped his wrists. "You can't take it off while the machine is still running— there's a chance you'll damage your neural pathways."

"Then turn it off, turn it off!" he shouted.

Sitara moved to Gretel's side. "That's enough. Turn it off."

"We're almost finished," she promised both Sitara and Edison. "Almost finished, my darling Eddy, my brave boy. Almost finished. You're very strong, I admire strong men like you. But I need you to be *honest* instead of strong. I need you to tell me what you know. Even if it's something you've never told anyone."

"I know things," he whimpered. "I've *done* things that I'm not supposed to do— a man in my position! Ohhh— can't you turn this thing *down* a little bit?"

"It's not the machine, it's *you*," Gretel cooed, as she caressed his temples. "And I'm so sorry, Mr. Crane, I'm very, very sorry. But you know there's only one thing that can stop the pain. The truth."

"I'm not supposed to tell anyone," Edison winced, as bolts of pain continued to lance his head. "I was told— if I said anything — I'd be blacklisted, I'd never work in tech again— help me, please, turn it off, turn it off!"

Sitara tapped Gretel's shoulder. "We're done here," she warned.

Gretel's face was now very close to her victim, and her arms almost embraced him. "Talk to me, Eddy. It's all you have to do. Just talk to me."

"In the ship's nuclear reactor," Eddy sobbed, "There are supposed to be five independent kill-switches, to prevent a runaway chain reaction. But there's only one. Kai'tzeen be my witness, there's only *one*."

"Good boy, my love, good boy," Gretel whispered in his ear.

"That's not all," Edison continued, still wincing. "The bulkheads. They're supposed to close automatically, if there's ever a puncture in the hull. So that the rest of the ship doesn't lose its air. But the detectors we installed— they're *salvage* parts — they might not work— we never tested them— we were supposed to buy them *new*—"

Sitara grimaced; the information was useful, but the method of obtaining it infuriated her. She turned away, unable to look at the man's face.

"Who ordered that?" Gretel asked him.

"He told me that if I said anything— Nooo!"

Edison was openly crying now. Sitara searched the side of the machine and looked for a switch or a button or anything that would turn it off. She opened access panels and scrolled through the data on its readout screens.

"Don't touch it," Gretel warned her. "You could give him a stroke."

"I'm ordering you to turn it off, now!"

"But he hasn't told us everything!" Gretel shot back. Turning to Edison, she caressed his face. "It's safe to tell me. I'll protect you."

"There's shortcuts like that all over the ship. On the construction cage, too. He said that if I told anyone— He would frame me for all of it— I'd be— Aaaagh!"

"Who threatened you, my love?" Gretel said to him.

He only screamed. His upper body convulsed. Blood began to trickle out his nose.

Sitara's body vibrated with the shock of what she was seeing and hearing. She ran to the machine's power cables and pulled them out of the wall.

The machine stopped. All the probes and sensors fell limp. The lights in the orb at the top of the machine went dark.

The man's screaming was reduced to sobbing. Gretel sat back, and fingered the arms of the machine's sensors. She looked to Sitara, her gaze full of anger and judgment. "He was about to tell us everything," she said.

"He was about to *die*, you scorpion!" Sitara said. She pushed Gretel out of the way to free Edison from the machine's headband.

His jaw hung slightly slack, and his neck had trouble supporting his head. Sitara helped him to his feet. "I am so sorry. I should have stopped it sooner. I am—"

He pushed her hand away and stood up. "Get away from me! Both of you," he said, rising unsteadily. "What is wrong with you?" Edison half-staggered out of the room.

Hearing the question, Gretel reflexively touched the gold trinolay flower on her necklace.

"I'm sorry! If I had known what this machine really does—"

Sitara apologized, as she followed him.

Edison didn't stay to let her finish, and he slammed the door behind him.

Gretel said, "They do this to themselves."

Sitara spun back to Gretel with a speed that made the disciplined politician reflexively raise her arms in defence. "I'm going out to get a fire axe," Sitara said. "If this thing is still here when I return, I'm going to smash it into little pieces, twist the sharpest parts into daggers, and shove them into every seam in your perfect cybernetic skin."

"They're the ones who lie," Gretel insisted. "It's not the machine. It's them. They do it to— to themselves."

Sitara shook her head, and marched away.

§ 38.

"Summary remarks for surveillance of target five: Legacy Aeternim Corporation, R-and-D facility and sales showroom," Glaive dictated into his Q-link. "There's a warehouse as big as an aircraft hangar, and there's an old-style rocket launch pad out back. I've seen two supply trucks arrive today, both of which carried a single container, and they needed a crane to offload it. Must have been something really heavy. Local management come and go by quad-copter. And this is also interesting: security is provided by a private military unit called Dragon Hill Security. They're outfitted in full body armour, combat-ready. Much better kit than the police around here. Please see my written report for exact specs. A final point: although my observation post was closer than one hundred meters and under no cover, still no one came to ask me what I was doing. So they're well armed, but maybe not well motivated. That concludes operations for today, at, uh, zero-one-thirty hours. Resuming operation after some shut-eye."

Glaive encrypted his report, transmitted it to his father via their private line, and returned to his hotel. When he awoke, the reply from his father was waiting for him: *Return to target five. Collect intel from interior of building. Make it your Priority One.*

Glaive leaned on the table, head in his hands, as he contemplated his new assignment. He looked over his photographs of the target as he ate a breakfast of coffee and army ration packs, more out of a sense of familiarity than an aversion to room service. He searched for the business card of the driver who traded guidance to the hotel for his jacket, he attached a comms bud to his ear and called the ID.

"Jumar Vaishya?" said Glaive, reading the name from the card.

"Who's this?" said the man's voice. Cautious.

"Lieu– Mr. Glaive."

"Who?"

"You're wearing my jacket."

"Oh! You're the fellow with no money."

"I've— fixed that problem now."

"Well then, I'm very glad you called. How can I help?"

"Come by the hotel, and let's talk."

"I— ah— don't provide that kind of service."

Glaive chuckled. "That's not what I want. I just need someone with local knowledge. And who speaks the language. Meet me in the lobby, and let's go for a walk."

Jumar met Glaive in the lobby. The two men stepped into the street. "There's a canal not far from here," Jumar offered. "Might make for a nice view as we talk, away from ears-for-hire. This city was built on a hundred little islands, many the ruins of drowned buildings. That's why there's canals and bridges everywhere. No other city like it, anywhere in the world."

He showed Jumar a printout of one of his photos of the Legacy Aeternim lab. "Do you know anything about this company?"

"Sure," said Jumar. "They make those robot arms and legs, for upgraders. Big spenders, those employees! It is a pleasure to get a call from there."

Glaive showed a photo of one of the security guards. "Any idea why they need an army for their security?"

Jumar laughed. "None at all."

"I need to get inside."

Jumar laughed again, louder this time.

"What— you can't help me?" Glaive asked him.

"I didn't say that," Jumar replied. "But it will cost you more than a jacket."

They arrived at the canal. Dozens of boats, heavy with sacks of coffee beans and sugarcane stalks and rice, pushed their way through the floating plastic bottles and dead fish in the water. On the quayside, workers in turbans and trousers and little else, as the heat of the morning was already intolerable, loaded and unloaded the goods from the boats, and sold them to the nearby shops. Glaive decided it was a good choice of a place to talk; the noise would make it harder for anyone to eavesdrop. Jumar led Glaive to a bridge over the canal, which afforded a good view of the ceramic and glass office towers of the city's financial district, a few blocks away.

"I've only heard stories about what they do in there," said Jumar. "Some say there's a vault under the building, where hundreds of people were frozen, just as they were dying. Hoping that in the future there'd be a cure for the disease that killed them."

"Cryogenics," Glaive nodded. "So they're not just about cybernetics. Any idea why they would be interested in space travel?"

"Space travel?"

Glaive showed a photo of a large machine being unloaded from a flatbed truck, in the lab loading docks. "I saw them unloading this yesterday. See the logo on the truck? Rammstein Industrial Motor Works— they make nuclear fusion engines for spaceships."

"Space travel. Huh. Maybe those towers aren't high enough for them."

"We're going in. I'll tell them I'm a potential investor, and that you're my translator. We'll do the tour, check the place out. At some point you slip away and go talk to the janitors or the admin assistants. The local people who do the real work in there. Find out things that they wouldn't tell a foreigner like me. Are you in?"

"Are you paying?"

Glaive looked around the bridge, to see if anyone was watching them. The bridge and both sides of the canal were full of people, all busy with their own business. Glaive reached into his pocket and handed Jumar a clip of Gayatrian rupees.

"This is a start," Jumar grinned, as he counted it.

"Meet me at the hotel at noon."

"See you round, Boss," said Jumar, walking away.

A heartbeat later, as Jumar was already half-lost in the throng of people, Glaive called to him: "Hey, how do I know you'll be there?"

Jumar grinned. "This is Lalkeela. You don't!"

§ 39.

Glaive had the hotel tailor print a conservative dark brown suit for him. But he wore a tie-clip he brought himself, which bore the image of a snarling raccoon carrying a sword: the badge of the Scavenger, his ship in the Arethusa Space Defence Force.

Jumar appeared at the hotel at noon, as promised. He had a new haircut, and he wore all new clothes: unblemished white shoes, maroon trousers, lime green jacket, a white shirt and a gold chain, from which hung solid gold trinolay. Glaive almost didn't recognize him.

"Good day Boss," he said. "Nice suit. Definitely not local, though. How about me? Do I look like your right hand man, or what?"

Glaive's half-smile showed he was impressed. "You bought this just today, didn't you?"

"This is Lalkeela, my friend," he replied with a grin. "Now I'm a high rolling, jet setting, globe trotting playboy, just like you."

"I'm just a soldier."

"Heh. It's all the same to me, boss."

Glaive handed him the keys to his rental car and said, "Let's go."

They arrived at the lab a few minutes later. An armed guard at the gate stopped them; Jumar directed the guard to the back window and to Glaive.

"Lieutenant Glaive, Arethusan Space Defense. I have an appointment."

The soldier nodded, then went back to his post to call the office and confirm Glaive's story. He returned a moment later.

"Your ID please?"

Glaive showed the gate guard the back of his left hand. The guard scanned the chip embedded there with an electronic reader, which told him that everything was in order.

"Parking is just to the left, sir. Have a good day."

Jumar parked the car. "So you got one of those under-the-skin IDs. I thought about getting one, but then I thought, no, that's not for me. What if someone steals it?"

"No one can steal it. It's under my skin."

"What if someone chops off your hand?"

"Is that a real risk around here?"

"Only if you don't pay your debts to certain people. Like the comms company."

The lab door opened for them, and a platinum-blonde woman in a sharp white blouse and pencil skirt greeted them. With her outfit and her almost albino-white flesh, she seemed tailor-made to match the lobby of the building: white walls with white accents and ornaments, white glass monitors, and soft white track lights where the walls met the floor and the ceiling.

"Welcome to the future, Lieutenant," said the woman, with a smile. "What will *your* Legacy Aeternim be?"

"I'm not here to buy, actually. I'm here to *invest*."

The woman's smile grew brighter, and she extended her hand to shake. "You must be Paladin Glaive! My name is Ivy Sterling. I'll be glad to give you a tour of the facility."

"I would like that very much. And my translator and I—" he indicated Jumar, "—would like to meet some of your people."

"It's a bit short-notice, but we can arrange it," the hostess grinned. "Shall we start in the lab?"

"After you."

The hostess led them down the hall and around a corner. They came to an area where the walls between the hallway and the lab were floor-to-ceiling glass, allowing visitors to see everything the researchers were doing.

"In this facility," said Sterling, "we are developing the next generation of cybernetic upgrades, designed to handle high-stress environments, including the heavy G-forces of fast-accelerating spacecraft, and the extreme cold of colony environments like Troth. Powered by the sugar and oxygen in the natural body's bloodstream."

"Is there a market for upgrades like that?" asked Glaive.

"We think there will be, very soon," she replied. "But as you have military experience, so perhaps you would like to see the prototypes for our newest line of upgrades?"

"Please," said Glaive.

The hostess led them down another corridor to a showroom. A row of naked people stood in glass cylinders along both sides of the room. With a closer look, Glaive saw they were not people at all but uncannily human-like androids. Not only the muscle-lines of their arms and legs, but also of the body and face, showed thin dark grooves incised in a sleek and plastic skin.

"We're planning to offer several models," Sterling informed them. "This one is your basic labourer model, for heavy lifting and for precision manipulations. The hands are modular, so you can exchange them for a variety of power tools. The legs and arms have extra servo-motors, to carry heavier loads or work in high-G environments."

"How much of the natural body does this model replace?" Glaive asked.

"Only the arms and legs," Sterling replied. "But there's an exoskeleton, to provide the natural spine and shoulders with extra support. And the cybernetic skin is more resistant to heat, cold, and injury."

Glaive nodded, and moved to the next model.

"This one's our latest pleasure model," Sterling described it, with a smile. "It features twice as many nerve endings on the skin, and all bodily measurements precisely proportioned to maximize evolutionary-psychological advantage."

"What you mean is, they're slim and curvy in all the right places," Jumar said.

"We can build to other proportions, and we also have male models, if the client prefers," Sterling told Jumar with a smile.

"Jumar?" Glaive said, absently.

"Boss?"

"I think you can go wait in the car."

A look of pained confusion crossed Jumar's face.

Glaive shot him a meaningful glance, and Jumar took the hint.

"As you wish, boss." He left the showroom.

Glaive nodded, then motioned for Sterling to continue. She moved to a third model and said, "This is the one we think will interest you the most: our combat model. Stronger limbs, tougher skin, fewer pain receptors. Standardized and replaceable synthetic muscle tissue in the arms and legs: no more battlefield surgery. IFF codes projected directly into the eyes. And you'll notice sharper contour lines in the face, to maximize psychological effect upon the enemy." She pressed an icon on her Q-link. The combat models' arms opened, and weapons unfolded from them. "Built-in area-denial weapon in the right arm, and short-range pistol in the left. These are last-resort weapons, of course, since there's not much room for ammunition. But the right arm can connect to a hydrogen supply line, to fire plasma bursts."

Glaive examined this one more closely than the others. "This is the first thing I've seen here which really looks like the future," he said.

"Sir?"

"The key strategic weakness of every army is the humanity of its soldiers," Glaive explained. "But this soldier— he'll march and fight for days without eating, sleeping, or tiring. He'll kill without hesitation, without remorse. An army of one, a god of war."

"I knew you'd like it," said the hostess.

"The generals will like it," said Glaive. He faced her. "Now, what are you working on that you don't show to the ordinary customers?"

"I'm sorry, I don't follow?" said Sterling.

Glaive stepped toward her. "I represent a significant fund. I want to see your longer-term revenue streams."

She paused for a heartbeat. "You already know we are the right investment for you. But are you right capital for us?"

Glaive cocked his head to the side. "Is it a matter of volume? Our family has been a world class financial force ever since my great-grandfather was President. Name something in Arethusa— we own a piece of it. I'm impressed by everything you've shown me so far. But I'm sure you have something under the counter. Something competitive. Definitive."

"As I'm sure you can understand, our partnerships and capitalization are heavily vetted. This conversation is part of my job," Ivy informed him. "I'm aware of course of your family, and since your aid has gone back to your car, I think I can let you in on one of our corporate secrets."

"That's better."

The hostess smiled. "You've heard of Lorelei Verlassen, the scientist who exposed the coverup of the Sentinel Probe last year?"

"We've met," Glaive confirmed.

"Oh! Well, then. Perhaps you've also heard of her Doomsday Argument," the hostess continued. "Our analysts looked at her numbers, and decided she was right. Civilization on Earth will no longer be viable in fifteen years. So, we're leaving."

"Leaving?" Glaive repeated.

"That's why we need the right kind of investors," the hostess confirmed. "You won't just be joining a company. If you're one of the top five hundred bidders, you'll be joining a *family*. You'll leave everything behind, forever. You'll do more than start a new life: you'll leave your old *self* behind, and become a new person, in a new world. A planet with no government, no regulations—

not even *history*. Nothing will hold you back from living how you want to live, or being who you want to be."

Glaive considered this for a breath. "Show me."

She gave him a sympathetic smile. "I'm sorry, Mr. Glaive, but I am not authorized to—" A flashing green light on her Q-link interrupted her. Seeing it made her smile. "Well! Wonderful news! The directors have decided to invite you to a preview of our exclusive offering. Please follow me."

Sterling turned on her heel and strode to the hall. "The best spacecraft engines ever built can get you to Lorelei's Planet in fifty years. That's still too long. But we at Legacy Aeternim found the solution. Instead of speeding up the starship, you make the crew live longer."

"How much longer?"

"With our next-gen hibernation pods: almost two hundred years."

Glaive whistled. "Impressive," he said. "But it would still be a one-hundred-year round trip. And you wouldn't recognize the world when you got back. Whole empires might have risen and fallen."

They reached the doors of the cleanroom. The hostess stopped, then stepped closer to him; her heels echoed in the hallway. "We're *not* coming back," she whispered in his ear.

Astonishment crossed Glaive's face. "You actually *want* a one way trip?" he asked, to confirm he heard what he thought he heard.

"That's right," the hostess smiled.

Glaive remembered to think like a businessman. "Then— what would be my return of investment?" he asked.

"Don't think of it as an investment," the hostess explained. "Think of it as a ticket, for the most exclusive party in the history of humankind."

The cleanroom doors opened to a preparation chamber. Sterling handed Glaive a dust mask, a hairnet, and a pair of gloves, and she took the same for herself. She removed her shoes and donned plastic slippers, and Glaive did the same.

"I can't let you bring any recording devices in here," she told him.

Glaive nodded, and dutifully removed his Q-link and his comms, and set it on a shelf.

"Are you ready?" she asked.

"Lead the way," said Glaive.

They proceeded through the next doors, which bathed them in an air shower. Then a third set of doors opened to the inside of what Glaive had thought was a warehouse. It was instead more like the interior of a tower or a silo: a circular space with a ceiling high enough to disappear into near-darkness. It contained hundreds of glass tanks, on multiple levels. Inside some of these tanks Glaive could see a naked human body, floating in a gelatinous liquid. Their faces, however, were clamped inside dark metallic masks, from which sprouted various hoses and wires. Other, smaller hoses ran from their arms and legs, delivering blood and other fluids to a pumping and filtration system. Life-sign readouts attached to the sides of these tanks indicated heartbeat, breath, temperature, and brainwave activity, all at the level of deep hibernation. Along the upper catwalks, several androids walked along, checking the empty tanks and preparing them for their eventual occupants.

Glaive said, "What exactly am I looking at?"

"Our newest ultra-long-term space hibernation technology. Volunteers like these provide blood products and other materials which we revert into stem cells and program for genetic compatibility with our passengers. In turn, our passengers can stay in hibernation for as long as supplies last. So, the more volunteers we can recruit, the further we can go."

"These people are volunteers?" Glaive marvelled. "Do they know what they volunteered for?"

"Oh yes," said Sterling. "They all sign legally-binding informed consent contracts." Ivy pointed to one such contract, sitting in a pocket attached to one of the pods.

Glaive leaned over a nearby pod for a closer look. "How long do their contracts last? How long do they stay in here?"

"Oh, once they go in, they never come out," Sterling told him. "Part of the contract. But we ensure their comfort by lacing their nutrient supply with dopamine. Their minds are enjoying the happiest dreams that science can provide."

"So they're all going to die in here?"

"This will expand their statistically-projected lifespan, and create an economic opportunity for their families. This way, they can at least be happy and useful."

Glaive lingered over the pods, stone faced so as to conceal his horror. He stepped down the corridor between two rows of pods. "I have to make a call," he said.

"Certainly. And would you like our investor information

package as well?"

"Please."

Back at the car, Glaive sat in the back seat, without speaking. His eyes studied the ceiling. His comms lay on his knee, waiting for him to touch the *Send* icon.

"So boss: want to know what I found out?" Jumar asked.

Glaive pulled himself back to the present. "Please."

"It's true. There is a fusion engine in the building. In the basement. I met a robotics mechanic in there, and he showed me where it was. Hundreds of robots putting it together. Damned crazy place to put it, let me tell you. When it's finished it will be too big to fit through the door. They'll have to tear down the walls!"

Glaive took a radmeter from his recon bag and measured the building. Something about fifty meters directly beneath the building was generating an unusually high count of alpha particles. He frowned at the reading. "Anything else?"

"He told me about the company's whole big-picture plan. It's to find a way to live forever. Drugs, genetics, cyber upgrades— you name it, they're working on it. *Kai'tzeen,* I wonder what that would be like, to live forever. You know, I heard that all the execs in the company are upgraders, and they've been running the company for near a hundred and fifty years. If anyone is gonna live forever, they will. Their head office is up there—" he pointed to one of the leaf-shaped skyscrapers in the city centre, "—so they can look down on us like the old gods of heaven."

Glaive acknowledged this with a nod. Then he noticed something missing from Jumar's new outfit. "What happened to your new trinolay?"

"Gave it to the mechanic so he'd show me the basement," Jumar said. "Didn't give him my card though. That was rude of me. But he spent the whole time telling me why religion is unscientific and stupid. Such an asshole. Still, at least the gold in my trinolay was worth something to him. How about you, boss? Are you a believer?"

Glaive was still thinking of the volunteers in the company pods. "I need your comms."

"My comms?"

"Can't use mine. They might be listening."

Jumar handed over his comms. "You better pay my long distance bill," he warned.

"I'll get you a brand new comms," Glaive promised. He

accessed a secure line to his father's office.

"Call-sign for voice-print," said an automated voice.

"Paladin Glaive. Priority: Urgent."

The line delivered some electronic beeps for a moment, and then his father's voice. "Son? I'm in a meeting. This had better be important."

"I've seen the interior of target five. They're building a fusion engine."

"That's not enough to trouble me on this line."

"For a starship. And they're not building it in orbit. They're building it *here*. And that's not all—"

"Right there, in Lalkeela?" said Sturgeon. "Heh. Interesting to see the Gayatrians show some audacity. Excellent work. Suspend surveillance of all targets, return to your hotel, and stay there until further notice." He disconnected.

Glaive realized the significance of his new orders. His view of the city changed. He saw a barber laying a towel over a client's shoulders with an elegant flick of the wrist. A barista opening a sack of coffee beans and inhaling the aroma. An artist painting a flower on to a little girl's cheek. Two street-cleaners opening their arms to embrace each other. These moments seemed to emerge from behind a cloud, as if he had arrived in an entirely different city: an older city, yet more caring, and more human. Perhaps it was the original Lalkeela.

"All these people," Glaive mused quietly. "They have no idea what's going to happen to them."

"Boss? You sound like you need a drink," suggest Jumar.

Glaive snapped his head forward. "Stop the car and get out."

"What's this about, boss?" said Jumar, stopping. He stepped into the street as Glaive got out with him.

Glaive was grim. "You have any family in this city? Any lovers? Any friends?"

"Sure, why do you ask?"

"Listen to me. You have to gather your people, and get out of town. Get as far away from this city as you can. And I'm sorry, Jumar. I'm very, very sorry."

"For what?"

"For what I think my father is about to do."

Jumar shook his head. "This is my city. I was born here. I'm not leaving for nobody."

Glaive was adamant. "It's not safe. Not even the kind of lack of safety you think you know. Take the car. Here's some money to charge up the battery—" he handed Jumar another clip of rupees, "—and get out of this city, *tonight*."

Jumar looked into Glaive's eyes for a moment. "I'm not having you report me for stealing your car. You think I'm stupid? What do you get out of this, anyway? You trying to steal my kidneys, or something?"

"I'm trying to save your life."

Jumar only walked away. Glaive was left to watch him disappear into a moving flock of people. They parted for him as he approached, and filled the space behind him as he passed.

§ 40.

"I spoke to the national controllers about this for over an hour," Hanfei said onscreen.

Lorelei could see the skyline of Yuzhow, the Chang'ren capital, in the window behind him. The broken and half-collapsed towers, the empty shells of burned-out tenements and office blocks. Jiandong kept out of the line of the comms camera, taking notes in Lorelei's office.

"We ran the numbers twenty different ways," Hanfei continued. "We want to help you. But most of them feel that the bombing of your platform will set your project back too far behind schedule. And behind budget. We have to make difficult choices. We have to rebuild our own country before we look for new ones in the sky."

"Well, thank you for trying," Lorelei sighed.

Sitara burst through the door of the office, slightly winded from running. "Lorelei— that scanning machine— it's—" Sitara began. Then she saw who Lorelei was talking to.

"Good evening Ms Kula," said Hanfei. "Or is it still afternoon in Vogelsberg?"

"Sorry to interrupt," Sitara said. "But this is urgent."

"Hanfei and I were just finished," Lorelei excused her. To Hanfei, she said, "I'll see you at the next council meeting."

Hanfei bowed, and closed the video connection.

"Chang'ren has stopped paying its dues to the Conference," Lorelei explained to Sitara. "Apparently, it's the opinion of their national comptrollers that our starship is a waste of time and money. I have to find a way to cut the budget by twenty-two percent, and still deliver the ship on time."

"I have to show you something," said Sitara. She moved to

Lorelei's panel and brought up the security camera records for the room where Gretel set up the neurographic scanner.

"This is— not what I was told it would be like," said Lorelei, as she watched the image of Edison Crane squirming in his chair.

They were most of the way through watching the interrogation when Gretel marched into the office. She had a story ready on her tongue, but the sound of Edison's screaming told her it was pointless to tell it.

Lorelei shut the recording off. "Enough," she said. She looked to Gretel for an explanation.

Gretel folded her arms and scowled. "It was *working*," she defended. "That last man you saw— he *knew* something. He was about to tell me!"

"You tortured it out of him!" Sitara accused her.

"I told you— the scanner doesn't work like that," Gretel insisted.

As Gretel and Sitara continued to argue, Lorelei escaped to the terrace.

Gretel disengaged from Sitara and followed her. "You have to understand," she said, "These are desperate times. We have enemies everywhere."

Lorelei said, "When are we *not* in desperate times?"

Gretel ignored the question. "Imagine how much more he could have told us— and what others could have told us— if Sitara hadn't stopped me," she said.

Lorelei said, "You told me the machine felt no worse than a pinprick. That man was screaming for his life!"

Sitara made a wide smile, glad of her friend's moral support.

"Either we use the neurographic scanner," Gretel concluded, "or you catch him in the act of setting another bomb and killing someone else."

"That's a false dichotomy."

"We don't have other choices."

Lorelei raised her voice. "We *always* have other choices," she declared.

Gretel smiled and reached out to Lorelei's face. "Lorelei, you just don't understand—"

"I do understand!" Lorelei replied, a crack of rare anger showing. "I spent eleven years in university. I gave up a normal life, normal jobs, relationships, all of those things. I made it to the highest level, all for one reason: so that no one would ever talk down to me like that again."

Gretel indignantly raised her head and shoulders. "I am third in line to be the Reichsgräfin of Stagsmarch! I can talk to you however I like."

Sitara joined them on the terrace, saying, "So you're ascendency class. That's why you have no moral conscience."

Gretel said to Sitara, "And *you* are a Gayatrian bottom-feeder with a gambling problem. That's why your ambitions are small."

"This isn't about me— it's about that man you tortured!" Sitara shouted.

Lorelei agreed with Sitara. "And when that man goes public with the story of what you did to him, you'll have to answer for it," she said.

"*You* will answer," Gretel told Lorelei. "You are the director of this project, not me. Or maybe you would like a different job?"

Lorelei said, "So, if you go down for this, I do too. Is that it?"

Gretel grinned. She touched the trinolay flower on her necklace and said, "It is time that you asked yourself one of the most important questions in life. What do you want. What do you want, Lorelei? To build a starship? Explore the galaxy? Expand human knowledge? To stand in the Courts of Heaven, and ask the gods why life is so unfair? These things have a *price*, my love. And are you willing to pay it?"

"And what if the price is my integrity? I can't pay that. That's who I am," Lorelei insisted.

Gretel made a small smile and said, "You won't miss it."

Lorelei didn't know how to reply.

"But as you said, we always have other choices," Gretel quoted with a smile. "So I'll have the scanner sent back, and you can find the bomber and build your starship in your own way. With my full support. And now I must be going. You understand of course, I'm very busy. You need anything: you know how to call me. Give my love to the family."

When she was gone, Jiandong said, "You didn't really win that argument. She just *let* you win. Now why would she do that?"

"Because she's a high-nosed poser, that's why," said Sitara.

Lorelei only stared into the empty space where Gretel vanished. "Give my love to the family," she repeated Gretel's words. "She knows I don't have one."

Sitara, seeing Lorelei's posture, moved toward her. "Don't let it get to you. I think we all need a drink," said Sitara.

Lorelei nodded. "*Ja*, why not. Din Mbembe used to keep a bottle of something in that cabinet over there."

Sitara went to the cabinet and poured a glass of westiller for the three of them, while Jiandong joined Lorelei on the terrace.

"Did either of you notice the way she asked you what you want?" Jiandong said. "How her hand moved to her trinolay, as she spoke?"

Both his friends shook their heads. "No; why do you ask?" said Lorelei.

"Because the question is theological; it's The Merchant's Question. They use it in catechisms."

"You think she's a priestess?" said Lorelei.

"She's a seeker, anyway," Jiandong surmised. "Did you see the look on her face? Serious, Judgmental. Just like a seeker would do."

Lorelei got to her feet again and said, "We're about to be tested again. On how fast we can find the bomber. And I'm sorry to say it, but Gretel's machine *did* narrow down the suspects on her list. There's only one left."

"Is it Gretel herself?" asked Sitara. "Please say it's Gretel."

"I know who," said Jiandong. "And I want to be the one who talks to him. He killed—" he paused to regain self control. "Because of him, one of my men died."

"The three of us will talk to him together," Lorelei decided. "Is he still on campus?"

Jiandong consulted his Q-link, and checked the log entries for the campus security checkpoints. "He left about ten minutes ago."

"What's his comms ID?" asked Sitara. "I can use it to track him."

"You can do that?" Lorelei asked.

"Not, strictly speaking, legally," she explained.

"If you get caught—" Lorelei said.

"It'll be fine, I've been doing this for years," Sitara assured her. "How do you think I caught my ex husband in that hotel with the android?"

"You divorced him for sleeping with an android?"

"No," Sitara replied with a pout. "I divorced him for not *sharing* it with me."

§ 41.

Downtown Vogelsberg was one of Éostray's best preserved mediaeval quarters. The streets were of bricks and cobblestones, sloping toward thin sewer grates that ran down the centre line: a practical design in mediaeval times; a picturesque one today. Corner posts on the timbre-frame and stone houses were carved with reliefs of grape vines, lemon trees, and flowers, often painted in cheerful colours. Store fronts in the old market square sold candlesticks alongside Q-links, nanotech pharmacies sat beside woodworking shops with hand crafted children's toys. The terraces overflowed with flower gardens, and the rooftops sported solar panels. Lorelei, Jiandong, and Sitara climbed a flight of stairs that led from the market square up to a nearby hill, where stood an ancient chapel and monastery. Once above the level of the mediaeval rooftops, they could see the ring of glass office towers, vertical farms, and wind turbines that surrounded the core, all shaped to match the contours of the hills surrounding the city. In the monastery courtyard, now serving as a restaurant, they found the man they wanted.

"We need to talk," said Lorelei.

"Can it wait until I'm done my beer?" said Din Mbembe.

Jiandong took his beer and poured it on the ground, and returned the glass to the table with a heavy thud. "And now your beer is done," he said.

Mbembe grimaced at Jiandong. "All right, let's talk."

The NavCom crew took their seats around him, positioning themselves so that he could not easily leave.

"You killed Lance Crassus," Jiandong accused him.

"Who? No— I had nothing to do with that. It was an accident — you were there!"

Jiandong showed him on his Q-link a copy of the Expeditions Council finance spreadsheet, with the embezzlement deductions highlighted.

"What the hell is this?" Mbembe asked.

"It's proof that you ordered the cheapest parts for the starship, and redirected the leftover money for yourself," Jiandong accused.

"How did you get this?"

Sitara interjected. "I'm very good with numbers."

"If you had done your job, all those people would have lived." Jiandong said.

"I didn't kill them!" Din insisted.

"But they died *because* of you."

"All right, I admit it, I told the purchasing managers to use the cheapest parts," Mbembe said. "But I'm not the only one taking the money."

The three friends looked at each other, to see if one of them was expecting this.

"All these invoices were signed off by you," Lorelei accused.

"I had to do it," Mbembe explained. "I knew someone might get hurt. But these were not the sort of people you say no to. You have to understand. They got around the security system in my house. They put cameras in my bedroom. They sent me videos of my children, at school—"

The panic in his voice made Lorelei uneasy. "You're saying someone threatened your family, to make you help them steal money?" she said.

"They also offered me a cut," Mbembe added. "Carrot and stick. Anybody would break."

"Who's doing that to you? When did it start?" Jiandong asked.

"It started just after you got your new job. Like I told you, I work for one of your suppliers now. We'd bill you for three or four times the price of what we delivered. Sometimes we delivered nothing at all. The extra money went to a private bank in Lalkeela. Numbered account. Don't know who owns it."

"I can trace a bank account easily enough," Sitara offered.

"But the money's only a perk to them," Mbembe finished. "What they really want is to force the Conference out of the race. That's why they hired *you* to run the project, Lorelei. You're a philosopher and an ecologist, and you're very smart, but what do you know about project management or space ship design? Did that never seem strange to you? They hired you because *they expect you to fail*."

Lorelei thumped her heel on the cobblestones. Her gaze swept from the city below, to the windows of the castle, to the sky above, and back to the cobblestones beneath her feet. She wandered off to lean on one of the chapel's walls, and scratch her head, and pull her hair.

Sitara stepped forward. "Who," she demanded. "Who wants us to fail?"

"I've already told you too much," said Mbembe.

"They'll never know you told us," Sitara promised.

"They have ways of finding out," said Mbembe. He looked at Sitara and said, "I think you already know about one of them."

Sitara did know. The thought of it made her grimace. She looked to Lorelei for direction.

Lorelei turned to Mbembe. "Go home, Admiral."

He didn't hesitate.

When he was gone she could not look at her friends. Instead she leaned on the railing to contemplate the city below.

"When I was doing my doctorate," Lorelei said, "I used to come up here, and imagine that when the night came, everyone in this city turned into poets, minstrels, and druids. There were art sellers and buskers on every corner. Pubs and cafés full of ideas. Everything was magic. I miss those days."

Sitara moved to her side. "Thinking of running away to the colonies? Leaving the honours race behind?"

"If I do that," Lorelei said, "I'll be forgotten."

Sitara put a compassionate hand on Lorelei's shoulder.

Jiandong joined them. "I'd say your name will be remembered for ten thousand years."

Lorelei frowned. "Sure. As the girl who failed."

"Then we have to win," said Sitara, with a cheeky grin.

"Didn't you once say that all you want in life is to have fun?" Lorelei asked her friend.

"Yeah, that was me," Sitara admitted. "But think of the fun we could have by exposing those people for the criminals that they are."

Lorelei smiled.

"That's not as easy to do as you may think," Jiandong reminded Sitara. "The honours race isn't a sprint. It's an endurance run. Little pups like us can sometimes beat them on the short tracks. But the big dogs always win the marathons."

"So what are you saying? There's nothing we can do?" said Sitara.

"We document and publish everything," Jiandong answered. "If someone kicks you, then you make sure the world knows exactly who is doing the kicking. It's the only way to kick them back."

"I want to do more than that," Sitara said. She turned to face Lorelei. "So, if there's a Q-link you want cracked, any private comms you want to open, or there's someone you know who needs more chaos in his life: you just ask. I can make it happen."

"You can do that?" Jiandong asked.

"Let's just say, between me and the networked q-bit computers in my apartment, there's a reason I was barred from all those casinos," Sitara said, with a sly grin.

Jiandong made a sly grin. "Can you get me unlimited grid access for free?"

"Sure, easily! Only a sucker actually pays for the grid, these days. In fact, I declare it's gaming night in Vogelsberg. Lorelei, want to come?"

"You go on," Lorelei said. "I want to sit here for a while, and do nothing. I never have time anymore to do nothing."

"You're not quitting the race?" Sitara asked.

"I'm taking a Blue Monday, that's all. After what the Admiral told me today— I need to be alone for a while."

"Don't say we didn't offer."

When her friends departed, Lorelei had the hill and the castle, and it seemed the whole city, to herself. She climbed up on the ledge that separated the castle grounds from the slope of the hill, so that she could sit on it, and survey the city below and the sky above. The night air was warm, slightly humid, but comfortable; it was one of those rare summer nights when the bright sharp lines of the daytime blended gently into the glowing pools and magic shadows of night. Stars began to appear in the evening sky, but very few, as the glare from the street lights washed all but the brightest away. She looked for the star that her probe came from, but could not find it.

When she turned to leave, she saw a semi-circle of flowers laid on the cobbles around her. The last person to place one there, a boy of twelve, realized that Lorelei saw him, and scuttled out of sight.

Lorelei picked up a handful of the flowers, and smelled them. She smiled at their sweetness. Then she shook her head, and threw them over the railing. She stepped on some of them as she walked away.

§ 42.

Early evening in Vogelsberg was the middle of the night in Lalkeela. Glaive had his hotel room vid-screen showing a classic movie, but he paid it no attention. Instead he lay on the bed with his Q-link, moving a green rabbit across its screen while trying to avoid the blue foxes and the yellow eagles.

He heard a low drumbeat in the air, a sound he hadn't heard

since the war.

From the balcony he couldn't see where it was coming from, so he climbed up the fire escape to the roof, taking his binoculars with him. In the distance, on the edge of the city and low to the horizon, he saw a fleet of helicopters. They were perfectly black against the dull orange-grey of the overcast clouds. The next alarm in his mind was started by a change in the usual rhythm of the car traffic from the city. He jogged to the side of the building that faced the busiest road, where he saw that the outbound lane of the road was jammed to a standstill with cars. People were scrambling around the road, some of them gawking at the fleet of armoured troop-carriers which drove up the inbound lane. Others abandoned their cars, and ran for shelter in the nearest building.

Glaive fumbled in his pocket for his comms. The screen showed him an error message: no service. He ran back down the fire escape to his hotel room, and tuned the monitors to a news feed. An anchorwoman was describing a sex scandal involving a national rallyfoot player and a pop singer. She paused, interrupting herself.

"I just received this report which says that all major roads and tunnels in and out of the city have been blocked by some kind of paramilitary force. Helicopters have dropped soldiers at various locations around the city, including the police headquarters, all the bridges and tunnels, and all the grid router hubs. Soldiers have covered their faces and have no national symbols or name tags on their uniforms— only their rank insignias. But the language they speak is—"

The signal from the TV station went dark, and then was replaced with an apology for technical difficulties.

"—Arethusan," Glaive finished for her.

He grabbed his kit bag, ran downstairs, and out the hotel's front door. The concierge was standing on the curbside.

"Have you seen Jumar Vaishya?" he asked the concierge "You know— my driver from yesterday morning. Have you seen him?"

"No," said the concierge, and he shook his head; but he did not take his eyes off the sight of a group of soldiers setting up a barricade, several city blocks away.

Glaive ran for the neighbourhood where he first met Jumar. As before, it was packed with people, but this time they were ferrying various boxes and bags from their shops and apartments into waiting trucks. Some of them haggled with the drivers, offering money or prized possessions in exchange for a seat for themselves or a family member. Glaive pushed his way through the mass of arms and heads and boxes and bags, shouting Jumar's name.

He ran back toward the hotel. The route took him past a group of soldiers forcing people out of their cars, so they could use the cars to build another barricade. On the other side of the scene he could see Jumar, arguing with a soldier. "But my house is just a few blocks away—!"

Glaive shouted for Jumar, but Jumar did not hear it over the blaring sirens, car horns, helicopters, and shouting. As Glaive watched, someone attempting to run the blockade in a speeding car. Jumar used the opportunity to dash past the soldiers.

"Jumar, over here!" Glaive shouted.

The soldier opened fire on the car. Bright red streaks of superheated plasma, burning through the air as they flew, struck the car in the front grill, and setting the engine on fire. Another soldier saw Jumar leaping over the barricade. He opened fire, striking Jumar squarely between his shoulder blades. The man fell on to the hood of a parked car, and rolled to the asphalt on the other side. Everyone who witnessed the shooting howled with outrage or with fear, and fled the scene.

Glaive ran to him, and examined the wound. His clothing and flesh were burned black, and his blood was oozing away.

"I told you to get out of town," Glaive told him.

"What's— wrong— with you—" Jumar groaned. He fell silent.

Glaive touched his hand to his heart, lips, and forehead, and whispered. "Summoner be kind."

A group of locals converged on Glaive, shouting something quickly in Gaietreyan, but he understood that they knew Jumar and they wanted to take him away. He picked up Jumar's body and placed it in the arms of the strongest-looking person in the group. They carried him away. Glaive took a last look at the soldiers as they built their barricade, and decided he had to leave the scene, too.

Finding an empty service alley between two office buildings, Glaive leaned his back on a wall, and slid down to the ground. He gave himself a few breaths to calm down. He could see people and cars passing by the mouth of the alley, but none appeared to notice him.

He took his comms from his pocket, found Lorelei's name in his contacts list, and called her.

At that moment, however, Lorelei was lying on her sitting-room couch in her apartment, asleep, yet still dressed. Her comms was in her handbag on the floor beside her, but the handbag dampened its ringing. She slept on, without stirring.

§ 43.

From the balcony of his hotel room, Glaive observed through binoculars one of the roadblocks that kept Lalkeela from moving. He watched the soldiers on it for a few hours, and made a mental note of their battle-readiness: the weapons they carried, the number of soldiers, the length of time between shift rotations, who they let through, and who they didn't.

He retrieved his duty uniform from his dufflebag: a practical outfit with a grey urban camo pattern, black boots, and a black beret with the badge of the Arethusa Space Defence Force. He polished his buttons and rank pins, and marched out to see who was on the barricade.

The pedestrians stayed well out of his way.

At the road block, two soldiers stepped out and pointed their weapons at him. Then they recognized Glaive's cap badge and shoulder flash. They lowered the rifles and stood up straighter, and called for their commander. A man with a ball cap instead of a helmet emerged from behind the barricade, and he almost tripped on his own boots when he recognized Glaive's uniform. But he controlled himself quickly.

Glaive, for his part, pursed his lips and remembered his training, when he saw that the barricade commander had blood stains on his uniform.

"I'm going to safety my weapon, and then we're going to talk," Glaive told him.

The barricade commander nodded. Glaive took out his pistol, removed the magazine, and then laid the gun on the hood of a nearby car.

"You put down your weapon rather easily," said the barricade commander.

Glaive said, "That was to protect you. From me. Now, who are you people. What are you doing here."

"We are the Sons of Courage," said the commander, and he handed Glaive a copy of the manifesto.

Glaive pocketed it without looking at it. "No you're not," he countered. "I know the kit you're wearing. Trained with it myself. Same boots, same guns, same radios. You're Arethusan Marine Corps."

"Some of us might have been trained by the AMC."

"So you were AMC up until what? Eighteen hours ago? What is this Sons of Courage crap? Who's giving the orders?"

"I don't have to answer any of your questions. Who the hell are you?"

"Lieutenant Paladin Glaive, Arethusa Space Defence Force. Now who are you."

"I don't have to tell you who I am."

"Yes you do," Glaive shouted, as he allowed some of his anger to show. "That's Standing Order Number One. When you are on duty and in uniform, and not in combat, whenever anyone asks you your name, you tell them. Name, rank, and regiment. Because we are citizens and soldiers in a professional army. Not mercenaries. And not bullies. We are proud of what we do; we are not ashamed of it; and we are *answerable* for it. And that's why we do *not* hide our names and faces!"

Glaive could see that his words were beginning to reach some of the soldiers staffing the barricade. But the commander remained unmoved.

"But we're not AMC," said the barricade commander, "We're a private security solutions provider. We have our own standing orders."

Glaive was too angry to debate the point. Instead he demanded: "Yeah? If you won't give me your name, then you'll give me your answer to The Soldier's Question. *What are you fighting for?* What are you fighting for? I will stand right here until I get your answer."

The commander grimaced at the invocation of a theological question. But he held his ground. "You can't threaten me like that," he said.

"*You* are the one threatening *me*. And everyone in this city," Glaive told him, shouting again.

"We're here to liberate this city," the commander barked back. "Didn't you hear about the bomb that blew up that orbital platform? Killed how many people? Who do you think planted it there."

"Nobody from Lalkeela."

"That's right," said the commander. "It was the aliens."

Glaive rolled his eyes. "So that's it? That's your answer?" he sighed.

"This city," said the barricade commander, "is crawling with aliens. And with their spies and sleeper agents. We are here to find them, and make sure they can't do any more damage."

Glaive needed another heartbeat or two of time to digest this information. "There's ten billion people on this planet," he said. "You can't put a barricade around them all."

"We can start with global keystone cities like this one. Go home and read the manifesto. And when you're done reading it, don't come back."

Some of the soldiers on the barricade sniggered. "Shut up!" the commander barked at them.

Glaive noticed that some of the locals were gathering to watch the argument, and some of them were filming the encounter with their Q-links.

"So you say you're liberating the city from *aliens*. Have you actually seen one? Do you even know what they look like?"

"You're not going to win this," said the barricade commander, as he took his rifle off his shoulder and held it in his hands.

"Neither are you," Glaive countered. "Because any minute now, the Gayatris will want their city back. You want to face their regulars in a straight-up street-to-street fire-fight? Because that's what's going to happen."

"The Gayatrian army doesn't scare me."

"It doesn't have to scare you. It only has to *kill* you. Look at your position: nice little barricade here, got your ammo stash here, your comms link there. And you've got what— six or seven men? Perfect for stopping civilian cars. Think you can stop heavy armour? Think you can survive an air strike?"

"We got what it takes," said the barricade commander, although his bravado was beginning to crack.

"No you don't," Glaive told him. "I've been scoping you. You have no heavy weapons, and no overwatch. And now—" Glaive gestured toward the people filming the encounter, "thanks to these good people recording us, Gayatrian military intelligence knows you don't have those things."

The barricade commander looked around him, and understood his position.

"So here's what we're going to do," said Glaive. "We're going to march to the nearest consular office of the Republic of

Arethusa—"

"So they can arrest us? They'll put us right back on this barricade again."

"—and then— *and then*— we'll dig in, and protect it. Because all the Arethusans in this city are going to run straight there for protection. And all the Gayatris who hate us for these barricades are going to follow them, with every torch and pitchfork they can grab on the way. Now you're going to do that, before a tank comes round that corner and sends you to the Summoner."

The barricade commander had no reply. He looked at his men to gauge their loyalty. Their hands were steady, but their eyes were watching the crowd and the distant street corners, with increasing worry. He jumped off his perch and stepped closer to Glaive, so that neither the crowd nor his soldiers would hear his next words.

"I hear what you're saying," he admitted, as he pulled his balaclava down, to let Glaive see his face. "You scoped our position about right. If the Gayatris bring in heavy armour, we're done."

"But you can't be seen taking orders from me," said Glaive.

"Not only that," said the commander. "I'm supposed to shoot anyone who gets as close to the barricade as you are now. But you're wearing an officer's uniform."

"Interesting position we're in."

The barricade commander smirked. "You could call it that."

"Any ideas for getting out of it?"

"Well," the commander said, as he scratched the stubble on his chin, "since you have this audience here, I could let you just walk away."

"And then, when I'm gone," Glaive added, "you could make *your own* decision to go defend the embassy. All right?"

The commander looked around the street for a moment, to give himself time to think. "All right then," he said.

"Good man," said Glaive. "Keep the watch."

"Keep the watch," the commander replied, as he stepped back. Glaive collected his pistol. The commander climbed back on to the barricade.

"Oh, but one more thing," said Glaive. "If this works, I should put you up for a commendation."

The barricade commander grinned, and wagged his finger. "Still not giving you my name," he said. Then he put his balaclava back over his nose and mouth.

"That's all right," said Glaive, as he tapped the body-cam on his uniform. "I got your photograph. The reverse-image search will tell me who you are."

"*Kai 'tzeen!*" the commander swore. He hefted his rifle and took aim. Then he remembered that shooting an Arethusan officer would not look good on camera. He swore again, and lowered his weapon.

Glaive smiled, and marched away.

§ 44.

The following morning, Lorelei awakened to the sound of her comms chiming. She had slept the whole night on her couch. The angle of the sun told her she was late for work by several hours. In her half-aware state she dumped the contents of her handbag on the floor to reach her comms, and answered the call.

"Lorelei? Where are you?" said Sitara. "The entire Council is here and they're really anxious to see you."

"I'm at home— sorry— I know I'm late. Tell the Council— something."

"I'll tell them you're coming. You *are* coming, aren't you? Also, have you seen the news from Lalkeela?"

"What news?" Lorelei asked. She turned on her Q-link and found a news feed showing pictures of Lalkeela, with helicopters flying overhead, and police in the streets fighting a losing battle with the soldiers on the barricades.

"A group calling itself the Sons of Courage published a manifesto on the grid, saying that the city had been infiltrated by aliens, and that they had come to protect and liberate it."

"Aliens? Seriously?" Lorelei exclaimed.

The news program cut to an interview with one of the soldiers. Only his eyes showed under his helmet; the rest of his face was covered by a khaki-green balaclava. "The bombing of the CNH platform was the first strike, in a secret plan to stop us from getting to space," he said. "We're here to make sure they do not strike again. It's all in the manifesto."

"That's not what happened!" Lorelei railed back, as though the man on the screen could hear. She grabbed her comms. "I'm coming straight over." She gathered the contents of her handbag together again, and raced to the CNH campus.

All fifteen members of the CNH Expeditions Council were

waiting for her in the castle's former ballroom, a space which had been converted into the Council's debating chamber. The councillors sat on their leather chairs around a large oval table. Most were relaxed: they checked their messages on their comms and Q-links, and smiled and cracked jokes to each other. But those who represented countries that had been attacked by the Sons of Courage sat quietly. They spoke to no one, and they glared judgmentally at Lorelei. Sitara and Jiandong were waiting there too, along with a small group of journalists and photographers, their cameras and Q-links ready for an official response, or an unscripted gaffe.

"They're saying it's aliens," Jiandong informed her, as he arrived.

"It's ridiculous," Lorelei told him.

"And it's not just Lalkeela," said Jiandong. "They hit a lot of other cities around the world." He pressed a few icons on the touch-screen built into the podium, causing the wall-screen to display a map of the planet, with symbols showing which cities had been occupied.

Hanfei Gao'Fu stood. "Madam director: much as this new development concerns us, today's meeting was called so that you could report the results of your investigation. I would be grateful, as would many others I'm sure, if we could preserve today's agenda."

"But my investigation isn't finished yet!" Lorelei protested. "Who called this meeting?"

"I did," said Alankar Sen. "You've had more than enough time with not enough results. And now there's a global crisis, which started when *someone*—" he looked at Sturgeon, "—told the world it was aliens!"

Lorelei now thought she understood what was happening. "You two have been arguing about this all night, haven't you? And now you want me to settle it for you."

No one answered her, although Gretel quietly chuckled. "Didn't I say she would see right through you?" she admonished her colleagues.

"I'm sorry, councillors," said Lorelei. "We've learned a lot in our investigation so far, but there's a few other possibilities I want to pursue—"

"Lorelei, in my business," Sturgeon interrupted, "if someone doesn't deliver the goods on time, she gets fired."

"This isn't like searching for lost car keys," Lorelei told him.

"We're looking for a saboteur."

"You've been looking long enough," Sturgeon concluded. "Find your saboteur, today, or find yourself a new job."

The gaze from all the councillors made Lorelei vibrate with stress. She breathed deeply, ran her fingers through her hair and scratched her head, and got to work. She looked at the map of Éostray, with all the occupied cities marked with icons. Using the Q-link on the podium she threw a dozen more documents on the big display screen: text files, diagrams, reports, spreadsheets, and photographs.

"Where there appears to be nothing, there's always something," she mused aloud.

Alankar leaned close to Sitara and said, "What is she doing?"

"She's solving it," she replied, with undisguised wonder.

"You think she can do it, right here and now?"

"I'd bet my job on it," the mathematician and former card shark replied.

They watched as Lorelei moved the documents around the screen, as if putting together a jigsaw puzzle. Alankar folded his arms and watched her with a furrowed brow. Sturgeon waved her off with his hand, and ordered a nearby android to pour him a drink. Gretel and Hanfei found their admiration of the scientist-philosopher growing.

Then Lorelei abruptly turned the screen off, and stood up. "I have it now," she announced.

Everyone prompted her for her answer. "This had better be good," said Sturgeon.

Lorelei took up a light-pen from her podium and waved it like a conductor's baton as she spoke. "The first thing you need to understand is that we were misdirected from the beginning. We believed there was a bomb on our platform, but we believed that because that's what we were told to believe."

"By Gretel Von Richter," added Sitara, from the side.

"Well, by everyone, really," Lorelei said. "And I went along with it too, when I should have known better. But Jiandong went to the platform personally, and so did a squad from CNH Security, and the Chang'ren Space Force. They took samples of metal and other materials from the blast site. Captain, tell them what you found."

"We found nothing," Jiandong answered. "No chemical residue from any explosives."

"And that's because, there were no residues to find. There

was, in fact, no bomb," Lorelei concluded.

The news was received by the councillors with breaths of disbelief and surprise. "How can you have an explosion without a bomb?" Sturgeon demanded.

"Plenty of ways," said Jiandong. "Ask your nearest engineer."

"After that," Lorelei continued, "we interviewed hundreds of staff people, here on campus and elsewhere, and learned basically nothing. However, Gretel suggested to me that we should look again at anyone who might have divided loyalties. She gave me a list of people, and she interrogated them here on campus, using a neurographic scanner—"

"She tortured them with it," Sitara reminded everyone.

Lorelei continued, "—And one by one, we found they knew nothing about the bomb. Then we came to our last suspect."

"Din Mbembe," said Gretel.

"*Genau;* exactly," Lorelei confirmed. "But instead of using the scanner on him, we *asked* him."

With that comment from Lorelei, Gretel felt Sitara's gaze bearing into her. But the seasoned politician denied the younger woman the satisfaction of a response.

"From the other interviews," Lorelei continued, "we learned that someone was embezzling money from the budget. Invoicing us for expensive parts, then sending cheap or broken parts, and keeping the difference in value for himself. We confronted Mbembe with that evidence, and he told us everything."

"So, Mbembe was the bomber." said Sturgeon.

"No, he wasn't," Lorelei informed her.

"But that rules out all the suspects on my list," said Gretel.

"But your list did not include *all* the suspects."

Gretel was worried now. "Then who was the bomber?" she asked.

"There was *no bomb*," Lorelei reminded her. "There was, instead, an accident. An ordinary, innocent accident, such as might happen on an orbital construction platform assembled with the cheapest possible parts."

"So then. Din Mbembe was skimming the budget. That's the end of it," said Alankar, satisfied the investigation was over.

"Alas, no. For he wasn't keeping all the money. He was sending most of it on to someone else. Someone who was threatening his family, if he didn't cooperate," Lorelei explained.

Now most of the councillors grew worried. They clucked and

muttered among themselves a little louder. Gretel grunted and rolled her eyes.

"The explosion on our platform was an accident that someone *wanted* to happen," Lorelei said. "Your choice of *me* as the director was part of the plan, too. As Mbembe himself told me: I was hired because you wanted me to fail. Just like all the other faulty parts on the platform."

Murmurs arose from her audience. Whispers asking whether Lorelei's claim was true; soft voices carefully distanced themselves from responsibility.

Lorelei moved on. "Whoever planned all of this, probably couldn't know exactly when or exactly how something would go wrong. But he would be ready for it; the accident would be the reason to further some other end he had in mind. Possibly this one," and Lorelei pointed to the map, with its red flags marking the cities that had been occupied by the Sons of Courage.

"How dare you!" Sturgeon barked at her, as he jumped to his feet.

Lorelei made an involuntary backward step away from him. But she gripped the podium, to steady herself.

"Look at the map again, Ambassador," she said. "Look where there appears to be nothing. Every city that the Sons of Courage occupied last night is a city where they assemble fusion engines for space ships. But none of the occupied cities are in Arethusa."

"This is outrageous!" Sturgeon fumed.

Lorelei made her opinion plain and clear: "This is reality."

"How about this for another one," Alankar shouted. "Sturgeon Glaive *wanted* an accident so that he could tell the world we were under attack by aliens!"

"You have no proof! No proof at all!" Sturgeon shouted back.

Calmly, and with no word of introduction, Lorelei pressed a button on her Q-link, which caused the wall screen to display a clip from Glaive's body-camera video footage. His voice filled the hall, saying: *I know the kit you're wearing; trained with it myself. Same boots, same guns, same radios. You're Arethusan Marine Corps.*

"This was posted to the grid by someone who smuggled a Q-link out of the city," Lorelei explained.

"Sturgeon, isn't that your son?" asked Hanfei.

Blood vessels on Sturgeon's forehead bulged. His fists vibrated with rage.

"But Arethusa is not my only suspect," said Lorelei. "I asked myself who else would benefit if the Conference starship died in the slipway? What if Mbembe was wrong? What if the embezzler didn't want an accident; what if he really wanted only the money? And just how deep in debt are you, Mr. Sen?"

"There are far more important things to talk about here," Alankar retorted. "Gretel's torture machine. Arethusa's puppet invasion of half the planet. That scorpion over there—" he pointed at Sitara, "—who once offered me a bribe!"

"And you accepted it!" Sitara immediately shouted back.

Alankar launched into a loud rant against several other councillors who he accused of corruption, and was silenced only by the bang of Lorelei's gavel.

"But Gayatri is not my only suspect," she declared.

"You have another?" asked Sturgeon.

"Yes," Lorelei confirmed. "Someone who thinks that building a starship is a waste of time and money. Someone who used the explosion on our platform as an excuse to stop paying his dues to the project. And finally, someone whose name appeared when we traced the bank account numbers."

She touched a few icons on her Q-link, causing the wall-screen to display a financial spreadsheet. It showed that the embezzled money was going into a private account held by Hanfei Gao'Fu.

Hanfei felt all the eyes in the room drill into him. "Someone had to stop the madness," he shouted. "Interstellar travel— it's a fantasy! Distances in space are too far— even the alien probe needed a thousand years to get here. Your starship gives people false hope. It will make people want things they cannot have— want to *change* things that must not be changed! That ship is a monument to the hubris of those who think they could do that which is denied even to God— the power to make new gods. Someone had to do something."

Hanfei fell silent when he noticed that his words did not justify his actions in anyone's estimation.

"Star travel— it's impossible," he pleaded one more time. But still no one moved.

Gretel, rising and facing Lorelei, clapped her hands. The other councillors soon joined the applause, and called out congratulations: "Great show, Lorelei!" "He was corrupt to the core, I always knew it." "Well done! Bravo!"

Hanfei, however, was growing red in the face. "*Hú li jing!* You will miss the days when your enemies were subtle," he swore, and he stomped out of the room.

Lorelei grinned, and almost laughed, as her pride enjoyed the praise. Then Gretel waved at the press gallery, inviting a cameraman down to the debating floor. She stepped on the podium beside Lorelei, and put her arm around her, as the cameraman took a picture. Lorelei she kept her arms stiff and protective at her sides. Then she noticed that a dozen people had formed a lineup, so that they too could be photographed next to her. The applause, meanwhile, carried on, and pricked upon Lorelei's skin like the drumming of a hundred fingernails.

"Meeting adjourned," she said. She left the room. Several photographers followed her, some of them jogging.

When she was in sight of the door to her office, Lorelei ran.

§ 45.

Lorelei's friends found her in the garden park that the CNH campus shared with the university. She was sitting under a tree, with a sketchpad and pencil in her hands, although she had made no drawings.

"Why aren't you answering comms?" asked Jiandong.

"I don't want to talk to those people," said Lorelei. "It's all a game to them. They actually call what they're doing a *race*. I don't want to be part of it."

"Too late," Jiandong said, as he and Sitara sat near her. "When you accepted the job of director, you became one of the horses."

What's more," Sitara said, "we took one of them down today. So we're not just running the race— we're winning it."

"You say that as if we accomplished something," Lorelei replied.

"We did! I know you hate the race, Lorelei. But if we have to run in it, then let's get as far as we can before we cannot turn back."

"It doesn't matter anyway," Lorelei lamented. "The damage to the platform will take months to repair. And Hanfei said it: the round trip would take a hundred years anyway. The race is over. Sixteen years, and it wasn't enough."

"That's it? The end of the world?" asked Jiandong.

"No. Just the end of *this*," she replied. She waved her hand at the arboretum around her, and to the students from the nearby university who walked about, debating things, kicking soccer balls and tossing discs back and forth, holding hands and playing with each other's hair, sitting alone under trees, thinking, wondering, dreaming.

Above it all, in orbit around the planet, workers in pods and spacesuits fitted six of the largest fusion-reaction rockets ever built on to a giant metal sphere.

Fifth Transmission: Chang'ren

Government type: Technocracy.

*Land area: 9.4 million square klicks, including 1.3 million
    square klicks of uninhabitable badlands and deserts.*

*Grid access: 9.89 citizens out of 10 have unique IP address and
    are registered with The Distributor; 2.1 out of 10 citizens are
    full-time virtual-reality immersed cybernauts ("dropouts").*

Largest city: Yuzhow. Population: 3.7 million.

§ 46.

Although Lorelei had grown up in a small town and loved the
countryside, she also loved the mediaeval quarter of Vogelsberg,
especially at night. But she was no longer a student at the local
university: now she was a celebrity. Strangers asked her to sign
an autograph, or to pose for a photo. Never in her life had she
met so many people who were glad to see her. Yet each
encounter felt like a role she had to play, and each performance
left her feeling a little less like herself. She searched the more
narrow, less tourist-travelled alleys for a small restaurant with a
table for one in an inconspicuous corner, and she made a mental
note to buy a pair of large sunglasses and a wide-brimmed hat.

On a cobblestone lane by a canal, she passed an art gallery.
Its front facade had been rolled up like a garage door, leaving the
space open to the night air. A small bar near the entrance served
wine to the visitors. A poster beside it advertised an exhibit
called "Imagined Planets". Lorelei stepped inside. Each painting
showed a planet in space; some showed several planets and their
star, some showed nebulae or the galactic disk among the
background stars. One of them showed Lorelei herself, in a tall
grass field on a hillside, looking up to the spiral arms of the
galaxy.

A member of the gallery's staff, recognizing her, handed her
a glass of white wine. Most of the patrons in the gallery
respected her space, although a woman approached her to say
she switched her university program to study math and logic
because of her. She could hear their soft voices whispering about
how magical it was to see her there, and wondering when her

starship will be ready to fly, and what might be out there in space for humanity to discover.

Passing by a painting of the probe as it might have looked before it crashed, she heard someone say, "Has anyone ever opened it up, to see how it worked?"

Lorelei realized the answer to that question was probably No.

§ 47.

The Seven's executive crew stepped off the plane that brought them to Yuzhow Spaceport, and lined up to face a battery of cameras and shouted questions.

"Doctor Verlassen! Is it true this is the first time you've seen the probe since you found it on Pluto?" one journalist asked.

"Yes," she replied. "And I'm grateful to the government of Chang'ren for letting me see it again, here in the great historic city of Yuzhow."

A small round of applause thanked her for her politic reply. Jiandong leaned closer to her and said, "That's what the controllers will be glad to hear."

Mary Drake, the journalist from The Contact, asked, "Jiandong, how does it feel to be back in your hometown?"

"It feels great," Jiandong said.

"Will you be visiting your parents or any old friends while you are here?"

Jiandong hesitated. "Only if the media will give us our privacy."

His remark earned for him a round of light laughter.

Claire Bennett, from the Times of Newgarten, said, "Sitara, what is your opinion of the security action in Lalkeela?"

Sitara glowered at the journalist. "It's not a security action, it's an occupation."

"That's an extreme way to describe it—"

"There's no other way to describe a thousand men with guns, harassing people at every road and bridge and tunnel—"

The first journalist spoke again. "But surely it's at least *possible* that aliens have infiltrated the city?"

"It's also possible that aliens have infiltrated *your brain*—!"

A policeman stepped forward "I'm sorry, ladies and gentlemen, but that's all the time we have for questions. I'm sorry, if everyone could please move along, sorry, very sorry, it's no problem."

The journalists dutifully shut off their equipment, packaged it in their carrying cases, and moved along.

The officer approached Lorelei and her companions, and made a quick salute, touching his fingers to his heart, mouth, and forehead. "I'm sorry. My name is Wang'chen, I'll be your manager for your visit to our glorious city, sorry, but if you would follow me."

"Our manager?" said Lorelei.

"Oh yes, sorry, your manager, yes, if I am acceptable to you. If not, that's fine, no problem, sorry, the distributor will assign another, it's okay, it's no problem."

Wang'chen led them through the spaceport and out the front door, where a city bus waited for them.

"We're taking the bus?" Sitara asked, astonished. "Don't you have cars here?"

"We do," said Jiandong. "But we've had to ration them. You only get one if your citizen score is high enough that you need one."

When they took their seats, the policeman at the door allowed other passengers to board. Then they departed the terminal, and headed downtown.

"What's a citizen score?" Lorelei asked.

"It's like the social credit system that we used to have," Jiandong explained. "It's based on things like your grades when you finish school, and whether you pay your bills on time. That sort of thing. It decides what kind of jobs you get, and where you can live, how much money you make, who you can marry, when you can have children. The higher your score, the better your choices."

"It sounds like it controls your whole life," Lorelei observed.

"It's not a person. It's a computer."

Lorelei shook her head. "If it were me, I wouldn't let a *machine* make those choices for me."

"Chang'ren— *Zhōnghuá,* in our own language— is the oldest continuous civilization on Earth," Jiandong said. "And in that time we've tried everything. Democracy, communism, feudalism, anarchy— we've done it all. Probably twice. These days most people think it's just easier to let a computer run things. It's not so bad. It gives you a dozen options. Keeps things in harmony."

"What happens if you turn all your options down?" asked Sitara.

"Your score goes down," said Jiandong.

"What happens if it goes down to nothing?"

Jiandong sighed. "It's best not to find out."

Lorelei opened a window and put out her head, to take in as much of the city as she could. "I've never been to Chang'ren," she said.

"If you want to see the city the way we do," Jiandong suggested, "then let's go upstairs." He reached for the emergency exit hatch in the ceiling; stopping only to check and see that their manager did not disapprove. Then, stepping on the backs of the benches, and with the help of the people already on the roof, he climbed up. Lorelei grinned, and followed; and Sitara followed next. They grasped the crudely-welded handrails to steady themselves, and took in the panoramic view of the city.

"Yuzhow is one of the oldest cities in the world," Jiandong informed them, with a note of pride. "There's no records that tell when the city was founded; it's like it's always been here, since the beginning of things. The Nocturnals threw everything they have at us— invasions, plagues, famines, a nuclear bomb— and we're still here. We will always be here."

"This city must have been so beautiful, before the war," said Lorelei.

"But we *won* the war," Jiandong reminded her. And he smiled upon the fire-scorched, broken, and roofless buildings; the skeletal skyscrapers, long-since deprived of their exterior cladding; the shanties made of flattened metal sheets, some of them set inside the empty shells of once-proud galleries and villas. The bus pushed its way through crowds of bicycles and rickshaws, colourfully clothed or painted as if to compensate for their surroundings. Most of the cars that Lorelei could see had their engines removed, and were pulled by donkeys or horses. Lorelei's nose squelched with the smell of deep-fried beetles and grasshoppers, cooked by roadside vendors.

"Yeah," said Sitara. "I'd say you did."

§ 48.

The bus arrived at the National Sailor's museum, in downtown Yuzhow. Long curtains and banners decked its portico, adding some colour and pride to the decrepit and cracked grey plaster and the weather-worn black bricks. The largest was the banner of Chang'ren: red, with a white dragon coiled across the midsection like a stripe, and a gold star above its head. Lorelei and her friends climbed down with the help of the driver and some other passengers. With officer Wang'chen leading the way, they passed through a gauntlet of journalists and celebrity-spotters. A few ran up to Lorelei or to Jiandong, and then turned their backs in order to hold up a camera and photograph themselves by the side of their heroes. Wang'chen allowed the first few, and then said, "Only one more, I'm sorry, only one more then we must go. I'm sorry. It's no problem. We must go."

Inside, they were led through an interpretive display area, with posters describing the story of how the NavCom crew found the probe. Monitors played the video that they made, telling the world about it. Yet most of the museum visitors moved quickly from one display to another; they read the first sentence or two, then photographed it with their comms, or photographed themselves standing next to it, and moved on. Wang'chen led them to a curtained portal. "It's just through here, no problem."

Beyond the curtain was a reproduction of the dome on Sentinel Base, where Lorelei found the probe. The same kind of supply crates and equipment lay along the periphery; the same kind of spotlights hung from above. At first Lorelei could not see the probe, as the bodies of a score of visitors stood in the way. They held their comms over their heads and snapped pictures of the probe and of each other, then stood still to examine their photos, selecting some for sharing on the grid, deleting others, then reaching up to take some more. As Lorelei moved closer, she saw the top and the corners of the probe's protective glass box, amid the forest of arms and cameras and comms.

Wang'chen pushed his way through the visitors to create a clear path for Lorelei and her friends to follow. With the space open to them, they moved to the centre of the dome, and found themselves closer to the probe than the reach of their arms. Yet with the bulletproof glass box protecting it, they may as well have been as far from it as the planet where it was found.

A short distance away, There was a wax dummy of herself, wearing a space suit, posed as if discovering the probe for the first time. The other museum visitors photographed themselves beside it, sometimes with their arm over its shoulder, grinning happily, and leaving Lorelei herself mostly alone. Lorelei folded her arms and narrowed her eyes at them. Her friends only shrugged, not understanding any better.

Wang'chen handed Lorelei a clipboard and said, "I'm sorry, we would like you to make a small statement, it won't take long, no problem."

"We were promised a few minutes to examine the probe on our own, after visiting hours. With the box open," Lorelei told him.

"You were? I'm sorry, we had to change the plan. Please read the statement, it's for the media, they're coming in shortly, no problem."

Lorelei looked to the clipboard and saw that it held the text of a statement Wang'chen wanted her to read. Then she noticed that the museum staff were ushering some of the visitors out of the dome, to make space for a small pack of reporters.

Jiandong said, "I've got my radmeter right here, but there's no way I can use it. Not in this crowd."

Wang'chen tapped an impatient finger the clipboard in Lorelei's hand, saying, "Read, read!"

Lorelei read it silently for a moment, then said, "I can't say this."

"It's no problem, it's only for the media, read, read!"

Sitara moved to her side. "The government only wants two minutes of political theatre. Nobody else is going to care."

"But half of this isn't true," Lorelei replied.

"They'll probably never let us come back if you don't read it."

The reporters gathered around, cameras and mics ready, their faces expectant. Then one more person entered the dome, and although the glare of the spotlights made it hard for Lorelei to see his face, still she recognized his formal posture and his neatly oiled hair.

Lorelei read the first lines from the clipboard out loud. "I, Doctor Lorelei Verlassen, of Éostray, director of the CNH Expeditions starship project, apologise to the world for—"

The man in the shadows folded his arms, and raised his chin proudly. The clicking of camera buttons and the bursts of their flashes made Lorelei take a step back. Wang'chen whispered, "It's okay, it's no problem, just read."

From somewhere in the room, Lorelei could hear the quiet voice of a translator, reading a transcript of her statement in the Chang'renni language. She looked to her friends; their facial expressions told her they knew what she was feeling.

Lorelei put the clipboard down and said, "For bringing to the attention of the world the proof that we are not alone in the universe—"

The translator stopped speaking into his recorder, and looked up, surprised. Wang'chen poked at the clipboard again, but Lorelei thrust it back in his hands. Hanfei, still in the shadows, grabbed the nearest museum staff member and whispered an order into his ear.

Lorelei said, "I apologize for believing that our civilization can *overcome* its problems, build starships, and explore space. But most of all, I apologise for *nothing*, and—"

A team of museum staff dashed into the space between Lorelei and the reporters, and they ushered everyone out of the room. Wang'chen grappled Lorelei and Sitara by the elbows and pulled them toward another exit; another police officer forced Jiandong to follow. Moments later Lorelei and her friends found themselves on the museum's shipping and receiving platform, with Hanfei Gao'fu standing in the door, blocking their return to the probe.

"You couldn't resist, could you?" he accused Lorelei. "All you had to do was read one paragraph. Less than a hundred words. And then you could have the close-up look at the probe that you asked for. We'd have removed the glass shield for you, let you scan the probe and take it apart. Sign your name on it, for all that I care. But you could not control yourself— you had to do things your way."

"The statement you wanted me to read was a lie," Lorelei told him.

"By reading it, you would have made it true," Hanfei declared.

"Yes, I know," she growled back.

"You *owe* me an apology," he asserted. "You *will* step in front of the probe, and our nation's media, and read that statement, exactly as written. Nothing added, nothing changed, nothing left out. Then you'll get your chance to study the probe for as long as you want."

"And if I don't?"

"Tomorrow morning, I will destroy it."

All together, Lorelei and Sitara and Jiandong blasted Hanfei with their shouting, Lorelei loudest of all: "What—destroy it? No! You can't do that! It belongs to the world!"

"That alien shipwreck is already the cause of too much

turmoil in the world," Hanfei hissed back. "And you yourself, Lorelei, have only made it worse. Your prediction of the end of time. Your song about how only you and your starship can save us. Do you not understand the effect that kind of talk can have?"

Lorelei remembered the times when people laid trinolay flowers at her feet.

"But I am a civilized man," said Hanfei, as he calmed himself, "I'm giving you another chance."

"You're asking me to tell the world I sold them an illusion," Lorelei told him.

"I'm demanding that you apologize for shaming me in front of the Council!" Hanfei shouted. Lorelei took a step back; it was the first time she had ever seen him angry enough to yell.

Then Hanfei controlled himself again, ran his oil-comb through his hair, and said, "I will have your apology before tomorrow morning. Or else, you will leave me no choice but to —"

"You always have a choice!" Lorelei interrupted. "Why do people say things like that? Have you no free will at all? Or do you always do what other people make you do?"

"Apologize," Hanfei growled at her, with an accusing finger pointed in her face, "and don't make me do something you will regret."

§ 49.

As the occupation of Lalkeela continued, Glaive settled into a daily routine. He would wake, shower and shave, have room service deliver breakfast, then spend the day watching the roadblock with his binoculars. In the evening, he would go to the lobby, pay his bill for the following day, and then order room service for dinner, so he could continue his surveillance of the roadblock. Sometimes he would chat with the hotel staff about how the occupation affected them. Some no longer had running water or electricity in their homes. Some were running low on food. On the evening of the one-week anniversary of the occupation, the hotel's system rejected his payment.

"That account belongs to the family fund," he explained. He put his hand on the counter and said, "Scan the chip in my hand."

The agent scanned it, checked the readout on his device, and said, "The readout says there's insufficient credits in your account."

"That can't be," Glaive said. "Try it again."

The clerk tried again, and shook his head. "No, still nothing. Do you have any other means of payment?"

"I could do a direct transfer from my private account— can I use your access?"

Glaive was led to an office and given a terminal. He checked his bank account balance on the grid, and found that it contained only twenty Arethusan credits. He thumped his fist on the desk: his father had cut him off.

Controlling his frustration, he returned to the clerk. "I'll arrange for the accounts manager to pay you directly," he said, hoping the clerk would be satisfied with that. He returned to his room, packed his possessions, and took them downstairs to load into his rental car.

Glaive drove to the local embassy of Arethusa. True to his prediction, the building's front garden was the scene of a loud protest. Around a hundred angry people shouted insults and chanted slogans, and sometimes threw garbage at the building.

He parked his car, took his bags, and pushed his way through the crowd. The protesters ignored him at first; but when he was close to the front of the throng, barely within sight of the door guards, someone recognized him from the standoff at the Sons of Courage barricade. As news of his presence spread through the crowd, people cheered for him, and slapped his back.

Glaive laughed, more from relief than from happiness. He pointed to the embassy gate and said, "I have to get to the embassy; can you let me through?"

They made a path for him to the gate. The ruckus of his arrival attracted the attention of the guards at the door: they let him into the fence line, but not into the building.

"Passport, please," they told him, though their expressions told Glaive they knew perfectly well who he was. The officer swiped its data strip into his Q-link, and frowned at the result. "I'm sorry, sir, but your passport is flagged," he said.

"Flagged? For what?"

"For security," the officer said.

"That's not a helpful answer. Let me talk to the station chief." Glaive stepped toward the embassy doors.

"I can't let you in the embassy, sir," the officer said, standing in his way.

"That's ridiculous! I'm an Arethusan citizen! My father is a national senator!"

"But your passport is flagged, sir."

Glaive grimaced at him. The guards, for their part, didn't like the effect Glaive's presence had on the crowd outside the fence.

Glaive nodded toward the guard house. "Can I use your comms?" he asked.

The guard checked with his officer, who gave his permission with a curt nod. Glaive followed him to the guard house. He entered the secret access number for the Glaive family penthouse into the vid-com on the wall. First it displayed the graphics for a comm connection in progress; moments later it displayed the furrowed and scowling face of the elder Glaive.

"I see that you did not stay in your hotel, as ordered," Sturgeon began.

"Someone froze my accounts," Glaive explained.

"Perhaps you can get your new friends in Gayatrian Intelligence to pay for it."

Glaive made a slight recoil from the screen. "Sir?"

"Or," said his father, "you could explain to me why someone who looked and sounded like you was captured on video threatening the boys on the barricades?"

"The Sons of Courage are AMC. They're us. But we're on a secure channel here, you don't have to pretend otherwise to *me*."

"Do not presume to tell me what to say, son. Remember who you're talking to."

"Who am I talking to?"

This made Sturgeon stop, his face frozen in surprise. When he found his words, he said, "I didn't quite hear you correctly there. It sounded like you were questioning my authority."

"They're *killing* people here. A man I knew, he had helped me scope the Legacy Aeternim lab, was killed for walking down his own street."

"You're a soldier. Men die in battle; you know that."

"Jumar Vaishya wasn't a soldier. He was just a local taxi driver, trying to get home."

"I don't care to know his name."

"All the targets in this city that I scoped for you have barricades around them now. Schools, hospitals, all closed. Nobody's going to work. Nobody can get across town, unless they submit to biometric scanning at those checkpoints. And they're not letting cargo ships come in. Soon the city will run out of food. And at night paramilitaries drive around with turret guns in the back, kicking down people's doors, shooting at anyone who didn't get home before curfew. They say they're looking for aliens, but they confiscate money and jewelry. They're not looking for aliens."

"Your point, son."

"Point is, we're the enemy here."

Sturgeon glowered for a moment. "The aliens are the enemy."

"Aliens did not kill Jumar Vaishya. We did. That makes us the enemy to a civilian population."

"Everyone who is not one of us is the enemy!" Sturgeon shouted. "You are an officer in the Arethusa Space Defence Force— you swore an oath to protect your country, if necessary to give your life for it. That is all the answer you need. The only reason you haven't been charged yet is because of me." Sturgeon glowered at his son, long enough to satisfy himself that he had control of the silence. "Let me tell you what we are doing in Lalkeela. We are bringing unity and sanity back to the world."

"Then why are we—"

"Have you ever wondered why, as a human race, we fight so many wars? The answer is because without war, human life is without meaning. Without an enemy to fight, we don't just become weak, we become *bored*. We lose purpose, we disengage. War also brings people together, erases their differences, gives them a common cause. All that's needed is a common enemy. It almost doesn't matter who the enemy is— it only matters that we unite and prove ourselves by conquering it. And now we have that enemy: and it is so different from us that it is not even human. What seems to you right now like a desperate injustice is only a minor stumble in a long march to a united world. That's what we're doing here."

"And when we've defeated our common enemy and the war is over, what do we do?" Glaive asked. "We go back to fighting ourselves again?"

"By then, there will be another enemy. And the war will never end."

"And history will remember you as the general who led the charge?"

"History will remember Arethusa," Sturgeon corrected him.

"Well then," Glaive simmered, "I know who my enemy is."

Sturgeon grimaced at his son, letting his silence make his statement. Glaive could see the wheels turning in his father's mind. But he folded his arms and glared back, making it clear he would not apologize nor retract his words; it was his father's turn to move.

"So. You picked your side. Good boy," Sturgeon said. "Now, stay where you are while I arrange to lift the hold on your accounts. Make yourself comfortable; it may take a while." He pressed a button out of view; then the screen reverted to its standby image. Glaive stared at it for a moment. He knew that his father understood him perfectly.

Footsteps approached the door: combat boots, he identified the sound. He put his sidearm in his belt, in the small of his back.

Two soldiers in full combat armour entered the guard house. A man in a business suit entered after them: a member of the embassy's political or diplomatic staff, Glaive surmised by the pin on his breast.

"You're the station chief?" asked Glaive. "Will you let me into the embassy now? I need an evac from this theatre."

The station chief motioned to one of the soldiers; the soldier activated his helmet camera and started recording the encounter. The chief said, "Are you Paladin Arko Glaive, Lieutenant in the Arethusa Space Defence Force, born in Newgarten, Arethusa, on May 10th, 2085?"

"What's this about?" Glaive replied.

"I need you to ID yourself, for the record," the station chief insisted. "Please present your passport and your sidearm."

"You're not my C.O., I don't have to—" Glaive said, but he noticed the soldiers had their fingers resting on the sides of the weapon, just above the triggers, ready to move.

Glaive showed the chief his passport. He kept his pistol hidden.

The station chief took the passport and handed Glaive a folded paper, stamped with an official seal. Then he said, "In the name of the President of Arethusa, and under the authority vested in me by the Emergency Standing Orders, I hereby discharge you of your commission in the ASDF, and I vacate your citizenship in the Republic of—"

Glaive's eyes shifted about the room as though the sky had changed colour. "Emergency Standing Orders?"

The station chief continued reciting from his script. "—of Arethusa. You are hereby ordered to surrender your weapon, your officer's badge, and your passport. If you do not do so, we are authorized to take all necessary steps to remove them from you—"

"You can't do that!" Glaive shouted. "I'm an officer— I was born in Newgarten—!"

"—Furthermore you are hereby notified that you are now *persona non grata* in all Arethusan territories and possessions. Effective seventy-two hours from this moment, all loyal and true Arethusan citizens shall enjoy full immunity from prosecution for crimes committed against you—"

Glaive stepped closer to the chief. "You're branding me *fair game?* This is total bullshit! There's supposed to be a trial first— oh, this is *his* doing, isn't it? He ordered this, didn't he?"

"—And may no one but the Summoner be kind to you," the chief finished.

Glaive stepped back, as he realized his father had won the round. He let the soldiers escort him off the embassy grounds, and into the unknown.

§ 50.

Glaive crossed the threshold of the embassy with a slight stumble, as one of the soldiers gave him a shove out the door. The protesters had been dispersed by the guards; some of their signs were lying in the ground, covered in footprints. He went to his rental car, only to see a tow truck pull it away.

A siren sounded: fifteen minutes until curfew. The street vendors and hawkers packed up their carts and displays; office workers and professionals dashed for their cars and taxis. A drone flew overhead, broadcasting commands from its loudspeaker. Glaive couldn't speak the language but he knew the message was a threat for those who remained outside after curfew began. Remembering his training, he made a quick mental stock of all the places within a fifteen minute jog where he could find shelter, information, or anything useful. He settled on a parking garage as a place to minimize his exposure to wandering paramilitaries. Entering it was easy: other nearby pedestrians had the same idea, and someone was holding the doors open for them and gesturing them to enter. Once inside, he saw that part of it had been converted into a shelter for people caught far from home when the curfew began. Mattresses lay in neat rows in the parking spots. Another area had become a social gathering spot with grid terminals and five-card finangle tables.

He lay down on one of the mattresses, and turned on his side with his face toward a wall, in the hope that no one would bother him. But someone tapped his shoulder and yelled at him in rapid Gayatrian; his gestures and tone told Glaive the mattress was for rent and not for free. Glaive apologized, and moved off to a different corner of the garage behind some parked cars. Another feature of his training: he knew how to get a few hours of sleep anywhere.

Glaive got up and peeked out the door. The street was empty of people. The silence made for a jarring contrast with the bustling energy of the city by day; not even insects risked breaking the curfew. He closed the door, made a quick inventory of his possessions, and found he still had his binoculars, camera, and pistol. Then he carefully slipped outside. He dodged around the pools of yellow-orange light beneath the streetlamps, and kept mental tabs on hiding places that he could reach quickly; a habit that served him well whenever the silence was broken by the buzzing of an overhead drone.

He came within sight of a Sons of Courage checkpoint. Floodlamps filled the street as far out as a city block in both directions. Bored-looking men with guns patrolled nearby. Glaive found a hiding place behind a flight of concrete steps leading into an office building, where he could watch from some safety.

One of the guards came close on his patrol. Glaive ducked back behind the stairwell, and readied his pistol. As soon as the guard came around the steps, Glaive fired two shots. Two bolts of super-heated plasma burned into the guard's head, dropping him to the ground before he knew Glaive was there. A third bolt to the heart ensured that the guard would stay down.

The action caught the attention of the other guards, who ran to the scene. One of them fell to Glaive's plasma bolts before getting half-way there; another fell before releasing the safety catch on his weapon. The last one ducked for cover behind a car. To reach him, Glaive only had to wait: his target was not a war veteran like Glaive, and might soon do something to give away his position. Glaive took the time to sneak around to a new cover, behind a garbage dumpster. The last guard made a dash for the safety of the barricade, thus revealing himself, exactly as expected. Glaive flanked him and silenced him with three quick plasma bursts to the head and heart.

When the soldier was dead, Glaive searched the body for

ammunition, money, anything useful. He found in the jacket pocket a digital key-card. "Perfect," he said, as he eyed a pickup truck with a turret-mounted gun in the back. He took the dead man's rifle and radio with him as he crossed town, feeling more confident, but taking no fewer precautions. He had a destination in mind, but he calculated that he had at least two checkpoints to cross to reach it. For the first one, he approached slowly, like a solder walking the control zone, and the soldiers on the barricade paid him no attention.

"You're back early," said the barricade's leader. Glaive didn't speak; he answered by shrugging his shoulders, and he kept walking.

Then the leader realized something was wrong. "Hey, who the hell are you?" he said. Glaive kept walking. The leader jumped off the barricade to confront him. When the two men were an arm's length apart, Glaive arm flashed forth; in less than a heartbeat the leader fell to the pavement with a combat knife buried deep in his throat.

By the time the nearest other guards understood what had happened, Glaive had already fired on them. Superheated plasma melted their clothes, flesh, and bones, just above the heart, into a bitter-smelling black hollow. Then Glaive stole another key-card for another truck. He launched it forward, smashing through the bars of the checkpoint, and speeding off into the darkness.

Glaive knew that within a few minutes every checkpoint in the city would hear about his attack on the barricade. The stolen radio told him that three drones had been dispatched to track him; moments later, he heard the buzz of their propellers in the air. At first he thought it strange that the drones were not firing on him. But when he reached his destination, he knew why. The entry gate to the Legacy Aeternim facility was blocked by another Sons of Courage barricade. This time, the soldiers manning it were ready for him. They opened fire on the truck from at least three directions. Glaive felt the first quiver of fear pass through his muscles. He knew that when the plasma bolts heated the car enough, the fuel tank would ignite. His gaze instinctively fixed on the engine heat indicator.

The truck's autopilot detected the overheating, and took control, slowing and searching for a safe place to stop and shut down. Glaive jumped out of it and rolled to the ground on the side of the road. The truck coasted to the Sons of Courage barricade and caught on fire, exactly as Glaive anticipated. He dashed into a nearby shopfront, took a position behind some shelves, and waited for the soldiers to come looking for him.

Moments later, they did; a team of seven, loudly barking reports and orders into their radios, and firing on anything that looked like it might be someone hiding in the dark: shrubs, public comms booths, raised flower beds. Glaive carefully peeked out from his hiding place and saw that the Sons of Courage were taking cover behind the burning barricade. Several bright flashes in the dark told Glaive that someone was firing on them from the roof of the Legacy Aeternim factory. Soon, the Sons of Courage team was down to three men. One of the drones crashed to the ground in front of the store, evidently shot out of the air by the company security.

As the last three Sons of Courage scrambled for cover, they came into Glaive's line of fire. He gave them one burst of plasma each, to put them down, and then one more to keep them down.

The security company ceased fire. The street quietened. No drones hovered overhead; the only sound came from the flames consuming the shell of the truck, and the rattle of the wind in the rubble. Glaive gingerly stepped out of cover, holding his rifle high. They shouted something at him in Gayatrian.

"You speak Arethusan?" Glaive shouted back.

"Put down your weapon and keep your hands up!" someone shouted back.

"Okay, I'm putting it down—"

He put his weapon on the ground. Three Dragon Hill Security men emerged from the burning barricade, weapons drawn.

"I surrender," Glaive told them. "Now take me inside."

"We're not the army, we don't take prisoners," said one of the guards. He raised his rifle, and took aim.

"I'm not one of them. I'm the one who attacked their position with the truck," Glaive stated.

"That was you? Hey, wait, I think I've seen you before. You're the guy from the vid, standing up to that goat-sucker on the barricade."

"Yeah, that was me, too," Glaive confirmed.

The guardsmen lowered his weapon. "Kai'tzeen's beard! It is you!" he grinned. "The whole world's talking about you! How'd you do it? You got ice-water instead of blood, or something?" He embraced Glaive in a rough and friendly headlock.

"I was a sniper in the war," said Glaive, as he gently pushed himself free.

"It's a hell of a thing to meet you! The name's Faceoff. That's my warrior name."

Glaive winced.

"What you doing out here in the middle of the night?" Faceoff asked.

"Trying to get the hell out of this city."

"Heh. Isn't everybody? But since it's you, maybe we can help."

The sound of drones approaching prompted them to jog back to the factory. They got the door closed just as two drones arrived and shone their spotlights on the wreckage of the barricade.

"We're due to rotate out of here tomorrow. They're taking us to Rio. Surfing, sunshine, and the sexiest girls on the planet. We could take you with us. For the special one-day low price of, oh let's say, twenty thousand."

Glaive grimaced. "I assume you mean Arethusan credits."

"Obviously I mean credits!" Faceoff laughed. "You can't buy anything with Gayatrian rupees anymore."

"The money's no problem. My father's a national senator," said Glaive. He knew that his father wouldn't pay it, but he gambled that Faceoff would believe him anyway.

"Rich boy, huh? Say, if you're dad's so rich, why do you need us?"

"My mission here was— off the books."

Faceoff studied Glaive's eyes for a moment. Glaive held himself steady, mindful of what he might have to do if the mercenary didn't believe him. A few breaths later, Faceoff laughed out loud and slapped him on the shoulder. "Ha! That's what I love about Arethusans. They got their fingers in everything."

Glaive grinned, and returned the pat on the shoulder. "Now I need to use your comms."

Faceoff pointed to comms on the security desk. "Not my comms. Fill your boots."

§ 51.

"I won't do it," Lorelei declared.

"But it's the best solution," said Sitara.

"The most *dangerous*, you mean."

"And I'm surprised you won't consider it. You broke into a military base on Pluto without thinking twice. Break-and-enter is like your trademark."

Jiandong laughed, but a stifling glance from Lorelei stopped him. "So you agree with her?" she asked.

"We're dealing with a man who is prepared to kill to get what he wants," Jiandong replied. "So when he says he will destroy the probe, I believe him."

Lorelei's glum face told them that she was no happier with that suggestion.

"He's not asking for much," said Jiandong, as he read the statement on the clipboard. "Just an apology for embarrassing him in front of the council. Which, Lorelei, you *did* do."

"So, the problem is not that he's an embezzler; the problem is that he got caught?" Lorelei reminded him.

"That's the choice he gave us," Jiandong conceded.

They sat in silence for a moment, contemplating their situation. Then Lorelei said, "He's bluffing."

Jiandong said, "You sure about that?"

"Well, no," she confessed. "But if he destroys the probe, the entire world will want to lock him up for it. He has more to lose than we do. He must know that."

"Do you want to take that chance?"

"It's the only choice I can see that isn't a turn in their stupid race," said Lorelei.

"Then that's it," said Sitara. "Tomorrow morning, we go back to Éostray, and hope that the probe is delivered to the next museum in fewer than a thousand pieces."

Jiandong and Sitara exchanged knowing looks with each other.

Later that night, Sitara sent a text message to Jiandong: *There's a fourth choice. We go in without her. I have a plan.*

Jiandong texted back to say: *I like it. Let's go.*

When he arrived at the museum, Sitara was already there, waiting for him, and applying makeup to her lips and eyes, using the camera and screen on her comms as a mirror.

"War paint," she explained to her captain. "They won't let us see the probe just for asking."

"What, exactly, is your plan?" her captain asked, a little worried about his role.

"A bit like your plan to get an audience with the bishop," she replied. "We get in the door because we're famous, and we get to the probe because we treat the gatekeepers with kindness and respect."

"That might not be enough. The probe is the most valuable artifact on Earth."

"Also, we hack the Distributor."

Jiandong's face flushed with panic. "You can't hack the—"

Before he could finish, Sitara handed him her Q-link. "When the guard isn't looking, you press this icon—" she showed him which one on the screen, "—and my program will do the rest." She opened the door, and strutted to the security desk, smiling for officer Wang'chen.

"Oh! Oh no! How is it you are here? What are you doing? The museum is closed— you cannot be here!" the officer startled. "If you stay, I arrest you."

"Is that really necessary?" said Sitara, with an innocent smile. "I know this seems very strange, seeing us here tonight. But we were told we could study the probe here for a while after hours, and, well, we lost track of time. That probe— it's really alien, isn't it? Have you ever seen it up close?"

Wang'chen grinned on one side of his mouth. "Miss Kula, in other situation, it would be no problem, honour to meet you. But as it is, I have to place you in arrest—"

Jiandong cleared his throat and tapped her Q-link, to tell Sitara the process it was runing was complete.

Sitara stepped closer to the officer. "Suppose instead of arresting us, we offered you something. To make things smooth for you."

Wang'chen eyed one of the security cameras for a second. Then he straightened his spine. "I am officer of law, Miss Kula."

"When I first met you," Sitara said, drawing closer to him, "I asked myself: you seem like a fine and good man. Surely your citizen score is high enough for something better than the police? Suppose we arranged for your score to— *rise*, a little bit."

"That not possible," Wang'chen snapped. "The distributor cannot be broken. Criminal offence to try, even if fail. I should arrest you for suggesting it."

Sitara said, "Check your score, on your comms, right now."

Wang'chen only laughed at her.

Sitara stepped closer again and said, "Just take a look. Could you do that for me?"

Wang'chen looked at her, then rolled his eyes and took out his comms. "I don't know why I do whatever beautiful woman tells me to do."

He read his citizen score. His eyes widened; he held the comms closer to his face, as if he did not read it properly the first time. "How did you—"

Sitara grinned. "I could— put it back where it was, if you prefer."

Wang'chen put his comms away. "No, no— but how did— that be not possible!"

"Before a system is truly foolproof," said Sitara, "you have to test it on every fool in the world."

"If anyone finds out you did this for me—"

"Yes, I know, we'll *all* be in trouble," said Sitara. "But we're all living dangerously these days."

Wang'chen said, "And all you want in return?"

"—Is for you to let us study the probe for a little while," she answered, "And then, forget that you saw us here tonight."

Wang'chen sighed, then said, "Follow me."

Sitara flashed him her most beautiful smile. "Thank you, you're a gentleman."

The officer took them through the museum, to the gallery that housed the probe. "I will be back when my shift done. One hour. Also, I have to lock you inside while you are here."

They stepped into the gallery. Wang'chen shut the door behind them. The locking mechanism echoed from above. They searched the wall nearby for a light switch. Finding one, they were rewarded with an unimpeded view of the probe, still encased in its protective glass box. It was alone; only the wax dummy of Lorelei kept watch.

"I can't imagine what Lorelei felt, seeing this for the first time," said Sitara, as she moved close to the plaque, with its alien figure drawings and cyphered numbers.

"I'm still having a hard time believing it's real," said Jiandong. They admired it together for a while. Then Jiandong dropped his backpack, took out an electric drill, attached a bolt driver to it, and began unbolting the case. He had to use one of the nearby crates as a step, to reach the bolts on the top bars. Then the two interlopers together lifted one face of the glass shield away. The probe was now theirs to touch.

"There it is. I almost feel like— like we should be kneeling," said Sitara.

Jiandong touched the plaque, and said, "This drawing here— these *people*— they're really *not human!*"

"It's *everything* Lorelei said it was!"

Jiandong reached for his radmeter, but before he scanned the probe he whispered, "By the Iron Ring of the Engineer, I shall fulfill my calling to the best of my knowledge and power, toward the perfection of any works to which I set my hand."

"What are you whispering?" Sitara asked him.

"Part of the pledge that we engineers take, when we finish our training and they give us our iron rings," he explained, as he showed her a faceted wrought-iron ring on his right-hand little finger. "Because this machine is— it's really alien, isn't it? I'm terrified of accidentally breaking it."

"I trust you," Sitara reassured him, as she placed a hand on his shoulder. "Anyway, it crash-landed on Pluto— it's already broken."

Jiandong thanked her with a quick touch to her hand. Then they both activated their radmeters and scanned the probe.

"Weird— it's like a thing that *we* might have built, a hundred years ago," Sitara observed.

"Indeed," Jiandong agreed. "Chemical rockets. Gyroscopes for orientation. Radio transmitters and receivers."

Scanning with her own radmeter, Sitara said, "Hydrogen-Phosphorus Q-bit circuits. This thing had a quantum computer!"

"This part here looks like a nuclear thermo-electric battery," said Jiandong, pointing to one of the larger spheres in the structure. "Long since gone cold now. But there might be enough trace to give us a more precise measure of how old it is — but wait, what's this?"

His radmeter was showing him a structure in another sphere, hidden behind the nuclear battery. It resembled a ring made of electro-magnetic coils, along with what looked to Jiandong like a ring of compressors and injectors. Another structure sat beside it, apparently designed to capture whatever might emerge from the coil.

He quickly checked around the rest of the structure and found several other spheres with similar structures inside them. Although they were all damaged in different ways, he saw enough to visualize in his mind what a complete and undamaged prototype might look like.

"But it's so *simple*," Jiandong wondered aloud.

"What's simple?" said Sitara.

"I think Lorelei was right," Jiandong proudly told her. "This thing *did* travel faster than light."

Sitara paused before replying. She looked at the broken heap of the alien probe, her expression quizzical, her mind doubting, but her heart hoping.

"I don't know for *certain*— not yet," Jiandong explained. "But I think this sphere contains a gravity-wave generator."

"A what?"

"Look at this—" Jiandong showed her the readout on his radmeter screen, "—here's where the plasma— probably plasma — from this sphere connected by these hoses— is compressed into a super-dense package using these magnetic coils. Then the plasma is injected into a toroidal vortex ring—"

Sitara didn't fully understand him. "I thought *nothing* can travel faster than light."

"That's correct," Jiandong replied. "But there's no limit to how fast *space itself* can expand or contract. Imagine that you are walking in a spaceport terminal, from the ticket counter to your gate. And you're walking on a moving conveyer belt. You'd still be walking at the same speed relative to the belt, but anyone who is not on the belt with you would see you walking much faster. That's what a gravity-wave generator could do. I don't know for sure but it looks like these structural arms over here were meant to reach out in front of the probe, grab on to the gravity of a distant star, and bend the fabric of spacetime in between— or maybe it pushes the quantum foam out of the way — then these identical arms reach out behind, so maybe they increase the *negative* curvature— so the thing would move like it was surfing on a wave of compressed and expanded spacetime — oh, this is— this is— the most— Well, *if* that's what I'm looking at here— almost wish I could take it apart—"

Wang'chen eventually returned to the gallery to usher them out. "My shift is almost done," he said.

Jiandong nodded. "I think I've got everything from the probe that the radmeter can tell us. Thank you, sir."

The officer escorted them to a fire door, and shook their hands. "I might go for very long holiday. Some place where food is good. Tired of protein bars and grasshoppers," he said.

The two scientists thanked him again. As they walked back to their hotel, Jiandong asked, "So how did you do it Sitara? How did you crack the distributor?"

"I didn't," Sitara grinned. "I cracked his *comms*." Sitara

showed him a program that was running on her Q-link. "Now whenever he checks his citizen score, his devices will redirect to my private server, which will show him a fake page."

Jiandong laughed, involuntarily. "He'll eventually find out," he warned.

"But by then, he'll have to admit he didn't arrest us like he was supposed to. And we will be back in Éostray. It's the perfect crime!"

§ 52.

Faceoff dropped a military-issue food ration pack on Glaive's chest. "Breakfast for heroes," he said. "Picked them off a truck this morning."

The rest of the mercenaries were at the security station, hooting and cheering together as they watched someone's grid-published video footage of a Gayatrian tank crushing a Sons of Courage barricade.

"Yeah! That's right, you had your fun!", they jeered at the screen. "Sons of courage? More like sobs of cowardice! Look at those guys run!"

"I told them that would happen," Glaive remarked.

He tore into the ration pack and ate the bar of dried fruit and compressed granola he found inside. He looked up to the ceiling. A heavier, louder noise was growing in the air. He walked outside to see what it was, and found a machine flying overhead, big enough and flying low enough to momentarily eclipse the sun. Its four wide fan-jet engines, one at each corner of the vehicle, roared to deafen anyone who stood below it. The wind they created blew the debris of the previous night's excitement all over the street. Faceoff joined Glaive a moment later, and they watched it fly over the factory and land behind it.

"That's our ride," he said.

"Haven't seen one of those quad-jet airlifters since basic training," Glaive remarked.

"Will you keep the rear guard with me while our guys switch out?" Faceoff asked.

"Sure."

They took positions behind the remnants of the barricade, but they stood casually. They could hear the rapid pops and claps of rifle fire echoing down the road, as the Sons of Courage were kept busy by Gayatrian infantry. But the sounds were distant enough; the streets and alleys surrounding the front of the Legacy Aeternim building were deserted. Faceoff invited Glaive to share some greenrock, but Glaive declined.

"Might be your last," he offered again.

"It's not my poison of choice," Glaive replied politely.

Faceoff pinched some of the fine greenish dust between his fingers and snorted it. "Never let it be said I didn't make the offer."

Glaive wondered what the grizzled mercenary might have meant by that last cryptic comment, and why he was handling the drug with his left hand. He stepped around the barricade, making it look as if he wanted a better view of the street, but actually to get closer to cover, in case Faceoff's right hand was on the trigger of his weapon.

"You know, I checked my account this morning. Your money hasn't come through yet," said Faceoff. "And I'm wondering why not. Didn't you say your father was some kind of rich guy?"

"He's a complicated man," said Glaive. "You'll get paid when we get there."

"What was it like— growing up rich?" said Faceoff. "Eating the best food. Sleeping with the hottest girls. Always someone there to do what you tell them."

"It wasn't like that," Glaive said. "Not for me."

"I looked up your old man on the grid last night," Faceoff continued. "He was a big-league rallyfoot player. Ran twenty laps a game, never any less. Then went into politics. I'd say he's a man who's used to getting what he wants." He sniffed another pinch of greenrock and said, "I was thinking: a man like him, he finds out his kid's in trouble, he'd be willing to do just about anything to get his kid out of it. But you told me he doesn't know you're here."

Glaive was convinced he knew Faceoff's intentions. "That's right," he said, while at the same moment switching off the safety catch on his weapon.

Faceoff emptied his greenrock supply. Then he raised his rifle. But Glaive had his rifle up and ready to fire first.

"Trying to hold me hostage, Faceoff? Don't be stupid," Glaive told him.

"Me and the boys figured you're worth a lot more than twenty grand."

Glaive slowly moved closer, keeping his weapon aimed between his enemy's eyes.

"Don't bother," said Faceoff. "When you were sleeping, I emptied out your mag."

Glaive smirked for a moment, then pointed his rifle at Faceoff's shoulder, and pulled the trigger. His rifle spat out a little green comet of superheated plasma, which burned through Faceoff's jacket and forced him to drop his rifle.

"Fuck!" Faceoff screamed.

"I'm career military, you idiot! Did you really think I wouldn't notice an empty mag?" said Glaive.

Faceoff scrambled for his rifle. Glaive shot him again, this time in the knee. Faceoff fell to the ground.

"All you rich boys are the same!" Faceoff hollered back. "I grew up in the real world— I had to *work* to get anything I wanted."

"Yeah. Life's not fair."

Faceoff scuttled across the ground toward his fallen rifle. "You can kiss your ride home goodbye, rich boy!"

"Don't touch that weapon, Faceoff," Glaive warned him. "Don't pick it up!"

"Fuck you!"

"Don't do it," Glaive repeated.

Faceoff glared at Glaive, his face shifting between fear and rage. He reached for his rifle.

Glaive shot the man three times in the heart. He stepped closer, and examined his target. He searched the body. He took Faceoff's extra magazines, as well as his comms and a wallet full of Gayatrian rupees. He put on the dead man's sunglasses, helmet, and Dragon Hill jacket, and covered his nose and mouth with a bandana.

Peering around the corner of the building, he saw the squad of mercenaries standing near their airlifter. He walked toward the lifter's security, faking a slight limp as he moved.

"Hey, there's Faceoff! What took you, buddy? Where's the rich kid?" one of them shouted.

In reply, Glaive gestured behind him with his thumb. Then he tugged on the shoulder of the jacket, to draw attention to the plasma burn there.

The mercenary grinned. "He tried to fight you, eh? You took care of him?"

Glaive responded by shooting him.

There were two more mercenaries on board the airlifter. As soon as they saw their friend go down, one reached for his pistol and the other unlatched his seat belt. Both of them were too slow, and they fell to the floor as Glaive's plasma bolts burned small holes in their heads. He hit the button to raise the ramp and close the cargo bay.

A hatch in the front of the cabin opened and the pilot stepped through it. "Is somebody shooting at—" he said. But Glaive's aim quickly centred on him, and he was dead before he finished his sentence.

The last person on board was in the co-pilot's seat. She squealed and put up her hands to cover her face. "Don't shoot, don't shoot!" she repeated.

Glaive recognized the voice of Ivy Sterling, the saleswoman he spoke to when he first scouted the factory.

"You armed?" Glaive said.

"No," she admitted, her hands still covering her face.

He grabbed her under the arm and pulled her out of the seat.

"Wait, wait! I can help. You need me," she insisted.

"What makes you so special?"

"There's a no-fly zone over the city," she explained, as she lowered her hands. "They'll shoot you down if you don't have a clearance code."

"I take it you have one?"

"And I'll use it to get us both out of here. But don't shoot, please don't shoot."

Through a side window, Glaive could see the security team who went around to the front of the building had returned, and that they brought a squad of their friends. Their weapons were raised and ready. Glaive released Ivy back into the copilot seat, and took the pilot seat for himself. He pushed the throttle up, and the airlifter was airborne. He knew that their weapons wouldn't damage the hull of the vehicle, but a lucky shot in the fan-jets might slow him down or make it harder to steer. Reaching over to the co-pilot's control panel, he pressed a button to activate the vehicle's combat AI.

"Combat AI Activated," said an electronic voice in his headcomms.

"Target all ground personnel within one hundred meters," he told the AI.

A hatch opened in the belly of the airlifter and a plasma gun popped out. It opened fire on the mercenaries. Some fell; others dashed for cover.

By then, however, the airlifter had sufficient altitude that

Glaive could accelerate and escape the city. He disengaged the combat AI, took off the sunglasses and bandana, and let himself breath normally.

A new voice crackled into his comms. "Dragon Hill flight 14, this is Gayatri air command. You have deviated from your posted flight plan. If you do not return to your flight plan you will be in violation of the no-fly zone."

Glaive opened the long-range radar on his heads-up display. It showed him that a Gayatrian interceptor was approaching.

"Gayatri air command, Dragon Hill flight 14," Ivy replied. "Requesting permission to file a new flight plan." Then she covered her comms and said, "Where do we want to go?"

"Anywhere," Glaive said.

Ivy told the air traffic controller, "We need a path to Vogelsberg, Éostray." To Glaive she explained, "It's the nearest company office outside of Gayatri."

"Transmit your clearance code," the air traffic controller requested.

Ivy entered the code through a keypad in front of her. Glaive watched the blip on his radar display get closer as he waited for the air force to answer. He kept the airlifter flying at a level altitude and a speed slower than the interceptor, to show his good faith. When the interceptor came within weapons range, he gripped the controls a little tighter, preparing for an evasive move, or a hasty eject.

"Dragon Hill flight 14, Gayatri air command. Turn about to bearing three-zero-zero and rise to standard cruising altitude and speed. We will follow you to the border. Air command out."

"Acknowledged," Ivy replied. Glaive programmed the instructions into the autopilot, and then let go of the controls. He rubbed his face in his hands.

"Thank you for not killing me," she said.

"I have no interest in killing anybody," he replied. He lay down on a bench in the main cabin. "Just wake me up before we get there."

§ 53.

Hanfei combed his hair at a seat near the buffet, where Lorelei would be unable to avoid him.

"Doctor Verlassen, it's a pleasure to see you. I trust you slept well," he said as he stood.

"What are you doing here?"

"I thought you might like some company for breakfast," he said. "We still have business to discuss."

"No, we don't," said Lorelei. She turned to leave the cafeteria, but she saw the way was blocked by a dozen or more waiters pushing wheel-carts loaded with a wide variety of breakfast foods.

"I don't know what your preferences are," Hanfei said. "So I ordered everything. Traditional Chang'renni delicacies. congee, steamed buns, green tea."

Lorelei saw he had been very generous, and some of the hotel staff snatched small items for themselves when they could. But she quickly surmised the reason for his generosity. "I told you yesterday, I will not read your apology," she said.

"If none of this is to your liking," said Hanfei, "there are many fine restaurants in this city which I would be honoured to take you." To his android butler he said, "Please bring up my car."

"I'm completely serious, Hanfei," Lorelei insisted.

Hanfei clenched his jaw for a moment, but controlled himself and smiled again. "I acknowledge we began this dance by stepping on each other's toes. But as you can see—" he gestured to the breakfast carts as he spoke, "—I can change my shoes. And if you can change yours then we may both enjoy a mutually beneficial turn round the floor. And when we part ways, we can part as friends."

Lorelei looked upon the breakfast carts again; her mouth involuntarily watered with the smell of the fresh fruits and the cooked meats. Hanfei believed that she was tempted; he took a plate and offered it to her in both of his hands, with a slight bow. Lorelei pursed her lips and shook her head; she took the plate and set it aside.

"Why did you do it?" she asked.

"To show you I am not so harsh as you think I am," he replied.

"No— I mean— why did you sabotage the starship? Funnelling money out of the budget? Wouldn't it have been simpler to vote against us when you had the chance? Chang'ren has a veto on the expeditions council— why didn't you use it?"

"These things are complicated," he said. "Certain appearances need to be maintained." He poured a cup of tea for both of them as he spoke. "We have studied you closely for these last few months. We know you take pride in being a rational person. Surely you see the rationality of our position? The speed of light cannot be broken. And for sub-light travel, interstellar distances are far too great. In sixteen years your starship will be less than half-way to the planet. The logical conclusion is that your starship will not save our world."

Lorelei did not accept the teacup. "And you want me to say as much, with the whole world watching."

"You can write your own apology, if you still don't like the one I gave you," Hanfei offered. "But if you continue dancing to your own song, I shall have no choice but to bring the music to an end."

"Why do people say they have no choice, when obviously they *do?*"

Hanfei did not answer; but Lorelei saw his fingers tremble as he raised his teacup to his mouth to drink.

"You won't destroy the probe," she told him. As the words left her mouth, her confidence returned. She picked a strawberry from one of the breakfast carts and ate it. "You can't get close enough to it, without thousands of people watching. If you tried to *scratch* it, every civilized nation in the world would demand your head. You'll be remembered forever as the man who destroyed the most important scientific—"

"—Discovery of all time: yes I know that's what you believe," Hanfei interrupted. "But I am not the only one who sees the probe differently. It's an illusion. Nothing but an illusion. It is the physical symbol of how desperate we are to believe anything, rather than the truth."

"What truth?" Lorelei growled.

"That there is no one out there," Hanfei explained. "That no one is coming to save us. And by your own calculation it is almost too late for us to save ourselves. If I destroy the probe, yes, half the world will hate me for it. But in time, the world shall see that I carried us back to reality."

"You plan to destroy the probe whether I apologize or not," Lorelei realized.

"I plan to keep my word," Hanfei countered.

Lorelei was no longer listening. She dropped her teacup on a cart and left the cafeteria. An android chauffeur standing by a long black car invited her to step inside. But she ran past it, in case it was Hanfei's car; instead she flagged down a passing autotaxi.

"Take me to the museum, quickly!" she told the autopilot.

She arrived at the gallery that housed the probe to find a team of workers dismantling the displays.

The probe itself was gone.

"Where is it?" she asked the nearest worker; he only shrugged, and showed by his gestures that he didn't speak her language.

She dashed to the loading docks; the security guards made no moves to obstruct her. She found the probe in the midst of a team of workers; they had dismantled the glass cage, and were now attaching explosive charges.

"What are you doing!" she shouted.

Wang'chen was one of the officers providing security. "We have change of schedule. It's no problem."

Hanfei arrived in his car, at the far end of the loading area. When he saw Lorelei, he stepped out, and leaned on the hood to watch.

"It's not too late for you to apologise," he said.

"And it's not too late for you to do the right thing," Lorelei told Hanfei.

One of the workers approached Hanfei, and reported something in the Chang'ren language. Lorelei gathered from Wang'chen's expression that he was none too happy with what Hanfei intended to do. The two men exchanged angry words; Wang'chen's hands moved to the clip on his belt which held his handcuffs.

"Hold," said Hanfei to his aid. "Ten seconds, Lorelei, or else I order my man to destroy it. Ten seconds!"

Lorelei ran to the probe and climbed on to it, and held its bars tightly, acting as a human shield. "Don't do it!" she cried.

"I'm prepared for the consequences!" Hanfei yelled, as his patience ran out at last.

"Are you?" Lorelei asked him. "Are you *really?* The whole world will know what happened here today. The whole world will know what kind of man you really are. Think what you're doing!"

Hanfei's gaze moved between Lorelei's stern gaze, and Officer Wang'chen's hands, ready with the handcuffs. Some of the loading dock workers were watching too.

Hanfei said to his workers, "Remove her."

When the workers hesitated, for they too were watching the Officer Wang'chen, Hanfei grabbed the nearest of them by the shoulder and pushed him toward the probe. "Do it!" he ordered.

Three workers forcibly pulled Lorelei off the probe. She struggled as much as she could: biting their arms, and stomping on their feet with her heels. Tears flowed freely from her eyes. But the three workers were much stronger. They dragged her to Hanfei's side. One of Hanfei's aids, meanwhile, produced a comms, entered an ID into its screen, then handed it it to Hanfei, who pressed the last button.

The probe exploded. All the hope and the confidence Lorelei had in the future transformed into screams of rage. "*Du Arschloch! Du Fickfehller!*" she howled.

Hanfei wore a proud smile. "Let her go now," he ordered, and then he got into his car. His entourage left with him.

Lorelei ran to the crater where the probe had been put down. Almost nothing remained that was not bent, broken, or blackened. Sitara, Lorelei recalled, had seen a man tortured; Jiandong had seen a man die. But Lorelei found herself staring at a blackened hole in the gravel where a moment before had stood the cornerstone of her life, her world tree, her ladder to heaven. She picked up a piece of shrapnel and flung it toward Hanfei's departing car. It cut her as it left her hand: not enough to hurt much but enough to draw blood. She shouted more insults at him, then sat on the ground in the centre of the blast crater, where her rage could turn into grief.

The sound of approaching sirens grew louder. Lorelei left the scene, half in a daze, and covering her ears as three fire trucks roared past her. As she crossed the service lane, a metallic glint in a privet hedge caught her eye. It was the alien plaque, embedded in the leaves, scratched but miraculously still intact. She checked to see how many cameras were watching her, and found that the nearest one had been damaged by the explosion, and that others were now behind the fire trucks. When the firemen were busy tending to those wounded in the explosion, Lorelei chose her moment. She took off her jacket and wrapped it around the plaque, hugged it, and carried it away.

As soon as she reached the street, she called for an autocar. Once inside, she reached for Sitara and Jiandong on her comms.

"Lorelei!" said Sitara, "Hey, did you hear there was an explosion at the museum? They're saying it's the probe."

Lorelei paused, considering who might be eavesdropping on her messages. "I can't talk about that right now," she said. "Listen, I need an empty diplomatic parcel sent to my hotel room. Can one of you arrange that?"

"Sure," said Jiandong. "How big?"

Lorelei hugged the probe tighter. "Just— big enough for about a dozen books. Big ones. College textbooks. You know the kind."

"You'll have it this evening," Jiandong promised. "By the way, you were *right* about the probe."

"Right about what?"

Jiandong sent to her Q-link a copy of the scans he made of the probe the previous night. "There's a structure on it which looks to me like a toroidal vortex ring. And here's plasma injectors, and a nuclear battery— which isn't a big enough power source, but everything *else* points to the possibility that this thing did travel faster than light."

"Faster than light," Lorelei whispered. She was too tired to celebrate the confirmation of her conjecture. But she was curious. "How did you get these scans?"

Jiandong was about to answer but Sitara spoke first. "Oh, you know. Sources."

Lorelei looked at the data from Jiandong's radmeter for a while. Some of her confidence returned. She said, "If it's all we have, it will have to be enough. Let's pack up. Time to go home."

"So soon?" said Sitara.

Grinning, Lorelei said, "We have a starship to build!"

Sixth Transmission: Éostray

Government type: Constitutional Monarchy.

Higher education: 6.2 out of 10 citizens is a university graduate (highest rate in the world); 29 of the 50 highest-ranked postsecondary institutions worldwide located here.

Religious attendance: 38% attend Communion assemblies; 13% attend minority group services; 49% declared agnostic or atheist.

Largest City: Vogelsberg, population: 173,800.

§ 54.

Exhausted, Lorelei pushed open the door of her apartment. She stepped inside, closed the door with a gentle kick, dropped her bags beside her boots, then dropped herself on to the nearest chair. Having lived much of her life in dormitories and university residence halls, she loved this apartment, and she protected the privacy it gave her. It was not simply the place where she could wear pyjamas all day, or eat nothing but cheese sandwiches for a week, all without facing anyone's judgment. It was the place where she could banish the noise of the world, and so possess her own thoughts, her own mind. With nothing but sunlight, fresh air, and bird song entering from outside, she gave herself the gift of a moment to be still, unbusy, and free.

She opened the diplomatic parcel that carried the probe's dedication plaque. She took the treasure to her writing desk, pushed her notebooks and pencils out of the way, and looked at it again under her reading lamp. New dents in its face obscured some of the inscriptions. But most of it remained legible, and the diagrams were still clear. It occurred to her that she might be the first sentient being to touch it since the plate was fitted on the probe, perhaps only hours before it was launched into space. She examined the diagram of the alien family. Their outlines were humanoid, and she smiled at the familiarity. Yet the three-fingered hands and the wider eyes made it impossible to ignore that the people pictured there were not human. A sense of accomplishment and pride surfaced in her thoughts: to have discovered this fragment of world-shaking history, yet also to be holding it secret, safe from those who wanted it destroyed.

"We found you," she said, remembering her first words when she first saw it. Then she added, "You're safe here, with me."

As she turned it over in her hands, the light from her reading lamp glinted on something inside it, as revealed by cracks and holes along its edge. It was perhaps no bigger than a pair of dinner plates, yet its weight made it feel as though it was made of solid lead. She peered closer, and realized that the plate was held inside a frame, and that the frame might be hollow inside.

Before she could investigate further, someone knocked on her door. Lorelei paused to hide the plaque behind a bookcase.

The man at her door had military haircut, though he had clearly not shaved in many days. He wore a navy blue pilot's coat over a duty shirt, both of which had small holes where the identification patches used to be. The stains on his pants was deep purple and black, the colour of the kind of mess a dangerous or desperate man might create.

"Lieutenant?"

Glaive cleared his throat. "Doctor Verlassen. I've— been banished from Arethusa." he said.

"Banished?" she said as she stepped back.

"I'm what they call 'fair game' now. If I ever go home, anyone can kill me and it won't count as murder. Can I come in?"

Lorelei softened her posture. She motioned for him to enter.

Glaive told her the story of his experience in the occupation of Lalkeela. On her Q-link he showed her the video of his encounter at the barricade with the Sons of Courage, describing his escape from the city.

"So that brings me to the favour I have to ask for," he concluded. "I need you to help me start a new life."

"I might not be able to give you that."

"You could give me a job working on your starship. Security. Analysis. Doesn't matter what it is. Doesn't even have to pay well. Just— something I can use to start over. A new life. A new home. A new name maybe—"

"You want me to forge identity papers for you?" Lorelei gasped. "I can't do that. For one thing, I don't know *how*—"

"Look— the way I see it," said Glaive, "I spared your life on Pluto. And you agreed that I owed you a favour for it. So I'm calling it in."

Lorelei shook her head as she thought about his demand. "If

you have nowhere to go then I suppose you can stay here for a while. I made the second bedroom in this apartment into a library; there's a couch in there you can sleep on. But as for a job, or forged papers— that's a *lot* to ask."

Glaive looked at her for a while without speaking, hoping that the seriousness of his gaze would impress his point of view upon her.

"So I'm asking a lot." He noticed the bruises on her arms and legs, and the bandage wrapping her hand. "What happened to you?"

"It doesn't matter," she replied.

"It does. Were you in a fight? I'm a soldier. If you need protection—"

"And what will I owe you for that?"

"Well, I need a job, and it looks like you need a bodyguard. There's two problems solved, right there."

"I don't need a bodyguard," she told him. "If anything right now, I need a time machine, so I can start this week all over again."

"But seriously, what happened? Did someone try to—"

"No," Lorelei insisted, and Glaive decided not to press the point.

"Have you eaten?" she asked.

"Not today."

"Go have a shower," she said, and she pointed down a hallway. "I'll ask the neighbours downstairs if they have any clean clothes that will fit you. If you're done before I'm back, you can have this." She handed him a bathrobe that was hanging on the back of a chair.

Glaive raised his eyebrows at it, but he accepted it.

A short while later, Glaive was freshly showered, and wearing a T-shirt and trousers borrowed from the neighbour. They sat across a coffee table from each other, eating a modest dinner of chicken strips on pasta with a white sauce.

"You cooked this?" Glaive marvelled, as he ate.

"Some of the ingredients came from the protein synthesizer," Lorelei explained. "But I did cook it and spice it myself, *ja*."

"Back home in Arethusa, we mostly eat energy bars on the go."

They ate in silence for a while: Glaive shovelled the food into his mouth as if someone was intent on stealing it from him.

"What's the rush?" Lorelei asked him.

"Old habit, from the war," he said. He slowed down, and sniffed from the wine glass before sipping it. His nose wrinkled.

"What is this?" he asked. "It smells like wine, but I don't know. Something's strange about it."

Lorelei politely concealed her surprise. "It came from a vineyard close to the boarding school where I grew up. Not the best, but it's all I had in the house just now."

"Real wine?" Glaive marvelled. "This is actual, real wine? Back home, 'Real Wine' is a brand name."

"That's twice you've mentioned your home," Lorelei observed. "Do you want to go back? Restore your citizenship, your officer's commission?"

Glaive leaned back in his chair and looked to the ceiling. "I don't know," he admitted. "Even if they reversed my banishment, which almost never happens, my father wouldn't have me."

"I've met your father. Would you *want* him to take you back?"

"Well— he got me a place in the army, always made sure I met the right people so I'd get the best jobs—"

"But that's not what I asked."

Glaive acknowledged it with a glum nod. "I don't know. I've never had to find my own way before. I suppose I'm an orphan now, just like you."

Lorelei dropped her fork on her plate with a clank that he found uncomfortably loud.

"What?" he asked.

"When I was a child, all my toys were hand-me-downs," Lorelei explained. "I didn't have parties on my birthday. In sports class no one picked me to be on their team. I wrote stories that no one read; I invented games that no one played; I made art that no one hung on their wall. The only place I could be myself was in the forests and fields outside the town, where no one would show off like they were better than me at everything. And when I turned eighteen, the headmaster handed me five hundred marks and said, 'Now you're on your own.'"

Glaive looked down. "I had no idea," he said.

"Of course you didn't; why would you," Lorelei replied. She collected her dinner bowl and walked to the kitchen.

Glaive stood up. "Here, let me do your dishes for you—" he offered.

"I don't need your help," she told him.

"What did you do after the headmaster kicked you out?" he asked.

In the place of an answer, Lorelei pointed down the hallway and said, "The first room down the hall is a library. There's a couch in there you can sleep on. Spare blanket and pillow in the closet."

"I am not your enemy, Lorelei. Why don't you trust me?"

"I don't know if I trust *anyone* anymore."

"What happened?"

"Didn't you hear?" Lorelei shouted. "They blew up the probe!"

"No, I didn't hear," Glaive replied. "I've been— off the grid for a while."

"I was there. They made me watch. Held me down so I couldn't stop them. All that's left now is—"

"What?"

Lorelei stopped herself. Her eyes reflexively darted to the bookcase where the time capsule was hidden. Then she felt her heartbeat quicken. She looked at Glaive, her head quivering *No*.

"You have a piece of it here?" he asked, and he looked where she was trying not to look.

Lorelei moved to stand in his way.

"Lorelei, I don't want to take it, or even touch it. I only want to *see* it. And I promise you, no one will find out about it from me."

Lorelei assumed he'd find it eventually. She took the plaque out and placed it on her writing table.

Glaive regarded it with his his hands held to his mouth, palms together, as if praying. The big eyes on the humanoid figures still made him want to panic and push it away. His fingers trembled. Adrenaline flushed through his heart. But he called upon his discipline, and forced himself to see it. Lorelei's evident comfort with it also helped him. He reached to it, but stopped himself when he remembered that he promised not to touch it.

"You're going to have to find a better hiding place for it," he said.

"It's safe as long as no one knows about it. And I mean *no one*." Her voice raised a little higher than her usual calm volume, Glaive couldn't tell if that was from anger or from fear.

"Does it do anything? Does it work?" he asked. "What have you figured out so far?"

Flight of the Siren

"Not very much," she admitted. She leaned closer to it, as she thought about it. Glaive leaned closer, too. Their faces were almost close enough to touch. They looked at each other. He made a small smile.

Lorelei leaned back. "I wouldn't make a good girlfriend," she said.

"I wasn't going to presume," said Glaive, as he leaned back as well, following her lead.

"I don't like dancing," she continued. "I don't watch much video, I don't return messages and comms. I *like* living alone. Going out, being friendly, talking about the day-to-day things, is like work for me. Most of the time I'd rather stay home and read a book."

"It must be lonely."

"Loneliness is my laboratory," she said. "If you want to create or discover anything genuinely new and beautiful, then you have to see and hear and think of things differently than other people. You have to look where it appears that there's nothing, where no one else will look; you have to go where maybe no one will follow. And if you find something that way, then the chances are people around you won't understand you anymore. You won't belong to the same world they do, anymore. But you have to *accept* that."

"That kind of thinking is going to kill you some day," Glaive warned. "Or drive you mad."

"Enlightenment, madness, death; three petals of the same flower," she said. "The search for knowledge always takes you to *one* of them eventually. Maybe that's why people stop searching."

He studied Lorelei's face, to decide if he believed what she said, or if she believed it herself.

"Please don't take this the wrong way, but— is that the the real reason you're building a starship?" Glaive asked her. "You feel disconnected from people down here, and you think the aliens up there will understand you better?"

"What? No, that's not it at all," Lorelei said, though she turned her face away.

"They might *not*, you know," said Glaive. "In fact we don't know whether they're still out there at all. No signals, remember?"

"There's an elevated infrared," Lorelei reminded him.

He shook his head. "I'm no scientist," he said, "but the aliens in this picture look rather a lot like us. What if they're so much like us that they fight *wars* the same way we do?"

Lorelei glared at him. "It would take too long for me to explain the stupidity of that answer," she muttered.

"They evolved," Glaive said. "That means competition for resources. If they're animals, like us, or even more like us, that competition is going to accelerate, amplify, at *some* point. That's how you get war. And war, combined with the kind of technology to get this thing all the way here? I've seen half that, and that's enough."

Grimly, he took a last sip of wine.

"I don't know what you expect to find out there in space," he continued. "But I expect to find planets covered in dead cities. If they compete for resources like we do, if they have rich and poor, and different nations and different religions, then it's basically inevitable. I expect wastelands, deserts, nuclear winters. And the survivors of the last war fighting yet another one in the ruins, not with guns and bombs, but with sticks and stones."

Lorelei stuffed the time capsule into a canvas shopping bag. "They found a way *out* of their wars," Lorelei insisted, "and so can we." Then she took the time capsule and moved to leave the room. "Tomorrow you'll have to find somewhere else to stay."

Glaive folded his arms. "You owe me. Remember? And now —" he nodded toward the time capsule, "—I know one of your secrets."

Lorelei felt the blood rush out of her limbs. "You wouldn't dare," she said. "You promised me!"

Glaive glare and folded arms reminded her that he had nothing left to lose. It was an effort for Lorelei to remain calm.

"If I do this for you," she said, "you'll keep this secret and you'll be out of my life?"

"Out of it forever," he promised. "Which will make both of us happier, I'm sure."

Lorelei stared at Glaive for a long time, then disappeared into her bedroom, taking the time capsule with her, and slamming the door on her way.

§ 55.

Gretel sat on Lorelei's desk, watching a newscast on the video wall.

"Welcome back, Lorelei," she said, as Lorelei entered.

"Why do you have a key to my office?" Lorelei asked, as she moved to turn off the feed.

"You were away in Yuzhow; someone had to mind the shop," said Gretel.

"I was gone for only three days."

"A lot happened in that time," Gretel said. "The police arrested your old boss, Din Mbembe, and charged him with embezzlement, and fraud, and— well the Council decided they just didn't like him anymore. So. Aren't you going to ask who the new admiral is?" she asked, as she tossed her brown curls over her shoulder.

"They picked you?" Lorelei guessed.

Gretel shrugged with false modesty. "Oh, I wasn't their first choice. But I know how to manage people, and get the best results out of them. An essential skill, for a big organization like ours. And for my first act as your new superior, I'd like to ask you to redecorate this office. Honestly, darling, I've warned you about your furniture before."

"No one talks about my furniture except for you," Lorelei observed, carefully.

"They're being polite, child."

Lorelei grimaced. "Do you have any *business* related priorities for me?" she asked.

"Oh. Yes. Aside from dumping your old boss, we had to dismiss another fifteen people. Over the same old nonsense as before: conflicts of loyalty. I've hired some new people—"

"If you used that *machine* on them—"

"No, I didn't have to. It was enough to just show them the machine."

Lorelei furrowed her brow. "It's *my* job to manage the staff on this project."

Gretel abruptly turned about to face her. "Lorelei, don't you *trust* me?"

"That's not what I said—"

"And do you believe me when I say that I want you to succeed?"

"I do— but—"

"So please, let me help, once in a while," Gretel crooned with a smile. "It means a lot to me, to know that you trust me. We're going to be colleagues here; but can we be friends, too?"

Lorelei paused, and wondered what Gretel might mean by

friendship. Gretel opened her hands and raised her eyebrows, impatient for an answer.

"I prefer to have very few friends," Lorelei replied, and she hoped that Gretel would hear in that answer what she wanted to hear.

"I adore you, Lorelei," said Gretel, clasping her hands in a prayerful gesture. "In fact I think you have a destiny. I'm so blessed to be part of it."

Lorelei smiled, and said, "I don't know if I have a destiny, but I do have *work*."

Gretel laughed. "Of course! I'll let you get back to it. But don't work too hard today— you've just come back from what must have been a very stressful time in Chang'ren. I heard about what happened to the probe— did you know the Arethusans actually *congratulated* Chang'ren for it?"

"No— I've been in transit all day—"

"Turn on the news, you'll see," Gretel told her. She activated the video wall, and surfed through several news channels until she came to one which was showing Sturgeon Glaive at a press conference.

"—destroyed the probe yesterday," Sturgeon was saying, "because its presence on our home world was a clear and present danger to all humanity. Scientists studying the probe found that even after a thousand years it was still transmitting data—"

"What scientists?" Lorelei exclaimed, as if Sturgeon could hear her. "No one studied the probe! And it was *you* who wouldn't let us!"

"—don't know exactly what was the *content* of its message," Sturgeon continued, "So, sure, it might have been sending pictures of us back to its creators. It might have been tapping into our comm nets. Or sending updates about its battery life. We just don't know. But the fact that it was transmitting *at all* was the problem. It means the aliens know where we are."

"The probe wasn't transmitting anything," Lorelei argued back.

"Chang'ren acted on behalf of all humanity; and today, we in Arethusa are pleased to show our gratitude and solidarity by withdrawing our membership in the Conference of Nations."

"Well— that's— unexpected," said Gretel.

Lorelei could only gasp.

Sturgeon let the applause die down, then said: "We have repeated for months that the starship will only antagonize and provoke whoever is out there. But the world hasn't listened to us. So, we have decided that we're not going to pay for it anymore. And we will be glad to rejoin the CNH at such time as it abandons that expensive and misguided— you know, the *design* of the ship is just ugly, too! Unbelievably ugly. So until the CNH comes to its senses, Arethusa will no longer participate in any CNH ventures. No more joint peacekeeping missions, no humanitarian aid or scientific exchanges, no more paying our membership fees. And none of our engineers working on your starship."

Lorelei shut the screen off. "He's just as bad as Hanfei. The probe was transmitting nothing, and he knows that, *die fickfehler* —"

"Easy there, my darling— where did that language come from?" said Gretel.

Lorelei shrugged her shoulders, and sighed.

Gretel nodded. "Don't worry about losing Hanfei, or Sturgeon," she consoled. "Men like them still live in the past. And there are other communities we can approach for help."

Lorelei thought she knew what Gretel was about to suggest. "If I take money from the Communion," she said, "everyone will think the Communion is trying to impose its values on the project. Can you imagine the crowds of protesters that would bring?"

"Your starship *already* fulfills the Communion's values," said Gretel, excited and self-assured. "It's the greatest advance of the human spirit since the first upgraders took the first steps on cybernetic legs. A point that many in the Communion seem not to understand." Gretel examined the dark lines between her fingers: the joints in her cybernetic skin. Then she snapped her attention back to Lorelei. "But never mind me. The point is, many others in the hierarchy read your paper on the *Kulturdammerung*, and they agree with you. They believe interstellar exploration could help push the threshold back to a safe distance in the future. They want to help. I want to help."

Lorelei was sure there were conditions attached to Gretel's offer. "The kind of help you gave me *last* time, with that neurographic feedback scanner—"

Gretel's smile vanished. "It helped! We both know it. And now you need my help again, and you don't have many other options."

Lorelei knew that Gretel was right, but did not want to show it.

Gretel rose and made for the door. "Call me when you're ready to swallow your pride," she said, and left the office.

Lorelei waited until she thought Gretel was far enough away. Then she crossed the campus to find Jiandong in his workshop.

"How close are we to being finished the new engine?" she asked him.

Jiandong removed his safety goggles and powered down his laser torch. "Nowhere near," he said. "We've managed to create artificial gravity waves here in the lab, but they were only seventeen microns wide—"

"How soon can you make them big enough to move a starship?"

Jiandong whistled with incredulity. "Honestly: no idea."

"Well, you've got six months," Lorelei told him.

"Six months!"

"That's when we run out of money."

Jiandong slammed his hand on a nearby table. "If I had another chance to scan the probe again, then six months might have been enough. You know, when Sitara and I scanned it, we found something that might have been an information matrix. Like those golden records they put on the Voyager probes, but in digital holographic. Who knows what it might have told us! But now, it's gone forever."

While Jiandong continued ranting, Lorelei's mind wandered. "What part of the probe did you think was an information matrix?"

"The dedication plaque. Not that it matters: the cleanup crew never found it."

Lorelei looked away, in the direction of her apartment. "I have to go," she said.

§ 56.

Lorelei ran home. She closed all the windows against the media drones that sometimes followed her, taking pictures for celebrity-chasing websites. She took the alien dedication plaque from its hiding place and held it in her hands for a while, imagining the knowledge it might contain. She scanned it with her radmeter, and found it contained several layers of integrated circuits and holographic databanks: technology familiar to her in its overall design, but alien in the details.

Finding that the edge held a ring of rotating clasps, she turned them and found that the front face of the plaque was a lid, like a treasure chest. It contained a silver disk embedded in the casing, that reflected a dim rainbow-like flare which seemed to come from an inner depth, as if below the table that the plaque was sitting on. Lorelei carefully touched it, and felt nothing.

An optical illusion— maybe a holographic information matrix? she wondered. But where does its power come from?

She found another disk embedded inside the lid. This one was black and featureless, and made of a thin film which depressed when she touched it. She also noticed that the rainbow-like flare on the silver disk disappeared when her hand covered the black one.

Photovoltaic cells!

Lorelei moved her reading lamp to shine directly down on the black disk. The rainbow-flare emerging from the silver disk brightened, and then projected the diagram that was etched on the time capsule's front face. The map of the origin planet was in three dimensions now, as was the sphere of the planet at the top of the diagram, and the family of aliens at the bottom. The writings and equations on the two flanks of the diagram now scrolled with more information.

She touched the holographic diagram of the family. The other features of the hologram vanished, and the star map expanded, nearly filling the room. One star in the centre of the map was topped with an icon resembling the alien family. She touched it, and the other stars flew into a celestial sphere surrounding her, and the home star produced a solar system with twelve planets, each with numerous moons, as well as comets and dwarf planets and all the orbital lines around the sun.

The icon of the alien family now stood over the fourth planet. Lorelei assumed this was the probe-maker's home world. She touched it; the star system rushed away, and the planet zoomed large, revealing all its continents, oceans, rivers, clouds, and cities. Lorelei touched one of the cities. The image of the planet became a rapidly changing series of holographic images of daily life in that city: people sharing meals, running along sports tracks, playing musical instruments, pouring offerings to their gods.

"So much like us", Lorelei marvelled. "The same families, the same houses—"

In the final series of images, the aliens raised sails on boats, looked at the moon with a telescope, flew a hot-air balloon, turned a dish antennae to face a distant star, launched rockets, and at last launched hundreds of probes like the one Lorelei found on Pluto, to explore the galaxy.

"—the same questions— *The same questions!*"

§ 57.

"It's amazing how much everything *looks* familiar, but different," said Sitara. "The shape of the fruit in that market stall is different. The style of their clothes is different. But they walk like us, they eat and sleep like us."

"It stands to reason they would be mostly the same," Lorelei said. "Their planet must have the same physics and chemistry as ours. So, it must have the same forces of evolution, too."

"They have *two* eyes," Sitara observed. "Why wouldn't they have one, or three, or five? Why wouldn't evolution find different paths on different planets?"

Lorelei smiled; pleased to have the answer. "With only one eye, you wouldn't have depth perception. With three or more eyes, your brain would have to process more information, but you wouldn't see any better than you would with only two. So, two eyes is the most efficient solution."

"I don't know— I just thought they would be more different."

Lorelei had the answer for that, too. "They probably *think* very differently than we do. Look at these three symbols on the pictures that have people. They're the same on the picture of the planet itself," she said, pointing to the symbols in the hologram.

"They use the same name for their planet as they do for their species?" Sitara asked.

"And that would be the most wonderful thing," Lorelei grinned. "Maybe they think of themselves as *part* of their world. Part of its ecology. That's so different from how most of us see things: always separate from each other. Always different, always— alone."

Sitara smiled and said, "You got us, Lorelei."

Lorelei squeezed her friend's hand to thank her.

Jiandong said, "Does this contain any technical information?"

"That's the best part," said Lorelei. She touched the image of the probe, still hanging in the air above the time capsule, and it changed to a three-dimensional blueprint, including all of its interior mechanics, and lines of text in an alien language which presumably described each part's functions and capabilities.

"We can finish the starship now." Lorelei concluded.

"We still need to translate this," said Jiandong.

"But it *can* be done—" Lorelei grinned.

"Not in six months," said Jiandong. "And not by the three of us alone, either."

Lorelei looked at the hologram for a while. "Then it will be my job to find us more time and more people. And to keep it secret."

"Secret?" said Jiandong.

"Can you imagine what would happen if someone like Sturgeon Glaive got his hands on this thing?"

"Or Gretel von Richter," said Sitara.

"She's our new boss now."

"*Kutte ke tatte!*" Sitara swore. "I am so beyond tired of having to be polite to her. Why hasn't she been arrested for what she did to that man with that— that horrible machine?"

"Because the police are on her side," said Jiandong. "You know this."

Sitara swore again. She did know it.

"So I want to put together a team," said Lorelei, returning to topic. "A kind of secret group inside the CNH, to study these designs and make it look like we figured them out by ourselves. So let's say, some time later this week, come to my office and bring two or three people who have skills we need and who you can trust. Bring the members of our old NavCom crew. Don't tell them what it's about. And then, we'll see what happens."

Sitara said, "What happened to you, Lorelei? A few days ago, the thought of doing something immoral almost gave you a heart attack. Tonight, you call us to your flat to help you plan the biggest conspiracy in all of human history."

Lorelei said, "They drafted me into their honours race. So now, what else can I do, but try to get ahead?"

Jiandong and Sitara exchanged knowing, resigned looks. Jiandong, who had been quiet for most of the last short while, grew circumspect and grim. "There's no way to run the race without shedding your human skin," he said.

"But we're the good ones in the race," Lorelei shot back.

Jiandong grimaced at her. "You're a philosopher, Lorelei. Remember what Amergin said? Evil men are certain of their goodness, and good men are worried about their evil."

"Lorelei and I," said Sitara, "are not *men.*"

"You *know* what I mean," he countered, as he rolled his eyes.

Lorelei touched the alien time capsule and said, "The terrible thing is, I *do* want the world to know about this. So if I am proposing a conspiracy, then it is a conspiracy of optimism—"

"—Hey, can we have hooded cloaks and secret passwords?" Sitara laughed.

"What I mean is—" Lorelei tried to explain, but Sitara was still laughing, and Jiandong was laughing too. She let herself relax, and joined them.

"I can see in my mind what it will look like when it's done," said Lorelei, as they settled down. "But who knows if we'll get that far, even if we have the best team. We're almost out of money."

§ 58.

New blueprints and spec sheets went out from Lorelei's office to the fabrication plants and suppliers which served the starship project. Their managers asked what the new designs were for, and Lorelei told them it was for an orbital arcology.

Within a month, Jiandong's lab built a larger model of their experimental gravity-wave generator, with help from the data they gathered from the plaque. Using smoke and lasers, they demonstrated that space itself would bend around it when it was turned on. Jiandong tossed his hardhat toward it, and watched it fall in a normal way until it got close to the device. Then it shot to the side, punching a hole in the laboratory wall.

Alankar Sen, reviewing the project's budget one day, saw the word *arcology* appear in a report. He smiled.

§ 59.

"Doesn't anyone in this organization knock before coming in here?" Lorelei asked, annoyed.

Alankar took a glass from the liquor cabinet in Lorelei's office and poured a westiller, and made himself comfortable in the chair behind her desk.

"And that's my chair," she reminded him.

"Indulge me for a moment; I'm here to help," he said. "Your project is out of money. My bank is prepared to make up the shortfall."

"Just like that?" said Lorelei, disbelieving.

"Just like that," Alankar confirmed.

Lorelei did some quick math in her head. "That's— almost a quarter of a billion marks."

Alankar nodded. "The money is just sitting in our databanks, gathering interest and dust. I'd rather see it go into the world and put people to work," said Alankar. "In fact we don't even want it back."

"You're not going to give me all that money for *free*," Lorelei observed.

"True," Alankar said. "But I think you will agree what we want in return is very fair." He sent a document from his Q-link to hers, and sipped his westiller again.

Lorelei read the contract. "You want to buy the gravity-wave engine?"

"Not all of it. Only a sixty percent stake," Alankar said. "A public-private partnership."

"We're going to *give* the design to the world, for free."

"See, that's the problem with public-domain research and development," said Alankar. "It isn't truly free. We pay for it with our taxes. And those taxes are never enough to get the job done. Or to do it *right*."

"That's because too many big players hide their money in tax havens so they don't have to pay—"

Alankar continued as if he wasn't listening. "So, *when* the public R-and-D fails, like it almost always does, people like me have to pick up the slack."

Lorelei glared at him. "When did you know that the Arethusans would stop paying their dues?"

"I had my suspicions back when Sturgeon Glaive started talking about alien signals coming from the probe. He could ride that fear train all the way to the presidency."

Lorelei nodded. "*Ja*, he probably could. And with him in that chair next year, the starship definitely will not fly."

Alankar smirked, then shrugged a shoulder. He said, "Your starship will run out of money first. And my family owns a bank."

Lorelei dropped her Q-link on the desk. "The Expeditions Council would never agree to privatize the project," she said.

"I'm *on* the council," Alankar reminded her. "I have already proposed the motion."

"You can't do that; you would be in a conflict of interest."

"Yes," Alankar grinned, "I would be." He laughed, and sipped his westiller.

When Lorelei regained her composure, she said "You don't seem to need me at all."

"But a positive signal from you might help persuade the skeptics on the council. Oh, and I almost forgot—" he took another envelope from a pocket and pushed it across the desk toward her, "—Your invitation to the bank's next corporate synergy forum."

Lorelei opened the envelope. "This is a ticket for a luxury cruise ship tour."

"Do you think our top-level meetings take place downtown?" Alankar said. "Look at it this way. You'll go on a legitimate business trip. You'll meet the other key people in the team, in a place with no cameras watching, so that everyone can be themselves. And you'll still be in charge of the starship. The Conference will have a forty percent stake in your engine design. That's forty percent of the wealth of the entire galaxy— all the minerals and real estate and energy in all the comets, all the asteroids, all the planets, all the stars. You want to buy a mansion? A private island? A starship of your own? A hundred starships? With a forty-percent stake in the biggest gold rush of all time, you could buy a sovereign nation."

Lorelei found herself smiling, as she imagined the things she could do with that much wealth. Homes and families for orphans like herself. Entire planets terraformed to resemble the forests and fields where she grew up. Then she realized what Alankar was imagining. She frowned. "It won't be *my* ship anymore. It will be yours," Lorelei said.

"Yes, it will be mostly mine," Alankar said, as he leaned back in his chair, relaxed and unconcerned, a smile growing across his face. "But you have to ask yourself the Merchant's question: what's your price? What will you give to see your starship fly?"

Several answers to that question moved through Lorelei's mind: among them, something she once told Gretel that she would never give up, but which Gretel said she would not miss. She made a brave face for Alankar. But her starship seemed in greater danger now, and the price of protecting it seemed smaller, less painful. Alankar's grin grew smug and satisfied. Lorelei's spirit faltered, and her gaze wandered into the distance.

Alankar sensed victory. "Don't take too long thinking about

it. The whole world knows about your little money-flow problem. The next offer to cross your desk might not be as generous as mine."

Lorelei was about to answer him, but her comms chimed. The name that appeared on the screen made her eyes widen.

"That's the next offer, isn't it?" said Alankar, and he winked and left the room.

§ 60.

Elsewhere, it was Jiandong and Sitara's turn to receive a surprise guest. When they arrived at the CNH Expeditions campus after lunch, they noticed a small group of people sitting in a circle on the grass. In the middle of the group, speaking to them in relaxed tones, was a man wearing the cloak and chain of a Communion Godspeaker. On the grass beside the group lay a small sign saying: *We are reading The Chronicle. Any questions?*

Sitara asked the security guard, "Yeah, I have a question: isn't religious recruitment not allowed on campus?"

"They're all employees," the guard said. "And the man in the middle says he is the Godspeaker of Newgarten."

"He is," Jiandong confirmed. "We met him, once."

They made their way across the campus green. The Godspeaker saw them and waved; Jiandong politely waved back.

Gretel von Richter was waiting by the entrance to Jiandong's lab. "You wouldn't happen to have a few minutes?" she asked.

"We're too busy today," Sitara said, and she attempted to push through them to enter the building.

"Surely you're not too busy to meet with your new admiral," Gretel smiled. "And it's such a beautiful day to be outside." She gestured toward an empty table on a patio near one of the campus coffee bars, where researchers from the starship project shared sandwich platters and doodled equations on the napkins. Jiandong and Sitara knew the invitation was not a request. They followed her to the patio and sat with her. When the coffee arrived, the Godspeaker of Newgarten came and sat with them.

"My lord, Godspeaker Rafferty," Jiandong greeted him.

"You may have heard that the starship is very soon to run out of money," said the Godspeaker. "The Communion is prepared to make up the shortfall."

Jiandong paused, then put on his best diplomatic smile.

"Great," he said. "But why talk to *us* about it? Why not talk to the Council?"

The Godspeaker said, "We like to investigate a project before financing it. To make sure the money will go where it's supposed to go."

Jiandong nodded. "Well, what would you like to know?"

"To start," said the Godspeaker, "are you confident in the people who work for you?"

"Oh yes," Jiandong brightened. "We have great people from all over the world working here. Maybe you heard: we managed to synthesize our own gravity waves."

"And how about you?" the Godspeaker asked Sitara.

"Very confident," she reported. "But some of my best people were fired, not long ago. And no one has officially told me why."

Gretel said, "They weren't good people; they weren't who they said they were."

Sitara gave Gretel a stern look, but Jiandong accepted that he wasn't likely to get a better answer than that.

Rafferty smiled. "And, when was the last time you reached out to the One-And-All?"

Jiandong shifted in his seat, and perked an incredulous eyebrow.

Sitara said, "I've never been much for religion. So, a past life, maybe? Why do you ask?"

The Godspeaker said, "I want to know what kind of people are part of the directing mind of this organization. Their morals, their values."

"I'm an atheist," Sitara replied. "But I don't see why that matters. What matters is that I can do my job."

"What matters is that we have only fourteen years left to save the world," said Gretel, adopting a serious tone, her distinctive vocal fry disappearing. "We read Lorelei's paper. Her logic was perfect. But she neglected to ask: what world are we saving? And who shall save it?"

Nodding with grave agreement, the Godspeaker leaned forward, his fingers touching the medallion on his chain, and said, "So. Who do you follow, miss Kula?"

"What? Really?" Sitara sputtered. "People don't just ask Noble Questions in friendly conversation like that."

"This *is* a friendly chat. It could *stay* friendly, if you answer honestly," Gretel said, letting Sitara grasp the unspoken threat.

Sitara paused to calculate her answer, knowing she would be

judged for it. "I've nothing against anyone's religion. But as far as moral guidance goes, I follow my own intelligence, and my own heart. I know what I'm here on Earth to do." Looking Gretel in the eye, she added, "And I know what I must *never* do, no matter what I might gain by doing it."

Gretel smiled. "It's good to see that you have boundaries."

Both Sitara and Jiandong grasped the judgment in Gretel's words. Sitara sipped her coffee, but kept her gaze on Gretel, daring the new admiral to look away first and so admit guilt.

"How about you, Captain Xiao?" Godspeaker Rafferty asked. "Whom do you follow?"

Jiandong knew there was no dodging the question. "Kai'tzeen said that each of the seven Celestials gave humanity *gifts*, as well as questions," he said. "The Muse gave us imagination, The Teacher gave us reason— you know the litany. When I was a boy, I once asked the family priest: why do we need the Celestials to teach us these things? Why can't we find them on our own? Aren't we smart enough? Aren't we capable? And the answer I was told was: no. We can never be more than children without their guidance."

"Childhood is the most sacred and blessed time of life," said the Godspeaker. His tone suggested he was quoting from a text.

"But eventually, we have to grow up," Jiandong countered.

Godspeaker Rafferty remained calm. "So you lost your faith," he said.

"I left the *church*," Jiandong carefully reframed. "There's a difference."

Gretel said, "You may want to consider coming back again." To Sitara, she added, "Both of you."

Jiandong said, "Why?"

"It presents the right appearance," said Gretel. "It shows the world that our top people are committed to order, fairness, courage, reason, charity, industry, and imagination. The values of the Communion. You can't have basic civilization without them."

"And if the organization's top people embody those values," Godspeaker Rafferty added, "then the Communion can provide funding."

Sitara said, "Well. Nothing's *wrong* with any of those values, at first glance. But I have seven more values for you. Signal, data, bandwidth, structure, network, language, and encryption. You can always count on them to mean the same thing from one day to the next."

Gretel stood up, and collected her handbag. "I have no doubt," she drawled. "Thank you Captain, it was a pleasure." To Sitara, she gave a cold stare. "Miss Kula", she said.

The Godspeaker also stood up. "The Celestials guide you, the Nocturnals spare you," he blessed them.

Before they left the patio, Sitara said, "Admiral Richter, I have always wondered, why is The Magician not a Celestial? Why is he one of the Nocturnals? He has the most interesting *question* of all twelve of them."

Gretel kept walking. "Don't answer her. We're on a schedule," she told the Godspeaker, tugging his arm.

The Godspeaker said, "Some other day, my child. Some other day. Keep the watch."

Sitara enjoyed the baffled and impressed looks of nearby witnesses, and grinned like a child who got away with stolen candy. When Rafferty and Gretel were out of earshot, Jiandong said, "What were you thinking, asking her that! With the Godspeaker standing right there, too."

"She *is* hiding something; isn't it obvious?" Sitara replied. "And after what she did, it takes all my energy to stop myself from screaming at her."

Jiandong understood. "But she's the admiral now."

"It's not like she can fire me," Sitara said. "I'm the one who translated the alien code. She needs me!"

Jiandong made a sympathetic smile, and shook his head.

When she returned to her station in the control room, she found that the system refused her password. She tried again, and was refused again.

Two campus security guards arrived in the control room. They found Sitara, and took positions on either side of her.

"Ms. Kula?" said one of them.

"Yes?"

"Good news," he said with a smile. "The Gambler has blessed you, and the next chapter in the adventure in your life has begun." They sent a document to her Q-link.

Sitara read it. "This is a termination notice," she said.

"Think of this as an opportunity."

"Who does this come from?"

"The management."

"Lorelei wouldn't do this to me!"

"Not her," he shook his head. "It comes from the

management."

Sitara looked at the note again, and saw that it was signed by Gretel von Richter.

She gathered her possessions from her station, and left the campus for her apartment: three small rooms half-way up the height of a pyramid-like stack of repurposed shipping containers, fixed in a cage of iron girders. She cleaned herself up, changed into a night-life outfit, and called an auto-taxi to take her to a casino. The eye-stinging lamps of media drones, the sea of welcoming faces, the free cocktails, the electronic songs from the gaming machines, flowed together for her into a glittering wash of excitement and promise. She took a seat by the five-card finangle table, cracked her knuckles, and played her first cards for the night.

By the end of the night, she stood between two security guards and under the unblinking eyes of several media drones, while the casino's footmen wheeled three dollies of system towers out of her apartment and into an armoured vehicle. She covered her mouth to conceal her weeping. A guard offered her a tissue, but she brushed it away.

"This," said one of the footmen, as he sent a document to her Q-link, "certifies that with the appropriation of all this hardware, your debt to the casino is paid in full. And this," he sent another document, "is your debarment order."

"You're barring me?" she sobbed.

"I'm sorry, but this is what happens when you bet more than you can pay, and lose."

Sitara stepped away, and sat on a nearby bench. "This is absolutely the worst day of my life," she lamented aloud to no one, on the edge of sobbing.

The footman moved to her side. "I'm sorry, but before I go, there's one more thing—"

"One more?" Sitara sobbed.

The footman opened his comms to its camera function. "You were part of the NavCom Seven crew. Can I have a picture with you?"

"Are you serious?" she bawled at him. "No!"

The footman made a sympathetic face, but still held up his comms. "It's for my son."

Sitara took the device and threw it into a nearby hedge. She stomped into her apartment, and slammed the door.

§ 61.

"No. I am not endorsing a private-sector buyout of the starship," Lorelei began. "And no, I don't know why the media is saying that I am. Please refer to our actual press releases, and not to some chat space on the grid—"

There was a pause on the other end of the call. "Having a rough day, are you?" Din Mbembe.

"I'm sorry," Lorelei sighed. "I've just answered that call thirty times today. Surprised to hear from you. Are you okay? Is your family safe?"

"I'm good. In fact I'm better than ever. And I might be able to help you. Shall we meet? The Morrigan's Pub, in an hour?" Din suggested.

"What's this about?"

"You'll like it. See you soon."

She arrived in the beer garden behind The Morrigan's Pub. A canopy of trees and a score of fairy lanterns hanging from wires, forming a natural ceiling. Lorelei found Din seated at the bench furthest from the entrance, with a pitcher of beer in front of him, and his own glass already half consumed. A clean glass lay across the table from him, and Din filled it for Lorelei as soon as he saw her.

"So, you say you're here to help?" Lorelei asked him.

"I'm here to help," he confirmed with a grin. He handed her a business card and said, "My new employers believe in your vision of a scientifically enlightened exploration of space."

Lorelei looked at the card. "Legacy Aeternim Corporation," she read from it. "Aren't they a biomedical company?"

"Biomedical research is our biggest and best known division," said Mbembe, "but it's not nearly the most *interesting*."

"I take it you work for the interesting one?"

Mbembe grinned. "Starship design."

Lorelei perked an eyebrow. "Why would a biomed company want to build a starship?"

Mbembe sipped his beer. "We'll get to that, but first: why would someone with your talent prefer to work for the CNH? There can't be many opportunities for you to get much further ahead than you already are."

"I get to work on the most interesting problems, with the most advanced technology, and the smartest people. And sometimes I get to do it in outer space. It's a good life."

"But your organization is in trouble, isn't it?"

Lorelei nodded. "It's no secret."

"Let me offer you another way to win the honours race," Mbembe suggested. "Join the winning team."

"The race doesn't interest me. Just the mission. And anyway, what team's that?"

"The private sector."

Lorelei looked at the business card again. "What are you selling, exactly?"

"Not selling. Inviting. Recruiting. Come work for us."

Lorelei perked an eyebrow at him again.

"Our company," Din explained, "has been in the starship business since you published your paper about the Doomsday Argument—"

"The Threshold of Cultural Entropy," Lorelei corrected him.

Din ignored her interjection. "And the company is not beholden to an oversight committee prone to outbursts of absurdist political theatre."

"Well, that *would* be a perk," Lorelei admitted.

"Back when I was your boss, I thought I had it rather good, too," said Din. "Money. Power. Access to classified intel. But it was always precarious. I never knew if I'd lose my job because some councillor had a temper tantrum. And when the council fired me," Din paused, taking another sip, "the company offered me a way to keep myself and my family safe. And now, I've been tasked with offering the same to you."

"Why me?"

"You're clearly smart and capable. And the company likes your story. An orphan girl from a small town, who became the most famous scientist in the world."

Lorelei furrowed her brow. "You make it sound like a fairy tale."

"Any job you want," Din said. "You're an ecologist by training: how would you like to be in charge of our terraforming research? We'll have you re-designing the biosphere of entire planets, fitting them for any kind of life you can imagine. I know what the Conference pays you— we can pay you a lot more. And we can throw in some good benefits. Including a chance for a whole new life, on a brand new world."

Lorelei smirked at him. "That's your sales pitch?"

"Well, it works on almost everyone else," he grinned.

Lorelei gave his offer some thought. "I want to finish my starship before moving on to anything else."

"*Your* starship?" Mbembe asked, a small smile growing on one side of his face.

"The Conference starship," Lorelei corrected herself.

Mbembe nodded. "So. My offer. It's a no?"

"It's a 'not today'."

"Well. Take your time to decide, I don't mind. At Legacy Aeternim, time is a deliverable product."

"Another marketing slogan?"

"No— ha ha!— but, time *is* the company's primary concern. We're working on keeping the Summoner comfortably far away. Money and profit is merely a means to that end."

Lorelei nodded. Then she finished her beer, and stood up. "I had better get back to the office."

"One more thing," said Din. "We've been studying your starship, like everyone else of course, and we noticed two structures that were recently added to the nose and the stern. They strongly resemble structures that were part of the alien probe. Can you tell me anything about them?"

"Not really," said Lorelei. "There's probably some policy that says I can't talk about work when I'm not, you know, at work."

"We also noticed the official published designs for those structures appeared a few days *after* they were installed. That's not a turn in the race, is it?"

Now Lorelei suspected that Din knew more than he let on. "I wouldn't believe everything you read in chat rooms on the grid," she said.

"And on the subject of the probe," Din continued, "A report said that when they gathered up all that was left of it, a rather significant piece was *missing*. My employers would be very interested to find out whether you know anything about that."

Lorelei studied Din to see if she could read his mind in his expression and demeanour. That was how she found that the pin on his lapel, bearing the logo of the Legacy Aeternim corporation, was also a body camera.

Quickly, she smiled. "Is your family safe now?" she asked.

"They are. For the moment. Thank you," Din told her. "We moved them to a colony near Troth. A third of a G has its advantages, but exercise and supplements are necessary to compensate. There are always adjustments to be made. And the company has a facility there."

"I'm glad they're all right. And now, I had best get back to work."

Din stood, and offered his hand to shake. "You will consider our offer?"

Lorelei hesitated, then shook his hand. "It was nice to see you today," she said.

§ 62.

Glaive was in Lorelei's library reading one of her books, when he thought he heard a creaking floorboard in another room, as if someone else was in the apartment. He went to investigate, but found nothing unexpected, so he returned to his book. A moment later he heard the creaking floorboard again. This time he took a table lamp with him: the nearest object he spotted which could serve as a weapon.

Finding no one there again, he checked the space behind the living room bookcase, where Lorelei kept the alien time capsule hidden. It was missing.

Glaive's heartbeat quickened. He moved back to the hallway that led to the library, but this time he leaned on the wall and kept his eyes on the door.

A man, wearing a dark uniform, a backpack, and a helmet, was in Lorelei's living room, tiptoeing to the door. There were three glowing red dots where his face should be. He carried the sack in which Lorelei kept the alien plaque.

Glaive threw the lamp at the man's head. The helmet deflected the blow, but Glaive's intention was more to surprise than to injure; it gave him time to leap for the rucksack. He grabbed it, then spun around to throw his weight into the intruder and at the same time land an elbow in the man's neck. It forced the man to fall over, but the man got a grip on the back of Glaive's shirt as he fell, forcing Glaive to fall with him. The two men wrestled each other for possession of the prize, and Lorelei's furniture suffered the consequences. Framed pictures fell from walls; wooden chairs were used as clubs and lost their legs; a bookshelf was thrown down. Somehow, the intruder got around behind him and put his neck in a chokehold.

Glaive escaped by pushing the man backwards out a window, smashing its glass and tumbling the intruder to the earth below. But in exchange for that freedom, Glaive lost his grip on the bag containing the alien plaque. He looked down and saw that the intruder had hit the ground in a cedar hedge, and the rucksack hit the ground near him. Glaive rushed outside, hoping to catch the man before he untangled himself. He arrived at the hedge only in time to see the intruder dashing down the street. Glaive followed; and soon found he was the faster runner. But the intruder still had a long head start, and appeared to have excellent knowledge of the city's smaller alleys and narrow paths.

Glaive caught up with him near the foot of an ancient stairway that led up one of the city's many green hills. Lurching for the rucksack again, Glaive missed and had to roll to avoid falling into a row of bollards. He regained his feet and chased the thief up the stairs, reaching the entrance to an ancient monastery. Glaive was still the better sprinter, but the thief tipped over everything in his path to create obstacles for him, including garbage bins and devotional statues of The Muse. A monk got in his way, and the thief cracked him in the head with the sack, knocking him unconscious. As the thief sped through the cloister, he dropped an egg-shaped object on the ground behind him. Glaive was on top of it before he realized that it was an explosive. Dashing to the nearest shelter, which appeared to be the ledge beside another stairway, he jumped behind it and covered his head. The egg exploded, sending bits of soil and grass and rocks all around. When it seemed safe to emerge from behind the railing and resume the chase, he saw that the thief walking to the edge of the hill, looking above and below, and typing a message into his comms.

Glaive tackled him. The move gave him a chance to rip the rucksack out of the thief's grip, pull it over his own shoulders, and retreat. The thief flipped himself back on his feet and looked around. He saw Glaive jogging away. So he threw another exploding egg. Glaive saw it bounce on to the ground in front of him, and so he kicked it back. The thief dodged out of the way; and it exploded harmlessly in the air above the slope of the hill. The thief therefore tried another weapon: a dagger, which he unsheathed from a holster on his leg. Glaive pointed at it and shook his head, silently warning the thief not to raise the stakes of the fight that high. But the thief rushed at him anyway.

Glaive grasped the thief's weapon arm and swung himself around, using the thief's own momentum to throw him off balance and disarm him. The thief lost his dagger, but stayed on his feet. The dagger was now in Glaive's hand. With a shake of his head, Glaive warned him again not to attack.

The thief charged anyway. Glaive adopted a sturdy fighting stance. The two men crashed into each other. A heartbeat later, the thief fell, with his own dagger buried in his heart.

Glaive looked around, and saw a small group of monks from the monastery watching him from the arches of the cloister. One of the monks examined the damage to the stonework caused by the first explosive egg, then looked to Glaive for an explanation. Glaive didn't feel like explaining anything. He pretended to lurch at them. They scattered away.

Next, he checked inside the bag to see that the alien plaque was still there. When he saw that it was, he relaxed. He walked down the stairs to the city again, shaking his head.

The sound of police sirens approaching the hill made him pause. He checked his exits and, choosing the path with the most cover from airborne drones, he dashed away.

§ 63.

When Lorelei returned home after work that evening, she found Sitara and Jiandong sitting on the front step outside, waiting for her.

"Hey, Lorelei. Do we have Alien Translator Club tonight?" said Sitara. Despite her cheerful words, Lorelei saw by her long face that something was wrong. Next she saw the broken window above, and the crushed hedges and glass shards below it.

"The plaque!" she exclaimed, and she rushed inside. She found some of the pictures on the wall were in the wrong place, the chair by her writing desk was missing, and some of the books on their shelves had been rearranged or dropped on the floor. She checked the space behind the bookcase where she typically hid the alien plaque, and found it missing. "*Sheisse, sheisse sheisse!*" she swore.

Glaive lifted his coat off the seat beside him, revealing the missing artifact.

"Oh, *mein Gott,* it's safe!" Lorelei exclaimed, rushing to hold it.

"Someone tried to steal it," Glaive explained.

"You didn't call the police, did you? I heard sirens today—"

"No, no. You don't want them to know we have this."

"I'll take it to the office. Hide it somewhere there. In case the thief comes back."

"He won't come back," said Glaive darkly.

"How do you know?"

He paused. "It's still a good idea to hide it somewhere else."

"I think I'll just keep it close to me from now on."

Sitara and Jiandong entered the apartment. "Is it safe?" Jiandong asked.

Lorelei nodded, "*Ja,* for now."

"I have some news," Sitara said. "Gretel sacked me today."

"What? She doesn't have the right to do that," said Lorelei.

Sitara showed her friends the termination notice on her Q-link. "According to this, she does."

Lorelei studied it for a moment. "What does *this* mean—'termination on moral grounds'?"

"Gretel did a background check on everyone. She asked me if I believed in the One-And-All. And I said no."

Lorelei shook her head. "She told me the other day that she let a lot of people go because they had conflicts of interest. I wonder if what she really meant was—"

"—they don't bow down to the Godspeakers in the Communion" Sitara finished for her. "You could be a thief, a murderer, anything. Doesn't matter. You just have to pray like they do."

"I think it's more than that," said Jiandong. "I noticed something about the new people she brought in to replace the ones she let go."

"They're all seekers, yeah, we know," Sitara said.

"They're also upgraders," Jiandong revealed. "Almost all of them."

"Like Gretel herself," said Sitara, catching on.

Jiandong said, "The Communion is not as united as it appears to be. There are many who believe human evolution has already reached its peak; that the Communion should focus on politics and culture. But others believe evolution can progress further, through technology. We could grow stronger, smarter, longer lived. Survive in the vacuum of space. Push the old gods off their thrones, and take their place."

Lorelei nodded, as Jiandong's remarks led to new conclusions in her mind. "Do you think she's replacing our people to control the starship, or to control the Communion?"

"Maybe both," Jiandong said.

"So that's what I have to do, to get back in?" Sitara burst out.

"Get an upgrade? I don't have that kind of money."

"There are few who do," Jiandong observed.

Sitara didn't hear him. "I want to *see* things— comets, planets, nebulae, maybe the whole galaxy from outside," she cried. "Who is she to tell me I can't have those things? Lorelei's starship was going to take me there. But apparently I'm not a good enough person. And if I can't find a new job in the next two months, I'll be deported—"

"Deported?" said Jiandong and Glaive, almost simultaneously.

"Remember when the refugees from the war came to Éostray? They made that new law, to justify kicking them out," Sitara explained. "But no one in this country will hire me for anything. I'm a foreigner here—"

Lorelei took Sitara's shoulders in her hands. "Sitara, you're one of my only friends. I'll find a way to protect you, and bring you back into the mission. I promise."

"Thanks, Lorelei. But I won't go back to the CNH as long as that goat-sucking rakshasa Gretel Von Richter is still in charge." She put on her shoes and coat. "I have to go now. Have to find a new job."

"Sitara, wait," Lorelei said, moving to her side. "I know about a job that would be perfect for you. Private sector. Legacy Aeternim."

"Another—job?" asked Sitara.

"Our old boss, Din Mbembe," said Lorelei. "He offered it to me, but you should take it instead." She rummaged around her desk drawers for the business card that Din gave her; finding it, she handed it to Sitara. "His company is building a starship of its own. I want to know how close they are to being done."

"So the job is being your spy?" said Sitara, as her spirits returned. "Yeah, I can do that."

Lorelei turned to Jiandong. "How— how do you feel about going to the Communion Assemblies again?"

Jiandong was much less comfortable with Lorelei's suggestion. "I haven't gone to an assembly in years," he sighed.

"I don't want Gretel to fire my chief engineer. Or my captain."

Jiandong smiled, appreciating the respect she showed him. "I know. But the last time I was there, I went through the motions, repeated the prayers, just like everyone around me. But it didn't feel like me anymore. It felt like some other Jiandong, one who does things out of obligation, instead of from an open heart. So I left, and I've never been back."

"If Gretel is replacing our people with her own, we need to know why," Lorelei added to her argument.

"The great irony is, I am still a spiritual man," Jiandong said, with a small smile. "When I left the Communion, I learned about the life of Amergin Morann, the scientist who discovered life on the moons of Jupiter and Saturn. The discovery inspired him to leave the Communion and invent a new philosophy. Cosán Eolais, the path of knowledge. How much do you know about it?"

"Not much," Lorelei admitted. "Just that it used to be illegal here in Éostray."

"It was," Jiandong nodded. "I believe the Celestials did not give us laws to obey. Instead they gave us questions to answer. So did the Nocturnals, and their questions are no less important — that's why they put Amergin on trial for blasphemy. I gave most of my adult life to exploring those questions. I know what my answers are; I know who I am. So when you ask me to join the Communion again, it is like you are asking me to say things I don't believe. To *be* someone I'm not. The Gambler asks: how far will you go? And my answer is, no further than this. I'm sorry. I can't do it."

Sitara nudged his arm. "Come on, Captain. If I can play spy with the cyborgs, you can play spy with the Godspeakers."

Jiandong rolled his eyes.

Glaive said, "What would you like *me* to do?"

"You've done so much already," Lorelei answered, not wanting to examine exactly how much. "I believe there's something *I* have to do for *you.*"

§ 64.

Lorelei sat across from Alankar Sen, behind her own desk in her own office and and in her own chair.

"My bank has— *very occasionally*— provided identity reassignment services for high-value clients," said Alankar. "But this man is an Arethusan outcast, and the son of a friend of mine."

"Is Sturgeon Glaive really a friend of yours?"

"Heh. No. In fact it pleases me to do something that will annoy him. And in exchange, you're willing to endorse my motion to partially privatize the gravity-wave engine?"

"To a maximum of forty-two percent, as I've just offered," Lorelei replied. "Not sixty. The engine was financed with public money; its majority-ownership should remain public. Besides: the rest of the council is more likely to support you at that level."

Alankar scratched his beard, lost in thought for a moment. Then he turned back to Lorelei and said, "Very well. We have a deal."

They stood and shook each other's hands. Alankar moved to leave.

"By the way: how low would you have gone?"

"Down to thirty five," he grinned. "Better luck next time."

Lorelei shook her head, but smiled. "Next time," she said.

§ 65.

Sitara took an autotaxi to Vogelsberg's corporate district, where the clay and timbre-frame of the old town mixed with the ceramic and glass of the new. Her destination stood high above its nearest neighbours; Sitara imagined that the view from the offices on its top floor must feel commanding. Reminding herself that the price of failing this interview would be deportation, she took a moment in the restroom to play her favourite dance tracks and put on her war paint.

She met Din Mbembe in the company's entry foyer: an all-white space with track lighting along the lines where the walls met the floor and the ceiling. Din wore an all-white suit, and appeared delighted to see her.

"Admiral," said Sitara.

Din grinned. "You don't have to call me that anymore."

"You were my admiral for many years, and you were always good to your NavCom crews," she said, by way of apology. She looked around the space and said, "Looks like leaving the fleet worked out well for you."

Din smiled. "Hanfei Gao'fu took most of the heat for the scandal. My family is now safe in Troth Base, and I'm going to join them there shortly. But first: the council fired you too?"

Sitara nodded. "I might have quit eventually anyway. The new admiral's approach to leadership is to throw flowers everywhere, and pretend everything's fine."

Din chuckled. "So you're here to find out if we might want you," he said. "I'm sorry to say, we're mostly looking for engineers. We already have plenty of mathematicians and data scientists."

"How much of your starship is already built?"

Din smiled. "I see what you're doing." He pressed a few icons on his Q-link, and then a hologram of a starship appeared in the space between them. It resembled a long cigar, with two wings in the midsection supporting its massive fusion engines, and a complex cluster of rings and spheres at the bow and stern. He pressed another icon, and most of the ship lit up; some parts of the gravity-wave generator dimmed to grey.

"You're nearly done," Sitara noted.

"But there's still more to do," Din said, gesturing to the grey areas in the model.

Sitara examined the hologram of the starship. "Your forward toroidal vortex ring can't be in front of your bow-shock deflector."

"The what?"

"Your starship will create a bow shock when it travels faster than light. Dust, gas particles, photons, anything that gets caught in the gravity wave will gather here—" she pointed to an area in front of the ship hologram, "—and won't be able to go anywhere because the ship will be moving faster than anything can bounce off."

"Because it's moving faster than light. Of course."

Sitara nodded. "But when you slow down, everything that got caught in the bow shock will fly forward, showering anything in front of you with gamma radiation. So you have to disperse all that material to the side, while your gravity wave is still on."

"Seems like you're already at work," Din said.

"I've been working on the Conference starship since the beginning," Sitara said. "I'm the one who translated the alien probe's dedication plaque. You could finish your ship without me. But it will take you ten times longer."

"You might be right," Din smiled. "You wouldn't happen to know what Lorelei did with the plaque, do you?"

She kept her gaze fixed on the hologram, and disciplined her voice to sound as natural as possible. "I assumed it was blown up with the rest of the probe."

"That's what everyone believes," said Din, as a slight smile grew on one side of his face. "But another part of my job is to find out what actually happened. The company drove a truck full of money up to my house and told me to give it to anyone who has information."

"Can't help you there," Sitara said, while wearing her best poker-face. "But if the company were to hire me, I'd bring everything I know about starship design. Including everything I know that has not yet been made public. And some things that never will be."

"When can you start?"

"What time is it now— two thirty? I can start at three. I want to get a coffee first."

"Perfect," said Din. "Because your flight leaves at five."

The first sign of concern crossed Sitara's face. "My flight?"

"The job is in Newgarten."

§ 66.

On the CNH campus green near his lab, Jiandong found the same circle of people who he saw the previous day, reading from the Chronicle and inviting passers-by to join them. He paused when he came close enough to hear one of them reading aloud: *My friends, beware the Nocturnals. For they delight in undoing the work of the virtuous, and their gifts are sink-holes on the road to civilization. Know their names: The Gambler who turns the wheel of fortune, The Magician who bestows glamour upon lies, The Madman whose passions lead to suffering and destruction—"*

On the other side of the green, Jiandong could see Gretel talking to a pair of security guards. He saw the way they pretended not to look at him. Then the two guards gave Gretel the three-fold salute, and walked toward him.

What the guards had done to Sitara, he realized, they were about to do to him. He breathed deeply, and then sat down with the Chronicle readers.

"Captain Xiao," said the apparent leader of the group, a man he recognized from the lab. "You're a seeker too! I had no idea."

"My parents were priests," he explained. "They read to me from the Chronicle every day, as I was growing up."

"Do you have a favourite passage?"

"Yes, actually, I do." He opened his hand to ask for the reader's copy of the book, and it was given. He turned to a page near the end.

When Kai'tzeen received the news that his exile was over, he gathered his followers and returned to his home town, singing songs of joy along the way. When he arrived at the village centre, he stood silent for a long while, and then he wept. His followers asked him, "Dear Kai'tzeen, why do you weep?"

Kai'tzeen said, "The people here say they have broken through the narrow pass. Yet their leaders demand severity, and the followers take pleasure in dealing judgment and punishment. The ways of the One-And-All are different. For the One-And-All is the sunrise in the morning, and the stillness of evening, and the sound of the peepers by the water at night. It does not hold a sword over anyone's head. But it plants fruit trees and flowers wherever there is earth to grow them. Therefore the man who loves the One-And-All shows kindness to strangers, brings medicine to the sick, shares food and shelter with the needy, raises up those who have been put down, and loves beauty wherever he finds it. For the One-And-All desires flourishing and happiness for you, and loves to play with the child in your heart."

Jiandong closed the book, and handed it back to the reader.

"He was a complicated man," said the reader. His posture suggested he wasn't speaking about Kai'tzeen.

Jiandong nodded, understanding. "He was not always a good man, but he wanted to be," he replied.

The two security guards nodded to each other, saluted Jiandong with a touch to their heart, lips, and forehead, and then they walked away.

Jiandong spent most of the evening after work showering, and meditating on The Magician's Question. He lit incense at his home shrine to Kai'tzeen, and poured a drop of wine before an image of Amergin Morann. But he could not recite the prayers. He had broken a promise he made to himself, and so he felt he could not speak to his gods again until he atoned.

He remained there, hanging his head, all night.

§ 67.

Sitara rode a glass elevator up the side of one of Newgarten's newest skyscrapers. Every few seconds it seemed the view became a different world: a smog layer, the crests of the century-old skyscrapers, then the pinnacles of the newest towers, some of them more than a kilometre tall. A tuft of blue sky emerged from between orange-grey clouds. It occurred to Sitara that it was the first time she had seen a star since returning home from the mission to Pluto.

"See that? A star!" she urged the others sharing the ride up.

Some of them looked, made an idle "Hmm" at the sight, and returned their attention to the red giraffes on their Q-link screens, running from the black lions.

Arriving at the top floor, the doors opened with the hissing of air pressure valves; Sitara forced a yawn to stop her ears from popping. Most everyone else in the elevator behaved as if this was normal. The corridor beyond had a second pair of sliding doors, which in turn led to a wide round space beneath a geodesic dome, where a chamber orchestra performed for ballroom dancers in the centre, and various guests and businesspeople in sharp-cornered outfits ignored them from the sidelines.

"I thought you were taking me to the design offices," Sitara said to Din Mbembe.

"Legacy Aeternim is a family," said Din, who had accompanied Sitara on the trip, "This is a good place to get to know your new brothers and sisters."

"Why are so many people here wearing masks?" Sitara asked, when she saw that many of the guests wore the heads of animals or cartoon characters.

"They're pop music stars, movie stars, politicians. Famous people who don't yet want it known that they are investing in the company." He waved toward the windows, where several media drones watched the goings-on from outside. When he saw Sitara's bemusement, he said "Think of this party like the next stage of your job interview. The company directors already know you have the talent; now they want to see what you're like in society. After all, if you get the job, you're going to spend a lot of time with us."

"On board the starship?" Sitara filled in the obvious blank.

Din nodded. He pointed to a woman at a nearby table, whose flesh was almost as white as the nearby tables and chairs. "Let me introduce you to one of our top marketing reps. If she likes your story, you can bet the management will like it too. Mind you, you're one of the famous NavCom Seven crew— there's a good chance she already knows your story."

The marketing rep saw Din and Sitara talking, and waved at

them to invite them to join her. Sitara put on her best society smile.

"Sitara Kula! Ivy Sterling, sales management, Lalkeela region," said the sales rep, as she stood and offered her hand for shaking. Sitara accepted, and Ivy pulled her close, to kiss her cheeks. Sitara kept her social smile on, though her spine stiffened.

"We are all so excited to see you!" said Ivy. "You're something of a hero to me. You came from nothing, worked hard all your life, and made it to the top. Didn't let anyone stand in your way."

"I had help, sometimes," Sitara quietly added. "And some good luck."

Din smiled. "You don't have to be humble among us. Our company wants the best people, and you're here because you're one of the best. Self-made and strong-willed. Just like us."

Sitara looked around. She saw a man stumbling among the ballroom dancers, his tie loose and his shirt buttons undone, an open wine bottle in his hand. He reached out to one of the dancers to steady himself, but pulled them both to the floor. At another table, Sitara saw a man kiss a woman on his right side, then kiss a second woman on his left while the first woman inhaled a pinch of greenish dust.

"Glad to be among my people," Sitara smiled, though an urge to run away rose up in her belly. "How many other candidates are here?" she asked.

"Five, including yourself, and Ivy here," said Din. "They might hire all of you, or none of you. Let's say, if you haven't been thrown out before midnight, then the job's yours."

Ivy produced a small tin from her purse and offered it to Sitara. "Want some greenrock? Pure as the day the gods were born." She opened it and Sitara saw it contained more of the greenish dust.

Sitara thought it possible that the offer was a test, and that any choice she made might be the wrong one. "Not today," she said.

"You'll have a drink, though."

"Oh yes," Sitara grinned. She pressed a button on the table, and a light appeared under her finger. She leaned close to the table and said, "Middlereach Estate Artemisium."

Ivy perked an eyebrow at Sitara's choice, then nodded approvingly. She inhaled a pinch of greenrock, and offered some to Din, who also turned it down.

"And what makes you think you'll get this job?" she asked.

Sitara smiled. "Well, I could recite my resume for you— all my skills and qualifications— but you're asking about something else, yes?"

An android arrived and placed Sitara's drink in front of her: a tall glass containing two fingers of a greenish sweet-smelling spirit, alongside a small decanter of water, some sugar cubes, and a perforated spoon.

"You want to know why *me*, instead of anyone else with the same resume, or a better one," said Sitara, as she placed the spoon over the top of the glass, then placed two of the sugar cubes on the spoon and poured the water over it, watching the sugar dissolve into the drink. Ivy smiled, and waited for Sitara to reveal her answer. Sitara finished the artemisium ritual and sipped the result, and gave herself a moment to savour it. Din smiled to see Sitara make Ivy wait for an answer.

"Because I actually don't care whether or not I get this job," Sitara said, with a smile. "I am one of only a dozen people in the world who knows *all* the science behind the gravity-wave engine. If you don't hire me, someone else will. Or—" she sipped her artemisium again, "—maybe I'll start *my own* company. Build my own starship. You're not interviewing me today. I'm interviewing you."

Din turned away from Sitara so that he could smile and laugh.

Ivy was smiling too. "Shall we let her in on one of our corporate secrets?"

"It won't hurt your chances," Din said.

Ivy rose to her feet and said to Sitara, "Would you like a tour of our starship?"

Sitara was sure this was a trick question, but she nodded. "Happily," she said, and stood up.

"Well," said Ivy, "why don't we start with the forward passenger lounge?"

Sitara took two steps away before she noticed that Ivy and Din remained still. Sitara stepped back to the table, and looked around to see if anyone else felt as uncomfortable as she did. But then, she realized what Ivy was showing her, and she smiled.

"I should have seen it when I came in here," she admitted. "The elevator doors. Air locks. So, you're building the modules here on Earth, and then you're launching them into space for final assembly. That makes sense. Cost effective. But this is a life-sized model, yes? It's clearly too big to fit in the cargo bay of a planetfall shuttle. And it's right in the middle of downtown."

"We're not going to use planetfall shuttles," said Ivy.

"Carbon-fibre cables lowered from orbit?"

Ivy only smiled.

The discomfort in Sitara's belly intensified into panic. "You're not going to— Is there a nuclear fusion engine in the foundation of this building?"

Ivy nodded. "Come, I'll show it to you."

"No, that's okay, I'll take your word for it." Sitara picked up her drink, and then set it down again and pushed it away from her without sipping it. "How many modules like this?" she asked.

"Twelve, in all. Three of them are right here in Newgarten."

Sitara looked to the windows.

"Yes, you can see one of them, just over there, almost three klicks away," said Ivy, as she pointed to another skyscraper: cylindrical in design, and topped with a similar geodesic dome.

"You can't launch a rocket in the middle of a city!" Sitara swooned.

"Why not?" said Ivy, plain and matter-of-fact.

"Because you'll kill thousands of people, that's why not!" said Sitara, breathless with indignation. "Din, you were so terrified that your family wouldn't be safe. What about all those other families? What about them?"

"My family will be safe, that's all that matters," said Din.

Sitara felt a mouthful of bile rising in her. She swallowed it.

"So, you say you don't care about this job," said Ivy. "That's fine with me; it gives me a better chance. But I'm curious. You've read Lorelei's Doomsday argument, I presume? Could you build your own starship in less than five years?"

"Five years? Don't you mean fifteen?" said Sitara.

"We took a second look at the numbers, factoring in the, ah, well, the *consequences* of our departure. Loss of capital and talent and— urban infrastructure. So perhaps you *do* need this job, if you want to survive what's coming. Or do you think five years will be enough?"

"This is part of the interview, isn't it?" Sitara asked, giving Ivy as well as herself a way to reframe the topic and so ease her mind. "You wanted to see how I might react to something morally outrageous?"

Din gestured toward the nearest surveillance camera, discretely embedded in the ceiling. "Everyone's being tested. Management's always watching."

Sitara regained her coolness, if only to disguise what she was really thinking. "Five years. If you're asking me seriously, then yes, it could be done. I would fit gravity-wave drives on some of the ships in the NavCom fleet. Then I'd help the Arethusan Space Defence fit them on their warships, so they could go looking for you."

Din understood what Sitara implied, but Ivy was reading her social media messages on her Q-link, giving Sitara only passing attention. "But seriously. What's it like to work with Lorelei? I've heard people say she's unemotional. Doesn't get social cues like normal people. Is she a good leader?" Ivy asked.

"She wouldn't have been a good fit in your company," said Sitara, without looking at Ivy. "If you told her that twelve skyscrapers around the world were actually starship modules ready to blast into space from the middle of their cities, I think she would take that very badly. I think she would do whatever it took to expose you, and stop you."

Ivy understood Sitara's real meaning. She put her Q-link down; her voice became more stern. "People say that we don't care about the little people," she argued. "But honestly: *they're* the ones who broke the planet. It's not our fault. They wanted better cars, nicer houses, faster computing, a new comms every year. We were only fulfilling demand. They could have chosen differently. But they didn't. And now that Lorelei proved they broke the planet, we have to do what it takes to survive."

"It seems to me," said Sitara, as she digested Ivy's world view, "that the person you should hire should be someone who can not only help you build a starship, but also build a civilization."

"Are you getting religious on me?" asked Din.

"No, I'm getting practical," Sitara shook her head. "You need people whose talents will be useful *after you arrive* at the new planet, not just in getting there. How many people can fit in your starship?"

"Five hundred investors and their families," said Din, "plus technicians, specialists, and the help. Maybe three thousand people in all."

"Are you going to need salespeople?"

Ivy gave Sitara a puzzled look.

Sitara pretended not to notice. "When you arrive, you'll create a new society, and the company will be the de-facto government, yes? It will put people to work, and it will have no competitors in its market. So, you're probably not going to need advertising designers or market researchers."

"We're not going to need mathematicians," said Ivy. "They don't *produce* anything. They're all theory, no application."

"Your mathematician is your all-in-one intellectual," Sitara said. "She can do your statistics. Your economics. Your data visualization. Your financial planning. And when the first generation of children are born, she can plan their education in math, science, and logic. Can your sales rep do those things? Any *one* of them, maybe— but *all* of them?"

A chime sounded from Din's Q-link. He read the message there, and said, "Congratulations, Sitara, you made the first cut."

"She did?" said Ivy, disbelieving. She checked her own Q-link. "No, there must be a mistake. Where's my name? This must be a data glitch. No, I know what happened: you hacked the network, didn't you Sitara?"

"I'm reading the same list as you," said Din. Turning to Sitara, he said, "It seems the directors like you."

"Hey, I *earned* my place in the ship!" Ivy blurted. "I was this company's top sales rep for the last eight years in a row. I outperformed my own records every year. I protected the company's assets in Lalkeela when those animals took over the city— and I fought my way out and survived, when the whole thing went to hell. I *deserve* to be part of this!"

Responding to her outburst, Din only shrugged his shoulders.

Ivy fled the room, her head down, her hand at the level of her eyes in a useless effort to keep people from looking at her.

Din smiled. "Would you like another drink?" he offered Sitara.

"Sure, thank you," Sitara accepted.

§ 68.

"Your new name is Jumar Kshatriya," said Alankar. "You were born in the city of Kumarlo, in Gayatri Pradesh, and you are thirty-four years old."

Glaive reviewed the new identity, in every conceivable form. Passport, employee ID, medical history. Everything.

"Can I ask," Lorelei began, "why didn't you choose an

Arethusan name?"

"*Kshatriya* is an old Gayatrian word for a warrior," Glaive explained. "And Jumar— that's the name of someone who— taking his name will remind me to be a better person."

Lorelei nodded. Alankar continued "You also have an appointment with a local cybernetic skin clinic, to change your face."

"I don't want it," Glaive said.

"I strongly recommend it," said Alankar. "And not just because of Arethusan authorities. It seems the local police are interested in you, too. Something about an incident at the old monastery. We can make that disappear, but we can't help with the Arethusans. Their facial recognition software is already worming its way into every security system in the city. Changing your face *is* your best option."

Lorelei looked at Glaive with curiosity.

"No surgery," he repeated. "No cybernetic skin. I don't want to see some other man in the mirror. Whatever name is on these cards, I want to stay being me."

"As you wish," Alankar acknowledged. "As for your new job," he said, "Head of security for the local branch of Lalkeela Pathfinders Bank."

"*Your* bank," said Glaive.

"Indeed," Alankar confirmed. "I like having ex-military on my team. Your predecessor in the position— *departed*, recently. So there was an opening."

Lorelei handed Glaive a shopping bag. "I had some new clothes printed for you today. New name, new suit. Happy birthday."

He smiled and accepted the gift.

"Go and try them on," Alankar encouraged him.

Glaive scanned the beer garden out of habit. "Be right back," he said. He took the clothes to the pub's bathroom.

"While we have a minute to ourselves," said Alankar to Lorelei, "Since Glaive— pardon me, Jumar— will no longer be protecting your apartment, I wonder if you have anything there which you might like to deposit in our vault?"

Lorelei's smile disappeared. "You heard about the break-in, *ja?*"

"The entire Council heard about it."

"Some furniture was broken, but nothing was taken," she said.

Alankar chuckled. "You're not a very good liar, Doctor Verlassen."

"I did move some of my valuables elsewhere, for safekeeping," she admitted.

"Wouldn't they be safer in our vaults? Protected by friends of yours like Glaive, who you know you can trust?" Lorelei didn't answer, so he pressed the point. "I know you have the plaque from the alien probe. And I know you don't like our deal to privatize the starship. You think I want to take your baby away from you. But no, not at all. I want my baby to grow wings and fly, just like you do."

"Your baby?"

"The ship was ours before the CNH bought it," Alankar explained.

"So you're trying to buy it back?" Lorelei asked.

"You want to sell it?" Alankar grinned.

Lorelei made a bemused face at him.

"But let me put my last card on the table," Alankar continued, "My bank is more interested in all the children that will come *after* this one. Thousands of them. Maybe millions. And even if those little heroes go adventuring into space and come back with nothing, they still need an engine to get there."

"We don't even know if it works yet," Lorelei told him. "You might be betting on a dead horse."

"That's the fun of venture capitalism," Alankar grinned. "It's like gambling with other people's lives. There's no other high quite like it. Not even greenrock."

Lorelei shifted in her seat slightly away from him. "What exactly are you getting at?" she asked.

"If you partner with us to develop the gravity wave to full commercial potential, you will have a majority share in the most important and profitable technology of all time. But if your baby were to fall into someone else's hands— however that might happen, and whomever they might be— I'm not sure they would be good parents."

Glaive returned to the beer garden, wearing the new clothes Lorelei gave him: a sportscoat, waistcoat, and trousers ensemble. It made Lorelei smile, and Glaive was glad to see her smiling at him.

"All this didn't cost you too much, I hope," he said.

"It cost her forty-two percent of her starship," said Alankar. He stood and made for the exit. "Think about my offer, Jumar.

You almost certainly won't get a better one." He swaggered out of the beer garden, confident in the brightness of his future.

"He's the man who sent the thief," Glaive said.

"I know."

He paused. "You really sold him almost half your starship, for me?"

"It's complicated."

"Once I go to work for him, I can make sure—"

"I have a plan to get my starship back, this afternoon."

"What do you mean?"

"That's— also complicated."

"Keeping secrets, are you?" he grinned.

"I'm allowed to do that," she laughed.

Glaive opened his hands, offering to hold hers for a moment. "Thank you," he said. "For all you've done for me, and for— for not letting power corrupt you, like it does everyone else. Thank you for being who you are."

Lorelei gave him her hands. They held each other that way for a moment. Glaive closed his eyes in a rare gesture of vulnerability.

Lorelei shook the feeling off. "I have to go to the office," she said. "There's a Council meeting today. I'd invite you to come and watch, but your father will be there."

"I don't care to see him ever again."

She gathered her jacket threw her purse-strap over her shoulder. "You can stay at my house until you find a new apartment— but— I'd like my library back soon."

"I think I can make it on my own now."

"Well," said Lorelei, when she was ready to go. "We're even then, *ja*?"

"Yeah. We're good."

"Okay. I'm going to work now."

The departed in separate directions down the street. But before Lorelei turned the corner that would have taken her out of sight of Glaive, she turned to look back at him.

At the same moment, he turned to look at her, and smiled. Lorelei smiled back.

A light-rail commuter train crossed the street, blocking her view of him. When it passed, he was gone.

§ 69.

"And most of these people," Jiandong explained, "were at the Communion Assembly yesterday."

Lorelei studied the list Jiandong gave her. It listed the names of the starship project's most recently hired staff. "You think these people are more loyal to her than to the project?"

"That's part of how the race is run," Jiandong sighed. "There is a bright side: she *did* pick some pretty good people. Engineers, scientists. And the *other* bright side is that the Communion is swimming in money. So now, the Council has to decide whether they want to sell the starship to a church, or to a bank."

"What does the Church want in return?"

"A seat on the council."

Lorelei looked away for a moment, then asked, "Do you trust them?"

"No, I don't trust them. But I *know* them."

Lorelei understood.

Jiandong headed toward the door. "Coming to the meeting?" he asked.

"I'll see you there."

After Jiandong left her office, Lorelei opened her Q-link, accessed the security camera footage for her own office, and selected the clip where Alankar said he was pleased to do something that would annoy Sturgeon Glaive. She opened an encrypted-anonymous message service.

"Please fwd to Senator Ambassador Glaive: Lalkeela Pathfinder Bank to create new identity for his son. Ambassador Alankar Sen, acting as agent of bank, approved contract personally."

She sent the message with the embedded video to Arethusa's secure alien-infiltration tip line.

Next she recorded a video message for Gretel. "Good afternoon, Admiral," she said into the camera by the video wall. "You asked me a few days ago whether I would support the proposal to create a seat on the council for the Communion. I've decided I *will* support it. If you need me to say so at the meeting today, then I will. See you there."

She sent the recording to Gretel's office. Then she wandered to the terrace. She contemplated the spinning of the city's many electric wind turbines, and sipped her tea.

Her sketchbook lay on a chair behind her, forgotten beneath a pile of meeting minutes and analyst reports.

§ 70.

"Madam chairwoman," said Sturgeon, rising to cast his vote in the council chambers, "on the motion to privatize forty-two percent of the Expeditions Starship project, the Republic of Arethusa *exercises veto!*"

Alankar Sen was the first to stand up and shout at him. "You can't veto that! We need this money to finish the ship!"

"I can, and I want to, so I will," Sturgeon shot back, over the voices of the other councillors who had similar points-of-order to yell about.

Alankar turned to Gretel. "Madam chairwoman, he's vetoing everything because he's afraid of aliens. It's ridiculous! Isn't there some rule that says members who don't pay their dues don't get to vote?"

"This time it isn't aliens," Sturgeon countered. "It's you. You personally, Alankar Sen, for providing safe haven to Arethusan outlaws." He pressed some icons on his Q-link, which sent to the wall-screen the video in which Alankar agreed to provide new identity papers for Glaive.

"How did you get this?" Alankar demanded.

Sturgeon dismissed Alankar with a laugh. He faced Gretel. "Since the honourable member mentioned aliens, may I have it on record *again* that the Republic of Arethusa believes the starship will provoke them. That ship must not fly!"

The council erupted in shouting. Gretel Von Richter, at the chairwoman's podium, bashed her gavel. Most councillors ignored her.

She screamed into the mic, her cybernetic body making it as loud and as jarring as a saw cutting through a steel girder. Everyone in the council chamber removed their earpieces and covered their ears.

"Since the member for Arethusa has exercised his veto," Gretel said calmly, "we may as well move on to our next item of business. A point of information. Over the last several days, I have been negotiating with another party who offered substantial funding to us. Enough to finish the ship and fly it for the next five years. And they do not require a partial privatization, so we don't need a motion to accept it. All they want in return is a seat at the Council. I can now reveal to you who that party is. Councillors, please welcome His Holiness Jerome Rafferty, Godspeaker of Newgarten, Arethusa."

The chamber doors opened and the Godspeaker entered. Most councillors clapped politely as he strode to the podium. Sturgeon folded his arms and grimaced; Alankar glared at Lorelei in disbelief. Lorelei smiled at them both.

At the podium, the Godspeaker ended the applause with a motion of his hand. "I know that some of you here are not believers, but if you don't mind I would like to begin with a prayer. For the sake of affirming the values of civilization. I would be very glad to see everyone stand up."

Most members of the council rose. But Alankar Sen walked out, glaring at Lorelei on his way. "Looks like you got everything you wanted.".

"*Ja*, I did. And I have to say, it feels good."

Alankar sniffed with disgust. "Have fun with it while it lasts."

"Is that a threat?"

He spun around to confront her. "Right now you've won. And you think you can do anything. But the Gambler never smiles on someone for long. Soon enough, he'll be smiling on someone else."

"Not necessarily *you*," Lorelei countered.

Alankar smirked. "We shall see."

Seventh Transmission: The CNHS Siren.

Length: 78 meters.

Propulsion: Experimental gravity-wave generator.

Max Operational Range: 103.5 light-years.

Crew complement: 27 (technicians, scientists, diplomats, linguists, and medical specialists.)

Max Time Between Resupply: 60 months.

Primary Mission: To explore the stars; to search for life; to better the human spirit.

§ 71.

The orbital tugboats guided the finished Expeditions Council starship out of the orbital construction platform. Lorelei and her team, along with key members of the Council, other officials and dignitaries, and twice as many reporters, watched from the observation dome of a nearby orbital station. They applauded when they saw the ship's running lights go on; some hugged each other.

"I don't much like public speaking," said Lorelei, as she took the podium, "so for right now, all I want to do is thank everyone who kept the name of the ship a secret. It was hard to choose. There were so many people who gave so much to the project— so much of their time, their heart and soul. What name could I choose, to honour them all? In the end, I decided to name it for something that says why we're going to the stars. A name that speaks to the urgency of our mission. But a name which also speaks to the allure of space, which is only the newest form of the ancient call of the unknown: the call to explore, to discover, and to wonder. And— I hope no one thinks this too personal— I named it after a ship that I made up for a story I wrote when I was nine."

Reporters leaned their cameras and mics a little closer to her.

"Ladies and gentlemen," Lorelei announced, "The Conference of Nations Starship Siren!"

Lorelei pressed a button on the screen of her Q-link. Winches attached to the side of the starship activated, pulling a curtain away and thus showing the name of the ship, proudly printed just under the observation windows of the forward deck. A floodlamp turned on, bathing it in white light. Applause rose from the witnesses. And finally, Lorelei touched another button, which activated an antique wooden ballista that sent a bottle of westiller flying from the observation platform toward the ship, to break upon its bow. Someone behind her opened another bottle of champagne, showering everyone nearby with bubbles. Pride shone through Lorelei's smile, as she received a lineup of people eager to shake her hand and congratulate her.

"You're winning, Lorelei," said Gretel Von Richter, when it was her turn. "Soon your starship will leave everyone in this honours race behind."

Lorelei thanked her. Part of her wondered if Gretel implied another meaning in that statement. But she had no time for that thought; a train of other dignitaries were waiting their turn to shake her hand.

Only Sturgeon Glaive refrained from the celebration. He stood near the observation window, motionless and unreadable, except to brush some stray champagne drops from his shoulders. He slowly shook his head. Then he took up his comms and placed a call.

"Are you in position?" he said. When he got the answer he wanted, he ended the call and left the party.

Lorelei saw him go, and moved to catch him on his way out, but a group of journalists got in her way.

As a planetfall shuttle left the orbital station, three other ships moved in. Though the new ships were dwarfed in size by the Siren, their sharp-angled boxy frames and their blue-and-white livery caught people's attention. Someone asked, "Those are not NavCom ships, are they?"

Lorelei said, "Blue and white? No. Arethusan Space Force." She looked over to the corner of the room where Sturgeon Glaive had been standing.

He was leaving.

§ 72.

"We tried to reason with them," said Sturgeon, gripping the edges of his podium as if to save his life. "We were patient.

Accommodating. Even humble. But they did not listen. And now it has come to this."

Lorelei leaned on a table in the observation lounge of the orbital station, watching Sturgeon's press announcement on a wall screen. She remained motionless; her arms were folded, her mind focused.

"As everyone knows," Sturgeon continued, "in a few days, the CNH starship Siren will fly to Neptune: a trial run of its new gravity-wave engine. Arethusa has decided not to allow it. And let me show you why."

Behind him, members of Sturgeon's staff unveiled a portrait of Lance Crassus. "This is the man who discovered the bomb on the platform," Sturgeon described him. "A humble technician, not quite the top of his class in college, but talented all the same. A husband and father, and a generous donor to his local youth rallyfoot league. He is the man who warned the rest of his crew to evacuate, and who tried to disarm the bomb. Selfless, courageous, and calm under pressure— one of humanity's brightest and best. And the first casualty in our first interstellar war. Please join me in a moment of silence, to honour him."

Gretel told her android assistant to order a bouquet of flowers for Lance's family.

"Very kind of you," Lorelei whispered to her. She told her own android assistant to do the same.

Gretel smiled.

At his press conference, Sturgeon gripped the podium again. "The lesson we must learn from his death is that humanity is not yet ready to face what's out there. And so, on my advice, the President has ordered the ASDF to blockade the starship—" gasps of surprise and outrage followed this announcement, "— and to blockade the planet Neptune against any NavCom support vessels. If the ship activates its gravity-wave generator, we will shoot it down."

"That man has lost his mind," said Gretel. "Our ship can go faster than light. Their ships won't see it coming."

"The trial flight won't go *that* fast," Lorelei reminded her. "We're aiming for only eighty percent of light speed. The warships at Neptune will have a few seconds to take aim."

Sturgeon Glaive continued. "We do not begrudge any nation the peaceful and scientific exploration of space. But it seems we Arethusans are the only ones who understand that Lance Crassus' death was a message from the aliens, telling us that we are not wanted in their galaxy. Well, I say it's our galaxy too! And we should be ready to fight for our place in it. And so we call upon the Conference— no, we *demand*—" he thumped his fist on the podium for dramatic effect, "—that the CNH starship be transformed into a warship. And we will not let it launch until the Council agrees."

"What will it take to get him out of the way?" Lorelei asked.

Gretel smiled. "I'm impressed, Lorelei. A year ago, you wouldn't have asked a question like that."

"I haven't changed at all," said Lorelei. "It's the world that changed."

Gretel perked an eyebrow, then smiled.

Lorelei gazed out the window at her starship, which floated under its own power now, and rotated to give its occupants a touch of gravity. "So many walls that stood in our way before we could get this far," she said. "Now we have a navy blockade. The final wall, it seems. But I don't know how to get around it."

"Part of your problem, Lorelei," said Gretel, "is that you think everyone is as rational as you are."

"If they're not, they should be," Lorelei shot back. She sat silent for a moment, tapping her fingers on the table. "What do I have to do, to make him see reason?" she said. "Do I have to do the same to him, that he's doing to me? Get the other navies in the world to blockade his colonies? Threaten him with a second *Gott-verdammt* space war? The world will unite, with *him* as its common enemy."

"If you're serious about starting the second space war," Gretel said, with approval, "then I'll be glad to introduce you to the Minister of Defence."

Lorelei now wondered if she should regret her words. "You actually *know* him?"

"Oh yes. He's one of us," said Gretel, as she touched the trinolay flower on her necklace. "And I am sure he would be most delighted to meet you. He's something of an admirer, you know. We all are. You're the fastest-rising, most successful new horse in the honours race since—."

Lorelei narrowed her brow and thumped her heel on the floor. "It's *your* race, not mine," she insisted.

"But you are very good at it, Lorelei," Gretel told her. "Some very powerful people are betting on you."

Lorelei held her breath, and looked at Gretel. She saw the perfectly symmetrical, almost cartoonishly feminine face, with its approving grin, its bouncing brown curls, and the groove-lines in the arms and shoulders that outlined her muscles: the signs of her cybernetic upgrades. Lorelei's hand moved to her breast, as if to calm the quickened beating of her heart. At the same time, the strange creature before her mirrored the action, and grew a bright smile.

§ 73.

Lorelei retreated to the cabin of a planetfall shuttle: one of the only places on the orbital station where she would not be hounded by VIPs, reporters, and well-wishers. With the din of their voices gone, the background hisses of air filters and the hum of electrics returned. The forward windows gave a view of the earth passing beneath the station in its orbit, shining dim blue-white light into the cabin, causing the stray hairs and dust in the air to glow like a thin mist. Lorelei hugged her sketchbook and a pencil close to her breast, as if she would drown without them. Sitara, Jiandong, and Glaive had followed her; their somber gazes moving between each other and the floor.

"And I suddenly thought: I was looking at Gretel, but I was *seeing* a reflection of myself," said Lorelei. "Of what I might become, if I carry on like this. And listening to myself talk: it was my voice, but Sturgeon Glaive's words. Calling for global unity through war. I had to ask myself, who do I want to be, five years from now? Do I want to be me? Or do I want to be one of them?"

"You don't want it to be Gretel," said Sitara.

"But she's the admiral of the fleet. I have to work with her. And there's no other way to make the Arethusans back down."

"Wasn't it you who told Hanfei that we always have choices?" Jiandong reminded her.

Lorelei looked to the floor. "*Ja*, that was me," she admitted. "But right now, that's the only choice I can see. You have to talk with people to reason with them. But that *arschgeige* Sturgeon Glaive is pointing guns. That's the exact opposite of talking."

"Lorelei, his son is sitting right there," said Jiandong, and he nodded toward Glaive.

"It's all right, Captain," said Glaive. "I know what kind of man my father is. And Gretel is right about him. He won't back down without a fight. It looks like he *wants* a fight. He probably thinks he can't lose."

"Still, I'm sorry I said that about him," Lorelei mumbled. She caressed her sketchbook for a moment. "Every other wall that stood in front of us, we climbed it by showing the world the logical and moral rightness of our position. But the way Gretel tells it, that has *never* been what really happened. I don't know who to ask for help. I don't know what to do." She pulled her legs up so that she could hug them.

Sitara was the first to break the uncomfortable silence. "Jiandong and I have done a few things for you that you don't know about." When she saw Jiandong's worried look, she added, "And we should have told you."

Jiandong nodded. He said, "Back when it wasn't certain that the council would vote to build your starship, I— might have— leaked— some confidential Council business to the Godspeaker of Newgarten. To get the support of the Communion."

Lorelei's eyes widened; her breath held in her lungs. "You could be *fired* for that," she told him. "And now it would be *me* who would have to fire you."

"Not only that," said Sitara. "On the same day he went to see the Godspeaker, I went to the city's biggest casino, and—"

"You told me you were going to a park," Jiandong interrupted to say.

Sitara shrugged, but she smiled. "I'm very good with numbers. And five-card finangle is nothing but numbers. I used to shark people like that all the time."

"Shark?" said Lorelei, not understanding what Sitara was saying.

"Gambling," Sitara continued. "Pretending to know almost nothing about the game, to make the other guy put down bigger bets. Then beating him. I'm good at that, too. The day Jiandong and I went to see the Godspeaker, I went to the casino and bet most of my back-pay at the finangle table. I won all of it back, and more. A lot more. And I gave it to Alankar Sen."

"You bribed him? You could go to *jail* for that," Lorelei said, alarmed. "Why did you do it?"

"He was going to veto the starship project. I had to put pressure on him."

"That's not all," said Jiandong. "When we went to Yuzhow, we bribed a guard to let us in after hours, so that we could scan the probe."

"You— bribed—"

"And if we hadn't," said Sitara. "You might not have found

out the plaque had a database inside it."

"And that thief who broke into your apartment, to try and steal it?" said Glaive. "I killed him."

"You killed someone for me?" Lorelei said, astounded.

"Yes I did," Glaive said, without pride and without shame. "Several men, if you count the ones I had to splash to escape from Lalkeela. I did it to protect the artifact, and to protect you."

"So those sirens all over the city that day: they were for *you*?" Sitara asked.

"I had to do it," Glaive defended himself. "He was a professional. He had good gear. And I'm a soldier."

Lorelei wrung her hands, as if to wipe away her moral distress. "Why did you do all those things?"

"Because we believe in you, Lorelei," said Sitara, moving to Lorelei's side, laying a sympathetic hand on her arm. "The discovery of your planet is the first piece of very good news that our lonely world has heard in a long time. And I won't apologize for what I did. Because I'm not sorry for it. Not in the slightest."

Lorelei ran her fingers through her hair and pulled on the roots. "The explosion on the platform, where all those people died— the torturing of those workers in Gretel's machine— the invasion of Lalkeela— all because of me," she said.

"People dreamed of new worlds because of you," Sitara reminded her. "People imagined a better future for themselves and their loved ones, because of you. And now we're going to visit another world, because of you."

"People are *dead* because of me!" Lorelei shot back. She pushed the plaque away from her.

Jiandong said, "Did you really believe that changing the world would be *easy*? Did you think that you could join that race of theirs without becoming one of them?"

"I am *not* one of them," Lorelei insisted, though she had to look away from him to say it. "I don't live like them, I don't think like them, I've *never* broken the rules like them—"

Glaive's voice cut through her denials and struck the reality that she had forgotten: "Yes, you have. On Pluto."

Lorelei felt the energy sap out of her muscles; she sat down, and acknowledged the truth of his words with a silent nod. Her tears, she realized, were formed of self-pity; she wiped them away. Sitara and Jiandong smiled for her, but their sympathy only further enervated her. She opened her sketchbook to one of her first drawings of the probe. Its lines were light and staccato, a testament to the fugue of imagination in which she had created it, and a contrast to the weary silence of the room. Her friends waited for her to say something.

"I used to know who I am," Lorelei said. "I used to know how to do the right thing. In these last few years I— I don't know. I stole things, I told lies, I made friends with people I knew to be corrupt. I told myself I was doing it to save the world. And now, what could I possibly do, how could I possibly —"

The drawing of the probe prompted a wave of clarity in her mind: faint and fragile, but real enough to grasp.

"I've got an idea," she said.

§ 74.

Prague Castle was a cluster of stone towers and palaces surrounding a thousand-year-old basilica, standing on a hill near the downtown of Éostray's capital city. It served as the hub of Éostray's government and the home of its royal family. Lorelei's autotaxi left her in the ancient cobblestone courtyard. As she approached the ornamental iron gate, a pair of guardsmen wearing colourful ceremonial uniforms and carrying pikestaffs challenged her in several of Éostray's languages: "*Ve jménu krále, přestaň! Halt, im namen des Königs!*"

More cars arrived, and from them emerged several reporters and their media crews. The two guardsmen maintained their discipline; though one of them momentarily darted his gaze toward the other.

"I need to see the King," said Lorelei, in her own language.

More soldiers emerged from the castle, with modern uniforms and rifles. One of them recognized Lorelei.

"Doctor Verlassen!", he said. "I'm sorry, but it doesn't matter how famous you are; you can't get an audience with His Majesty like this. No one can."

"I have something for him," said Lorelei. She opened her rucksack and showed the guard what was in it.

"Is that—?" said the guard commander. His eyes seemed to grow twice as big.

"It is," she confirmed.

The reporters and camera crews crowded closer; they, too, gasped when they recognized it.

"Let her in! Let her in!" said the guard commander. The

ceremonial guardsmen lowered their weapons and opened the gate.

"No media," said the commander, as the reporters and camera crews tried to follow.

Lorelei, Jiandong, and Sitara were led to an elegant reception hall in the castle. Judging by the gold-framed paintings, the silk curtains, and a hologram table similar to the one in the NavCom Seven lab, they presumed this hall was in a private area of the palace, not shown to tourists. After a short wait, a middle-aged man in a white shirt and trousers, a green housecoat, and bare feet, entered the room. Two curious Czech wolfdogs followed him. The guards bowed or curtseyed, as the protocol required, as did Lorelei and her friends.

Lorelei held the time capsule out for him and said, "Your Majesty. I've been keeping this to myself, these last few months. But it doesn't belong to me. It belongs to the world."

Although he had been told what to expect, the king was no less awed to see it than the guards and media crew had been. He admired it for a long moment.

"And by bringing it to me, instead of to the council," he said, "you make it appear that you are above the honours race, while in fact you have taken first place today."

Jiandong and Sitara made a quiet chuckle. The king smiled at them, letting them know he saw the comedy too.

Lorelei said, "Even so. I think you might be the only one I can trust to take care of this."

The king accepted the plaque from her hands, and admired it for a moment.

"I saw your broadcast from the NavCom Seven," he said, "and I've been following your career, ever since."

"Really?" said Lorelei, almost disbelieving.

"Oh yes— my court is full of admirers. I wonder if you are planning something equally bold to end the blockade of your starship."

"I don't have a *whole* plan, yet," Lorelei admitted. "But coming to you with this—" she gestured to the plaque, "—was the first part of it."

The king grinned. "If you want, I could launch my missiles at the Arethusans. In less than twenty minutes, the blockade would be over."

"If we did that, we would have another war," Lorelei said, with a quiet uncomfortable laugh. "But that's not what the starship was supposed to be about. It was supposed to demonstrate that we could be more curious, more co-operative, and less narrow-minded, if we chose to be. It was supposed to show that we could be the kind of people who don't need to hate each other to feel a sense of purpose. Who don't need a common enemy to come together. It was supposed to show that we could be better."

"In that respect," the king asked, "do you feel it has succeeded?"

Lorelei pursed her lips and breathed, not sure how the king would like her answer. "I don't know," she admitted. She looked to the floor.

The king smiled. "I respect that kind of honesty," he said. Gesturing toward one of his attendants, he said, "Tomorrow, the guard will escort this artifact to the Royal Science Foundation. It's time we had a full team of experts to study it. The public can see it in the museum on weekends." Nodding toward Lorelei's friends he added, "The executive of the NavCom Seven, as well as this officer from Arethusa, can see it whenever they want."

"Sir," the attendant acknowledged, and he took up his comms to issue the orders.

"Captain Xiao," said the king, "if you want to take a photo for your column, please do," the king invited.

Jiandong, startled by the invitation, held up his comms to take the photo of the handover. The king gestured that Lorelei should stand by his side for it. The access to the plaque, and to the king himself, she realized, was a large advantage in the honours race. Having her by his side was also an advantage to him. But for tonight, she chose to imagine that he gave her this advantage because he believed in her, and in her vision.

"Ever since your election, I wondered what it would be like to meet you," said Lorelei. "I didn't imagine it would be like this."

The king smiled. "In my position, I almost never meet people like you, either."

Lorelei looked down, to hide that she was beaming with pride.

The guard commander cleared his throat: a polite sign that Lorelei's time with the king was over.

"One more question," said the king, and everyone stopped. "Lorelei, if I may ask: when you trespassed on that base station, on Pluto—"

"Yes—?" said Lorelei, expecting to be chastised.

"What was it like?"

Lorelei looked up again, and grinned.

§ 75.

Lorelei enjoyed the sight of the Expeditions campus green filling with reporters and camera crews.

Gretel pushed her way through the scrum and stepped up to her. "Who let them in here?" she demanded.

"I did," said Lorelei.

"There's a protocol for press conferences!"

"This isn't a press conference," said Lorelei.

"No? It looks like one."

"It's a scientist— me— " she touched her breast, "—and some of my scientist friends—", she gestured to Sitara and Jiandong, "—talking about science, on the steps of a scientific institution."

The nearest journalists chuckled to hear it. Gretel, however, frowned. "Some of them seem to be under the impression that you have a statement to make," she grunted.

"It happens that our conversation may interest other parties," Lorelei smiled. "So, I invited two or three more friends to come and listen."

Twenty camera crews activated their equipment. A dozen media drones buzzed overhead. Gretel wanted to argue the point further, but the field of electronic eyes made her step down.

"You're wondering why I gave the artifact to the King of the Éostrayans," said Lorelei. "He was the first person I could think of who has nothing to gain from it. Who wouldn't treat it like a trophy. But is powerful enough to keep it safe. The knowledge it contains belongs to everyone in the world. Not just to me, not even to the Conference. So, my team and I put together a data package, containing everything we learned from it. All the engineering specs that we used to build our gravity-wave engine. Hundreds of photographs and sound-bytes of life on the alien planet. And we are making it free to everyone, right now."

With a signal from Lorelei, Sitara pressed a button on her Q-link, causing the data package to change its security setting from secret to public.

"And the address for all this data is in everyone's messages, as of— right now," Sitara said. She pressed another button, sending the message.

A commotion of surprise spread across the green, as most people's comms toned with the arrival of Sitara's signal. Gretel stepped forward again, a rebuke ready to fly from her lips. But the commotion among the reporters changed to applause. She stepped down again.

"So even if the Arethusans destroy our starship," Lorelei said, "the rest of the world will build new starships, and leave men like Sturgeon Glaive behind. And if he was here today, I'd say to him: would you like to come with us?"

Seeing Gretel's astonishment, Lorelei said, "And you too, Gretel. And your friend the Godspeaker. In fact—" she addressed the media again, "I would like to invite *every* member of the Expeditions Council to join me on board the *Siren*, for the first flight."

"The test flight to Neptune, or— to the planet?" Gretel asked.

"Both flights, if you want," Lorelei confirmed. "For some reason that no one has explained to me, the ship already carries enough supplies for thirty people for a year. So I plan to make the formal invitation at today's council meeting," said Lorelei. "You'll be there for that, I hope?"

Gretel said nothing; only glared at her. She turned to the sea of cameras and put on her best smile.

§ 76.

Sitara's desk at the Legacy Aeternim office was in a tightly-packed cluster of stations in the middle of a wide and mostly empty white room. The distance from her desk to the door gave her time to look busy whenever anyone entered and approached her.

Din Mbembe's footsteps echoed, so that they sounded like they came from everywhere. He rolled up the sleeve on his shirt, to show that the muscles on his fingers and arms were outlined with dark inset groove-lines. He grinned like a boy with a birthday gift.

"You're an upgrader." Sitara noted.

"Just my hands and arms, right now. I'll do my legs later," said Din. He stretched out his arms, admiring them. "They're extraordinary things. Delicate enough to do brain surgery. Tough enough to punch through a brick wall."

"They're beautiful," Sitara agreed.

"You might want to consider an upgrade for yourself. While you can still spend the money."

"What do you mean?"

"Lorelei published the specs for the gravity-wave engine. So we'll be finished our starship *far ahead* of schedule. I'm going to take a few day's holiday. See a few sights I've always wanted to see, before I never get the chance again. Do you have any family? You should visit them."

"Do we have a launch date now?"

"Soon. Very soon. It's coming. I can feel it— it's coming!" As he walked away, he spun in circles, with his arms outstretched. "Goodbye, old Earth. You were the cradle of humanity— but we cannot remain in the cradle forever."

When he was gone, Sitara booked a flight to Vogelsberg.

§ 77.

The pilgrims formed an orderly line leading to the temple's inner enclosure, and the Lucky Sun Company's kiosk that sold incense sticks and paper trinolay flowers, blessed by an android in priestly garments. Each pilgrim bought their choice of offering, then recited a prayer and placed it in the bowl before the ancestor's shrine, conveniently placed next to the kiosk. When Jiandong's turn came, he held his paper trinolay for a moment, and reminded himself why he agreed to go through the motions.

When the ceremony was over, one of the priestesses touched his arm. He looked, and the priestess put her hood down.

"Ambassador Von Richter!" he greeted her with surprise.

"Can I ask a question?" she said.

"Of course."

Gretel motioned towards a bench that overlooked a small water garden, and they sat together.

"What is your work?" she asked, and she touched the trinolay emblem that hung from a string around Jiandong's neck.

Jiandong grinned. "The Engineer's question."

Gretel said, "I'm sure you've struggled with it your whole life."

"I have certainly encountered it, many times."

Gretel smiled, but her gaze told him that she wanted an answer. He considered how to speak his truth to someone who could dismiss him from his job if she didn't like what he said.

"When I was little," he said, "I used to like being the last person in line to give an offering to the ancestors. By then, most people were already leaving; the sanctuary was mostly empty. So, it was easy to imagine that the ancestors really saw me. All the Celestials, too."

"How about today?"

"I think they don't care about the paper flowers. Not really."

"The ceremony still matters," Gretel reminded him. "It is the rehearsal for the deference and respect that we all owe to each other."

"I know," Jiandong agreed. "But I think the One-And-All notices the people who care about each other, spontaneously and without calculation. People who try to do something with their lives, whatever their rank and station."

Gretel looked to the sky as she considered Jiandong's answer. "You're certainly succeeding; you built a device that bends the geometry of spacetime."

Jiandong grinned at the phrasing of it. "The most I've ever expected from myself is to do the best I can with what I've been given. The One-And-All can take care of the rest."

Gretel smiled. "That sounds like something the heretic Amergin might have said."

"Useful advice, all the same."

"The hierarchy studied Lorelei's work very closely," Gretel continued. "They concluded that she is correct. Civilization on Earth cannot be preserved."

Jiandong leaned back. "You just told me your work is to preserve it."

"And so it is," she replied. "But not necessarily here on Earth. So we are selecting a crew for the Siren's maiden voyage," said Gretel, with a girlish grin. "I'd like you to be part of it."

Jiandong looked down to the water, this time to conceal his surprise. "Isn't that Lorelei's job?"

"Not for the test flight, to Neptune," Gretel clarified.

"That flight will be unmanned. Everything on autopilot. In case anything goes wrong."

"A few of *our people* will be on board," said Gretel, leaning closer to him so he would understand her hidden meaning. "More will be waiting in the support ships at the destination. When the Siren gets there, our team will disable the autopilot, and take control. Then the rest of our people will board. From there we will go to a virgin planet, to start a colony. Where we can live a life of purity and harmony."

Jiandong sat up straighter and looked at Gretel, his eyes wide. After a moment's struggle to find the right reply, Jiandong said, "You're asking me to help you hijack the ship, and then leave everything and everyone behind."

"I know it's a lot to ask," said Gretel, as she touched the side of his face. "But my dear Jiandong: I've read your journalism. I know what's on your mind. You are exhausted by this world. You hate the politics. The little races for attention that people run. This is a way out."

Jiandong noticed that Gretel's other hand was now inside his thigh. "I don't 'hate' the world," he said. "But I don't think much of some of its people."

She removed her hand, and patted his knee. "Don't answer me today. Think about it. But do answer soon. Talk to your family first. And then, come join us. A new world is calling. I can feel it— it's calling."

§ 78.

The pilgrims lined up to board the spaceplane that would take them to the Siren. Dressed in red robes with black hoods, they chatted amongst themselves, laughed, praised the One-And-All for their good fortune, and hugged each other. Jiandong moved among them, receiving congratulations from some of them for designing the gravity-wave engine, and agreeing to be part of The Plan.

Three, however, wore cloth wraps under their hoods, hiding their faces. If anyone approached them, they saluted with a touch to their hearts, lips, and foreheads, but did not speak.

"Those three took a vow of silence for the journey," Jiandong explained to the seekers. "Best if you leave them be."

The spaceplane departed Vogelsberg spaceport, and a few hours later docked with the Siren. A technician greeted them with the three-touch salute.

"The space traffic controllers expect this shuttle to be full when it lands on Earth," said the technician. "And I don't mind saying, everyone on my team is glad to get off this boat. In case the Arethusans shoot us down."

Jiandong said, "How soon until you're done here?"

"We just turned on the auto pilot," said the technician. "You know how to shut it off?'"

"I do," Jiandong nodded.

"Then my team and I can go." She gathered her tool kit, then put her hand on Jiandong's shoulder and said, "Summoner be kind."

Jiandong furrowed his brow. "That's optimistic."

"I know you're not going to die," said the technician. "But you're not coming back either, so it feels like the same thing."

Jiandong nodded. "You know the Summoner's Question?" he asked.

"*Ja,* it's 'What are you living for?' And the answer is—"

Jiandong patted her on the arm and said, "Forget what it says in the Chronicle. Find the answer for yourself."

The technician hugged him. Then she stepped off the planetfall shuttle, leaving Jiandong and the pilgrims on their own.

§ 79.

The flight deck of the Siren was spacious and comfortable. Combining the features of a computer centre and an observation lounge, it was designed to give whoever sat in the captain's chair the best view of the monitors. There were no windows: the walls and ceiling were a single dome of holographic displays, updated in real-time to give the occupants the impression that they sat on the outer hull of the starship, able to see everything around. In fact they were deep inside the starship's central hull, shielded from interstellar radiation. The gravity came from the ship's rotation: Jiandong tested it by tossing one of his shoes in the air, to see where it would land. It curved to one side as it fell, and hit the floor near the edge of the room.

"So, if you're facing the bow, we're rotating clockwise," he reported to everyone in earshot, as he put the shoe back on. "And now, everyone, I need a moment with these three pilgrims," he said, gesturing to the three whose faces were veiled.

"Who are they?" one of the technicians asked.

"You'll find out when we get there," Jiandong said.

The technician gave the three-touch salute, and left.

The three pilgrims removed their veils and threw down their hoods.

"That was the easy part," said Glaive.

"I thought it would be harder to breathe, wearing this," said Sitara, dangling the scarf at the end of her arm.

"When is the ship programmed to leave?" said Lorelei.

"Less than an hour," said Jiandong.

Lorelei looked to Sitara and said, "Over to you, now."

Sitara grinned. She checked the time on a nearby display. "The info-dump is pre-programmed on my private server. It should go public right about now—"

Somewhere in Vogelsberg, where her private server was housed, thousands of Legacy Aeternim documents uploaded themselves to Arethusa's alien-infiltration tip line.

§ 80.

In his office in downtown Newgarten, Sturgeon Glaive's comms was ringing. but the senator was too busy to answer. After the tenth ring, his secretary opened the door.

"Senator Glaive, we have a— oh!" The secretary did not expect to see the lingerie-clad gynoid in the office, dancing for him.

"I told you— I'm in a very important meeting!" Sturgeon shouted at the secretary.

"Sir— the call is from the President's own chief of staff." He handed Sturgeon a Q-link which displayed an official document. "He says that the President is pulling the fleet off the blockade."

"But we *need* that blockade! Wasn't he listening to me? That ship cannot be allowed to fly until our fleet is FTL-ready," Sturgeon roared.

"I know, sir. But we received some new intel. The secret starship you were looking for— it wasn't all in Lalkeela. Some of it was *here*."

"What do you mean, some of it?"

"They built their ship on the ground, in twelve separate pieces. Three of them are here in Newgarten. Disguised as skyscrapers."

Sturgeon looked out the nearest window. One of the Legacy Aeternim buildings was less than a city block away. He saw ground troops blockading its entryways, and hundreds of drones and helicopter gunships converging in the air around it. A few blocks further beyond, he could see a flood of smoke and ash cascading through the city streets, enveloping everything below the third floor, preceded by a racket of sirens, horns, and crashes.

The windows trembled with a low yet powerful rumble. From the apparent source of the spreading cloud, Sturgeon saw a bright flash. A skyscraper had shed its outer shell with a series of explosions, revealing a tall and wide cylinder, covered in the unmistakable silver sheen of heat shields, and flanked by gantry cranes. A cone with a cluster of reaction-engine rockets capped the summit.

"Kai'tzeen!" Sturgeon swore.

The rumbling of rocket engines swelled louder. The gantry cranes fell away and the cylinder lifted itself up on a column of rocket fire. Sturgeon squinted at the brightness. A second avalanche of smoke and glass washed through the city, drowning all other noises, and breaking Sturgeon's windows. He and the secretary flipped the desk on its side and took shelter behind it.

"All those people down there—" said the secretary, looking at the crowds of pedestrians running away, coughing, falling over, and fighting for seats in taxis and buses.

"How did they keep a secret like that?" Sturgeon wondered. The secretary glared at him. But his eyes were hypnotized by the giant rocket, as it passed through the clouds and out of sight.

Then he spun on his secretary and ordered her: "Take me to the spaceport."

§ 81.

On the flight deck of the Siren, Lorelei and her friends saw that the Arethusan warships were moving away. "The plan is working!"

But a new blip on the display made Lorelei slow her celebration down. "An orbital pod is approaching. I thought all the pilgrims were already on board?"

Jiandong looked at the display. "It's got a CNH transponder. I had better go down to the airlock and see who it is."

Moments later, the pod docked on one of the Siren's airlocks, and Gretel boarded the ship. Instead of her usual business attire, she wore the cloak and the hood of a Godspeaker. She was followed by two people who wore the same tabard as most of the pilgrims, but they had helmets and ballistic masks. Their eyes were like telescopic lenses, and glowed green.

"Admiral!" Jiandong greeted her. "I thought you were going to join the second wave."

"I heard that three Godspeakers joined the team. I want to

know who they are," Gretel said.

"The ship is due to spin up the gravity wave in twenty minutes," Jiandong warned her.

"I'll come with you as far as Neptune," she said. "That gives us hours."

Jiandong had to acquiesce. "I saw them going toward the flight deck; I think they wanted to see the new holography display."

"Take me there."

As he led her down the corridor, he took out his Q-link and typed a message to Glaive. Gretel asked, "Is that the override?"

"The whole operation's a failure if it doesn't work."

"Of course."

Allowing Jiandong to lead her from a few steps ahead, she was able to enter some commands into her own Q-link.

§ 82.

"They'll be here in two minutes," Glaive warned, when he received Jiandong's message. "And she has two cyborg warriors with her. Fuck— fighting on board a spaceship is the worst. Better go hide somewhere."

"What about you?" said Lorelei.

Glaive opened his cloak and showed her that he was carrying a compact plasma carbine.

"Where did you get *that?*" she marvelled.

"I work for a bank now, remember?" he grinned. "Now go."

Lorelei pulled a lever on a wall, causing a trap door in the ceiling to open. A ladder descended, too slow for Lorelei's liking in the minimal gravity. When it came in reach, she grabbed it and pulled it down. She and Sitara climbed up and away; Glaive closed the trapdoor after them and put his Godspeaker disguise back on.

A moment later Gretel arrived on the flight deck, followed by her two cyborgs and by Jiandong. Glaive stood in the centre of the room, facing the bow of the ship.

"Lord Godspeaker! It's a welcome surprise to see you," said Gretel, approaching him reverently. Then a moment of puzzlement crossed her face. She looked to Jiandong and sad, "Where's the other two?"

Glaive dropped his hood and mask, and shot one of the cyborgs. Its head exploded off its shoulders. The second raised his right arm; the barrel of a plasma rifle extended from his forearm and locked itself place with the fighter's hand on its trigger. It aimed for Glaive.

Jiandong attacked it from behind, wrapping his pilgrim's veil around its neck, pulling it off balance. The move gave Glaive a chance to shoot it and kill it.

Gretel, surprised by her fighter's defeat as well as by the swiftness of it, stepped away from Jiandong and circled the room, to get to a place where she could see both Jiandong and Glaive at once.

"I *do* know you," she said to Glaive. "You're Sturgeon's boy."

"Not anymore," he said.

"And you, Captain Xiao. You're a traitor," she said to Jiandong. She dropped her cloak and raised her arms. Plasma guns emerged from them, much like the ones Glaive had seen on the models in the Legacy Aeternim showroom. She pointed the barrels at each of the two men. Glaive instinctively aimed his weapon back at her. Jiandong carefully stepped toward the lever that opened the emergency exit.

"If you shoot me," said Gretel, "I still have time to kill *him* —" she pointed at Jiandong.

"If you shoot him," Jiandong told her, "I'll eject the ship's power core into space. You and your pilgrims will all stay right here, until you go to jail."

"So will you," Gretel countered.

"Then we can share a cell."

Glaive knew that Jiandong was bluffing about the lever, but he rolled with it. "So there's your choices, Gretel. You can go to jail, or you can die. And in both cases, we don't leave orbit."

Gretel activated her plasma guns; a row of indicator lights showed that the weapon was charging its first rounds.

Glaive shook his head at her. "Don't do it."

Gretel made her intentions as plain as the rage on her face.

A proximity alarm sounded; the tactical display showed a dozen drones approaching the ship.

§ 83.

Alankar Sen stepped through the airlock, followed by four of his own cyborgs. On his orders, they shot and killed two pilgrims who dared to ask them what they were doing. The rest scattered out of his way.

From down a side corridor, Sitara and Lorelei witnessed the murders. They froze in place for a moment. Without averting their eyes from the scene of the crime, they reached out and held each other's hands.

"The ship was finished barely a week ago," said Lorelei, "and there's already blood on the decks. Come on, Sitara, we have to warn Glaive."

"I can't believe it," said Sitara, unable to look away from the bodies of the pilgrims.

Lorelei turned Sitara's face toward hers, to make eye contact. "I know, but it's happening, so we have to— make something else happen," Lorelei told her. "It looks like they were going to the flight deck. Let's follow."

Lorelei started walking, but Sitara grasped her hand and stopped her. "Shouldn't we be going *away* from the men with the guns?" she said.

"They're taking over my ship," Lorelei replied.

"I know— but it's only a ship. We can build another. Let's go to the escape pods!"

"If this ship doesn't fly then there won't *be* another," said Lorelei. "And all our work will have been for nothing. I won't have that."

Sitara squeezed Lorelei's hand again and said, "Do we have a chance?"

Lorelei paused. She closed her eyes for a heartbeat, then opened them again and said, "A small one. Maybe. I don't know."

Sitara held her breath. Her mouth shaped some words that did not become sound. Then she said, "Okay."

§ 84.

Alankar Sen stepped on to the flight deck. Both Glaive and Gretel pointed their guns at him. But when they saw Alankar's cyborgs, they stepped back.

"I knew this ship wouldn't be empty," said Alankar. "Some people are so predictable."

"That might include *you*, too," said Gretel.

Alankar took a pistol from inside his coat. "I have been lied to, and pushed around, and manipulated, and ignored, and *played*— by too many people! Including by that darling of the world, who can do no wrong, Lorelei Verlassen—"

"You watch the way you talk about her," Glaive warned.

Gretel noticed the whiff of anger in his tone. "You, of all people, protecting her? Now I've seen it all!"

"Enough!" Alankar yelled. "Enough. Enough."

"What in the world do you *want*, Alankar Sen?", Gretel drawled. "You say you've been played, when the truth is that you've been given everything you've ever asked for."

"I told you what I wanted. This ship was supposed to be Gayatrian. My ship. The Conference took it from me. I'm here to take it back." He pointed his pistol at Glaive, then at Gretel. His cyborgs took aim at both of them as well. He said, "If you both agree to leave this ship right now, then you can take my shuttle. Stay on board, and I will kill you."

A chime sounded from the communications panel.

"Don't answer that," Gretel ordered.

Alankar motioned for one of his men to answer it anyway. "It's my technical team, come to disable the autopilot. If I don't let them in, they'll know something's wrong."

The cyborg opened the comms channel. The panel's monitor activated, and showed everyone a head-and-shoulders image of Sturgeon Glaive, sitting in a military situation room. Behind him lay rows of monitors staffed by a dozen women and men in uniform.

"Whoever's on board that ship— stand down, or I will open fire on you!" he demanded.

Silence stilled the flight deck for a heartbeat, and then Gretel began to laugh.

"I'm serious!" Sturgeon insisted. "We have surrounded the Siren with a swarm of nuclear-armed drones. In less than five seconds I can blow you all into atoms. But that's not what I'm here to do. I'm telling you to shut down the gravity wave!"

Gretel only laughed louder. "You ridiculous people! You're all the same!" she cackled.

Alankar pointed his gun back at her, and then saw his hand was trembling. He yelled aloud to steady himself enough to pull the trigger.

That was the state of the room when the door opened, and every gun inside it pointed at whoever was about to step through.

It was Lorelei. She saw the guns, and immediately put her hands in the air.

When Glaive saw her, he put his weapon aim back on Gretel and Alankar. "Don't shoot her— I'm warning you— don't do it!"

Lorelei gave herself a few heartbeats of time to see all the weapons aiming at her, and to feel the fear. Then she said, "So— it's— nice of you to join me."

Alankar said, "What? Join *you*?"

"On the mission," Lorelei stammered. "To the planet. Just like I invited you."

Gretel said, "This starship belongs to the Communion now."

"It belongs to me," Alankar repeated. "My people laid the keel, paid for it, and built it. Now you get off it!"

"*Everyone's* starship," Lorelei shouted. "This doesn't have to be the kind of race where someone must lose for someone else to win. This doesn't have to be a race at all— look, you're staking your lives now!"

"That's how we know we're committed," said Gretel.

"Have you thought about what will happen if one of you shoots first?" Lorelei asked them. "Everyone else will shoot back, and then *all* of you will die. And what will that accomplish? We'll all be dead together."

"I'm not afraid to shoot first," said Alankar. "If that's what it takes to get respect then that's what it takes."

"Is that the kind of respect you want? The kind that comes from fear?"

"Better that, then no respect at all."

Gretel pointed one of her guns at him. "You'll get none from me for trying to take over my ship. God gave me this mission— God will *reward* me for killing you."

"God will reward you?" Lorelei interrupted. "What kind of god rewards people for murder? For torture? For lies? And how do you know if you're really hearing the One-And-All, or if you're only hearing the echo of your own pride?"

"Your side is pointing guns at us too," Gretel snapped, then gestured toward Glaive.

Lorelei looked. Glaive now had two guns, one in each hand, to point at Gretel and at Alankar. Lorelei stepped toward him, hands back in the air, and said, "Will you be the first to put the guns down?"

"If I put my guns down, they'll shoot us," Glaive said.

Lorelei said, "I know that's what they say. And probably what you've seen happen before. But *someone* has to be the first to show a little trust."

She turned to Alankar and Gretel and said, "You could try it too. As soon as you see him lowering his guns, you could lower yours. All together. Like you're dancing. Dancing, seeing each other as people instead of as *things*. Lowering your guns, *trusting* each other. You trusting him. You, trusting her. Both of you, trusting me. Trusting, dancing, and *running for the escape pods*."

Everyone flashed their guns back up again.

"See, while you were pointing your guns at each other and looking at me, you didn't notice that I have two other friends on board the ship," said Lorelei.

Everyone looked at the place where Jiandong had been standing, and saw that he was gone.

"They've gone to the engine room. They're taking the cooling rods out of the nuclear fusion core. The warning system should be alerting us right about—"

Alarm bells sounded in the flight deck. Red lights lit up on every control station.

"—Now," Lorelei finished.

"Why are you doing this?" asked Gretel.

"There should be just enough time for you to evacuate your pilgrims," Lorelei told Gretel. And—" she looked to Alankar, "—to get your, um, big soldier guys, back to your shuttle. And, Senator," she addressed herself to Sturgeon Glaive, still listening on the comms, "you might want to pull your drones back, before the explosion destroys them. Unless—"

"Unless what?" said Alankar, Sturgeon, and Gretel, almost simultaneously.

"Unless you want to come with us." Lorelei said. "See, as soon as your people are off the ship, we will try to stabilize the reactor. And if we're successful, then we'll fly this thing to Neptune. Together. Or, actually, maybe, all the way to the planet. The ship is already provisioned. Want to be one of the first people from Earth to set foot on a new alien world? Want to be one of the first voices that tells everyone back home what we found?"

Lorelei's audience looked to the stars that surrounded them. For a moment, they forgot that they were looking at a holographic projection. They imagined that they were already exploring space.

"You're really willing to destroy your own ship, and yourself with it, just to teach us a lesson on— what?" said Gretel.

"I'm trying to find a way out of the honours race, for all of us," said Lorelei.

"But it's all his fault!" said Gretel.

At almost the same moment, Alankar said, "But she and her people started it!"

Sturgeon Glaive, also talking over the others, said, "Never! Arethusa goes first, or no one goes!"

"That's what's wrong with you," Lorelei told them.

For a moment, the authorities glanced at each other, wondering what she meant.

"The Madman's Question," Glaive said, as he caught on to her meaning. "She had barely set foot on Earth again after two years in the Kuiper belt, and you put her in that show trial. She put the Madman's Question on you."

"And now," Lorelei finished, "you have answered it."

Alankar dismissed the implication with a grumble; Gretel only glowered coldly.

"It's the honours race, that's what's wrong with you," Lorelei named their madness, finding that she had their attention now. "It's a disease that looks like health to those who catch it. A poison that makes those who drink it feel good. It stops you from seeing the smallness of all our lives, the complete pointlessness of our hatreds, under the immensity of the cosmos. But the same immensity is also full of beauty, and wonderful things. We could be out there, exploring it. Couldn't you want that? Couldn't at least one of you want something like that?"

The armed fighters in the room kept their weapons up for a few more heartbeats. Whether through Lorelei's appeal to their better natures, or the fear of standing on board a ship that was about to explode, Gretel and Alankar backed away from each other, toward exits on opposite sides of the flight deck. Slowly, with their eyes never wavering from each other's weapons, they reached for their comms and ordered their people, almost in unison: "Evacuate the ship!"

Gretel's pilgrims filled the escape pods, and launched themselves to safety. Alankar's shuttle, crewed with his mercenaries, detached from the airlock and rocketed away.

"I'm not going anywhere," said Sturgeon, grinning. "You want to blow up your own ship, you go right ahead. I'll even help."

"Question for you, Sturgeon," said Lorelei, as she selected a few icons on the comms console. "When you deployed those drones, did you go through the proper chain of command?"

Sturgeon made a pained expression. "I don't answer to you."

"But you do answer to your President," Lorelei reminded him. "Which is why I am patching this conversation over to his office. His people are probably watching, and telling him what's happening. And I expect he will withdraw the drones, any moment now. They are *his* drones, after all. Not yours."

Sturgeon straightened his spine. He whispered something to someone off screen. A moment later, the drones retreated to a safe distance.

Lorelei said, "It's not too late for you to join us here, too."

Sturgeon laughed, and shook her head. "Where others go, we go first. That's how it is."

"Well then," said Glaive, with an icy tone, "you better keep the watch."

Sturgeon gritted his teeth at his son, and ended the call.

Glaive put his guns away, and put his hand on Lorelei's shoulder. Lorelei stared into the space Gretel and Alankar had occupied, and shook her head.

"You tried," Glaive said.

Lorelei put her hand on his, and said, "I don't understand why they didn't want to come."

"I do," said Glaive. "They're not yet ready to let go of their illusions."

"You let go of yours," Lorelei said.

"Mine were taken from me."

Lorelei nodded. "Still. The starship was supposed to bring everyone together. And when they had the chance— well, you saw for yourself. I'm a failure."

"You sure of that?" Glaive questioned her. "Look where you're standing."

She looked, and found herself standing at the command station. The readouts on the monitors told her the ship was fully fuelled and provisioned, free from its moorings, and ready to fly. Lorelei traced her fingers over the rim of the clean control surfaces and hand railings, reassuring herself that they were real. She admiring the sleek new touch screens: a pleasant change from the switches and keypads of the old NavCom Seven. In the holographic view of the space outside, the Earth turned beneath her in full blue and green glory. The NavCom support ships floated nearby in perfect station-keeping, some launching pyrotechnics to celebrate the Siren's first flight. Beyond the Earth and its halo of ships and satellites, there lay the sphere of the stars: no longer distant and untouchable, but now inviting, welcoming.

Summoning.

Lorelei smiled, and wiped a tear from her eye.

The engine's alarm lights stopped; Sitara and Jiandong returned to the flight deck. Glaive and Lorelei turned, their fingers still half-tangled together.

"Well, it worked," said Jiandong.

"What worked?" asked Glaive.

Sitara said. "Sorry if we scared you. The plan was to fake our nuclear core meltdown *after* we got to Neptune. But Lorelei told us to do it here."

Glaive laughed. Lorelei laughed with him.

"We better fly this thing," Lorelei said. "Pretty soon they'll realize the core meltdown was faked, and they'll be back." She stepped out of Jiandong's way, so he could reach the command station.

"This is your ship, Lorelei," said Jiandong. "Take the captain's station."

Lorelei furrowed her brow, then returned to the command station and put her hands on the railing. "Disengage auto-pilot. Transfer the ship to a higher orbit," she ordered.

Glaive, at the pilot's station, smiled and entered the commands. Lorelei recited the pre-flight systems checklist: her friends confirmed that everything was online and ready.

"Are we ready to go?" she said, when the checklist was done.

Sitara said, "We just need you to say something inspirational. You know, for posterity."

Lorelei made a nervous smile, then said "With these small steps into this new world— oh, I don't know— let's just go and meet the neighbours."

The thrusters oriented the ship toward Lorelei's Star. The space around the fore and aft gravity-wave generators rippled, as if they were pebbles dropped in water.

The Siren then appeared to vanish, leaving a momentary streak of red-shifted light in its wake.

§ 85.

"Sixty percent of light-speed. Seventy. Seventy-five."

We still don't know if it will work.
"Eighty. Eighty-five. Ninety."
I might be about to kill us.
"Ninety. Ninety-five percent. Ninety-seven percent."
We should have done more tests.
"Ninety-eight percent. Ninety-*nine* percent!"
I wonder if I should hold his hand.
"Ninety-nine point four. Ninety-nine point seven."
Ja. I think I need to hold his hand. Maybe her hand too.
Maybe the four of us should hold hands.
"Ninety-nine point eight!"
Maybe— just this once— I should admit that I'm afraid—
"Ninety-nine point nine percent—"
Oh Summoner, be kind to us—

§ 86.

One hundred and eighty days later, after traveling at around twenty-two times the speed of light, the CNH Siren arrived within twenty AUs of Rhinemaiden 74-B, the binary star system orbited by Lorelei's Planet. The view of space as seen on the flight deck passed down the spectrum, from the purples and blues of the upper bands where the doppler effect had shifted everything, then fading to black as space resumed its normal appearance. New stars and new constellations surrounded them. Two suns shone to welcome them, one bright and yellow, the other slightly larger, more reddish, and dimmer. The four friends danced and jumped on their chairs and hugged each other, and screamed and laughed and cried.

When they settled, they scanned the space for planets. This required several hours of careful telescope work, searching for points of light that seemed to move against the background stars while the ship sailed closer to the suns. They found five terrestrial planets and several gas giants. One of the terrestrials was in the habitable zone, where the energy from the sun was enough to allow liquid water: neither too hot, nor too cold. It matched what they knew about the origin of the probe that crashed on Pluto: a discovery that now seemed half a lifetime ago.

"Any organized signals?" Lorelei asked. "Lasers? Microwaves? Radio?"

"There's something from the fourth planet out," Sitara

reported from the comm station. "A repeating pattern. Might be a nav beacon! Too weak for us to detect from back on Earth."

"Somebody's home!" Lorelei breathed, excited. "Broadcast the greeting signal. Let them know we're here. And set course for the fourth planet."

The fourth planet was an ocean world, blue and cyan in the twin sunlight, glowing with blooms of bio-luminous microbes on the night side. Thousands of red and white islands grew from this sea, in wide archipelagos where the greater islands shepherded long chains of lesser ones until they disappeared from the eye. White wispy clouds gilded the planet around the poles. One white moon hung in the planet's gravitational grasp: its bright but cracked surface suggested a crust of ice, perhaps with a liquid ocean beneath. A halo of satellites orbited the planet in every direction, flashing the reflected light of the twin suns through a thin haze of dust, speckled and glittering like an aura. Lorelei and her crew held their breaths in awe. Jiandong touched his hand to his heart, lips, and forehead, in religious salute. Sitara and Glaive hugged Lorelei, and hugged each other. Then Lorelei sat on the floor, and let loose her tears.

In the wonder of the moment, they did not notice a small flashing red light on a tactical display.

"And what about life?" asked Lorelei. "Any organic markers in the spectrograph?"

"Still searching," said Jiandong, checking a readout on a nearby science station. "I think I know why we found the elevated infrared. The planet is saturated in greenhouse gases. All the lands outside the polar zones are deserts—"

Then she ship shuddered. Alarm klaxons sounded; red lamps flashed warnings. The gravity on the deck seemed to lean to one side, as the impact changed the way the ship rotated.

"Did we just hit something?" said Sitara.

Jiandong, reading the monitors, said, "Looks like the planet has its own asteroid belt. No— it's a garbage belt! We got hit by a piece of dead spacecraft!" He showed his friends camera images from one of the ship's antennas, where a jagged hole appeared at the place where a large metal cylinder, twisted and broken from some ancient accident, had struck the ship. The tactical display showed a dozen similar objects within a thousand-klick range.

"That couldn't have hit us in a worse place," he reported, as he examined more monitors and readouts. "Our fuel is burning out of the hole, and pushing us off course."

Sitara pointed to a navigation readout and said, "It's worse than that. It's pushing us to crash into the planet!"

Jiandong ran to Sitara's station to see for himself. "Get to the landing shuttle!" he shouted.

They ran to the corridor, pushing themselves off the walls as the low-G allowed, to the shuttle bay. The damage to the ship was spreading: one failed system caused another to fail in turn. Bulkheads closed, to keep the cascade of failures contained. When they reached the last bulkhead before the shuttle bay, they found it already half-closed. The four survivors pushed off the walls to reach it and squeeze through. First Jiandong, then Sitara, then Glaive escaped to safety. But Lorelei saw it snap closed at almost the same moment that she touched it.

Lorelei pulled on the bulkhead's manual release, but it did not move. "Something's blocking it," she told her friends. "I can't budge it!"

"Get to the escape pods— we will find you!" said Jiandong, shouting through the bulkhead's window.

"The escape pods are gone— those pilgrims used them all!" Lorelei reminded him.

"They didn't take the ones on the flight deck," Sitara said.

Lorelei put her hand on the glass. "Don't let me drown out there. Find me."

"We will," Jiandong and Sitara promised.

Glaive said, "Now go!"

Lorelei ran. In some corridors the walls became floors, as the ship rotated off-axis, changing the direction of gravity. Short-circuiting wires, flashing alarm lights and klaxons, and a thinning atmosphere, made the distance a struggle: she half-ran the first corridor, and half-staggered the next. Finding the flight deck sealed behind bulkheads, she donned an oxygen mask from a nearby emergency locker, and searched for the manual release for the bulkhead. The alarms quietened, and her eyes began to dry: the warning sign that the ship was depressurizing. She wrenched the bulkhead open, threw herself into the flight deck, and found an escape pod: a cone-shaped craft with three seats, not much fuel, hibernation equipment in case of a long wait for rescue, and a heat shield for making planetfall. She climbed in, and pulled the launch lever. The pod closed, and rocketed out of the ship.

Into the silence of space.

§ 87.

The pod opened. Lorelei drifted awake.

Everything was blurry to her hibernation-exhausted eyes. But soon she could make out that she was under a grey geodesic dome, with several spotlights shining down on her.

She sat up; her muscles felt weak. She rubbed her eyes, then flexed her fingers and wiggled her toes.

"Hello? Hello!" she called out. "Is anyone out there?"

She climbed out of the pod, stumbling at first, then pulling herself back to her feet by grasping the pod's handrails.

She was not alone. Three people, two adults and a child, all clad in white, stood nearby. They seemed glad to see her, and also curious. One of them stepped forward, and smiled. Her eyes were larger than a human's eyes, and her hands had three long and spindly fingers.

She reached out to Lorelei, in greetings.

Author's Notes

From the age of about six or seven, I built fleets of starships using Lego bricks from incomplete and mismatched sets. At nine years old I wrote my first science fiction story: it was about a group of rabbits who build a rocket ship, but on their first launch something goes wrong and they found their ship on course to crash into Jupiter. Probably in the same year, I read Arthur C. Clarke and Ray Bradbury for the first time. Thinking brave new thoughts about space and time cannot help but do weird things to a young mind. One of my teachers compared reading such books to experimenting with drugs. I was told not to read them until I was older. Naturally, therefore, I read them anyway. My generation was promised routine spaceflights on vehicles like the Space Shuttle, orbital hotels with rotational gravity, and permanent colonies on the moon, perhaps also on Mars, all before the turn of the millennium. And I wanted that future. I was crazy for it.

Many years later, as a grad student in philosophy, I met Prof. John Leslie, just after attending a lecture he delivered on the Carter-Leslie Doomsday Argument. Although I ended up writing my thesis on a different topic, I bought his book *The End of the World* right away, and it stayed on my bedside table for many years. Around the same time, a fellow grad student told me about the Alcubierre Warp Drive, then only a few essays in academic physics journals, now a well known (among nerds like me, anyway) hypothesis that spacetime might have no limit to how fast it can expand or contract. By sharp contrast with the Carter-Leslie argument, Prof. Alcubierre's paper made the future look more like *Star Trek,* and less like *Mad Max.*

Many more years after that, I became a college professor. For my summer vacation one year, I read Asimov's *Foundation* trilogy. And I read Whitehead's *Adventures of Ideas* which describes how civilizations are driven by a force of "formulated aspirations" (starship engineering?) and at the same time by an opposing force of "senseless necessity" (complex system collapse?). At about the same time, several NASA-funded scientists published an essay about a mathematical model they had invented, which shows how "over-exploitation of either

Labor or Nature results in a societal collapse."[1] I searched political science journals looking for more statistical models like it. I found, for example, that The European Union's Global Conflict Risk Index uses only twenty-four indicators to predict whether a country will experience large-scale armed violence in less than four years.[2] In October of 2018, the International Panel on Climate Change warned that only twelve years remained to do what is necessary to limit global warming to only 1.5 degrees Celsius above pre-industrial levels.[3] And Stephen Hawking, the world famous scientist, predicted that humanity had only one hundred years to colonize another planet, or else we would face extinction.[4] All these things came together with the sci-fi that my old teachers wouldn't let me read but were secretly proud that I read anyway. The point of all that is to say: Lorelei's Cultural Entropy calculation, and her gravity-wave engine, while only fictions at the moment, are nonetheless plausible.

A third feature of Lorelei's planet, the honours race, probably needs no explanation. I borrowed the term from political observers who lived during the ancient Roman empire. Yes friends, that sort of thing has been with us for *that* long, at least. It is one of the bigger reasons why kids like me got three job-killing economic crashes, a never-ending war in the Middle East, willful inaction in the face of the climate crisis, and a resurgence

---

[1] Motesharrei, Rivas, Kalnay, "Human and nature dynamics (HaNDY): Modelling inequality and the use of resources in the collapse or sustainability of societies. *Ecological Economics* Vol.101, May 2014, pp. 90-102.

[2] Halkia Stamatia, et.al, *The Global Conflict Risk Index: (GCRI): Regression model, data ingestion, processing and output methods.* (Luxembourg: Publications Office of the European Union, 2017.)

[3] IPCC, 2018: *Summary for Policymakers.* In: Global warming of 1.5°C. An IPCC Special Report on the impacts of global warming of 1.5°C above pre-industrial levels and related global greenhouse gas emission pathways, in the context of strengthening the global response to the threat of climate change, sustainable development, and efforts to eradicate poverty [V. Masson-Delmotte, P. Zhai, H. O. Pörtner, et.al. (eds.)]. World Meteorological Organization, Geneva, Switzerland, 32 pp.

[4] Julia Zorthian, "Stephen Hawking says humans have 100 years to move to another planet". *Time*, 4th May 2017.

of fascism, instead of colonies on the Moon.

Finally, I should say a few words about Lorelei herself. I visited Germany in 2004, where I learned about the Lorelei, the siren-spirit who lives in a bend in the river Rhine, and who lures sailors to their deaths. When I first thought of writing science fiction, I wondered what a futuristic version of that story might be like. Instead of a rocky cliff on a river bend, what about an entire planet? Next I wondered: what if the starships that crash on that planet were called there not simply by the song of a faerie woman, but instead by the prospect of an answer to a big philosophical and scientific question? And then a new correspondence appeared to me, connecting the Lorelei of legend with goddesses of wisdom from other cultures: the greek muse Urania, the gnostic aeon Sophia, as examples. Lorelei lives in a world that has been with me since my childhood, and I have loved her the whole time. I hope you have enjoyed meeting her too. You will meet her again some day soon: a sequel to this book is already in progress. The siren will fly again.

Brendan Myers
Gatineau, Quebec
November, 2020

About the Author

Brendan Myers, PhD, is the author of eighteen published books in philosophy, environmental ethics, history of ideas, spirituality, urban fantasy fiction, and game design. He's run three successful fundraising campaigns on Kickstarter, presented a TED talk, and hunted for fairy tales in seven European countries. Originally from Elora, Ontario, Canada, Brendan now serves as a professor of philosophy at Cégep Heritage College, in Gatineau, Quebec.

Other fiction titles by Brendan Myers:

Fellwater
Hallowstone
Clan Fianna
Elderdown
The Seekers
A Trick Of The Light

Select nonfiction titles:

The Other Side of Virtue
Loneliness and Revelation
A History of Pagan Philosophy
Circles of Meaning, Labyrinths of Fear
Reclaiming Civilization

For more information, please visit brendanmyers.net.